MURDER
AT THE
WORLD'S FAIR

A De Cenza Murder Mystery

ARTHUR COLA

ARPress
45 Dan Road Suite 5
Canton MA 02021

Hotline: 1(800) 220-7660
Fax: 1(855) 752-6001

Ordering Information:
Quantity sales. Special discounts are available on quantity purchases by corporations, associations, and others. For details, contact the publisher at the address above.

Printed in the United States of America.

ISBN-13: Paperback   979-8-89389-892-7
          eBook   979-8-89389-893-4

Library of Congress Control Number: 2024923845

The Pieta of St. Peter's by Michelangelo

NEW YORK WORLD'S FAIR 1964-1965

DEDICATION

To my wife Donna, our children, my grandchildren and family who are the light of all my adventures past and present, I present this tale. And for all who seek to find beauty and love, friendship and faith, truth and thrills may this story present you opportunities for discovery.

TABLE OF CONTENTS

VATICAN PAVILION CEREMONIES
NEW YORK WORLD'S FAIR 1964-1965
OCTOBER 31, 1962
NEW YORK — 3:00 A.M. .... ROME — 9:00 A.M.

CHAPTER ONE

BLOOD ON THE PIETA

The bright sunlight streamed through the discolored glass panes of the otherwise darkened and stark warehouse. Its shafts of brilliance were more tones of sickly yellow than the poet's naming it golden light. The almost barren interior space it illuminated was broken up by a large gleaming Carrara marble statue. The purest white marble statue sat on wooden pallets designed to carry such weight and also to be easily moved.

Climbing across the figures making up the statue was a fit and trim man in a blue smock which was covered in glistening marble dust. That Christmas snow appearance, the light crystal-like kind, of dust itself was of the purest white in color. It would be found in the Tuscan mountains, where the likes of Michelangelo almost five centuries earlier would have roamed as he chose his marble for his sculptures. In fact the statue on which this dust covered young man precariously balanced himself was being chipped at by him. Those powerful arms would and could take up a challenge from any man much larger than he. But not this day, for he was carving into the marble sash that which was to be his final effort to recreate that which Michelangelo had those many centuries ago. With a mallet type hammer and chisel, he chipped away at the fine pure stone brought to America solely for him to work on. Chosen by the man in the smock in those Tuscan hills it was then shipped from Italy. That was almost two years ago. The last bits of fine marble chips exploded out of the words now being formed. Each letter of those words was identical to those which the iconic master artist of the Renaissance Era had carved on his own work.

"That's it. It is finished," he jumped off the statue bumping into a wooden table filled with sculpting tools, a bucket of water, polishing chemicals and cotton cloths. He steadied himself and began to gaze at his creation now bathed in streams of sunlight. Then he read the Italian words he had just finished carving. "Created by Michelangelo Buonarroti of Florence," he sighed. "And like you who all Italy called rightly, Il Divino Michelangelo, I stand before my work alone." He pulled a linen cloth from the pocket of his smock, dipped it into the bucket of water. Climbing onto the edge of the pallet, he reached over and wiped out some marble dust which collected in the letters he had just completed.

Jumping off the pallets, this time landing firmly on the cement floor of the empty warehouse, he took in the results of months upon months of constant sculpting. Speaking in Italian he proclaimed the work to be completed. "I think that the 'Divine One' himself would be pleased with my recreation of his Pieta." His eyes took in the Holy Mother Mary cradling the body of her son who had just been taken down from the cross. Dropping the damp cloth into the bucket, he began to speak to the statue in English. "My heart wishes that I could have carved on that sash across the breast of the Mother of Our Lord the truth about who created you, Created by Giovanni Gaglioni of Abruzzo, Italy." He slumped against the figure of Christ and lowered himself onto the wood of the pallet. "See this, this place is no warehouse. It's St. Peter's Basilica in Rome. The Pieta has just been put on display and people are in awe of it. And yet the credit for its beauty, for its rendering of the final scene of the act of salvation, was being attributed to another. I can see me now in the midnight hours sneaking into the Basilica. Like you did in your time, I am carving the truth of who sculpted the most revered work of Christian art in western civilization. But alas I am not you, and this place is not St. Peter's. And I cannot take credit for a work which I was hired to recreate."

The daydreaming Giovanni Gaglioni lowered his head into his dust covered hands. A sprinkling of dust fell from his thick almost black bushy hair which like the one he idolized hung below his ears. Unlike his Renaissance idol however, he was clean shaven. He rose and touched the hand of Christ, caressing it as he looked at the crucified one. "Michelangelo, I think that you would approve of how I was able to retain the vision you presented in your Pieta. I even used the type of tools which you did. No power drills, no mechanical anything was used on my recreation of your masterpiece. See the youthful appearance of our Blessed Mother as she holds the one called Messiah, Savior, Lord and Son of God. And does not the Lord Jesus look exactly as you portrayed him to be after the Crucifixion? See how peaceful he is now that His sacrifice is completed."

Tooting horns of tugboats out on the Hudson River just a couple of blocks from where he stood talking to his statue of the Pieta interrupting his one sided conversation. It brought him back into the warehouse, away from the Vatican of five centuries ago. The sounds of whistles and trumpets blended with the pounding of nails. He was reminded that those boats were practicing for the welcoming of the original Pieta by Michelangelo. The nail pounding with automated tools were the sounds of placing the final boards on the stage platform where the dignitaries were to stand the next day. The Archbishop of New York, Cardinal Spellman, would be joined with prelates and civic leaders to welcome the priceless masterpiece arriving from Italy.

Had Giovanni Gaglioni been able to peer out those slightly open windows high above him, he might have been able to catch a glimpse of the activity on that stage as the final decorations were being affixed to it. The Flags of Vatican City and the United States of America flew over the stage. The Gold and White colors of the Vatican flag were used in the bunting surrounding the platform as were those of Red, White and Blue of the United States. Since he could not, he just listened and dreamed of his work being recognized as worthy of praise. But the praise he sought was not from a tugboat whistle. It would come from the lovely lips of one he admired, no adored but in the recesses of his heart. But such words could not be uttered by him. In the real world beyond the warehouse walls he was a nonentity whereas Sheila Murphy was the companion of the man who hired him to recreate the Pieta. That man was Carlo Battista called by everyone the "Signore Battista" or just "Signore."

The very thought of his boss, made him jump up and look about for the tarp. He wanted to cover the statue not only to surprise the Signore but to present a concern he had about it. He caught sight of it lying neatly folded under the work table similar to so many he had seen back in Italy and if he had a chance to look, in the work sheds across America. He went to pull it out and unfold it. Noticing as he did so a brochure which announced the New York World's Fair on the table. He took hold of it unfolding it on the table, placing the hammer on one end of it and the chisel on the other end. His long narrow fingers pressed against the open interior. "There you are," he pointed to the symbol for the Vatican Pavilion on the map. "There Divine One is where your Pieta shall be placed. Millions will come to see it and not one shall come to see mine. The Signore tells me that one day mine shall also be enjoyed by many. We shall see. For when that happens, the love I hold in my heart may be revealed without fear. I shall be an accomplished man." The tooting of the horns brought him back to his task.

Pulling out the canvas tarp and laying it flat on the cement floor, he began to pull it up and over the statue. Though on the short side his strong muscular arms had no problem lifting it up; it was just the awkwardness of insuring that the marble fingers of Christ or the Virgin Mary did not get caught in it that was an issue. Slightly older than his idol was when the original Pieta was created, the twenty-eight year old artist tucked the canvas covering at the back of the statue and patted it. "We are ready, are we not?"

A deep throated booming voice answered his question. "I should hope so. The ship, the Cristoforo Columbo will be docking just down the street at the 44th Street pier tomorrow."

The startled artist popped his head up from behind the tarp covered statue. He brushed his long dark locks from his face. His wide cocoa brown eyes rivaled those of "Elsie the Cow" seen in billboards across the nation advertising milk. Those eyes did not focus on his boss; rather they were drawn to the vision of stunning beauty which stood arm in arm next to him. Dare he even crack a smile? He did not.

"Signore Battista, you gave me a fright. I was just finishing up…"

"Forget all that; is it done?" Two wide eyes as clear as the blue waters of the Caribbean squinted. His pudgy fingers grasping a half smoked equally thick cigar tightened their grip causing the tobacco to crunch and then break in two. He tossed the smoldering remains across the cement floor.

The blue smocked man began to embrace the covered marble, the marble dust sprinkled off his hair and cotton smock as he did so with such tenderness as one would think that his lover was soon to be in his arms. "Si Signore, but…"

He was cut off as Battista rushed wildly to him and grabbed him by the collar of his smock. "Gaglioni, what is this 'but'? The Pieta's ship docks tomorrow just down the street from where we stand. It is essential that this statue be done. Is the piece done or is it not; the ship which brings it is just outside the entrance to the river."

As he spoke and Giovanni quivered in his hold, three rather threatening looking men stepped into the sun light beyond the doorway through which they had just entered. The woman stood stoically in place as the men flanked her. Only her eyes gave indication of the fright within her. On the fairly warm April afternoon, she was wrapped in a mink coat with a collar pulled up until it touched her golden, though bleached, blond hair held in place by whatever hair spray brand she used up that morning. Her black pumps began to scrape and then run across on the cement floor. She rushed to Battista now shaking the artist, who was too frightened to speak at all, let alone answer a question.

She tenderly touched the hands of Battista now pulling the smock collar tightly around the neck of Giovanni. "Carlo, my dear, how can he answer if he cannot breathe?" She flashed a grin revealing perfectly white straight teeth surrounded by ruby red lips, also applied that morning.

The three gruff looking men stood directly in front Battista and Sheila. One hand was thrust under their suit coat jacket. Each was quite tall and muscular they could easily squish the artist and certainly didn't need the gun they now fondled under their jacket. Nevertheless, they awaited their orders and said nothing as they stood like the marble statue under the tarp, cold as stone.

The hold was loosened. The round head covered with a black fedora hat turned. His piercing blue eyes began to widen. The wrinkles around his eyes softened as those on his brow did. He smiled at her and nodded understanding. Then turning to Giovanni, he patted his cheek softly.

"Now Giovanni, my boy, forgive my… shall I say excitement. It's just that we have planned for this day for so long that…well we just can't afford any type of delay. The masterpiece is arriving; if we are to present the gift to the city, your statue my boy, then it must be ready. You do understand… caspice?" Battista placed his arm around the woman's waist; she who in her twenties was a good thirty years younger than he. "Sheila, you always know how to quiet my nerves and settle me." He waved his other hand at the three men who took one step back and dropped their hands to their sides. The bulge of the gun still visible under their jackets caused no ease of nerves on poor Giovanni.

The artist's watering eyes froze on those deep green eyes of Sheila Murphy being squeezed by Battista. At twenty-eight, he was much better suited for such a lovely and soft spoken woman than the beast of a man who held onto her, he thought despite his fear. She cast back a slight smile and gaze of understanding his misery at that moment. She thought Battista took no notice of the exchange; he then took hold of Giovanni by the waist and held him and Sheila close.

"Now then, where were we before…well before the excitement? Ah yes, you were going to tell me about the marble weren't you Giovanni?"

Giovanni Gaglioni shuddered and Battista could feel his body tremble. He released Sheila and turned into the artist face to face. He placed a kiss on each of his cheeks and then patted them gently, his pudgy fingers caressing them before being pulled away.

"Now see how I love you. I make Sheila here jealous…" he turned and winked at the woman. She returned a nod and broad smile with cast down eyes to feign embarrassment. Returning his gaze into those dark eyes of the one he kissed, he began a history lesson of sorts. "How do you return this love I have for you my friend? Was it not I who plucked you out of the Belle de Arte school in Florence to give you what your heart yearned for; that is to work on marble of your own? Did I not take you to Rome and gain permission to have you study at the feet of Michelangelo's Pieta in St. Peter's itself? And when you had studied and measured and created drawings and models of clay, did I not proclaim you to be as good as the master, Il Divino Michelangelo, himself?"

The would-be artist began to relax in what had now become an embrace. "Maybe the Signore Battista really does love me and was just excited and concerned about the project," he thought to himself before he answered. "Signore Battista, you make me to blush and feel shame to have appeared so ungrateful for all you have said is true. I shall be always in your debt. I will choose my words more wisely in the future."

"Yes that's it; words…they are so important wouldn't you agree Sheila," he twisted his body so as to take in her reaction while still embracing Giovanni.

She delivered an approving coquettish smile while her emerald eyes pierced the very soul of Giovanni Gaglioni the recipient of a welcome embrace rather than the strangle hold of a few minutes prior. The shuddering of the artist's body made Battista think that he was still apprehensive though in truth it was Sheila's smile and those green eyes which sent the shiver through his being.

"Why Giovanni you still shake. Perhaps it's the boys," he turned toward them so that he could address the still stoic statue-like henchmen. "Giuseppe, Stephano, Andrew, you make our Giovanni scared. Relax, go have an espresso or wait at the car for me."

"Yes Signore Battista," Andrew Jackson spoke for the three. He gave a shove to the others and they made their way outside where a black Cadillac limo sat with its engine running. The driver dressed in formal livery wear and cap was leaning against it smoking a Pall Mall cigarette. The music of Elvis blaring from the interior of the car drowned out the call from Andrew to him.

"Sacha, the Signore says for us to get an espresso…hey idioso… are you deaf?" The three now stood in front of the non-responsive driver. Andrew took hold of the driver and shook him. "Now do you hear me?"

"For Christ's sake get your hands off me. You made me miss the best part of the song…" he began to sing song the lyrics. "Love me Tender Love me…see I can't remember now."

"Who the hell cares about that asshole with the hip movement?" Andrew had released the driver, but not before he took the cigarette from his mouth and tossed it aside. "These things will kill you one day."

"So now the big man is a doctor," Sacha laughed boldly but not totally without fear as he gazed at the three linebackers now forming an arc of flesh around his slender frame of a body.

"Cut the crap and get in the car," Stephano stepped into the confrontation. "The Signore says that we should go get an espresso. Take us to Mulberry Street."

The stunned driver looked directly into Stephano's dark eyes which now picked up the afternoon sun which caused a spark of red to shoot out from them or so it seemed to Sacha. "Are you crazy, we're on 44th Street and Little Italy is past Prince Street which is south of 2nd Street."

Andrew didn't wait for Stephano to answer. His large hand grabbed hold of Sacha's crotch and squeezed his balls. The resulting scream left the driver doubled over before Giuseppe shoved Stephano and Andrew away. "Idioso, get in the car, all of you."

"He deserved it; he defied the Signore's order." Stephano pushed his way past Giuseppe. He walked behind the car to the other side entering it with a loud slam of the back door. Giuseppe followed without a word and entered on the passenger side rear door.

"There, now those big bad boys are gone," Andrew caressed the cheek of the still unnerved Sacha and then with his other hand tenderly took hold of his crotch. "There now, does that feel better?"

"What the hell…stop it, if the Signore knew what you really liked he'd kick your ass."

The tender strokes suddenly became a vice lock grip, Sacha grimaced and sweat began to pour off his brow. "And who's going to tell the Signore anything…you Sacha? I'll cut your dick off first and shove it down your throat."

"I didn't mean anything by it, honest Andrew; you just scared me that's all."

"That's a good boy," the grip loosened. "Who'd want you anyway male or female?" Andrew gave a shove to the driver. "Now take us for an espresso; you know this city better than any of us. There has to be a Trattoria closer than Little Italy."

"Sure Andrew, right away." The nervous Sacha slipped behind the wheel, glanced at the two in the rear seat through the rear view mirror as Andrew entered the car.

"Move your ass over Giuseppe and let a real man in." The bravado was taken very seriously by his co-worker and protector of the "Signore" for he and Stephano had seen what an angry Andrew could do to a man, even one as big as them.

Sacha lowered the window separating the rear of the limo from the driver's area and turned his head toward the back seat. He almost laughed at the sight of what he envisioned to be a see no evil, hear no evil and speak no evil trio of thugs. The laugh was not because of the sight of Andrew now licking his lips with his wide tongue, while Giuseppe was using his little finger to dig into his ear and Stephano was rubbing his eye saying that something was in it. But he dared not provoke them again by ridiculing them. "There's a little place on 42nd St. in the theater district which would be perfect for getting a quick espresso and getting back to the Signore."

He pulled down on the gear shift and off they sped down 44th Street toward Broadway.

Inside the warehouse, all was quite calm. Battista still hugged the now calm artist and Sheila applied more lipstick as if she really needed it.

"Now then, see they are gone, there is nothing to fear my boy… nothing at all. Sheila and I are here and we love you, don't we my sweet thing?"

"Huh, oh most assuredly Carlo my love, we love everyone especially one who is about to make millions for us."

"Let's not be crass my dear, Giovanni is a modern day Michelangelo," Battista then focused on Giovanni. "He is your idle is he not?"

"Si Signore, he is the idle of all sculptors and painters and even architects for he is the genius in all three fields."

"Is that so, well right now we are interested only in marble and what can be made from it; so tell me what is the 'but' about and why is the marble covered?" He released the shaken artist from his grasp with another pat on his cheek. "And do watch the words you use, we wouldn't want another misunderstanding would we?"

Giovanni glanced at Sheila, who cast an ever so gentle smile toward him and stepped back to adjust the tarp. "Si Signore, of course Signore… no misunderstanding to be sure. The 'but' and the covering both answer your question. The statue is covered for it is about to be revealed BUT for one little thing…"

"There's that word again, Giovanni." Battista's face began to get flushed with streaks of red. "Is the marble ready or is it not?"

Giovanni began to pull on the tarp. "Let the marble speak for itself Signore." He gave the tarp a quick tug and it began to cascade down off the marble revealing a replica of Michelangelo's Pieta.

Both Sheila and Battista gasped in wonder and joy.

"Signore Gaglioni, this is magnificent there is no 'but' about it." Sheila walked up to the now smiling artist and planted a kiss on his cheek. "Look Carlo how the sunlight makes it sparkle with holy light." She crossed herself and knelt at the feet of the Christ being held by Mary, his mother. Just under the collar of the now open mink coat lay an ivory white lace shawl. It purposely covered her shoulders and the low neckline of the pink rather tight fitting dress she wore. She pulled it up so as to cover her head in prayer. It was a natural instinct and not thought out nor planned; the emotion of seeing such perfection in art struck her to the core of her being.

Carlo Battista stood awestruck watching her devout posturing before the statue and its artist, who didn't quite know how to react to this sudden act of piety so unlike the Sheila he saw when she was with Battista. The gleaming white statue radiated something that Battista with all his connections around the world with his import and art business could not define. He once again took hold of Giovanni and kissed him on each cheek.

"Sheila's words are true my dear Giovanni, this is perfection as if the actual Pieta of St. Peter's where in this place and not on that ship in the Hudson River. I cannot imagine as to how you could say 'but' in presenting this masterpiece to us this day of days. See how it glows with a holiness which would defy that most learned of the art world to identify this work as a copy."

"You are too kind Signore, but…"

Battista dropped his embrace and held Giovanni by the shoulders at arm's length. "There's that word again, how can you use it in the presence of such perfection?"

"But… I mean my point is that its gleam is too bright, I think. Michelangelo's statue is 465 years old. Would it not be slightly duller in the sunlight?"

"Nonsense, who has ever seen it since it entered St. Peter's in natural sunlight? No one has; for it has never been moved from the Basilica until this year when the Pope himself gave the permission." He patted Giovanni's cheek once again. "So you see, there is no 'but', there is only perfection." He placed his arm around the blushing yet nervous artist's shoulder and called to Sheila. "My dear, come to Giovanni and tell him that what I say is true. He will believe you."

The young woman rose with a slight touch to the feet of the crucified Lord. The lace shawl turned into a veil covering fell down to her shoulders as she approached the artist. That same sunlight which was causing the marble of the statue to gleam now shone upon her so as to make a halo effect surround her head. Giovanni trembled as she approached. Her loveliness in his mind was to rival the gentle face of the Virgin Mary of the statue he just created as the Master called Il Divino Michelangelo had envisioned. The Divine One had created not an elderly Mary holding her thirty-three year old son but one with youthfulness and sublime beauty of gentleness.

Battista watched virtually dumbfounded as he had never seen this pious…devout side of his lover. His eyes watched her every move as she fell to her knees before the artist and began to kiss his hands. Giovanni glanced quickly at his patron who brought him to America to create another Pieta to rival the original. Could he just stand there and accept such devotion and ignore the feelings of his patron? His mind began to spin, his body to tremble as her lips touched his hands which he instinctively withdrew. He attempted to wipe the fresh ruby color of her lips from his hands while she crumbled to the floor while praying.

"Hail Mary full of Grace the Lord is with thee…"

Only the shout from Battista stopped her words. "What the hell are you doing Sheila? Stop it right now." He grabbed hold of her arms and brought her to her feet. "Have you gone mad? This is just a piece of marble and this nothing of an artist is just someone hired so that we could make millions and live our lives in such luxury as to be the envy of monarchs and presidents."

Her weight though in truth lighter than sugar plums dancing in one's dreams fell on him as if she were a sack of potatoes. He tried to keep her on her feet.

She only called out all the louder, "Hail Mary full of Grace the Lord is with thee."

"Stop it I say," Battista slapped her in the face with the hope of bringing her out of whatever trance-like state she had fallen into. He shook her again and again.

Giovanni stunned at first suddenly had the courage to act. "Stop it Signore, you are hurting her." He took hold of Sheila and swung her away from Battista's arms and into his own. Holding her in his strong well developed sculptor's arms, they ran behind the statue. The rage in Battista's face could be seen as it became deeper shades of crimson. Gently he lowered Sheila onto the floor with her back up against the back of the Virgin Mary. She was confused, shaken, and distraught.

"Show yourself, you insignificant piss ant. You ingrate who would take the woman I love, the woman who I made into a princess among New York society, how dare you defy me."

Giovanni Gaglioni understood all that Battista was saying was true. He was nobody, a struggling would-be-artist in Florence when New York tycoon Battista picked him for greatness in the art world. Some would call him a businessman while others referred to him as the mob boss. Whatever he truly was, the Signore plucked him into a life beyond his wildest imagination. He was brought to America to begin work on a noble project. For his efforts he was to be paid a sum never dreamed possible as a youth in the Academy *Belle de Arte*. He lowered his head next to Sheila's and whispered that he would go to speak with Battista. She began to shake her head back and forth saying, "No, no, do not trust him."

"But he is my patron who made me what I am. I must do him the honor of explaining how I feel about you. I need him to know that I didn't mean it to happen." He looked into her watery eyes and spoke to her. "How your eyes burned into my heart and I had no defense to stop the flaming desire to see you, to hold you, to touch you."

"Please Giovanni, do not tell him such things…you don't know what he's really like. He is not selling your statue to the Cathedral as you think, he is going to switch it with the real Michelangelo Pieta and ransom it for millions or sell it on the black market."

The shock of hearing those words struck the artist as if bricks had hit him. He fell backwards onto the cold cement floor. "No, the Signore promised that once the statue was completed that I would be introduced as its creator. He said that my career would be set on a course to fame in my own right, able to create my own pieces from my own thoughts."

Sheila struggled to speak. The fear of what might happen to Giovanni flowed through her like her blood rapidly pumping through the heart. Still she was torn between loyalty to Battista and her own secretly held love for the artist. Her voice faltered. "It's all a lie Giovanni," she sank into a daze, just staring out into space. He lowered her onto the floor placing the balled up shawl under her head.

Rising slowly with a lasting final touch of her hand, he walked to the side of the statue. Battista was pivoting round and round looking for his men, the ones he had sent away.

"Signore, I do not mean to hurt you. I have done all that you have asked of me. But now I must know the truth. Did Sheila say the truth to me? Is my statue not going to be sold to the cathedral to serve as a lasting memory of the Divine One's Pieta at the World's Fair?"

Battista was now pacing to and fro his anger reaching rage; pausing to light a cigar and then tossing it aside and pacing again. He looked about for his goons once again and realized he had sent them away. It was just he and the artist in the cavernous warehouse with the changing light as the afternoon sun became the evening sun. The rays now illuminated the base of the statue rather than directly on the figures of Jesus and Mary. He stood frozen in his steps with a beet red face and fist pounding into his hand. "You have betrayed me," is all he said before he lunged for Giovanni who quickly ran to the other side of the statue at the feet of Jesus.

"That's not true Signore. I am grateful for all you have done for me. But the heart does not always work as it should. I did not mean to insult you."

"So you admit it. You love my girl, my princess, my lover."

"I am guilty of loving one whom I may never love. But I love you too as my patron as my friend as my sponsor to this nation."

With speed unlike any Giovanni had ever seen in a track star who was trim and cheetah-like, the 200 pound, five foot ten inch Battista leapt at him. Battista crashed into the hundred and thirty-five pound slender but powerful and now shocked artist. With fists as large as those of Michelangelo's David he began to swing without thought or direction. One of those punches crashed into the smooth face of Giovanni who screamed in pain and struggled to get out of Battista's vice-like grip. More blows landed on his face, then stomach, then chest. "I hate you. You deserve death for what you have done to me."

As Battista shouted Giovanni's knee struck him in the groin. The artist was free as the Signore bellowed in agony and anger at the same time. Standing behind a wooden work table holding his sculpting tools of chisels, hammers and polishing materials, the artist took a piece of cloth saturated with water and polishing ointment and placed it on his chin. "Signore, per favore, please stop this rage before…"

He never finished his thought. Battista now on the other side of the table lifted it and tossed it aside. The metal tools rang like bells off tune as they hit the cement floor. Now only three feet of space lay between the two. The rage in Battista's eyes and the fear in Giovanni's eyes grew in that moment of confrontation. In a swoop down to the floor, Battista grabbed hold of a heavy chisel used to cut the folds in Mary's gown and veil. He swung it violently without aim as he once again lunged for the artist. Giovanni tried to outrun his patron and circled back to the statue. At the base of it an awakening Sheila was coming to.

She gasped out, "Stop this…"

Both men paused to stare at each other. Only the statue of the Holy Mother with her son's body given in sacrifice for all people stood between them. Giovanni understood the message for he brought it to life as had Michelangelo almost five centuries prior. Battista however saw something quite different; it was a hammer lying at his feet. He slowly leaned over to pick it up, throwing the chisel aside as he did so.

"And now traitor to the heart and our friendship," He clutched the hammer firmly in his thick hands. Here is what shall be done. Look good for what you see will be the last you shall ever see of your work." Battista raised the hammer to strike a blow to the face of the Virgin Mary. He grinned like a Cheshire cat before attacking his prey.

Giovanni screamed as in excruciating pain and tackled Battista before the hammer struck the marble. "Not the marble Signore, not the symbol of our faith."

As the two plunged to the cement the hammer flew from the grasp of Battista across the floor crashing not into the marble but into the shattered tool table. The two men now rolled across the floor each trying to place a blow into the other's face, kidney, stomach and ribs. The two hundred pound man had the advantage as they managed to get to their feet. Battista literally lifted the shaken artist off the floor. He hoisted him up with one hand under Giovanni's arm and the other firmly entrenched on his crotch area. He swung around to toss him into the marble statue. At that moment Sheila crawling out from behind the statue pulled herself up on the arm of the Holy Mother Mary and thrust herself into Battista. She had managed to interfere with the power of the toss. The might behind throwing the artist was diminished as Battista lost his balance. He was falling backwards from the impact of Sheila's body hit. As he tumbled back, Giovanni flew into the hand of Christ gashing his head. Blood gushed out and ran down the robes of Mary. He slid down to the base of the statue motionless. With a scream of anguish, Sheila bouncing off Battista made her way in a crawl to the fallen artist. She cradled him as did the Virgin Mother directly above her, the sunlight now illuminating a human Pieta.

Battista tumbled into the broken pieces of the tool table and fell to the floor in a daze which focused on the marble depiction and the human depiction of sorrow and sacrifice. Slowly he tossed aside the pieces of wood in which he was tangled and rose. "Look at you," he shouted. "You do not mourn for me, but for one who betrayed me." The hammer which had crashed into the trashed tool table caught his eye. "Tramp, that's what you are; nothing but a whore who gives herself to anyone who would cast a wandering eye toward you." His rage erupted once again as he took hold of the hammer and raised it above his head. "Death is what you both deserve."

Fearing that the statue was in danger once again, Sheila gently rolled the body of Giovanni off her lap and stood to face Battista, her arms were spread wide to protect the statue as she stepped forward to meet her one time lover. "Carlo, you cannot do this…you cannot destroy such beauty." As the last word was uttered the hammer came crashing into the back of her skull. She fell backwards onto the body of the unconscious artist.

Battista still in a rage shouted, "So is the end of all traitors." He stood over their still bodies. Then throwing the hammer aside, he ran to the warehouse doors hoping to find his goons.

As the 44th Street door slammed shut behind him stillness followed. It filled the warehouse with an eerie quiet. The marble dripped the last of the blood from Giovanni Gaglioni's wound and mixed with Sheila Murphy's blood seeping into the folds of Mary's marble gown at the base of the statue. Two eyes fluttered and then a groan of pain was uttered. Slowly the body moved and beheld another body; then followed the wail of grief and heartbreak.

Giovanni cradled Sheila in his arms and rocked back and forth, humming a tune which accompanied the words which she had prayed just minutes ago, Ave Maria Gratia Plena, Hail Mary full of Grace…and as he hummed he thought of the love they shared. It was an innocent love shared through a smile or touch of the hand, a kiss lightly given in the shadows of the now blood stained statue. It was a kind word of encouragement when the Signore was on one of his harsh barrages against the unfairness of life and how he would get what was due to him. He glanced up to the face of the Christ, no longer in pain but at peace and then to that of His mother, serene and accepting of the sacrifice just made on the Cross. But in his heart there was no peace, no serenity; for within it began to burn the desire for revenge. As the beating heart seemed to speed up he lifted the body of the one he loved. They loved in silence for most of their time together. He lifted her lifeless body. Her golden hair was streaked with almost a sunset red color from her blood. Holding her before the Pieta for a moment, he then placed her body over that of the Christ in the arms of Mary.

"Now rest my sweet. I shall return with him the one who took you from me. I promise as I stand before you that shall I make him repent. But for now sleep as did Juliet of old and wait for my return. I shall join you in heaven as I could not in this life." He kissed her lips, still warm, tenderly; then taking the lace shawl once used as her pillow, spread it across her body as a shroud. "May the angels be with you as you enter paradise my love."

Staggering to the door with a throbbing head and a broken heart, he took sight of the weapon of murder. He picked up the hammer he used with chisel to shape and bring forth the Pieta copy. "Ah, my friend, you shall be used one more time to bring justice to this place."

He pushed open the warehouse doors and entered the crowds and traffic of 44th Street just as a black limo pulled away. His vision still blurred with tears made it difficult for him to discern whether or not it was the Signore's car or just another black Cadillac.

CHAPTER TWO

ENCOUNTER ON 44TH STREET

The dazed artist leaned against the steel door of the warehouse rubbing the blood and tears from his eyes. People were hustling down the sidewalk taking only a quick glance at the blood spattered man who seemed to be drunk and disoriented as he couldn't stand up without wobbling. He grabbed onto the door handle to steady himself. Yet despite the horror of what just happened, his eyes tried to follow the limo as it slowly made its way toward the dock area. Traffic was thick with vehicles in the late afternoon as the Cadillac made its way toward the river where the barge which would hold the Pieta after being lowered from the Cristoforo Colombo was docked.

Inside the limo chaos reigned. Battista was shouting at his henchmen who kept telling him that they only did what he ordered by going for an espresso. None of the three dared to ask why he was covered in blood. A bar towel hung in front of the rear seat suspended on a shelf bar which held crystal glasses and bottles of whiskey, a decanter of water and wine. He grabbed the towel and began to wipe his hands over and over again.

"Okay, okay enough of your excuses," he paused and looked at his navy blue suit coat and pants each stained with blood as was his white shirt and polka dot red and blue tie. His hat was long gone still on the floor of the warehouse. The fight drew blood but most of it came from the bashed skull of Sheila. The realization of what he had done began to sink into his bruised head. Taking the water decanter he pulled out the stopper and let it fall to the floor of the car. Pouring the water onto the towel he began to wipe his face and hands. Then he rubbed down his suit coat but to no avail. The rubbing only spread the life force of Sheila further into the wool and silk fabric. His bloodshot eyes began to look over his supposedly well trained body guards. This is how he referred to them whenever they were present in a public place. They settled on Stephano. He was almost exactly his size.

"You, Stephano, take off your clothes," he ordered.

"What? Signore, you've got to be kidding me, no?"

"I am not. I need to look presentable when you drop me off at the Port Authority Building where the gathering will take place for the planning of the arrival of the Pieta at the Dock."

But Signore, what…how can I protect you naked?"

"I don't think I'll need your underpants but we shall see, in any case the boys will buy you some clothes later. There's been an accident as you can see and you and me, we are near the same size, so your clothes will have to do, time is of the essence if our plan is to work."

Andrew was taking particular delight in the request. "Here let me help you get out of your clothes Stephano." He began to loosen his colleague's tie and unbuttoned his jacket. "Giuseppe, help me out here."

The four rather large men were cramped enough in the back with Battista now stripping down and not waiting for the banter to cease. Finally he called for an end to their talk. "Just strip down Stephano and quickly," then he yelled up to Sacha. Keep the windows up, they're tinted so no one will notice our undress and turn off into that alley ahead so that I can get out."

Stephano pushed Andrew away, "I can do this myself."

Andrew laughed. "I was only trying to help." His eyes glowed as the well-formed physique emerged from underneath the black suit and white shirt. He wore no undershirt so his chest hair covering him like a carpet was exposed.

Battista was sitting impatiently waiting while Andrew and Giuseppe tried to keep a straight face seeing their Boss only in his boxer shorts and crew neck white cotton tee-shirt and Stephano in his white Jockey shorts.

The quiet one Giuseppe had to speak, if for no other reason than to insure that they would not be blamed for yet another issue.

"Signore," Giuseppe began hesitantly. "Your shirt and shorts, they are stained, no?"

"Shit, that they are…the accident, there was a fight, then he crashed against the statue and bled and then…" he actually became a bit emotional. "…and then she fell cracking her head and blood was everywhere, so you see you need to get back there to clean up the mess before they are found. I left them there holding onto each other. She betrayed me, but you three… you shall never do to me what she did. You give me the clothes from your back to save me, eh Stephano?" Battista leaned over Giuseppe and kissed the naked man on each cheek and then on his lips. Andrew snickered audibly. Battista was oblivious as he made his delicate request.

"I will need your underpants, so make it quick, per favore."

Sacha pulled into the alley just a block away from the Port Authority Building. Battista was soon into Stephano's clothes and with a pat on his cheek offered his thanks for his unselfishness. "You shall not regret what you have done for me this day, Stephano. This I promise you. Here, at least cover yourself with my pants such as they are. And you two, you will get him some clothes after the chore is done."

"Yes, Signore, right away," the two said in unison.

"No, not right away; you have to do the chore first."

"But Signore, you never told us what that chore is," Giuseppe meekly offered.

"Did I not; of course, I am distraught…you know over the accident. Go to the warehouse and you will find them in each other's arms," his voice quivered. "There is a tarp there which is for the statue, use it to wrap them in it. What you do with them must be discreet; no one must know what was taking place with the creation of the statue. So crate up the statue as planned and call for the others to meet you to load the statue onto the flatbed truck as planned tonight but get them there now. Then clean whatever mess remains and leave no trace of any of what you may find. Capisce?"

Andrew was over his mocking attitude toward Stephano as well as the pleasure in seeing him in his natural state. "Si Signore, we understand completely. Stephano put on the pants and the Signore's jacket. We will need your help such as it is. We'll get Sacha to help also, if the car can be parked. Signore, one question more if I may?"

"But of course, but hurry, time is of the essence."

"The two of whom you speak, we understand that one is your…your companion Sheila but who is the man, not Giovanni the artist?"

"That's exactly who it is, the traitor to my heart, my love, all that I did for him."

The three hulking men looked at each other, eyes wide with shock and mouth open with no words but an "Aha" coming out. The thought that such a puny man could steal such a woman from their Signore was beyond their thinking.

"We shall do as you ask," Andrew finally got out then with another thought, "Sacha call a cab for the Signore. We cannot have him walk alone on the streets, he might be recognized."

"Ah, my Andrew, you love me," Battista patted his cheek and swung open the door; he leaned back in and told them that the key to the warehouse door was in his pants pocket. He then walked to the street with Sacha.

As soon as they were out of sight, Stephano ordered the other two out of the car. "Get out, let me dress in peace at least." He held the Signore's pants and coat over his lap.

The limo out of sight though he continued to look down the street but all was still blurry. His head was still throbbing. The blurriness was due to his sight being impaired with blood and tears. The disoriented artist was being bumped into and pushed aside over and over again by passers-by. Finally he made his way back to the warehouse door. His smock splattered with blood sealing the remains of the marble dust into every fold made him appear to be an unkempt panhandler to most who saw him. He pulled on the handle, there was a rattling sound but it did not open. He pulled harder and still it did not budge. He became agitated and pounded on the metal door until he was quite exhausted and slid down to the ground pulling up his legs and weeping uncontrollably. The doorway was recessed from the sidewalk. Once again he looked like a panhandler beggar often seen in the deserted doorways of old buildings around the city. Several people walking by dropped some coins at his feet; he never noticed until some voices unfamiliar yet kindly seemed quite close to him.

"Hey there, are you okay?" asked Ron De Cenza as he stooped down placing his hand on Giovanni's shaking shoulder.

The artist shrugged and attempted to move away from the touch never lifting his head. He scooted away from the voice only to bump into another person. Feeling trapped, he lifted his head looking towards the direction of the hand which touched his left shoulder. He rubbed his eyes with the sleeve of his smock and saw a younger version of himself. A slender young man with thick black hair and large cow-like cocoa brown eyes not particularly tall from what he could tell as he was kneeling. Those eyes looked at him with genuine care not as if he were some derelict street person. But then he noticed another person behind him and felt the presence of one kneeling on the other side of him and someone behind him. He was surrounded and began to shake.

"Leave me alone, I'll shout for help."

The plump usually jolly fellow to his right side jumped up and pushed his friend who stood behind him. "Clarence, he thinks we're muggers or something worse."

The older man looked at the nineteen year old and shook his head. "Well what do you expect? Look at him, obviously someone beat him up and tossed him aside like trash."

Clarence was almost twice the age of Bob Wentz to whom he was speaking and also Ron De Cenza at thirty-six years of age. He was tall and light in hair and fair skin announcing his heritage from northern Poland. Bob didn't know how to respond to the sarcastic remark. So he just looked at him with a gapping mouth. He wasn't alone in looking for the right words. Ron and the one who stood behind him also were at a loss. That was unusual for Ron and for the dashing young black guy from the heart of Chicago. Actually all of them were from the windy City. That is except for Ron; he insisted on claiming his family was from Oak Park Illinois just across the street from Chicago as he would say. They were in New York for the World's Fair. Others were on the trip with them as well. Clarence as the elder of that group, in fact was the eldest. All were seminarians of the Latin School of St. Benedict Abbey in Lake Como Wisconsin. Not that

Giovanni or any of the curious folks now gathering and watching the scene unfold in the doorway of the warehouse, could tell. They were dressed in casual wear at least for them. That consisted of black pants, white shirts and an Abbey jacket which was black with gold lettering stating the name of the Latin School. All were also wearing black leather dress shoes rather than sneakers which would have been more practical as they were exploring New York City since their arrival a few days earlier with their Latin professor Father Gregory OSB (Order of St. Benedict) and mentor Brother Anthony.

Clarence took charge of the situation. He knelt down in front of the battered man more to block the view of the curious. To the other three he motioned to form a barrier between him and the gathering crowd. "Sir, we're not here to hurt you. We are seminarians, men studying for the priesthood, do you understand?"

Giovanni nodded understanding.

"Good, now my name is Clarence Chekowski, and this smiling fellow is Bob Wentz, and next to him is Ron De Cenza the one who first came to your aide and finally that is Isadore Johnson whom everyone calls Iggy. If you will let us we would like to help you, it appears that you are hurt and in need of medical attention." He glanced at the others. "Get rid of the crowd."

Bob went into action and pulling Iggy with him addressed the onlookers. "There is nothing to see. All is well, just a slight mishap."

Iggy added, "We're his friends and will take care of him."

As the crowd dispersed, Clarence continued. "Ron do you have a handkerchief?"

"Yes, here, it's clean." He pulled it out of his pocket and held it out to Clarence.

"Good, now sir, my friend is going to wipe your face. It appears that you have been bleeding, a lot I might add."

"There's no time, I must get in. She's all alone. I must get to her."

The four were all now kneeling in front of him. "She, is there someone with you?" Ron asked.

"Yes, Sheila Murphy she's…" Giovanni couldn't go on and broke down once again, lowering his head into his knees which he held in a fetal position to his face.

Ron impulsively leaned into him and placed his arm around him. "Listen, it's going to be all right. We'll help you get to her. Where is she exactly?"

The other three looked on with a bit of apprehension as they had heard stories of violence in New York and this guy though emotional was obviously in a fight but on who's side and over what? Thoughts of drug deals, gang warfare and robbery swirled in their heads. They may all be from the Windy City but except for Iggy none of them had been exposed to violence until that frightful day on the beach on the Abbey grounds when a man bloodied like this man before them, came down the grassy knoll with a blade in his stomach calling out 'killer, killer' and collapsing in the arms of Ron to die there. The horror of that day and what was to follow as the life of Ron was threatened still haunted them despite the culprit being apprehended. So they feared for Ron who was once again holding a bleeding man.

Before Giovanni had a chance to answer, Ron saw the gash on the artist's head. "Guys, look at this, he's really hurt. We need to get him to a doctor."

"No, no, I must get to her." Giovanni released his legs and grabbed hold of Ron.

The other three made a move to pull him back. Ron told them to hold back never removing his gaze into the eyes of the artist. "It's okay, sir, we will help you first. Now where did you say this Sheila was?"

That gaze which pierced the very soul was returned by Giovanni. A sense of trust was forming as he replied. "She's inside, there." He pointed to the door he attempted to open.

"Well what's she doing in a dump like this?" Bob spurted out without thinking.

The sorrowful eyes turned to see who would speak in such a manner. Bob was mortified and apologized. "I am so sorry. Sometimes my tongue gets ahead of my brain."

"Ah, but you are right to call this place as you say, 'a dump' but what we do here was noble until this day."

"Really, that's cool; what were you doing anyway?"

"Bob, really? Not now," Ron chided his closest friend. "Listen, sir, one thing at a time; we will get you to Sheila, maybe she can hear our pounding on the door and open it for us. Guys, make some noise on that door."

The three rose and started to pound on the metal door. The metallic sound echoed in the recesses of the warehouse.

Giovanni began to slump into Ron's hold. "No amount of noise shall bring her to us; only the trumpet of Gabriel can raise her now."

The three instantly stopped which was fortunate as another crowd was beginning to form.

"What are you saying? Gabriel… as on the last day when we'll all be raised for the Last Judgement; I don't get it."

"Really Bob, a future priest and you don't get it. He means that the dead shall be called forth. This Sheila must be dead." Clarence whispered the later thought in his ear.

"God have mercy on us, not another dead person. Look at him, what if he…you know murdered her." Bob ran behind Iggy and held onto him. "He's full of blood Iggy just like that guy who died on Ron."

"Will you guys zip it, we can hear everything. We're only three feet from you."

"Sure Ron, whatever you say but be careful," Bob was serious as he was when he first discovered what the murderer at the Abbey was up to with Ron and his buddies.

"Ignore him sir, he's a worry wart…we'll look around for a way in, it appears that…"

"She is dead, she hears no more. She laughs no more. She kisses me no more."

"We are so sorry sir…" Ron and the others made a Sign of the Cross over themselves.

"Thank you, but he is out there," Giovanni raised his arm and then pointed out to 44th Street.

"I get it, you mean the murderer…I mean you didn't do it, right?" Ron asked fearing the answer and a repeat of all that happened with the murder in the Abbey.

"The Signore, he did it, he lied to me, he pretended to care for me and be my friend but he sought only money and now all is lost and she is gone."

"Ron, this is getting out of hand, who's this signore guy?" Bob was now holding onto Iggy and Clarence so tightly that they squirmed with pain in their arms.

"Sir, you've been through a lot, this we all can see. We'll call the police and they will get us into this building and then we can find this Sheila of whom you speak…"

"She rests in the arms of Jesus and Mary, there you will find her."

The seminarians shot glances to each other which spoke to their confusion as to what was meant by the battered and obviously shattered man. As usual, Clarence had a clarification or so he thought.

"Yes, that's true; one day we shall all hopefully be embraced by the Holy Mother and Our Lord when we enter the kingdom of Heaven, should we prove worthy."

"Ah yes, of course in heaven all will be as it should be." Giovanni sank back into a sullenness of quiet reflection, perhaps imagining Sheila in heaven with the Lord or just wondering what would be his fate once he found Battista and brought him to justice.

"Clarence, I don't think the gentleman quite meant what you described as yet anyway," Ron tugged on the artist to bring him closer to him and whispered, "Sir, am I correct in what I just said?"

"Huh, oh…heaven yes of course… call the police…what?" he then looked at Ron's worried face and asked a question. "Why do you keep calling me sir?"

Ron answered that it was because he had never told them his name and that they were trying to be respectful.

"My name, yes, of course…how could you know, you just met me and took pity on me but a few minutes ago." The artist shook his head as if trying to clear his thoughts so that he may express them better. The movement caused him pain expressed in his eyes and seen as he held the side of his head where the gash lay raw and open, though the bleeding had subsided. "My name is Giovanni Gaglioni. I am an artist who was befriended by the Signore who I betrayed after he found me at the art school in Florence and took me into his patronage so that I might learn sculpting without the fetters of the academy's rules."

Now Ron, as well as the others, was really confused for Giovanni made it sound as if he had done something unforgivable. But Ron thought about his words. He tried quickly to understand them in a manner which the others could not. Then it flashed like bolts of electricity in the synapsis of his brain. This man did not mean that he killed Sheila but that in some way had caused it to happen thus he was guilty. Clarity set in, because back at the Abbey in Wisconsin when the wounded man died in his arms, he had once chosen words which implicated him in that man's death.

"Okay guys let's not jump to conclusions shall we. Remember what happened on the beach not that long ago."

The others nodded their understanding.

"So it's Giovanni Gaglioni is it, well it's nice to meet you. Just in case all of us hovering over you has been a bit disquieting may I introduce myself and my friends to you once again. I am Ron De Cenza, that tall distinguished looking guy is Clarence, the smiling one next to him is Bob and then that one on the end is Iggy. Do you remember?"

"I do, mi piacere… I am pleased to meet you though I wish it could be on a different occasion than this…" Giovanni interrupted himself and went back to what Ron had said about calling the police. He explained that calling the police would be a bad idea until he could show them inside the warehouse and better make them understand why he said Sheila was in the arms of Mary and Jesus. He never finished his explanation for another idea had exploded in his injured head. "Mama mia, of course, the loading dock… signori, we must get to the other side of this building. There you will find another entrance, one through which we might enter and…" he could not finish and the guys let it go unsaid as they excitedly helped him to his feet and made for the loading dock of which he spoke.

One could hardly call the open corridor between the warehouse and the next building over an alley. It was very unlikely that any kind of vehicle could travel on its brick pavement; it was a pedestrian walkway at best. It did, however, save them the need to go around the entire building. Once through it, they found themselves just a few feet from the truck dock area which slanted downward from 45th Street to the shipping dock. "Ah it's here, see this truck; it is scheduled to leave here tonight," Giovanni began to share. "So perhaps we have beaten them here and we can save Jesus and Mary and my Sheila."

The guys were just as confused as ever, but Ron just kept pushing them on. "How about just seeing what's inside the warehouse. It might make sense out of all he has said." They walked alongside the flatbed truck. The arm of a hoisting crane stuck out over the side right next to them. Climbing up the cement stairs they came to an overhead door the size of a two car garage door. It was locked shut. Next to it however was an entrance door and it had glass panels on the top half. The presence of glass was a lucky break for them since that door was also locked. Scrounging around the dock area, Iggy found a piece of cement broken off the edge of the dock.

"Guys, I think we can use this," he called out as he lifted the rather large hunk of cement. Bob ran over to him, while Clarence and Ron held onto the still weakened Giovanni whom they carried most of the way down the corridor with linked arms for him to sit upon.

Bob arrived with Iggy holding the cement piece. "So who's going to do the honors, while we pray that there is no alarm system? You do realize that this is called breaking and entering which is a crime."

"Since I have nothing more to lose let me do it, Bob." Giovanni wobbled his way to Bob and took the stone, immediately throwing it at the glass panel over the door handle. It shattered with little detectable noise thanks to street traffic just beyond them. "Whew, that was heavier than it looked and I work with stone."

The four seminarians gave the artist a gentle pat on his back and praise for having the guts to smash out the window, as Iggy put it. Ron in the meantime knocked out the small pieces sticking out of the frame and stuck his arm through the panel. In a moment the door unlatched and they entered a cavernous area where the natural sunlight still shone upon the white stone statue in the center of the warehouse. They were seeing the stone from the back. As they approached Giovanni became more unsteady. He had to be held up by Ron and Bob so weak had his legs become. As soon as they came near the white marble it was clear what Giovanni had meant about Jesus and Mary but more than that; they found the lace shrouded body of Sheila resting on the sculpted body of Jesus being held by Mary. It all began to make sense but not soon enough. The four cried out in shock as the blood stained Pieta revealed just how horrific the crime was. Giovanni fell to his knees before the lifeless body of the one he loved in silence for so long. His weeping brought the four to their knees two on either side of him.

Ron placed his arm over Giovanni's shoulder. "Would you like us to say a prayer?" he quietly asked. A nod indicated that he would.

The four began to pray the Lord's Prayer. As they prayed the Amen and were about to begin the Hail Mary, they heard a noise. It was coming from the front door which was locked or so they thought.

"God have mercy, Ron what should we do?" Bob was beside himself. "It's the police. I just know it. We're all going to be arrested and go to jail on Riker's island in this city. Once there we will be beaten and God only knows what else by the criminals locked up there and then…"

"Shut up Bob you're frightening Giovanni." Ron glanced around the warehouse. He saw the crumbled tool table, a black fedora hat and tools strewn about the floor and the tarp lying at the back of the statue and that was about it. "There's got to be a phone here. We can call the police if it's not them at the door."

Giovanni informed them that there was no phone, in fact there was nothing but what they saw except for a bathroom in the corner across from them. "The Signore, he wanted complete isolation and privacy for the surprise which all the time was nothing but a plan to steal and that's why my Sheila lies there…wait, here." He took the hammer which he had shoved through his belt. "This is what killed my Sheila…"

"Oh God almighty, Giovanni, don't touch it," Ron quietly shouted. It was too late.

Giovanni knelt with the hammer in his hand. Ron quickly took the blood soaked handkerchief from his jacket pocket and took the hammer, wrapped it and then asked Iggy to unzip his backpack. He placed hanky and hammer into it. "Now let's get out of here. Once they notice the broken dock door window it will be all over for us. So we can't hide in the bathroom…" he paused. "Unless it has a window, does it Giovanni?"

"Si, a small one above the stall."

"It will have to do. Follow me. Once we see who comes through those doors we can decide if we climb out that window or give ourselves up to the police."

The four made a bee line to the bathroom holding Giovanni as they had in the walkway. Once inside Ron tore off sheets of toilet paper, wet it and placed it over Giovanni's wound on his head. "Clarence, do you have a pocket knife?"

"Don't be ridiculous, why would I have such a thing?"

"I have one," Iggy said as he rummaged through his backpack trying to avoid touching the hammer. He pulled out a Boy Scout knife. "Always be prepared, that's what they told us."

"I could kiss you Iggy, but there isn't time," Ron whispered as he took the knife and began to cut into the cloth toweling in the dispenser. "This will help us break and climb out the window if needed and be used to bind up Giovanni's head. Now Bob, get to the door and peek through the crack. Let me know what you see. And shut off that water, whoever it is they will hear it running."

One last wad of toilet paper wetted by Clarence and it was turned off.

From the crack opening made with the door left slightly ajar Bob peeked through. He had a clear view across the vast open space of the warehouse with only the statue with Sheila upon it between the bathroom and the front doors. Giovanni couldn't be near that door to watch what may be taking place. He sat in the stall holding the wet wad of paper to his head.

"There're three guys coming in," Bob announced.

"Christ, what's with that lock; it wouldn't open for love or money," complained Stephano as he entered swinging open the door with such force that it banged up against the wall with a loud thud. He walked in trying to hold the blood stained pants up and shirtless with only the suit jacket also streaked in blood covering his upper torso. "Let's get this over with, I need decent clothes and fast. I feel creepy in the Signore's clothes let alone what's all over it."

"Shut your face; the Signore will reward you; he said so." Andrew scolded. "Come on…oh Jesus look at this…" his powerful arms opened as if ready to present something special but they shook with abhorrence. "So this is what the signore called an accident."

Stephano ran up to the statue and froze at the body of Sheila. "He murdered her, that's what he did. It's Sheila and her head is crushed in." He gently returned the lace shawl over her face. "She was so sweet to me, always a kind word when I was down when the Signore yelled at me. Where is that asshole artist who did this, I'll kill him with my bare hands." He turned and looked around the almost barren space. He kicked around the tools about the floor as the other two knowing the truth in their hearts stood motionless. "And you Jesus," he pointed to the statue of the dead Christ. "Why did you let this happen?" he kicked the chisel across the floor in a growing misplaced anger.

Finally, Giuseppe yelled, "Stop Stephano, it's not what you think."

The usually quiet one got in his face. "And who's going to make me, you or the faggot next to you?"

Andrew didn't hesitate; he threw himself into Stephano and tackled him to the floor. Each screaming slanderous insults about their manhood and genitals they rolled across the floor trying to get each other in a strangle hold. As their shouts rang through the building, Ron and Clarence watched over Bob's shoulder while Giovanni began humming the Ave Maria again while rocking back and forth on the toilet seat oblivious to Iggy holding onto him.

Giuseppe in vain tried to stop the fight. He placed his hand under his jacket and suddenly a shot rang out echoing throughout the warehouse as one calling out from a cliff in the mountains waiting to hear one's voice returning. The shot ringing throughout the building did what it was intended to do. Andrew and Stephano lay on their backs having pushed each other away. Giuseppe was standing at their feet swinging his gun from one to the other.

"Have you no respect? What did Sheila do to deserve this," he pointed to her lifeless body, her arm dangling over the arm of the Jesus part of the statue. "Kill that son of a bitch Gaglioni not each other."

Stephano pushed himself up into a seated position. "That son of a bitch didn't do this Giuseppe."

"How can you say that, look there she is and where is he?"

Stephano risked getting to his feet while Andrew did the same. "Exactly, my friend, where is he? The Signore said that we would find two bodies here and yet there is only one. That could only mean that he thought both were dead; think about it." His hand rested on the signore's fedora. He took hold of it and then tossed it aside.

Giuseppe lowered the gun. "But he professed love for them both; how could this happen?"

Andrew spoke calmly so as not to excite either man. "They betrayed the Signore," he picked up the hat. "It's as simple as that, he told us so. Maybe it was an accident and maybe Giovanni did attack the Signore and Sheila got in the way but that's not our call. We have a job to do; the movers, they will be here soon to take the statue. It must be made ready, now get the tarp over there."

"Why, who cares about a statue anyway. That asshole artist needs to be found." Stephano stood with bowed head in front of Sheila's body.

"Stephano, get a grip," Giuseppe placed his hand on the distraught man's shoulder. "Let us do what we have to do and then we'll find Giovanni and find out the truth, what say you?"

There was no reply. The gentle giant of a man simply took the tarp and spread it out on the floor next to the statue. The other two did not make a move, they knew better. He then took the body gently off the body of Christ and laid her at the edge of the tarp, recovering her in the lace shawl. "We should say a prayer or something for her. In the name of the Father and of the Son and of the Holy Spirit; I remember that's how we should start to pray. But what should we say?"

Andrew and Giuseppe took their place on either side of him. "I can't remember my First Communion prayers," stated Giuseppe what about you Andrew do you know any?"

"It's been a long time, but here goes. Lord, Sheila was a good woman who always was sweet to Giuseppe, Stephano and me too. Bring her to heaven. Amen."

"Amen."

In the bathroom there were also three answering Amen and one still singing softly the Ave Maria not knowing what was taking place at the base of his statue.

"Okay that's it, now roll her up in the tarp and…"

"And what Andrew? You will not toss her into the river like trash," Stephano grabbed the gun from the inside jacket pocket.

"Don't get excited, we won't do that. Stephano take hold of that end; Giuseppe, you hold the middle and I'll take the head. We'll put her back onto Jesus just like we found her. And then we'll seal the statue up as planned in the crate."

Ron patted Bob on the shoulder as he suggested that they get out before the thugs find them. The three stood at the door of the stall. "Giovanni, we need to get out of this place. But we'll come back with the police and give Sheila a proper service."

Bob closed the bathroom door with a lightly heard click. He didn't want Giovanni to take a final look and see her lying on the statue and being covered in the tarp. Ron stood on the toilet bowl tank and wrapped the towel he had cut around his hand.

"I wish I had that cement rock now," he punched the window. It creaked but didn't break. He punched it again and it cracked. One more time he punched the cracked piece; it fell out onto the street side. Piece by piece he pried the remaining glass pieces out of the frame. "It's clear, Bob, you go first. Come up here, I'll boost you out."

Beyond the closed bathroom door, the pounding of the crate pieces could be heard thus concealing any noise which the breaking of the glass may have caused. One by one they climbed out that window and dropped to the sidewalk below. Their jump from the window disturbed but a few people walking by. Iggy ended up explaining that they were on a scavenger hunt to those who looked at them with suspicion. Just as Ron was about to pull himself up to the window, the bathroom door opened and Stephano entered.

"I need to take a leak. I'll fill the bucket with water while I'm here." He dropped the bucket to the floor and headed for the urinal located next to the stall wall behind which Ron now crouched down on top of the toilet set.

The peeing seemed endless to Ron who thought that he must have a bladder the size of a horse to pee so long. But at last it ended and he began to fill the bucket and wash his hands as he did. The dispenser of course had only a fragment of towel exposed as Ron had cut it away but he managed though why one could only guess as the bucket when filled over flowed and got him wet anyway. He left the door open as he brought the bucket out. Once Ron heard the resumption of crate building and sloshing of water and mop, he jumped to grab hold of the window frame and pull himself up and through the window. Hanging down briefly he called to the guys, "They're crating the statue, we need to get a move on and get the police."

Clarence immediately hailed a cab and the five crammed into it. "Hotel Lexington," Clarence directed the driver.

CHAPTER THREE

THE CAB, THE HORSE AND STITCHES

The artist Giovanni Gaglioni crammed between Ron and Bob. Their pal Iggy was sitting on Clarence's lap, his mind silently coming to grips with what just happened. So too was the artist Giovanni Gaglioni. He looked out the cab's window watching the crowds of people now filling the street. There was plenty of time to people watch as the cab was at a standstill. What Clarence hadn't realized when he hailed the cab was that they would be caught in rush hour traffic in midtown Manhattan which they had to cross. That crossing would take them through Times Square and toward the East River near which was their hotel. To the guys he seemed transfixed on the sights and sounds surrounding them. The cab inched toward Broadway which he studied not with interest more like an escape from what just happened. He began to rub his smock trying to remove the blood soaked marble dust absentmindedly.

"Signore Gaglioni," began Ron. "Is everything okay, ah… va bene with you?"

"Si, grazie…I mean yes thank you. It's just this smock, so dirty and…" he looked down at the blood stains. "Well I am not presentable for your people where you take me."

Bob chimed in, "Oh them, you don't have to worry about them, one, Matthew, is a farmer's son and had to muck out cow shit from the barn, another, Quinlan, is from the Ozark Mountains of Missouri and grew up with outdoor plumbing until he was five years old, then there's the French guy, Francois but we call him Frankie, but really he's from Quebec in Canada. I guess he could be considered a posh type of guy but he's an okay guy. Then there's Jerry. He's from Miami at the tip of Florida where it's hot as you know where in summer time. He's use to being all sandy and wet from the beaches there. Finally you will meet Andy Dooley. Well he's just a Hoosier from Indiana. In Chicago we'd call him a kind of a country bumpkin, but you'll like him. That carrot top head of hair will probably make you want to paint him or something. Oh and then there's Jim Beck, he's from Chicago like me and Iggy, but he's from an old Polish neighborhood of the city, very religious but big and strong as an ox."

"So many people, Bob, am I to meet this day. How can we explain my appearance and this head." Giovanni tugged at the cut up towel now wrapped around his head as a precaution in case his wound began to bleed again.

Ron shot a look to Bob trying to tell him that he just put the guy on overload with information on total strangers to him. "Listen, forget everything that Bob just told you. Just think about going to school and seeing a bunch of fellow students like when you were in art school in Florence. Here, put on my jacket it will cover up most of the…the stains. When we get into the hotel lobby no one will pay attention; that is if this cab ever gets to move." He poked Clarence on the other side of him. "Clare, will we have enough money to pay for this jaunt?"

"Don't worry about that, if we don't we'll get Father Gregory or Brother Anthony, one of them should be able to help us out."

"Lordy, I forgot about them. The guys will be able to accept Giovanni here kind of like you, an older guy but they are a different story… and that's exactly what we have to create for them."

Clarence ignored the reference to his age which was even older than that of the artist. He focused on the Latin professor and the Brother whom they saved and who helped them with the murder case at the Abbey. He was appalled that Ron even thought to make up some type of cock and bull tale to tell their professor no less. Yet he looked at poor Giovanni, so beaten up physically and emotionally that he controlled his tongue lashing.

"We cannot lie to Father and certainly not to Brother Anthony who is like one of us, especially to you know who."

"I'm sitting right here on your lap Clarence," Iggy's face began to shimmer with a burgundy color in his caramel colored skin. "This artist guy... sorry Giovanni for saying it that way but it's true nonetheless. Well you don't know me as I am and as Brother Anthony is, you may be scandalized."

For the first time since they met the Italian artist, he cracked a slight smile as he looked at Iggy over Ron's shoulder. "So you are like Andrew then, is that it? I mean you like the male form as opposed to the female form. Am I too, how do you say it...blunt?"

The guys sat quietly with a smile on their faces just waiting for Iggy to respond.

"No Giovanni you are not too blunt, you have hit it on the head if you pardon my term use. But I am going to be a priest; that means I cannot let such attraction be a part of my life, do you understand? And I cannot risk that others learn of my nature, so to speak, or they will kick me out of the seminary."

"Iggy, such a cute name... I meant no insult; that's what got me in this situation in the first place. I went to a good art school in Firenze... Florence to you. Many there were like you and they were in good company historically for so too were such artistic giants like Da Vinci and Michelangelo, though the latter one denied it publicly. So your nature, as you put it, is safe with me." Giovanni reached over Ron and took hold of Iggy's arm and gave it a shake.

A sudden jerk of the cab and they were thrown backwards. They were on the move and crossing the Times Square area.

"Praise the Lord, we are finally on the move. Hey, Giovanni look out there, that's Times Square with all its bright lights and theaters, neat isn't it? But you've probably seen it a hundred times, but for me it was only my second time and for these guys their first time just earlier this week. We explored it on the way to the 44th Street dock to see where the ship will bring the Pieta for the World's Fair."

Giovanni managed to scooch up on the seat to get a better view. "You are wrong Ron, I have seen only a little of Central Park because the Signore lives on Central Park West. I have seen only what is between the apartment and the warehouse where I carved my Pieta. And pardon me if I boast too much; I did so in a way similar to that of Michelangelo almost five hundred years ago using only hand tools. You see time was important to the Signore. Everyone calls the Signore Battista by that name. He would say it worked against us…but it was he who made it so not me. I worked every day for hours trying to replicate the Master's work for the purpose of having it presented to the Cathedral. It is to be a memory of the visit of the actual Pieta coming from St. Peter's in the Vatican to America. But it was all a lie. Sheila told me the truth. The Signore intends to steal Michelangelo's Pieta and replace it with mine so that he might make millions from the black market or ransom."

Everyone began to talk at the same time. Each expressed shock and the need to stop this Signore person. Everyone agreed to help save Giovanni's statue for what it was originally intended. Watching the face of the artist Ron knew something more than just the saving of his statue was on his mind. So he assured him that honoring Sheila so that she might have a proper burial would be part of any plan. The eyes of the artist sparkled at the mention of her name. He was most grateful to all. Yet at the same time he kept looking at their school jackets imprinted with the Abbey's name.

"But you are students, not like me in the art school, but studying for the priesthood. Does such preparation make you able to face such a man who would murder and do this," he pointed to blood stained towel wrapped around his head, "to another person?"

Iggy smiled and poked Ron in the ribs. "Oh, you'd be surprised to know what we can do, especially this one."

In the chaos of chatter, Bob rolled down the window of the cab. He stuck his head out and spotted a mounted Policeman a few cars back of them.

He began to shout, "Officer, officer we need you; it's an emergency."

The cab driver slammed on his breaks and the five were thrust into the window partition between him and the passengers in the back. He opened the window in that partition. "What the hell do you kids think you're doing? Get your head back in the car; I can get a ticket for that."

Ron pulled Bob back in, "He's right, what are you thinking?"

"Oh my Jesus, I don't know Ron, it just seemed the right thing to do at the time. We have to save the Pieta don't we? You don't have to be the one who always has the solution do you?"

"What the hell do you mean by that?" he dropped his pursuit of an answer. The big blue eyes of Bob were telling him to shove it. So he tried to be rational. "Well yes of course we want to save the statue. But not like mad men, screaming for the police. We have to get our story straight and then tell it to the police and Brother Anthony."

His approach didn't work. Bob felt insulted. Iggy was offering his own take on the situation. The driver was in a panic. The mounted policeman was headed toward the cab.

"Everyone keep calm; Giovanni, it's going to be fine don't you worry, our friend here is just a little too enthusiastic about saving your statue and all." Ron went into thinking mode.

Clarence in the meantime had his own idea. He leaned into the partition window. "Driver…" he glanced at the ID card hanging from the visor, "I mean… Oscar, we are not all kids as you can see. Just move this cab along. I will quiet the kids."

"Christ Clarence, we're not eight year old kids. Did you have to say that?" Bob jammed back into the seat and crossed his arms around his chest with his lower lip coming up over his upper in a most grand pout which would make any eight-year old proud indeed.

"Stop pouting, that's exactly how you acted when you shouted from the window…" Clarence was interrupted by a rap on the roof of the cab.

All five heads turned to the sound with Bob looking up and out of the window. There sitting on his horse was the mounted policeman. "Oh hi officer, may we help you?"

"Well young man someone called to me from this cab. How can I be of help to you?" the officer bent low in his saddle and peered into the cab. "A bit crowded, I'd say. You should have taken two cabs but I'll let that go for now. So what's your problem?"

"Well, I… I was just calling you to…to tell you that my friend Ron here has something to ask you." That's him just on the other side of the guy with the towel wrapped around his head.

"Son, is that true, what's the problem that he can't tell me."

Ron squeezed out from between Giovanni and Clarence and pulled Bob out of the window while gently shoving Giovanni to Clarence's side. Now he sat at the window. He was thinking of how he would wring Bob's neck when they got to the hotel. That's when what his best pal had said gave him a brilliant idea.

"Well it's like this officer; our friend here is visiting your fair city from Italy; ah…he's part of our school group. See the jacket, St. Benedict Abbey that's where we come from in Wisconsin just north of Chicago."

"So your friend is Italian, well my grandmother on my mother's side came from Italy as well. Young man, do you speak English?"

Giovanni found his tongue after several tries. "Yes sir, I do, not too good but I do."

"Well then, where do you come from in Italy?"

"Oh you wouldn't know it; it's a small town in the forest of the Abruzzo province called San Pietro Avelana in central Italy."

"Well no kidding, well that's her province as well, maybe your people knew her people. Her name was Doratina Settefrati."

"I am sorry to say that I do not recall that name, a fine sounding name to be sure; but then I was sent to school in Tuscany and maybe didn't have a chance to meet your family."

"Well that's too bad; now on my father's side; his people came from Ireland, County Mayo in fact but you wouldn't know them for sure. So then, what did you say your problem was?"

The bantering had given Ron enough time to polish a story line or so he hoped. He explained that their friend was working on an art project for the World's Fair and slipped and fell hitting his head in the process. "We were going back to our hotel to tell our professor, Father Gregory, but this traffic as you can see is making it difficult. We think he may need medical attention. See his head is bleeding."

"So it seems; let me see what I can do." Officer Brennan blew his whistle and began to move traffic away from the cab as best as they could. When a car space opened on the other side of his horse he got down and opened the cab door. "Now let's get this young man some help. Come on out all of you. I'll put your friend up on the horse and we'll go just around the corner, there is a Doctor's office there and they can help you."

Clarence paid the driver and was the last to leave the cab. "Ron, this is crazy, we don't have money to pay for medical treatment." He pulled Ron to his side. "Maybe we should just tell the officer the truth about what we saw and what Giovanni told us about this Signore person."

"Really, and then what, get Giovanni arrested for being part of a plot to steal the Pieta? No, just go along with the Officer's plan."

Just off Times Square in the middle of rush hour, the hordes of people stood in amazement as if they were tourists. If they were New Yorkers, they probably were thinking that a movie scene was being practiced. In either case, Officer Brennan was leading the way holding onto the horse's reins. Giovanni was in the saddle clinging for his life on its horn. The four seminarians followed alongside the horse, occasionally forcing out a smile. Tourists flooded around them as they made their way taking pictures and laughing about how frightened the guy on the horse looked. One of them even commented that they never thought such courtesy and concern would be found in New York City of all places. When they got around the corner and to the brass doors leading into a tall building of gray brick, Giovanni was helped off the horse and after thanking Brennan profusely they entered the black and white tiled lobby with banks of elevators on each side of a long corridor. At the end of that corridor were more brass and glass doors behind which were the medical offices. Large gold letters trimmed in black announced that they were entering the "New York Medical Center." Below those in smaller letters, it read, "Time Square Center."

Ron walked up to the unadorned functional reception desk. Despite its Spartan appearance it did display a small stand-alone poster card announcing the World's Fair. The image on the card was that of the Vatican Pavilion and superimposed over it was a picture of the Pieta. He made no comment about the Fair but stuck with the story he had told Officer Brennan. The nurse was most accommodating until she asked for their insurance information. They had none. This forced Ron to tell her that she should contact their professor who would give them the insurance information from St. Benedict's Abbey.

"I think that it would be best to contact this professor yourself, young man," she placed the phone on the raised counter's ledge.

"Sure, thank you maam…" he dialed "O." Yes may I have the number for the Hotel Lexington, no I didn't try information; I dialed "O" for operator. I see, I need to dial "411" okay then thanks for your lack of help."

Clarence poked him in the ribs. "Stop being so juvenile, just dial "411" like at home."

Iggy and Bob were consoling Giovanni on some chrome framed cushioned chairs opposite from where Ron and Clarence stood. The artist didn't understand the poking and the talk of '411.'

"Yes, I need the number for the Hotel Lexington. Thank you I'd appreciate you connecting me." He shot a glance of "Oh My God, what if this doesn't work" to Clarence. "Yes hello, this is Ron De Cenza, I am a registered guest with my school St. Benedict's. I need to speak with…" he hesitated and at the last minute asked for Brother Anthony instead. "Yes thank you, I will hold on."

Clarence took the receiver and covered the mouthpiece. "Why Brother Anthony?"

"Cool it, he'd be more likely to understand that's why and also Father Gregory might feel obliged to tell the Abbot and then all hell will break loose."

While this drama was unfolding on Sixth Av. Off 44th Street, Stephano had just entered the bathroom of the warehouse building with another bucket of bloody water to dump. Each time he did so, he would curse the artist who he was convinced had killed Sheila despite what had been pointed out about the Signore. This time he felt a cool breeze over his head. He turned and looked toward the window over the stall and pulled open its door. Small pieces of glass were scattered about the floor and on the toilet tank.

"Andrew, Giuseppe get in here; I think I found the way Gaglioni got out of the warehouse without us seeing him out front," he yelled.

The two ran to him and just as they reached the door, there was someone pounding on the dock door. "Shit, it's the movers already. Stephano stay in here, they can't see you looking like that."

When they got to the dock door, they saw more broken glass, this time just one panel of the door was broken out, not the whole door frame. On the other side of the door a hulk of a guy stood with heavy beard and bulging arms instructing them to open the dock's delivery door even before Andrew got the back door open.

"You're early, you'll have to wait a few minutes while we make sure the crate is solid and ready to be transported," Andrew told the driver of the truck. "So wait here on the dock or the truck whatever you want. We'll be right back. Giuseppe will tell you where the truck is to be taken with the package."

Andrew entered the bathroom. Stephano was dumping the contents of the bucket into the toilet. "Make sure no blood can be seen in the sink or toilet bowl. The movers are already here so I need to check on the package."

Stephano threw the bucket down and stormed into Andrew's face. "I don't like this Andrew, we were supposed to make a switch and that's all, now we're covering up a death, maybe even a murder and for some foreigner too."

"Cool your jets; he's Italian just like you…"

"Bullshit, I'm American born and raised not like that faggot…"

"Watch your mouth Stephano or those will be the last words you ever speak." Andrew was quite sensitive about his attraction to guys.

"Oh yeah, well just try to touch me. I'm the one who stripped down in front of all you assholes. I'm the new favorite of the Signore, he said so, so just try something I dare you…"

"Shove it, and just follow me. We have to make sure the crate is sealed tight."

With a kick which sent the bucket flying into the stall and crashing into the bowl with a splash and clank, Stephano followed Andrew to the crated statue on which the body of Sheila laid wrapped in the loose end of the tarp. He mumbled something about Andrew wanting to get a piece of his backside but thought better than saying it to his face.

Besides the floor being wet from scrubbing off the blood, it was now clear of all the tools and broken pieces of the table. These had all been piled at the delivery door and would be taken away with the crated statue. Andrew stood in front of the crate and pronounced it to be sealed and identical to the one coming from Italy on the ship. "See even the top has been painted orange, like the one on the ship."

"So what, once they open it and find poor Sheila, they will know it's a fake. Then what are we to do when the Signore finds out that we crated her with the statue?"

Andrew slowly turned to face Stephano; he walked with even paces so as not to pose a threat. Within inches of his face, Andrew placed his hands gently on the lapels of the blood stained suit coat which belonged to that of the Signore Battista. He rubbed his hands on them and glanced down at Stephano's bare chest and smiled. "We need to get you properly dressed for the reception later tonight at the United Nations." He patted Stephano's cheek, "Come on; let's get the show on the road."

Stephano didn't know what to say or do as he touched his cheek where it was patted and wiped it as if removing some disease. He then followed Andrew as far as the bathroom. "You said that they can't see me, so I'll wait in here."

"Smart boy, as soon as they're gone we'll look for Sacha and get you properly dressed. It's almost 5:00 p.m. he should be driving by soon to get us."

Clarence being the only one over twenty-one, besides the patient, was at the reception desk signing the release papers on behalf of St. Benedict Abbey. Ron came out of the examination room with Giovanni who had been stitched up and sported a gauze pad covered with a wide bandage on the right side of his head just partially on the forehead itself. He was holding a bottle of pain pills just in case the headache persisted and some ointment in a packet to apply to the wound when the bandage was changed the following morning. Iggy and Bob ran up to them.

"So how did it go, did it hurt?" asked Bob.

"Of course it hurt, dumb wad," answered Ron for Giovanni who didn't quite know how to react to the question. "He'll be able to let the wound breathe in a couple of days when the bandage comes off. Then next week we have to get the stitches removed. Giovanni why don't you go and sit with the guys, I need to see if Clarence needs any help."

The three returned to the row of chrome framed chairs alternating with gray and purple plush cushions.

"Clare, how goes it?"

"How goes it? That's all you have to say? Well it goes like shit that's how it goes. Brother Anthony may have been kind on the phone, but they'll be hell to pay I can feel it in my bones."

The words were no sooner out of his mouth than through the second set of brass doors with glass panels came strolling in the short Filipino priest in the full habit of the Benedictine Order and the god-like Apollo looking Brother Anthony also in the habit of a black cassock like robe covered with a scapular panel on front and back on which the cowl or hood hung. The cassock robe was tied with a black leather belt. They both ignored those on the chairs and walked directly up to Ron and Clarence standing frozen in place.

"I'm sorry boys, but I felt obligated to tell Father about this situation." Brother Anthony stepped back and let the priest approach.

Clarence handed Father Gregory the release form and bill. "We still owe ten dollars. The insurance didn't cover it all."

"Is that so," the priest turned. "Brother Anthony do you have ten dollars on you?"

"I'll check." He reached into the slit on the side of the cassock and into the pocket of his black pants underneath. Pulling out a hand full of cash, he began to count the multiple bills, mostly singles. "There, here's ten dollars Father."

"You are most kind." Father Gregory addressed the nurse behind the counter. "I believe that this should settle the outstanding balance for the treatment."

She quickly counted the bills and verified that it would indeed cover the balance. She then took the bill from him and stamped it Paid, then handed it back to him.

"You are most kind," the priest turned to address his students. "And now may we meet this victim of circumstances as you put it and get the real story behind the injury? Mr. De Cenza perhaps you should do the honors as you seem to have had all the answers when we spoke on the phone."

As they approached the three on the chairs, two stood and pulled up Giovanni to do the same. Then Bob offered a chair to Father Gregory and Brother Anthony. Iggy pulled other chairs around to form a tight circle so that all could face each other and hear each other easly. It would also make eavesdropping difficult. It was evident that the nurse was eyeing them from behind the counter listening in on what was being said.

"Sit down gentlemen; I would like to hear the truth before we go back to the hotel." Father Gregory's tone had a hint of worry in it as he focused on the bandage affixed to Giovanni's head. "However before you begin Ron, may I point out that all your classmates are in a state of, if not distress, certainly concern. Your absence from us all day is a worry. It seems Ron that you think you know how to traverse this grand city because you have visited it when you were sixteen. May I point out that perhaps you allowed yourself a bit too much confidence in your exploratory skills?"

Ron turning a bright red was about to offer an excuse, counterargument perhaps even an apology but thought better of doing anything.

"Now then, I have had my say. Shall we begin to hear from Clarence first as he's the eldest in your class and our Abbot Lawrence thought him to be a fine example to you all."

The compliment which really wasn't one at all shook whatever clarity Clarence may have been able to present. Yet, as an obedient seminarian, he began as best he could. "Let me begin by saying that we were having a delightful time today as we explored the city. Ron took us to see St. Patrick's Cathedral and then across the street to Rockefeller Center where we went to the top of the Rock and saw the sprawl of New York below. Then off to Times Square and walking past the Theaters so that we could decide which play or musical we'd like to see if we could afford to do so. That's when we, that is, all of us as one, decided to go see the reception dock."

"Dock, as in where a ship moors?"

"Yes Father, exactly. It's the one where the ship carrying the Pieta will transfer the statue to a barge. I think its name is Challenger…not the ship the barge's name. The ship's name is the Cristoforo Colombo, you know Italian for Christopher Columbus."

"Thank you for the detail Clarence but I think Father wanted to learn about that," Brother Anthony pointed to Giovanni's head."

"Sure, I just wanted to be thorough. After all we are scheduled to perform ushering duties to the visitors when the Vatican Pavilion opens in a couple of days. Anyway, on the way to the dock, that's when we met

Giovanni Gaglioni an artist from Italy." He ended without any clarification of how they happened to meet the artist. Nor did he make any reference to the wound on his head.

"Indeed, Brother and I are most pleased that you enjoyed your exploration of the Cathedral and theater district. But how did you come upon this young man from Italy?"

Iggy and Bob began to speak at the same time but Ron stopped them before they even began. "Father, Brother Anthony, let's not drag this out any longer. I am the one who broke into the warehouse and believed in this man's story. I am the one who led the others into harm's way by doing so."

Father Gregory held up his hand. He thanked Ron for such honesty and confession of guilt but that didn't answer his question as to how they had come upon the injured man. Nor did it address why they had to break into a warehouse because of his story, let alone what was inside that building.

Ron took the not so subtle hint and got to the point. He began with an analogy to the Parable of the Good Samaritan which Jesus told about a traveler who was beaten, robbed, stripped and left to die in the gutter. He told them of how many people saw a bloodied hurting man in the warehouse doorway yet chose to ignore and run from the sight. He became rather dramatic in his laying out the scene on 44th street but it served to paint the picture of what actually happened.

"We didn't want to be like the rich man or priest who ignored such plight and injury, we just had to be like the Good Samaritan. So when we saw Giovanni here in agony and so bruised, we offered him our help."

"Yes, that's how it happened Father, honest," confirmed Bob.

Brother Anthony had to add his own observation with a question as well. "Gentlemen, I call you friends because that's what you are to me and we all know why. So I commend you on your effort to be a Good Samaritan, but why on earth did you not go directly to a hospital and have this poor man helped?"

Before Ron or any of the others could respond, Giovanni spoke. He addressed Father Gregory and Brother Anthony by name telling them that he learned of their great courage and kindness during the murder incident at the Abbey. The priest and Brother were not particularly pleased that a total stranger had learned of the scandalous event. They chose to say nothing. The artist told them how he learned of them in the cab ride during which the policeman helped them reach the doctor and receive treatment. But more than that, he answered the Brother's question by telling them of the missing part of the story.

In a weak voice, with a throbbing returning to his head, he continued. "They found me on the ground just beyond the sidewalk in front of the warehouse building, empty of everything except for my work and the materials needed to complete it. But I will come to that later, first I must tell you about Sheila Murphy. To look at her, with such blond hair as to rival sunlight and red lips as to make you seek a forbidden fruit from the garden of Eden you would understand how my heart grew fond of her. I work for a man who is most demanding and from this," Giovanni pointed to the bandage, "I learned with a cruelness hidden quite well." He returned his focus on Sheila. "She offered me a kind word and a smile to lift my spirits when I felt that my work wasn't being appreciated as it should be. Today was such a time when a smile was offered and a hand touched in innocence."

"So where is this Sheila now?" asked Brother Anthony.

"She is in the warehouse still, for when we broke into the building to rescue her others who protect the Signore came to find me and end me. Your students took me away and hid me. They helped me to escape. But my Sheila they could not rescue for she was with the angels already."

The priest and brother exchanged a glance of understanding that the woman must be dead. They expressed their most profound sorrow for his suffering and her death.

"Brother, ask the nurse to use the phone. Call the police. We must return to that warehouse and find Sheila." Father Gregory took Giovanni's hand. He consoled him on what was obviously a heartbreaking loss.

While the Brother did so, Giovanni knelt before the priest. "And you will give her the last rites Father, she would like that. You will find her resting in the arms of the Holy Mother and our Lord."

"Of course my son, we know those who believe are with the Lord."

"Father," Ron quietly interrupted. "He means what he says quite literally. Giovanni is a sculptor who was commissioned by this Signore person to reproduce Michelangelo's Pieta. Sheila rests on the statue of the body of Jesus being held by Mary."

"My sons, I cannot speak," he dropped his professorial speech and used the pastoral language as he went to each of his students and embraced them. Coming to Giovanni he placed his arm around his shoulders and walked with him toward the brass doors. There they waited for the police to arrive in prayer, which for Giovanni meant the humming of the "Ave Maria."

CHAPTER FOUR

QUESTIONS AND REVELATION

The bells of St. Patrick's Cathedral across from Rockefeller Center and the old Cathedral Basilica of St. Patrick's near Little Italy at Mulberry and Prince Streets and all the Churches in between them were ringing out the 6:00 p.m. evening hour. At that moment through the first set of brass doors facing 6th Ave. off 44th Street there entered a rather tall man in plain clothes. His attire spoke law enforcement. It consisted of a dark blue polyester suit, light blue shirt and navy blue solid tie. He was accompanied by two uniform cops with pistols drawn.

Standing petrified at the second set of glass and brass trim doors, Father Gregory and Giovanni watched as they made their way toward them past the bank of elevators. The four seminarians and Brother Anthony now stood behind them equally unnerved. Ron in particular knew what it was like to be interrogated about a crime but with the added dark cloud of being a suspect. Thus his heart sank for he knew Giovanni would be the prime suspect as the investigation began. After all he had used the hammer now in Iggy's backpack. When they found Sheila they would surely conclude the crushed head was the result of blunt force trauma. His mind spun out various scenarios, each of which he tried to address internally as he watched the police officers close in on the door.

One of the uniform officers opened the door, the seven beyond it instinctively stepped back to give the plain clothes officer space to maneuver as he entered with a small flip pad of paper in hand. He acknowledged their presence with a smile and a nod of his head. Then he directed the officer at the door to guard it. No one was to enter or leave for the time being. To the second officer, he ordered that he should speak with the doctor on duty and the nurses as to what had taken place in their offices which resulted in the urgent call to Police Headquarters.

Now he was able to focus on the Priest, Brother, the Seminarians and the cause of the call, the injured man. Taking note of the circle of chairs he invited them to take a seat and pulled over one for himself. But as they went to the chairs, he began to direct them to a particular seat which resulted in Ron being on his left, Giovanni on his right and directly opposite him the priest and brother. The other guys were directed to the seats in-between. The circle being filled as he desired he finally spoke.

As he introduced himself as Detective Sargent Brandon Malone, Ron let out a moan of sorts and muttered to Bob on his other side. "Another Irishman, just like Detective Sargent David Monahan. I hope he is as understanding."

The Detective Sargent poked Ron in his arm. "Perhaps young man you would like to share your comment with all of us and then tell me why you hope that I am an understanding person."

"It was nothing Sir; we just know a kind and understanding police detective just like you back in Lake Como, that's in Wisconsin near our school."

"Indeed, well I would certainly be thrilled to hear all about such a policeman who would warrant such acclaim as you seem to have for him. First I'll need all your names, ages, occupation. Secondly, tell me why you are here in New York City all the way from Wisconsin. Finally you sir," he patted the arm of Giovanni. "From you I will need a statement as to how you were injured as well."

The introductions began in the reception area now void of nurses at the desk. Some began to feel that the room had become hot; others that it was getting cold and all agreed that the air was so thick with tension that it could be cut with a knife. Yet no one addressed those issues, rather they answered as they were directed to do. Through it all, the Detective Sargent Malone jotted notes on his pad. He would ask them to repeat something when he fell behind in his note taking which periodically happened when his Parker pen gave him trouble. Then he would shake it and lick the pen point and continue writing.

He found out that Ron and Bob were both nineteen that Iggy was twenty, and all were part of the Latin School of St. Benedict Abbey but all were to study for the priesthood for the Archdiocese of Chicago, their hometown so to speak, though Ron clarified that he lived in Oak Park just across the street from the Windy City. When he heard that Clarence was thirty-six, he became a bit perplexed. Clarence explained that he was what the Church called a late vocation and that he already had a degree from Lewis University in teaching. Father Gregory explained that he was their Latin teacher and responsible for them as they performed their duties of ushering in guests at the Vatican Pavilion who would come to view Michelangelo's Pieta.

"You probably already know that the Holy Father, Pope Paul VI granted permission for it to be brought from Rome for the World's Fair. It's due to open in a few days."

The Detective Sargent informed him that he was well aware of the time table for the ceremonies and opening of the Fair.

There was a bit of a commotion when it was Brother Anthony's turn when he announced that he was in charge of the Ministry caring for the gay community by his order.

"So you're going to save the gays from going to hell, is that it?" asked the Detective Sargent.

Brother became outraged but couldn't get any words out to express how he felt without perhaps ending up in jail. Iggy jumped from his chair and was pulled down by Clarence. The little man from the Philippines however set the policeman straight.

"Detective Sargent, our Lord has already saved all people if you remember your Catechism. It's not a matter of having all the answers to get anyone into heaven but to provide support, encouragement, understanding and the opportunity to experience the love of God…you do believe in God, I presume given your name."

Now it was the Detective Sargent's turn to feel warm and uncomfortable. "I beg your pardon Father. Sure I go to Church…ah sometimes. I went to

Catholic School as a boy too, right here but on Staten Island by the Statue of Liberty's island." He felt as if he were being closed in as those eyes around the circle blazed outrage and then sought out Iggy with sudden softening and compassion. It didn't take him long to figure out that the young man was probably one of those gays he had just condemned to hell. "I am so sorry. I didn't mean that all gays were going to hell like automatically…but you know, we all need saving and right now I need to be saved from putting my foot in my mouth. So if we could continue…"

During this heated then cool exchange, Giovanni realized that he was next in line to give his story. He suddenly felt hot and took off the school jacket which Ron had given him. The Detective's eyes were instantly drawn to the blood stains on the smock.

He was not alone. Every pair of eyes in that circle of chairs zeroed in on that smock. Once taken in they flashed their gaze on the Detective Sargent. Each was trying to figure out how this bushy auburn rather unkempt hair man would react to the sight. As for Father Gregory and Brother Anthony, they like the detective were also viewing the gruesome sight for the first time, but they like him managed to say nothing and show no emotion whatsoever.

"Just give me your name and then tell me why your smock is splattered with blood," Malone directed quietly while touching Giovanni's arm in a gesture meant to quiet the artist's nerves and offer support but which resulted in tears and quaking.

"The blood…it is mine…" he hesitated trying to form the words and then broke down in sobs as he held his hands to his face. "But it also that of my Sheila…"

"Your Sheila! Who is this woman and how is she yours?" Malone waited for no answer, he bellowed to his uniform officers at the door and questioning the medical staff in the examination room. "Van Buren, O'Hara, get yourselves into the reception lobby on the double."

Officer O'Hara stationed at the door was at the back of Malone's chair in seconds while Van Buren ushered in the doctor, two nurses and receptionist behind the counter and told them to wait there. He then joined his partner behind Malone. Both knew what the call meant. That is a potential criminal may be taken into custody depending on how the questioning proceeded.

Giovanni was now on the verge of hysteria. Ron jumped out of his chair just as Brother Anthony rose from his but was pulled down by Father Gregory. "Let Ron handle this Brother, he has been with him all day."

Ron knelt in front of Giovanni now bent over and weeping. "Giovanni, it's going to be okay…va bene. Take a deep breath; no one is here to hurt you. None of us will let them."

The big brown eyes which could match those of Ron peeked out from the hands which covered his face. "I will say the wrong thing. I will use the wrong words…I cannot talk of it…of Sheila."

Ron shouted over to the receptionist counter. "I need some Kleenex; do you have some back there?"

The receptionist held up a box. Her hand was trembling.

Van Buren left his position to fetch it from her. "Listen kid," he began as he handed the box to Ron, "the Detective needs his questions answered here or at the station, savvy?"

Taking the box from the officer, who could stand up easily to the goons who they saw in the warehouse, he replied that he understood. Then he looked at the Detective Sargent. "Sir, Giovanni is an artist brought here from Italy. He is not entirely comfortable with our language as you might note. May I tell you what the four of us saw earlier today and what Giovanni told us; it may help him to calm down." Ron pulled two pieces of tissue from the pop up box and handed them to Giovanni.

"If it will get the story out, then do it," Malone was trying to be patient.

"Thank you," he turned to Iggy on the chair next to the artist. "Iggy would you mind sitting over by Bob?" As Iggy transferred places, Ron handed the box to Giovanni and sat down. He glanced at the priest and Brother and then noticed the print hanging above them. It was one of those pastoral scenes meant to bring on calmness and relax the patient. A stream flowed through a forest area of lush green leafed trees; through their branches sun light filtered down and sparkled on the flowing water. He took a deep breath and prayed that he wouldn't use the wrong words as Giovanni put it and remain calm. He was well aware that sometimes his Italian heritage made that difficult at best. He grabbed a tissue from the box now resting on Giovanni's lap and wiped his brow.

He tried to be as accurate as possible, pausing when a thought may not have been clear to get reinforcement from one of the guys. Malone had handed his pad to Van Buren; he was to keep the notes. He wanted to focus on Ron's words and Giovanni's reaction to them.

All went along smoothly as the story of how they found the beaten Giovanni Gaglioni on the ground just outside some metal doors on 44th Street on their way to view the reception area for the Pieta. The Detective heard about the Parable of the Good Samaritan as well. Father Gregory rolled his eyes thinking that such drama was over the top. But Malone took the story with grace. Then Ron had to explain how they broke into the warehouse from the rear of the building at the loading dock. Malone looked up at his men. They understood that this was breaking and entering according to the law. However the mitigating circumstance of trying to rescue Sheila was taken into consideration. When he found out that Sheila was dead and that her body was on the statue of the Christ bring held by his mother, a statue that Giovanni hand carved out of marble, he jumped to his feet.

"God almighty, sorry Father," he began to bellow orders. "Van Buren, tell Jones in the squad to call for back-up. They are to meet us at the warehouse on 44th Street near 6th Avenue and pronto. Listen all of you who were with this man," he pointed to Giovanni. "Are you sure that she was dead? Sometimes people appear to be dead but are only unconscious."

Giovanni began to weep again. "But she is gone Detective, I held her after she was struck with the hammer, the very hammer which is in his pack on his back." He pointed to Iggy.

"Oh my God, I completely forgot that I had it," he tore the backpack off and handed it to O'Hara.

Officer O'Hara methodically opened the pack and peered inside. "There's something here all right and it's wrapped in a blood soaked handkerchief if I'm not mistaken."

"Don't touch it," ordered Malone. The circle was now in chaos as both priest and Brother were beside themselves as to how to protect the four seminarians who knew of a murder weapon and chose not to report it immediately and for sympathy for the artist who had now thrown himself into Ron's arms. "Giovanni Gaglioni, who does this hammer belong to?"

"I…I would say it's mine. I use it on the chipping of the marble as I carved the statue."

"You leave me no choice," he looked for his officers. Van Buren was just entering the reception area. "Van Buren, cuff this man on suspicion of murder."

Ron and the guys went ballistic, each yelling that it was an outrage and that Giovanni was innocent. "You can't do this," he took hold of the artist and pushed him through the chairs and toward the doors. "Of course the hammer is his, as he said but he wasn't the one who used it on Sheila. It was this Signore guy, his boss. You didn't let me finish the story of what happened." Ron pressing against Giovanni squeezed him against the glass as he inched his way to the door itself which led to the corridor. The medical staff began screaming with fear and outrage for they saw a gentle soul when they treated him.

O'Hara dropped the backpack and pulled his gun. "Stop, do not let me use this Ron De Cenza." He held the gun with two hands and pointed it at Ron's chest.

The teen and the artist froze along the glass. Malone shouted. "Put away that gun O'Hara before someone gets hurt. You over at the counter, quiet down. You aren't helping the situation. And as for all of you," he pointed to the guys in the school jackets. "You had best keep your comments to yourself until I hear the entire story. Sorry Father, Brother but these teens and that guy Clarence should really know better than to harbor a potential criminal. They have concealed a possible murder weapon from us, and wasted our time with stories of the Good Samaritan when the so called real murderer, that is if they are telling the truth, gets away."

"My profound apologies, however if you knew a bit more about what Ron had just experienced not long ago, you may have a better understanding of why he would want to protect Giovanni from being accused falsely of murder."

"Is that so, well he can fill me in on our way to this warehouse where all of this supposedly took place. O'Hara, take Ron and Giovanni to my car and stay with them. The rest of you may ride in the squad cars waiting outside." He walked over to the shaken medical people. "I am sorry for this little bit of confusion. You are free to go for now. Should I need you, I shall contact you…oh and thank you for your statements to Officer Van Buren."

Outside, Officer Van Buren was ushering Ron and Giovanni into the unmarked black Chevy sedan with a portable red gumball light affixed to its roof. It was flashing a revolving light and attracting a number of locals and tourists heading for Broadway to the scene. Officer Jones had to get out of the car, summon the drivers in the other two squads to create a space so that everyone could get to their assigned vehicle. Bob was insisting that he go with Ron as they were a team. O'Hara was unimpressed and sent him to ride with Father Gregory in the squad in front of Malone's car. Brother Anthony, Iggy and Clarence were to ride in the first squad car.

When Malone entered his car, all was in order and ready to head out to the warehouse. "Are we all comfy gentlemen?" He plunked himself down between Giovanni and Ron, crawling over the former to do so. "Now then, why didn't you call the police as soon as you found Giovanni in this state laying on the street no less?"

The car began to inch its way into traffic. Sirens were now turned on to facilitate their progress which was still slow nonetheless. They were headed for the docking area of the warehouse as that's where Ron said they could get in easily since he broke the backdoor window. He hadn't of course, Giovanni actually broke the window. But Ron felt that such details would only cause further harm. The information did not impress Malone, who informed him that he just admitted to breaking into a building.

Ron leaned over Malone to get Giovanni's attention. "You see, even I use the wrong words."

Malone gently pushed him back to his side. "You may think that you're cute with your comments young man but this is New York City and we don't take breaking the law lightly. But I'm not pressing you about what you did. If you really want to help Mr. Gaglioni, I need the evidence and information which may help me prove his story. For instance what does this Signore person look like? Most of which I have yet to hear thanks to the hammer issue and your attempt to break the law yet again."

The walls of the car seemed to be closing in on Ron. Still without his jacket which was back on Giovanni, he also felt a chill. April nights in New

York could be cool and that it was as they finally approached the warehouse building. And all that Malone learned was that the Signore had come to see the statue with Sheila. He was dressed in a fine silk Armani suit with a black overcoat and wearing black fine leather gloves. Sheila he learned was a vision of loveliness in a mink coat, pink dress and lace shawl under the coat's collar. When Giovanni mentioned the shawl he had to pause to control his emotions. Finally Malone was told how a copy of the Pieta was created by the suspect and that it was against the marble of that statue that Giovanni had banged his head when thrown into it by the Signore. Who that mysterious boss, as the artist referred to him was, well that had yet to be presented. The cars were pulling up to the actual dock and formed a line to block any traffic attempting to come to the building or leave it for that matter. The entire building was surrounded. Pedestrian traffic was guided to the other side of the street.

Officer Perry Jones opened the door of Malone's car. "Sir, the building is surrounded."

"Thanks Jones, give O'Hara and Van Buren assistance with the others. Bring them to the receiving dock door there." He pointed to where Ron had told him they could enter and then asked Ron and Giovanni to get out of the car.

Standing at the back door and seeing the broken panel, he glanced through the panel. The interior was in darkness as the shadows and nightfall itself crept over the city. He tried the door handle and it was not locked. "Okay gentlemen follow me. Our first task is to find a way to get some lights turned on."

Giovanni told Malone that he could direct him to the electrical box which he used many times as he worked at night on the Pieta. The three entered while the others waited with the officers on the cement stairs leading up to the door and delivery platform. Giovanni led them to the left of the door and flipped open the box's cover. He pulled up the main switch handle. Large metal shaded overhead lights came to life and the interior was adequately bathed in light. As soon as the interior was illuminated, Giovanni looking across the cavernous room screamed and began to run in circles around the center of the room, where he knew the statue should be. Ron followed yelling, that "it's gone, it's gone."

Malone chased them inside and ordered them to stop. Ron ran up to him and emotionally pleaded for him to put the guns away that Giovanni was just upset about his statue and Sheila not being in the warehouse. O'Hara and Van Buren waited for the order to holster and got it. Jones held the others just inside the back entrance door.

Malone called everyone to the center of the room. "Now then, as you can see, the statue is not here. Also there is no body, no murder victim. In fact I can't see any sign of human activity or anything which may indicate that someone was here let alone carving a statue out of marble. So here's the 64,000 dollar question; where is the murder victim?" He turned so as to be within inches of Giovanni's face, a face now lined with worry and grief. "O'Hara, look for prints on all the doors. If someone was in here there has to be some sign of their presence…"

Ron interrupted the Detective Sargent. "Sir, look at the floor; it's wet."

Malone went down on one knee and rubbed his finger across the floor near where he stood. "It's damp, not unusual for an empty building on an April night." Then he shot a grin at Ron. "Okay I see your point. Van Buren, take samples of this residue and check for something other than water at the lab. Now young man does that satisfy you?"

"If you'd pardon me just for a moment; Bob come with me. Clarence and Iggy take the officers to the back door. Show them where we entered and look for pieces of broken glass which may match that of the missing window panel in the door."

"Well, Father, we seem to have a budding Detective on our hands."

"My son, you don't know the half of it."

"Mr. Gaglioni, you'll have to come with me. I need to check on those two. From now on you'll have to be like mustard on a hot dog."

The confused artist turned to the priest. "Padre, what is this mustard on a hot dog and how do I become such?"

The priest smiled and patted him on the shoulder while explaining it just meant that he would have to be near the Detective Sargent at all times. Malone laughed and pulled on the artist's arm to have him follow. "Brother Anthony, I think we must also be like mustard on the hot dog as far as being near these seminarians."

They followed Malone and the artist to the bathroom where they found Bob and Ron in the stall with Ron standing on top of the tank as he had done when breaking the window for their escape. Just as he was looking down from his perch at Bob, he noticed something in the toilet bowl. "Bob, take a look in the bowl, is that what I think it is?"

"Ah, I hope not. All I see is some pieces of rope stuck at the bottom where the crap goes down."

"Exactly, and that proves that someone was in this bathroom besides us that is." Ron saw the gathering crowd at the stall door. "Great, we've made a discovery while checking out this broken window which I broke so that we could escape the goons."

Malone was getting perturbed. "Listen kid, I am tolerating your shenanigans because I want to believe you. After all you're studying to become a priest and all. But this is getting to be a "B" movie plot and I don't intend to be the dumb cop unjustly persecuting this innocent victim." He pointed to Giovanni with his thumb as if no one would know what he was doing.

Bob interrupted the comment with an excited remark. "Wow, do you really think this could be a movie plot? I wonder. Maybe Murder in New York City could be the name; and just maybe we could all have parts in it, you know to give it an authentic feel. What do you think Ron?"

"Brother Anthony, take my friend's temperature. He is either hallucinating from a fever or he's smoked some weed. Maybe you can figure it out."

They could not hold it in, and the laughter broke a little of the tension though poor Giovanni had no clue as to what a "B" movie was or how this terror he was living could be a film plot.

"Shit Ron, I never touched pot in my life, you know that." Bob's words sank in. "Oh my God, I'm sorry Father."

Malone put an end to the nonsense by calling attention to the toilet bowl once again. Ron went on to explain that the window was broken because he broke it with his hand wrapped in the toweling from the dispenser. He pointed to the sink area. That toweling also served as a temporary bandage on Giovanni's head he went on to say. Then he asked him to look into the bowl and describe what he saw.

"Now I said stop the nonsense. We have to find a murder victim or this friend of yours is going to jail for putting the New York Police force on a wild goose chase and you four will be right there with him."

The reaction was expected, panic from Bob who thought he'd get raped, protestation from Clarence as if he were Clarence Darrow in court, and a burgundy color raising in Iggy's face. Ron however remained calm. "Just do me the favor Detective Sargent, pretty please." He folded his hands as if in prayer and bowed to the Detective Sargent which Father Gregory thought to be impertinent but said nothing.

"Okay, but this best be something…all I see is slightly discolored water and a couple of strings or rope pieces stuck at the bottom."

Ron jumped off the tank. "Exactly, and that proves that someone used this for something other than going to take a…a poop," he smiled at the priest and Brother Anthony. "Those are pieces of mop head rope, I'm sure of it. If you test them you might find remains of blood and that would prove that there was a murder."

Malone bellowed, "O'Hara get…"

"I'm right here sir."

"So you are. Go get the evidence collection kit and get those things out of the toilet and tested."

"Yes, sir," O'Hara scurried out.

"Now as for you young man, let me just point out a few things. One, blood would indicate someone bled not that he or she was dead. Two, we would have to match the blood with the victim and we have no victim; and three…" Malone was at a loss for words. "Oh yes, and three how do we know who put the mop in the toilet and how is this Signore person part of all of this?"

Now it was Ron's turn to be at a loss for words but of all people it was the Italian artist who found words. He identified the goons as really being the security team for the Signore. And he named them; Andrew Jackson, Stephano Rondini, Giuseppe Mortelli and the limo driver too, one called Sacha Dumbroski. Malone jotted their names on his pad, ripped out the sheet and called for Van Buren this time. He was also right at the bathroom door. He told him to have the names checked out.

"I'll have it radioed in right away sir." And off Van Buren ran.

A more amiable Malone was becoming evident. "Well now we're getting somewhere. All we have to do is find these three and the mysterious Signore. Exactly why do you call him so and who is he anyway?"

Once again it was the Italian artist Giovanni Gaglioni who filled in the missing information. He did so with a sense of courage which he felt growing within himself. That confidence was due to Ron proving that the four Seminarians and he were in the warehouse and he could verify the people involved. He proudly announced that the term signore was a title like Mister in English but it also meant Lord and the Signore was Lord of all who served him, including himself, for he commissioned the copy of the Pieta. "So we just call him as do most of his people the Signore. His name is Carlo Battista."

Malone became apoplectic. "Are you out of your mind, Carlo Battista, as in the tycoon of the Import/Export Art business who most people call the mob boss of Manhattan but behind his back? He has connections around the world and dines with the Governor at the drop of a hat. In fact he's at some hifalutin event tonight at the United Nations. A lot of my guys are guarding the area right now.

"Oh my Lord, Father Gregory, the United Nations; we're supposed to be there to help serve the guests and meet the Ambassador from Italy and the Vatican representative since we will be working at the pavilion. And aren't you and Brother Anthony supposed to be with the Abbot?"

The eyes of Giovanni Gaglioni brightened and revenge grew in his heart.

Through the broken window of the warehouse bathroom the sounds of chimes from the Churches of New York City filtered in. They announced the 8:00 p.m. hour.

United Nations Headquarters

CHAPTER FIVE

INTRIGUE AT THE UNITED NATIONS

Father Gregory and Brother Anthony were in a quandary. What Ron had pointed out was quite accurate. They were supposed to accompany the head of their Abbey, Abbot Lawrence, to the United Nations where a gala was being hosted by the Nation of Italy on behalf of the Vatican which was not a formal member of the United Nations. However, given the historical significance of Michelangelo's Pieta coming to the World's Fair the Cultural arm of the United Nations felt it important to celebrate the arrival of the statue at the 44th Street dock. That highly anticipated arrival had the city abuzz with excitement. At the same time it was unthinkable not to be present to support their students who were trying to save the Italian artist from being arrested.

As the last chime of the bells rang out, the two Benedictines huddled just outside of the bathroom door to discuss their options.

Inside Malone found himself to be in a quandary as well. Still shocked to hear of the accusation that the Signore was none other than a prominent business tycoon with mob ties, he knew that he had to tread carefully not rush in as a bull in a china shop. But how to follow through with the investigation and not offend half the elite of New York City at this gala was his dilemma to solve and quickly. So now he huddled with O'Hara,

Van Buren and Jones to lay out a plan to gather information about Carlo Battista while keeping an eye on him.

While all this huddling and secretive conversations were taking place in and out of the cramped quarters of the bathroom, Ron and Bob still stood in the stall with Giovanni. Clarence and Iggy placed themselves at its rust laden door now swung open. Why they thought that their presence could protect their friends was another matter. But they stood like soldiers ready to protect their own. They locked their arms and faced inward to offer moral support.

"Ron," began Bob, "how about going out the window like we did earlier?"

Ron climbed back on top of the tank and pulled himself up to the window's ledge. He was peeking out over the broken frame which he had caused. He could just see squad car lights flashing. "Nope, they're all around us." He jumped back down. "In any case, what would that prove other than that Giovanni here is guilty?"

The silence which followed was only broken by the sniffling of Giovanni as he tried to hold back his fear and tears. A man of his age, twenty-eight, he thought, should have more courage, grow two and stand up to the Signore. The image of Sheila's body on his statue brought on a more sensible approach. It would take more than just him to bring down the Signore let alone getting through his body guards.

Gathered around the sink were Malone and his officers. The Detective Sargent was drawing some type of diagram on the mirror over the sink with a bar of soap. Clarence listened in on their conversation.

"Now this is the reception hall, just a rectangular room off the General Assembly Hall. Our men should already be there to help with security. The problem is that this is international territory and we have no jurisdiction. We are there only to assist with security because of all the big wigs attending," Malone explained.

"Well then how can we arrest this Battista guy?" Jones inquired.

"Arrest, you're way ahead of the game Jones. First we need to find out if that artist guy's story is true and until we find the body, that's going to be difficult to prove. But we can keep an eye on him."

Clarence inched his way back to the stall door. "Listen up; the Detective is drawing some kind of diagram on the mirror. He is talking about the reception and that Battista person."

Just the name of the Signore sent shivers up and down Giovanni's spine. But in Ron's eyes a bright light seemed to shine. "Clare, that's great news. The reception, we all need to get to that reception. If what Giovanni says is true…I mean accurate, we know it's the truth right guys?" his eyes locked on those of the artist. "Sorry Giovanni just the wrong words again. So where was I? Ah, right…we're supposed to be at the reception anyway to help with the serving of the guests. The other guys are probably already there. The question is will Malone let us go or put us in jail." He paused as he sat on the toilet tank. "Well we'll never know until we ask."

Iggy and Clarence dropped their locked arms and Ron strolled out of the stall. He stepped up to Malone and tapped his shoulder just as he was placing an "X" in various spots on the drawing on the mirror. At the same time Father Gregory and Brother Anthony were entering the bathroom as best they could. Given the amount of people in it already, that was no easy task.

"Pardon me, Detective Sargent, but I have a request to make."

"Ron, I'm kind of busy right now, we have a security issue which needs attention."

"Exactly and we have a service duty needing attention and both are at the same place, the reception at the United Nations building." Ron glanced over to the priest. "Isn't that right Father?"

The priest didn't know why he should go along with the scheme which he knew his student was formulating as he spoke. At the same time he did know that at least part of what he presented was true. His students were to help as servers at the reception and that could be considered a service duty of sorts. "Quite correct Ron. Detective Sargent Malone, this reception… it is the high point of the celebrating the eminent arrival of the Pieta. All of us are supposed to be there, but under the circumstances…"

Ron interrupted his professor. "Right you are Father. Under the circumstances we cannot let a possible criminal get away with whatever he's plotting. If Giovanni is accurate in his story," he shot a grin to Giovanni. "Battista may very well use this gala as an opportunity to sell the real Pieta which he intends to steal. All kinds of rich collectors will be attending, don't you think?"

"What, are you crazy? No one can steal the Pieta. It's under such security that you would think that it was Jesus and his mother in the flesh. We are trying to find the actual murderer if we haven't already done so." Malone glanced at Giovanni pitifully sitting on the toilet bowl seat cover. "Besides that we need a body to prove that a murder was committed in the first place. How on earth did you come up with this cockamamie idea of stealing the statue?"

"Bob, bring out Giovanni please."

Bob pulled out Giovanni from the stall. He gave him a little pat on the back and a slight shove. Then he, Clarence and Iggy formed a backdrop right behind him. He stood in front of the Detective and Ron not quite knowing what to do and certainly what to say.

Malone however had plenty to say. "You, don't tell me that you're behind this stealing story? Murder isn't enough for you is that it?"

Ron slipped to Giovanni's side and locked his arm into his, hoping to bolster his resolve. It seemed to work. He felt the artist taking a deep breath and standing tall stretching out his backbone as he did so.

"Detective Sargent I shall try to find the correct words. I stand before you with a heavy heart. I wish to help with the catching of the one who killed my Sheila that's true. But also today I learned of the plan to steal the Divine One's statue of the Pieta. I was outraged, that is true. I told the Signore that he lied to me. I was told that my statue was to be a gift to the Cathedral so that the people of America could always remember the visit of the real Pieta at your World's Fair. That is why I carved it in the similar manner that Michelangelo did almost 500 years ago. Then this morning, Sheila tried to protect me. I was shouting at the Signore about his lies. He took me and beat me and I did the same to him but to protect myself. That's how I got this wound on my head. He threw me into the statue, my statue made with love. And that's when the one I loved in secret came to help me. She tried to calm down the Signore as she often had to do when things didn't go his way. She herself he struck with my own hammer, this you do not believe but it is true. He took it off the floor after he broke the tool table on which my carving tools were laid out.

Malone was visibly moved but took control of himself. "I see. Mr. Gaglioni. Please try to understand that it is not that I do not believe your story. But I must find a way to prove that it is true. It is your hammer which probably has your fingerprints on it which you just admitted to being the murder weapon. So you must see my position in all of this. These teenagers and that man," he pointed to Clarence and gave him a look that he should know better. "They seem to think I can just go and arrest this Signore guy. I can't but I can go to the reception and try to find a connection. We will watch who this Battista speaks with and now that I know that stealing is part of the plan, to learn if such a plot exists."

"That is all I can ask," replied Giovanni. "But do not think he plans to steal the statue from the pavilion at the Fair. This is not his plan. There will be a switch; mine will replace the real one."

"Good God man, how does he plan to do that?" Malone grabbed the loose fitting school jacket which Ron had given him and pulled him closer.

"That I do not know, for as I said, this I just found out today." The trembling returned. The fear was back.

Malone let him go. "I am so sorry; I didn't mean to frighten you. Okay, men let's get to the United Nations. And as for your students Father, they will perform their duties as intended. You Mr. Gaglioni will have to stay with my officers."

Ron protested. "No way, sir, can't you see that he is the one person who could set off Battista who thinks he's dead. He could be disguised as one of the seminarians, an older one like Clarence. Please we promise to keep him with us."

"Father Gregory, Brother Anthony do you accept the responsibility for this man? Should he escape you will be held responsible as will these young men."

Brother Anthony walked to Giovanni and placed his arm around him. "He shall never leave our sight."

"Then let's get there…wait how can you seminarians go dressed as you are?"

Again, Brother Anthony stepped in. "We'll stop at the hotel and pick up their cassocks; surely there's an extra one for Giovanni. It's very near the United Nations so it won't take long."

As they made their way to the waiting squad cars, lights flashing and sirens ready to be sounded, Father Gregory pulled on Brother Anthony's sleeve. "That was an interesting statement of acceptance Brother."

"Why thank you Father; and it's absolutely true, no matter where Giovanni will be so will I be, if you get my meaning."

"I believe I do Brother, let us hope that it will only have to be at the reception."

Having retrieved their cassocks at the hotel, the squad cars crawled to 42nd Street. They picked up some speed on the way to 1st Ave. on which the UN was located. The thirty-nine story Secretariat administrative building of green glass could be seen rising high over the East River and was easily distinguishable even in the dark. Along the line of the Flags of the Member Nations they passed and turned into a drive leading to the main doors. These were located at the end of a low winged building. It had a small dome not easily visible from their angle. It was situated over the General Assembly area where all member nations would meet and vote on critical issues facing the fragile peace of the world. They also addressed humanitarian, cultural and heritage issues. Since the UN is an international territory within the borders of the United States it has its own security force and agencies to see to its operation and maintenance. However, when there is a large attendance of dignitaries and guests these agencies and guards are supported by local police as back up and traffic control. That's were Malone's men came into play.

Malone led his primary investigative officers to the entrance doors followed by Father Gregory, Brother Anthony and the seminarians, including the fake one. The priest presented the credentials of the Abbey and invitation. The group was admitted with no issue. Brother Anthony who actually lived in the city and thus had also visited the UN in his formative years and Ron De Cenza who was there when he was sixteen were the only ones who had ever been on the UN tour. But that was some time ago so they depended on the guards and police officers posted in the Lobby for directions to the Reception area. They walked parallel to the blue wall on which hung the portraits of the past Secretary Generals of the United Nations and under the open balcony corridors which overlooked the vast lobby. Off to the side of the General Assembly chamber were a series of reception rooms where the gala was being hosted by Italy and the Papal See which is the official name for the Vatican.

Just as Malone passed through its doors out came a young woman of about twenty with flaming red hair worn down to her shoulders. She was in a full length gown of light blue chiffon over a satin like material which shimmered. Clutched in her hand was a cloth sequined purse of the same color as her dress. The skirt of the gown was what is called "A" line in that it flared a little as it met the floor. The bodice was sequined like the purse and had a scoop neckline which revealed no cleavage. Despite that absence, her breasts were well defined and would be a challenge to one's vocation. From her neck a simple gold cross hung on a fine thin gold chain. One would have thought her to have come from Galway or some other town in western Ireland but in fact she had come from Wisconsin and was half Italian heritage on her father's side. Malone and the officers passed her by with little notice other than professional observation. However, when the clergy group came upon her, they all stopped with awed expressions.

"Susan, is that you?" exclaimed Ron as the others gathered around her.

"Ron, what a surprise; your friends are already inside. But they are serving the guests. My do you look spiffy in your cassocks boys and Clarence you too." She had not noticed the priest and Brother Anthony as yet as they chose to stand away from the guys when she approached. Each knew of her rather demonstrative ways and they were quite right. She proceeded to kiss each of the seminarians on the cheek until she arrived at Giovanni. "And who is this charming man, Ron? He's not a member of our Abbey of that I am quite sure." She kissed him anyway and Giovanni began to blush.

Taking hold of her arm, Ron began the introductions. "Susan Liguri this is Giovanni Gaglioni from Italy. He's an artist…"

"Italy, the land of romance and music and art; of course you are an artist." She took him by the arm and began to walk him into the reception hall to the relief of the priest and brother. "My you look like an older Ron De Cenza, you could be brothers. How did you meet?" She tightened her squeeze on his arm.

Giovanni looked for help from the guys behind them.

Brother Anthony suggested that Ron diffuse the situation so that they could implement their plan. He would take the others and set them in their positions. Father Gregory agreed. The priest was to seek out the Abbot and assist him in making the rounds of introductions to visiting prelates and dignitaries.

"Bob, you stay with me. You know what happened the last time Susan and I were together alone."

Receiving permission they sprinted up to Susan and Giovanni. "So Susan, what brings you to the UN?" Ron squeezed between her and Giovanni and Bob took her arm on the other side.

The red faced artist was only too pleased to be relieved from her clutches or so it seemed to him. Ron took hold of his arm and the four were now linked. They made their way to the small stage where a band composed of strings and brass were just finishing the William Tell Overture by Rossini. The familiar piece excited the guys who were fans of the Lone Ranger TV series not because they were familiar with its composer and the classics in general. They paused in a trance-like state for the flourish as they imagined their heroes on Silver and Scout riding off to a new adventure. Susan pulled them back into reality.

"Really, the theme of the Lone Ranger show, how gauche can they get. Come on boys we have work to do."

Bob was offended. "What do you mean Susan, it's so cool and at such a posh party to boot."

"Really, do you even know that the great classical composer Rossini created it? Don't bother to answer. It's apparent from the look on your faces that it's only the horses with the Lone Ranger and Tonto on them that excites you."

Giovanni chimed in that he thought the Rossini piece was quite effective in his William Tell Opera.

"There, now here is someone who knows the classics." Susan pulled away from the guys so that she could turn and face the artist. She shot him a smile. "You Italians, so…well so charming."

The blood began to boil beneath Ron's skin. But why it should as he was to become a priest and give up such banter and flirtations he wasn't able to address, so he stated the obvious. "We were kids Susan, when we watched the show. So how would we know where the music came from?"

"Well you're not kids now Ron, so let's get to work here." She sent Clarence and Iggy off to circle the Reception Hall from the opposite end, by the bar.

They made their way toward the stage area. Their formation of four abreast with locked arms however made it difficult to traverse the room. Ron spotted a small tall table on which was a lighted votive candle encased in a stone-like holder. He led his little group to it before anyone else did. The four of them now circled it. Once there he returned to the initial question which was never answered. "So like I said, why are you here Susan?"

She smiled coyly and winked at him. "Why do you think?" She was more than a Midwestern plain talking girl. She had the charm of the South in her. She was raised in Georgia before her father accepted an adjunct professorship at Loyola University in Chicago. Her mother became a widow a couple of years after. By then Susan was a student at the University and her mother found the job at the Abbey in Wisconsin. The point was that she used that southern charm to full advantage whenever she deemed it necessary.

Ron began to stumble over his words as the blood rushed to his face. That was a dead giveaway that she was getting to him once again. Back at the Abbey he found himself in her amorous embraces and got so aroused that he ejaculated all over himself, an incident that he would never forget or live down. He was not about to allow that to happen again. Even so, there was a forbidden attraction to her. That was despite his knowing that what she did in flirtation was really a defense mechanism to stave off advances that she didn't want. All that changed when she met him as the new seminarian at the Abbey Latin School. He was innocent and kind, not bad to look at with that boyish grin and big brown eyes. And he was so respectful to the point of having to run away from her advances though at the time she hadn't realized why.

Giovanni felt the tension in Ron's body as he stiffened his posture. He stepped in. "Signorina…"

She flashed her sparkling green eyes at him. "Signorina, how lovely a term."

"It's Italian for Miss, nothing more… but still Signorina Susan I am most pleased to meet you. But as you can see we are preparing for the priesthood and must not how you say, be close with the women, do you understand my meaning?"

She turned cool like ice in a Coke. "Unfortunately I do, but I thought you my dear Giovanni…with such a romantic name might be in disguise or something like that…"

"But how did you know?..."

Bob and Ron were about to choke half to death they were coughing so hard. She grabbed hold of Ron's wrist and squeezed it until her pink painted nails were about to pierce his skin. "I didn't but thanks for the inside information Signore Giovanni." She turned directly into Ron's face. "Ron De Cenza, you let me in on this caper of yours or so help me I'll expose you to all these big shots in this room including the Archbishop over there."

"Bob, did I do something wrong?"

"No Giovanni, it was just the words used that's all."

"Ah, the wrong words again, mi dispiacere, I am so sorry."

Ron took hold of Susan and whispered in her ear. "Make no expression of any kind, pretend that I'm whispering sweet nothings into your ear."

She pushed herself away from him. "Right and you in the cassock of the Church, very believable; just tell me what's up. And you don't have to go all Rock Hudson on me. I am resigned that you have been called to serve the People of God, unless of course you have changed your mind."

"I have not, so give it up. The weakness of the flesh will not take hold of me tonight. There's a murderer in this room, I think."

Romance was dropped like a hot potato. "No kidding, where?"

"That's the problem; I don't know him, only Giovanni does so that's why he's dressed like one of us. He has to identify him for the Detective Sargent."

"Okay boys, what can I do to help? I have my ways as you well know."

"Don't go there Susan, we get it," Ron looked at Bob with a look of a sad puppy dog.

"Signorina Susan, you wish to help us, no?"

"The answer is Si…er yes to that question."

"Ron, Bob, I see a spark in her; one I think which can help us. It's like my Sheila." Giovanni momentarily got silent and reflective. "She like my Sheila can excite the men which we cannot do."

Bob laughed. He was thinking of Brother Anthony and Iggy and how they could excite the right man easily.

Ron poked Bob in the ribs. "Stop it before you attract attention to us. Okay, I see your point Giovanni but would this Signore of yours be open to another woman so soon?"

"Ah not him, but his security men; the ones we saw at the statue…" he again became reflective and shook it off. "Two of those three… they like the women."

"And are you saying that one of them does not like the women?" Bob asked with a thought already popping into his head.

"Si, that's true; Andrew likes the young men. So the Signorina would not do good with him…"

"Ah, but the Iggy or Brother Anthony might be the very ones who could, given what you are saying Giovanni." Bob was grinning.

"Okay, okay I get it. We have to distract the three from the Signore but where the hell is the Signore?" Ron knew only too well what this game of allure and attraction could do.

"Ah, he's the big man talking with the Archbishop who the Signorina pointed out."

The heads of Ron, Bob and Susan turned to check out the man. He was no longer in Stephano's clothes but in a black tuxedo with silk lapels and a red rose in the button hole. Instead of a black tie, he wore a red bow tie. He stood out like a sore thumb even in a crowd bejeweled and sequined to the hilts. But mostly that was due to his henchmen hovering near where he spoke with the Archbishop and another clergy man who Ron identified as Abbot Lawrence of the Abbey where they attended Latin School.

"Oh my Lord, Ron we can't get the Abbot involved in this; not again."

"No kidding Dick Tracy. Bob, we have to concentrate on distracting the thugs first and following the Signore unless…no it can't be. There's no way the Abbot or the Archbishop is involved with his plot to steal the Pieta."

"Don't be a dope Ron, our Abbot is too good; he even forgave me for what I did to you."

"Stop it, don't bring that up again Susan…it's too embarrassing."

"Well I thought it was all too cute and innocent."

"Well you weren't accused of murder and had to admit in front of Detective Sargent David Monahan, Father Gregory, Brother Anthony and his cops what happened to me."

Susan smiled and cast her eyes down to offer an apologetic look. "Well I suppose you're right from a boy's point of view and messy too from what I have heard, not having personal experience in that sort of thing of course."

"There you go again; you just can't help yourself can you. Let's embarrass the seminarian and maybe he'll off himself again…oh my God, what did I just say?"

She patted Ron's cheek. "Calm down honey. I said that I am resigned to give you up. In any case older men are much more experienced in love; she flashed her eyes at Giovanni."

Ron leaned into her, not that he wanted to after what she said and what happened in their past together. But he had to for the sake of Giovanni or was it? "The victim of the murder was Giovanni's girl, so cool it with him."

"Got it," she moved slightly away from Ron and turned to Giovanni but not with the coquettish eyes as before. "So, where are we in your plan?"

Ron tried desperately to remove himself from the emotional entanglement and memories, which he had whenever Susan Liguri was around. He focused on the plan which wasn't even a plan as yet. He spoke up quietly yet forcefully. The plan such as it was required them to get the three thugs away from their boss so that one of them might follow the Signore Battista around without possible detection and hopefully catching him is a clandestine conversation of some kind. They had to approach Iggy or Brother Anthony and ask them to place themselves in harm's way by flirting with Andrew. Susan was excited to do the same with Stephano and Giuseppe. Ron still felt that she was in real danger, so unless she could flirt with only one at a time, it would be a "no go" for her involvement. Ditto for Brother Anthony; Iggy would be a back-up for him or vice-versa.

Now that the plan was laid out, they had to find Iggy and Brother Anthony which was not hard to do. As they turned to leave the table, there stood Brother Anthony, Clarence and Iggy.

"I promised the Detective that I would be with Giovanni at all times; so don't be so surprised." Brother Anthony smiled at the artist. "We weren't able to catch much of what you said, but we did hear my name as well as that of Iggy mentioned."

"I am most grateful for your watching over me Brother Antonio… Anthony, such a strong saint's name."

"Yes it is isn't it; but were it not for Ron and Bob my name would have been a disgrace to our Abbey. So Giovanni I owe them not only my good name but my life."

"Brother, you're embarrassing us; how about getting to the plan which I'm afraid may be asking too much from you and Iggy."

They looked around the filling room. More and more guests arrived to congratulate the Cardinal Archbishop and his people for having brought the Pieta to America. Brother Anthony became quite aware of how many more ears there were to listen in on juicy gossip. Too much attention was being drawn to what now appeared to be six members of clergy gathered about one stunning young woman. To some of the guests now eyeing the growing group it was a temptation waiting to happen; to others it was a scandal. In both cases their gathering at the little cocktail table was garnering too much attention. "We need to split up. Clarence, make the rounds with the others from the Latin School. Please tell them to stay away from Ron, Bob, and me."

"Hey what about me?" asked Iggy.

"Go with Clarence Iggy, I cannot have you involved in whatever plot these two have cooked up, not if I heard correctly. Is it true that one of the Signore Battista's body guards seeks young men?" Brother Anthony was loyal to his vows but understood what had to be done. He felt obligated to help out with the all too familiar scenario which he rejected long ago.

Iggy wouldn't follow Clarence, who left in a huff as he wanted to be part of the plan.

Bob suggested that they start to roam around the room, but seven of them would make them even more obvious. So it was decided to break up into two groups, one would have their sights set on Stephano and Giuseppe and the other on Andrew. Giovanni would have to be with the group which had Brother Anthony for obvious reasons. Just as that decision was made who should walk by them but Stephano. He brushed against Susan. She giggled out a sweet "Well big guy, watch where you're going."

His eyes bulged from his head as he looked her up and down approvingly. "Forgive me Miss…how about giving me a name?" His huge hulking physique towered over her and the others except for Brother Anthony who could have given him a run for his money.

Without the slightest hesitation she cut off Ron's attempt to squish the exchange. "It's Christine and you're forgiven. Such a big hunk of a guy like you makes it difficult to move through this herd of cattle without touching them." She smiled with just a bit of teeth showing.

His focus was now all on her.

Brother Anthony had swung his arm around Giovanni turned him from Stephano's view and walked him away from the table. The chit chat began. All would be lost if the body guard of the Signore got even a glance of the artist. If the flirtation didn't go well, it would be the end of their hastily contrived plot and maybe them as well. Luckily the plan was playing out before it was even explained to the Brother. They had to run with it.

"It is rather crowded and I see that your glass is empty. May I bring you a refill?" Stephano after the humiliation of stripping in front of his colleagues and the Signore and enduring Andrew's cutting remarks about his manhood had a chance to prove that he was a real man. He wanted to demonstrate that he was not like Andrew. He had a chance for a conquest in his mind and went for it despite the need to keep the Signore safe.

Susan, alias Christine, was in her element and enjoying a bit of fun. "Now I gave you my name and you have yet to introduce yourself."

"I beg your pardon Miss, my name is Stephano Rondini."

"That's Italian isn't it?"

"Yes, it is but I have been in this country since I was a boy."

"Is that so; well you certainly aren't a boy any more. Italians are supposed to be hot blooded romantics, I hear. Is that true?"

Stephano was now blushing and acting like a boy with a crush rather than what he truly was. "That, you will have to learn for yourself Christine."

"Is that so; well then, let's just take a little walk to the bar and discuss life and love, shall we?"

As they departed, Ron, Bob and Iggy let out an audible sigh of relief.

"Holy cow Ron, no wonder she got you all hot and bothered…"

"Don't you dare say it Bob or I'll clobber you right here in front of the Cardinal."

"Calm down pal, I didn't mean to have you relive it. Though if I was being truthful, I wish that might happen to me; that is if I weren't becoming a priest." Bob quickly added with a reddened face.

Iggy stepped in between them and ended their testosterone conversation. "So it looks like it's just us, so what's the plan?"

"Oh nothing at all, we just need you to flirt with one of the thugs who we saw in the warehouse wrapping up poor Sheila's body. He protects this Signore person who is a murderer. We thought Brother Anthony could do it since he's had experience with guys before taking the vows that is. But he's off with Giovanni as he promised. So it's you we need to distract Andrew enough so that we can follow Battista without being caught. We hope to catch him making plans to steal the Pieta and right here under the nose of the UN, the Cardinal, and all these people. So what do you think?"

"What I think is that this is nothing more than a walk in Bug House Square in Chicago where guys go to get picked up or to pick up other guys."

"Holy shit Iggy, you know of such a place and in Chicago? I live there too and never heard of it."

"And you Bob have probably never tried to pick up a guy."

"Well of course not, but then I'm not…oh Christ I am so sorry, I didn't mean to insult you."

"It's okay," Iggy patted Bob's cheek. "I am who I am and have given it up for a higher purpose. That is apparently until this moment. Now in performing my duties I am right back in Bug House Square so that we can save a life, go figure. So Ron, where's this Andrew guy. Have you seen him yet?

Ron craned his neck to scan the room. "I can't see him. Did you get a good look at him in the warehouse before we escaped?"

"Not really I was too scared then, what with the body being wrapped in the tarp and the Pieta right there with her body placed upon it."

"Well look for a well-built guy with shoulders like a football player and hands to match. Just like that Stephano who just left, he'll be wearing a Tux."

"That's it, what's his coloring, skin tone, eyes, hair, height…"

"Oh yeah, well he's at least 6 foot two, dark eyes and short dark hair and…well he kind of looks like you Iggy, as far as skin tone is concerned that is."

"So then he's like me huh, a charming personality with jovial outlook on life and one who can speak on any topic including cute guys…"

"Crap Iggy, he's gay like you and of your race as well. There now I've said it. I made it a racial thing as well as a societal thing. Back in biology class at the University, Dr. Bond would frown on me for not being able to discuss people without alluding to their race."

Iggy hugged Ron and squeezed him tightly. "I love you for your honesty. But don't get frazzled, I'm not insulted. Just point me to the guy and I'll get him distracted or my name isn't Isidore Johnson."

"Well then you're in luck, there he goes," noted Bob. "It looks like he's looking for the bathroom. See how he's kind of running toward the hallway."

"I'm on it and I have to get to that men's room before he does or this isn't going to work." Off Iggy literally ran, circumventing dignitaries that ordinarily would have him gasping with disbelief.

That left Ron and Bob awkwardly watching over the crowd. "So how do we distract the last bodyguard, Giuseppe?"

"You got me pal." Ron instead had seen the Signore himself leaving the company of the Cardinal, Abbot Lawrence, the Ambassador from Italy and another idol from his childhood who had inspired him to become a priest, Bishop Fulton J. Sheen. "You look for Giuseppe but keep a distance and I'll see what I can do with the Signore."

Ron gave Bob a light punch on his arm and turned to leave. He walked right into the Detective Sargent Malone.

Iggy was panting and had to splash some water onto his face as he ran into the men's room just before Andrew got to the door. He just looked up as Andrew ran through the door unzipping his pants. He noticed the young man noticing him. "Christ, people think I'm a camel or something I swear." He ran to the urinal and relieved himself with a sigh. "Wow, never thought I'd make it."

He said this approaching the sink at which Iggy stood dumbfounded. Andrew really was a stunning guy, and he shot him a smile. "So how come you're dressed like a priest? Your eyes didn't say that you're a holy Joe." He soaped up his hands and rubbed furiously.

"That's because I'm not a priest. I go to a religious school and we all have to dress this way."

"No kidding, what a drag on getting the girls eh," Andrew snickered.

"I suppose so if I were into that sort of thing."

"What! Are you one of those queers I hear tell about?"

"Are you?"

Andrew got into Iggy's face. "Who you calling queer boy? I ain't no faggot, I just like what I like."

"And I like what I see right here too."

"So that's your game. How much are you charging?"

Iggy smiled coyly. "Oh not much, just enough to get me by; it's expensive this New York town."

"That it is, but are you worth it?" Andrew closed in on Iggy and tugged at his cassock. "You're a bit nervous, is this your first time for hire?"

"Well we're in the UN building, that's kind of nerve wracking for me, how about you."

"Well boy, it's like this," he grabbed hold of his crotch area. "If you like it, I can give it to you, UN or in the alley, it doesn't matter to me."

Iggy deflected the talk of nerves and told Andrew that the UN was prettier what with the marble sinks, good lighting and mirrors and all so handy to get looking good afterwards. Andrew took the bait and shoved him into one of the stalls. "Now let's just see what you've got under that dress of yours, shall we." He began to unbuttoned the cassock one button at a time.

Ron was having issues of his own. Malone wanted to know why he and the others weren't serving the guests as they were supposed to do. Ron tried to explain that with their being so late there was no chance to get instructed and assigned so they had to wait.

"Where did your friends go?" the disbelieving Detective Sargent asked.

"A couple got thirsty and went for a drink. Iggy went to the bathroom and there's Clarence," he pointed, "with my classmate Quinlan over on the other side of the room. Speaking of the bathroom, I think I have to go, so if you'll excuse me…"

"Just a minute Ron, hold it. Where is this Signore guy, have you seen him?"

"Yes I did. He was talking with the Cardinal and my Abbot right over there by the windows. Wow, look at all those city lights, cool isn't it?"

"Yeah, beautiful, go pee and get Giovanni to me. I need to know what this guy looks like."

"Yes sir, right away."

Ron ran down the corridor and into the men's room. Splashing water in his face, he heard a voice coming from the stall. He froze. The voice was that of Iggy.

"My oh my aren't you the man, so big and hard all over."

"Well you're not too bad yourself my man, you're not chubby at all under that dress. You are well put together."

Ron was pounding the marble sink top. *My God he's going to have his way with Iggy, I can't let that happen,* he spoke to himself. He turned to walk into the stall and shock them into stopping whatever was taking place.

The bathroom door swung open and who should prance in but the Signore. Ron was sure it was him as Giovanni identified him earlier and the red bow tie was a giveaway. He went to the stalls and not trying to see if the closed doors were locked he pushed open the first one. "What the hell, what's this?"

Andrew spun around pants unzipped. He fumbled with the fly and tried to zip it up. "Signore, I was just telling this queer that he'd better watch out or he'll be laid out flat by someone not as forgiving as me for looking at me at the urinal."

"I don't pay you to get off on my time. Get your ass out there where I need you. The meeting is set. Meet me at the room two doors down the hallway."

"Yes sir, right away." Andrew scurried out as Ron covered his face with water in his hands. He was humming a Beatles tune so as to make sure that the Signore hadn't thought he overheard something.

"You," the Signore pointed to Iggy quivering at the side of the bowl, the cassock was a ball of black cloth on the floor behind him. "You're lucky I came in when I did. Shut your mouth and there'll be no trouble, got it?"

"Yes…yes sir, I was just trying to earn a little cash that's all."

"What, he wasn't attacking you?"

Now Iggy didn't know what to do, so he threw Andrew under the bus. "Well, not exactly; I got this ten dollars from him." He pulled out the Hamilton from his shirt pocket.

"Well get your ass out of here, I have to go."

Iggy picked up his cassock and squeezed past the big man. The door slammed behind him. Ron turned around and Iggy plowed right into him and hugged him crying that he had failed.

"Hush, he'll hear you."

From the stall they heard the Signore. "Imagine Battista with a faggot on his payroll. Oh well, it's a new world. Ahhh…"

"Come on, let's get out of here," Ron whispered.

Out in the hallway, Ron was consoling Iggy. He told him what he did was very successful for he now knew where the meeting was to be held. "Look there's Andrew down the hall. He's going into that room. Let's duck in here." Ron opened a door next to the men's room and found it to be the Ladies Room. "Ah, not here, come on before he comes out."

"Ron, is that you?" The voice was that of Susan. "Come to the first stall."

Bob and Ron crept into the Ladies Room and knocked on the door. It opened and Susan stood there applying lip stick while holding a little mirror. "I needed privacy. Stephano is at the bar ordering drinks. I think he likes me."

"Are you crazy? Just keep him occupied and remember that he is a hired gun and is vicious."

"Cool it Ron, it's all under control. How did you boys do?"

"Iggy did very well. He got us the location where the Signore is going for some kind of meeting. It's right down the hallway."

A sudden click of the door served notice that someone had entered. There was a knock on the stall door. "Occupied," Susan answered. "You better get out of here." She squeezed past the boys, her chest rubbing across that of Ron.

He began to sweat and she peeked out of the stall door, saw no one. She stepped out of their way. The boys made for the door. Just as they got into the hallway out came the Signore from the bathroom. He noticed Iggy who immediately planted a kiss on Ron.

The Signore walked right up to them. He tapped Iggy's shoulder. "So you didn't take my advice huh? After more money, eh?"

Iggy lifted his head from Ron's lips and smiled. "This is quite the place for quick cash. This trick gets a kick out of doing it in public, what a world eh?"

The Signore shook his head and Iggy went back into the kissing mode until the big man entered the door into which Andrew had gone.

"Sorry Ron, he thinks that I'm a prostitute so I had to play the role. Are you okay?"

"Yes, I'm okay but did you have to be so rough?" He rubbed his lips. "I think you bit me."

"Sorry, but I had to think quickly."

They had a good laugh and ran down the hall to the room past the one where the Signore had entered. They found Bob lying across a beige and gold French provincial sofa. "Hi guys, I followed that Giuseppe to the room next door. How did you do?" He propped himself up and swung his legs down, pulling up his cassock to his knees.

Iggy fell into the sofa while Ron pulled up a chair from the table in the center of the room. He noticed a bar next to the sofa. "Let me get you some water Iggy." While at the bar, he had a thought. "Here Iggy take a drink. Poor Iggy, he almost went the whole way for us, not like me back at the Abbey. He's one hell of a brave guy."

"No kidding, Iggy, did he hurt you?"

"No Bob; thanks for asking. He's just a scary one that's all."

"Hey guys, I have an idea. We're supposed to be serving the guests right. Well I'll just make up a drink tray and waltz into that room next door as soon as we hear voices. Maybe I can pick up something they say or at least see who this Signore guy is talking with."

"No way; it's too dangerous. Ron, they killed that poor Sheila and almost did Giovanni in for just a kind glance."

"Nope, I'm going to do it Bob. Go listen at the wall while I make up a tray. Iggy you earned your rest, sit tight."

"Hell no, I'll peek out the door and if clear then you can go."

"Actually that's a good idea. I need to appear to be coming from the other end of the hall, if I have something from the bar."

A few minutes later Iggy was watching the hallway holding the door ajar just enough to see. He gave Ron the sign to get ready to sprint out. Bob was at the wall with a glass to his ear. "I saw this in the movies, now I'll see if it really works." Fortunately it did.

Ron noticed the phone on the end of the table. "Listen guys, if I get in I'll press the intercom button on the phone there if there is one and dial the extension on that phone over on the table. We should then be able to hear what's going on."

"Lordy, Lordy where is that Detective and his men. We need back up, just like in the movies."

"Got a grip Bob, this is not a movie. It's real life. Cops aren't just around the corner waiting to help out in a crisis." Ron slowly crept to the door and Iggy opened it wide. He sprinted out and was in the reception room in no time at all. Pulling his credentials from his pocket, he hung it around his neck and went to the bar with an order for a private party. While waiting for it to be prepared, he saw that Susan was still occupying Stephano's time. *"Well at least she's out in the open and relatively safe,"* he thought.

Just as he picked up the prepared tray, up came Clarence with Quinlan at his side. "Ron, what's up with the spying stuff? Clarence told me everything," stated Quinlan of Missouri.

"And Clarence has a big mouth. We didn't want to involve you guys, not yet anyway. If what I am about to do works we'll get together back at the hotel to plan our next step. Tell the guys to hold tight. What I am about to do will either make our day or it will be my last day on this planet."

Clarence forbade Ron to go with his tray. "Get real; this man is a murderer with mob ties. How can you expect to combat that with a tray of booze?"

"Get out of my way Clarence. Iggy and Bob are placing their life on the line and if I don't get into that room, they may be found out." With that being said, he picked up his tray and walked toward the corridor through which he had just run. Proud that he could balance the tray with the wine bottles, and some Irish whiskey, a container of ice and glasses, he walked slowly down the corridor only to see both Andrew and Giuseppe at the door. They had seen him, he had to proceed. Arriving at the door, the two stopped him. "I have to deliver an order for refreshments."

"The Signore didn't tell us anything about ordering booze. Hold on, I will check." Giuseppe opened the door and called in. "Signore there's a kid out here saying he has an order of booze for you."

"I didn't order any drinks."

"I told him you didn't," Giuseppe was about to close the door.

"Giuseppe send the kid in, I think my friends and I are thirsty. It will help with our discussion."

The four men at the table, two on each side of where the Signore sat, laughed.

Ron entered and looked for the location of the phone; thankfully it was not at the meeting table but on a side table by a sofa similar to the one next door where his pals were nervously waiting for him. He made for it and set the tray on the side table. "Should I pour, sir?"

"Yeah, what do you have?" the Signore asked as he sized Ron up and down wondering why he looked familiar to him.

Ron explained that he had two kinds of wine, Chianti and Roscato and Irish whiskey and seltzer. The Signore ordered the Chianti. The others ordered the whiskey over rocks with a dash of seltzer. With his back to the meeting table, Ron pressed the intercom button and dialed the extension next door. When he turned to serve the drinks, the Signore called him over.

"Have I seen you before kid?"

Ron couldn't lie not when it was obvious that the Signore was about to recall where he saw him. "Yes sir, it was out in the hallway a little while ago. I was with a friend."

"Oh yeah, you were the one with the queer guy. Look at this innocent face my friends." He squeezed Ron's cheeks. "But under this holy robe, oh my what have we here" He laughed and grabbed for Ron's balls. "Imagine, in this place with all these holy ones walking around this guy had the nerve to make money for a kiss and maybe more if I wasn't there to stop it eh kid?"

Ron pressed out a wide smile after making a silly move to avoid the hand but letting him grab for him. "One has to live, sir."

The Signore laughed and patted Ron on the ass. "They're all around us my friends. I tell you even in my organization his kind is there. It's a changing world. You can go kid, here's a little something for your trouble."

Ron accepted the fifty dollar bill with another toothy smile and hastily went for the door.

CHAPTER SIX

SPYING BY PHONE

The four pair of eyes watched Ron with empty tray in hand open the door. None of the four cracked a smile, even when the Signore made a wise crack about the kid being so handsome and what a waste it was to the women of the city.

The door swung open letting in the harsher light of the hallway into the meeting room which had recessed lighting and table lamps to give it a more comfortable feel. Two heads turned. Their faces sparked an order from the Signore. "Hey kid," he bellowed. Ron froze in the threshold and turned to face him. "I need one more favor and there's another twenty for you if you can produce for me."

Ron was red in the face, not knowing what to expect next from this Signore person, who thought his blush was cute. He shook his head and poked at the grim looking burly man to his left. "See what a waste, what a waste."

The man with the long black hair greased back as if he were one of the bad boys on the street corner eyeing the passing girls remained silent. He just rubbed his fingers along the side of his head to make sure that the hair grease was doing its thing.

Ron took that gesture the wrong way and had a flashback to the barn at the Abbey. It was an image he had spent months trying to forget ever happened. "Sir, you are most generous, but my boss will miss me should I stay a minute longer and then there goes my job."

The Signore raised his large body from the leather back chair and grinned from ear to ear. "Don't worry kid, I'm not asking you to hustle anyone. I want you to find my body guard Stephano. I don't think you can miss him. He looks likes these guys right behind you."

"Signore, I can go for you," offered Giuseppe as he pushed Ron to the side and stepped into the meeting room.

"Nonsense Giuseppe, you have done quite enough for me this day." He offered a genuine smile of appreciation as he ran his fingers up and down the silk lapels of his tux. "You just have a seat, you too Andrew, you look tired. Have a glass of wine and listen carefully to us."

The two goons slowly walked to the side table, Ron held back a gasp as he watched the phone and hoped that they didn't notice the light over the intercom button. Fortunately they did not; the wine took all their attention.

"So kid, like I was saying…my man, he's quite the big guy with the hair like this man next to me but he wears a tux like mine but black tie not red. There will be a bulge under his jacket, if you get my meaning. You'll know he's my security man."

"I get the drift sir. I'll be right back with him." Ron ran, before anything else could be said. He headed straight down the hall into the reception room and once again collided with the Detective Sargent. "Oh my God, am I glad to see you. There's no time but have your men ready at a moment's notice. The Signore is having a meeting down that hallway."

"Then I'll just go bust it up and arrest him on suspicion…"

"You can't do that; it would defeat the whole plan the guys and me…"

Malone interrupted, "Plan what plan? And who said you should be planning anything let alone doing so without me?"

"Really, now you intend to scold me like I'm ten years old. Anyway I am working and on an errand for a guest and he's quite important so please let me do it. Just get your men at those doors leading out to the main lobby of the UN building. By the way, do you guys have Walkie-Talkies?"

"Why the hell do you need those?"

"Forget it, just stay by the phone at the bar. I will call the bar and ask for you when I need you to take action. Will you do that for me? Trust me, if this goes as planned, you'll have a case. Right now you and I both know you don't have one. Oh and keep Giovanni and Brother Anthony near you and away from that hallway. I don't want him to know that he's not only alive but with the police, so hide him. You see that guy with Susan, he can recognize Giovanni but not me so let me do this please."

"I can get busted for this but okay, and call me as soon as you can."

"Will do…look there's Brother Anthony with Giovanni; make sure they stay away from the bar until I get that man in the tux and lead him away." Ron pointed to Stephano who was standing at the bar while Susan was seated on a chair next to him with her arm draped over his shoulder and laughing to beat the band. Making his way through the crowd and avoiding conversation with his pals scattered about the room, he saw Clarence and motioned to him to go to the bar. He did so immediately for he could order a drink because he was well past twenty-one. Ron pulled on his ear and pointed to the bar trying to signal that he should listen to what takes place there.

Malone watched his antics amazed that Clarence actually understood the signal. He pulled out his walkie-talkie and ordered his men to the outer doors of the reception room hallway.

Ron approached and Susan saw him from the corner of her eye. "Oh Stephano, just saying your name makes my heart pound a little faster." She giggled convincingly.

"And just seeing you sparkling like the dawn of the sun makes something else on me throb with desire." He grinned, winked and took a pose which emphasized his manliness.

She didn't flinch. It was usually her talking that way to rouse a guy for the fun of it and well did Ron know that. She played along in her Southern Belle persona.

The bang of the tray being dropped on the bar by Ron ended their banter. Ron moved his hand across his neck. Susan was supposed to cut off the conversation and let him take over. She did not.

"Well how rude, young man; that noise could just make me jump right out of my dress in fright."

Stephano had what he needed, a chance to be the hero. "Hey punk, get lost. The little lady doesn't need you making her night a fright, do you honey?"

"Well bless your heart, I should say not, Stephano honey bun."

The goon puffed out his chest and moved to place himself between Ron and Susan behind whom he was standing. "I said get lost punk." He pulled on the cassock collar ready to shove him away.

It was a scene from David and Goliath as the hulk of a boorish man stood towering over the little shepherd boy. And Ron had his stone with which to hit him right between the eyes and not even touch him. "Sure, I'll just go tell the Signore that you told me to get lost and that's why you didn't come back with me."

"Bullshit, how would you know the Signore; who are you anyway?"

"I work here at the UN. The Signore is down that hall with two fellas called Andrew and Giuseppe. He promised me twenty bucks if I bring you back. So when I heard this pretty Miss sparkling woman call your name, I knew I had the right guy and that's all's to it." Ron's bravado made Susan's eyes twinkle as she went with the flow of the act.

"Well honey bun, who is this Signore person? I mean is he so important that you would have to leave me here on this chair all alone?" She stroked his five o'clock shadow on his cheek ever so gently.

Stephano began to sweat profusely and stepped away from them. He turned to face them both. "He's my boss, and I must go. So kid, lead the way."

"Well you sweet thing, I'll just have to come with you. Your boss won't mind would he?" She held out her arms to him all the while smiling sweetly so as to melt butter.

Ron with mixed emotions of fear for her and one he couldn't quite understand poked her in the back. She ignored him.

Stephano slipped his hand under her arms and lifted her off the barstool and softly placed her on the marble floor. "Once he sees you, sweetie, he'll understand why I was delayed." He placed his arm around her waist. "Okay kid, lead the way."

Walking right between them, he gave Susan a look of disgust and walked toward the hallway. He knocked on the meeting room door and opened it. The Signore was laughing as he told the men at the table the story of seeing the kid outside the men's room kissing another guy.

Susan tapped Ron on the shoulder. "Why honey is that man talking about you? Why aren't you a frisky boy?"

Ron clinched his fists, hiding them in the folds of his cassock. He proudly announced that Stephano was found.

"Ah, Stephano…go sit with the boys and have a glass of wine. You did well kid, come get your tip." He slipped his hand in his jacket pocket and took out a wad of bills, then pulled out a twenty. He waved it at Ron, who got slapped on the ass by the greasy hair guy as he passed him. "But you brought more than my man, who is this charming little lady?"

Before Ron could utter a sound and give her real name, she spoke up. "Why my name is Christine Galucci from Georgia originally but Chicago now. Stephano was so kind to me, me not knowing a soul except for the Consul General of Italy, he likes me."

"I bet he does and from the look on Stephano's face, he's not alone in his admiration. How old are you little lady?"

She stumbled a bit but got into character again. "Why my mommy told me a lady should never be asked her age."

"That young huh, well I'm afraid that the party is over for you and the kid here. Why don't you take him and show him a good time, we have business to take care of now."

"Why aren't you the sweetest thing? But I think he likes boys from what I just overheard as we came in. But I'll try…come along boy." She tickled Ron under his chin. Then with that lily white index finger of a goddess, she motioned to him. "Follow me honey."

Ron was ready to explode but had to play the role thrust upon him. "Sure honey bun and maybe you can get me a real man with those twinkling eyes of yours. Then again he may not be able to see them what with all the mascara slapped on them." He stalked over to her and grabbed her arm and pulled her out the door, slamming it behind them.

"That will be some show, eh boys? And now gentlemen, we get to work." The Signore opened a leather bound folder set in front of him.

Out in the hallway, Ron was pulling Susan to the room next door.

"You let my arm go Ron De Cenza. Who the hell do you think you are? You're not even my boyfriend." She pulled his arm off her arm and dropped her Southern accent.

They stood glaring at each other in front of the walnut colored door of the next room. Inside, Iggy and Bob with notepad in hand sat listening to the beginning of the Signore's meeting.

"Boyfriend, you'd let your boyfriend treat you like I just did, it figures."

"My boyfriend would respect me too much to treat me like you just did, so there."

"So buttons on your old man's underwear; I wouldn't be your boyfriend if they paid me."

"But you obviously would be a boyfriend to someone who paid you from what I heard." She really got to him.

Ron was fuming and so red faced as to burst a blood vessel. "That was just Iggy and me. We had to act quickly and since he had already gotten action from one of those goons in the men's room; that was the first thing that came to mind."

"So it's Iggy and Ron sitting in a tree, K I S S I N G…, she stopped singing, "quite the pair to rock those leaves right off that tree."

"You…you make me crazy. I'm going to become a priest and you make me out to be a male whore."

She smiled then giggled. "I make you crazy?"

"Oh my God in heaven, come on, the guys are waiting inside." He took her hand and pulled her inside the room. "Look who I found?"

Both heads popped up from staring at the phone. "Susan," exclaimed Bob, "Why on earth did you bring her here Ron?"

"Right, this could be dangerous," added Iggy.

"Me bring her; not quite. And she's not Susan. Oh no, she's Christine Galucci from Georgia and then Chicago." Ron swished his cassock back and forth and fluttered his eyes.

"Now you just stop that, you have no room to talk." She slapped his hand. "Imagine two future priests kissing in the hallway like streetwalkers, why I declare." She began to laugh at her own Southern accent picked up again for effect. Then she just plopped herself on the sofa between Bob and Iggy who immediately jumped off the sofa.

"You told her, Ron how could you? You know it didn't mean anything. It was just a way to save our ass, so to speak."

Ron took Iggy by the shoulders and looked into his teary eyes. "I wouldn't do that, the Signore who saw me with you told his goons and some guys around that table…shit the meeting. What's going on with the meeting? Everyone be quiet." He leaned over the side table and looked at the phone with its green intercom light illuminated.

A welcomed silence fell over them as they listened in. The only voices they could identify were those of the three goons and the Signore; the other four men never uttered a word except for the greasy hair one and that was only a grunt when he patted Ron's ass in passing.

It became clear that one of those men was overseeing the water transportation at the 44th Street dock. Another was in charge of ground transportation which seemed to be a backup if the first part of their plan failed. Another was taking care of arrangement for the equipment needed to hoist the Pieta in the crate from the barge. That's when the switch would be made with the copy Giovanni made which the guys had seen crated up with the body of Sheila. And that was the part of the story which no one mentioned at the Signore's table; because none of them knew what Andrew, Giuseppe and Stephano had done with Sheila's body. The one voice not heard from finally was heard. Someone named Francesco Mondera was to organize hoisting equipment which was needed to switch the crates.

When the discussion got to speaking about possible trouble, Andrew poked Stephano who poked Giuseppe.

"Signore, gentlemen," began Stephano. "You need to know that when we entered the warehouse to dispose of the bodies and crate the statue, we found only that of Sheila…"

The Signore exploded as he had done with Giovanni and murderously with Sheila. He threw the leather folder across the table and pounded on it with his fists. His wine glass tumbled over; he grabbed hold of it and threw it at his body guards. "And you tell me this now, when all the plans are made? Gaglioni must be found and dealt with."

"Yes Signore, immediately, of course" the three began to stumble over each other's words. "We do know one thing." Andrew was speaking. "He climbed out of the bathroom window for the window was broken, which means he was hiding and saw us."

"I'll go check your place on Central Park West. He knows no one in the city and he would have to get clothes, even money to get out of town."

"Don't be an idiot Giuseppe. He'd never go back there, everyone including the doorman would tell me he was out without you and that would send an alarm. No he is still in the city, the question is where." The Signore began to calm down and think of possibilities. "He might even be here at the gala; after all he has the credentials and knows the Bishop."

As this took place Andrew began picking up the broken pieces of glass and noticed the green light on the phone. Stephano, did you touch the phone?"

The guys and Susan next door began to panic. They were trapped in that room and had to go past the other room to get out of the area. Iggy ran to the window. "It doesn't open."

"Oh my God Ron what are we going to do, we're going to get killed, oh my Lord," Bob was in a panic grabbing hold of his friend.

Susan glanced around the room and at the entrance door. "We have to make a run for it; it's the only way out."

Ron ran to the door and opened it a crack. "Susan's right. You two take her back to the bar at the Reception. The Detective will be there, don't ask me how I know, just do it. I'll follow.

"No way in hell Ron," Bob had gained back some courage. "I'm not abandoning you."

"Will you listen, it's the only way. Get Susan to safety now." He opened the door and waved them out. Iggy took hold of Susan who ran up to Ron and kissed him on the cheek.

"I'm sorry Ron; you are a brave man." She ran out with Iggy.

Bob was next and slammed the door shut. "I am not leaving you alone to face the music. We die together."

Ron gave him a quick hug. "No one is dying tonight." He went to the phone and dialed the extension at the bar. Malone standing next to the bar phone picked it up. "Detective is that you?"

"Yes Ron; it's Detective Sargent Malone." He made sure he used his name.

"Get your officers ready and get Clarence to alert my friends. We're making a run for it. The Signore knows someone is listening in on his planning session, I'm sure of it."

A drum roll from the small band which had been playing a series of Verdi and Rossini pieces drowned out Malone. Onto the platform stepped the Italian Ambassador to the United Nations and the Bishop of Brooklyn, the Most Rev. Brian McEntegert. The Bishop welcomed the guests and offered his appreciation for their support of the project. He then began to explain what would be happening over the next two days as the ship docks. He talked about the Pieta and another priceless sculpture called "The Good Shepherd," which was created in the Second Century. The audience learned that is the oldest known statue depicting Jesus. Both would be unloaded on April 14th. The Bishop went on to explain that the priceless art pieces were to stay overnight on the Barge which would then make its way around the battery and up the East River to Flushing Bay where they would be transferred to flatbed trailers and brought to the Vatican Pavilion. "Here tonight is the Captain of the barge named Challenger, Ben Olsen." The applause was deafening. It provided Ron and Bob a great opportunity to race down the hallway and into the reception area, yet they hesitated for one more listen.

In the Signore's meeting room they were still trying to lay blame for the phone being used while their meeting took place. Andrew, Giuseppe and Stephano emphatically protested their innocence as the one in charge of providing strong arm protection stood before them as the primary inquisitor. He was a good size man who could rival the physical size of the three body guards though about twenty years older than them. His glaring hazel eyes looked for a twitch, a nervous reaction, a flinch of weakness as he grilled the three men. It was clear that Ben Westridge had plenty of experience in breaking down men even before he laid a hand on them.

"Signore," Stephano pleaded. "You know us; we are loyal and would not do such a thing."

"Basta, enough," the Signore cried out. "This man stripped naked for me just this morning; why would he then betray me tonight."

Westridge turned toward the table ignoring the shocked faces of his colleagues who focused on the stripping part rather than the importance of how that impacted their plan being listened in on by an unknown person. "Was anyone else in this room besides us?"

One of the three, now snickering, spoke. "We four have sat here waiting for the Signore for at least one hour prior to his arrival. No one came in." It was the man with the greased back hair who responded.

"Francesco is correct; we sat and shared how we could help each other with the switch." Jeffrey Rafferty rose and walked to Francesco Mondera. "But there was another who entered when all of us were present. Surely Francesco would remember as he patted him on his ass most tenderly."

Francesco bolted out of his seat and shoved Jeffrey into the wall. His arm was at his neck. "Are you saying that I'm a faggot?"

Westridge pulled Rafferty off Mondera. "We cannot fight among ourselves or all is lost. Rafferty is right, that kid was in here serving us the whiskey and wine. And stop your craziness; even the Signore patted the kid's ass. It's a Latin thing."

The Signore was red in the face but managed to remain silent. He was sure Westridge had just insulted the ways of the Italians and Spanish Latinos.

Westridge, ever observant saw the red face and addressed the unspoken issue. He had not insulted anyone; it was more of an observation of playful customs he told them. "If it was true that such a playful act of affection indicated something else then many of our most honored men of football and basketball would be accused of the same. So Francesco calm down and let us reflect on this boy who is certainly no boy but a shrewd street punk."

The two men returned to their chairs and the Signore sat down as well. Mondera muttered something about his tie being ruined.

Ben Westridge turned his attention back to the three body guards. "Two of you came into the room at the same time as the boy did. Where did he go?"

Stephano not being one of the two, shrugged. Andrew and Giuseppe agreed that the kid simply served the wine and whiskey from what they could see from the doorway. That's when the fourth voice still not heard up to that point was raised. Antonio Penne finally had something to say.

"My friends, I am sitting here at this corner end of the table nearest the door. It faces the table where the tray was placed by the boy. I saw the phone there but no light shining from it. Once the bottles, ice bucket and glasses were placed there, the phone was no longer visible as you can see now; nor did I have a reason to look at it anyway."

The red face was fading away and the eyes widened as the Signore began to put the pieces of this puzzle together with the kid as the missing piece. He first thought and then thought of another. "Ah, but there is yet another punk involved in this little escapade to learn too much. Andrew you also know of him, if you don't know him shall I say intimately. Though I would say that what I saw in the stall was truly quite personal. And later I saw that same punk kissing the kid who served us. In fact did we not all laugh about this at Andrew's expense?"

Andrew jumped to his feet and pulled out his gun from under the tuxedo jacket. "I'll kill that little prick and cut his dick off and shove it down his throat while the kid watches and then I'll do the same to him." He headed for the door.

"You will do no such thing Andrew, sit your ass down. You see we have forgotten one other. A certain Christine Galucci from Georgia and did not she say currently in Chicago?"

Ron had just opened the door when Antonio Penne spoke. Bob was about to turn off the intercom and make a run for it but paused to hear one last kernel of what they thought. "Oh my God, Ron, he's going to kill you and cut off your…your thing and Iggy too." He ran to Ron who had closed the door and was leaning against it.

"Stop it, they'll hear you. I have ears. I heard and now they're talking about Susan; good thing she gave them an alias name. There's no time to lose, let's bolt and get to Malone. This time he can arrest them." He opened the door; the hallway was empty, all the guests had gathered at the stage to hear the Bishop and Ambassador. "Okay the coast is clear, let's boogie." He shoved Bob out the door and they made a dash for it.

Now it was Stephano's turn to voice some kind of outrage. "That sweet flirty way of hers lured me. Shit, I fell for that little ass and nice tits."

Giuseppe, the only one who was not duped in some fashion spoke. "She would not have gotten away with that shit with me. Before she dies, she'll learn what it means to speak to a real man in that way."

"What are you really saying about me?" Stephano was about to take a swing at his colleague.

"Calm yourself Stephano. We only know that she was in here. Perhaps your charm did work on her and a future might be had. It would be a waste to eliminate such a lovely thing until we know if she's another Sheila. Does anyone recall her near that table where the phone is?"

Ron and Bob had a clear view of the bar as they ran into the reception room. Malone was standing at it with Susan and Iggy on one side of him and Brother Anthony and Giovanni on the other. Clarence was just leading all the guys to the bar as Ron and Bob sprinted to it and dropped on the floor behind it. "Susan, Iggy get yourselves behind the bar and on the floor."

The fear in his eyes made them bound for the back of the bar. Iggy placed a bar towel on the floor so that Susan would not soil her dress. Ron watched the gesture and wished that he had thought of it.

Malone was now speaking to Clarence and the guys. "There are too many of you; it attracts attention. Split up. You two," he pointed to Quinlan and Matthew, "go to the Men's room. You two," he pointed to Frank and Andy, "you go to the ladies room. All of you stand in front of the door. Make sure no one enters or leaves it until my officer gets to you. Now, Clarence, take these two with you and stand at the doors of the food preparation room. Again make sure it's empty and if not that no one leaves it. Brother Anthony, you and Mr. Gaglioni stay close to me." Clarence left with the tan muscular Jerry Metcalf of Miami and Jim Beck, the big guy from Chicago who could kick ass if need be.

The guys left and Malone talked over the bar to the four on the floor. "Okay, they're gone. What happened?"

"Arrest them, that's what happened," Bob spurted out. "They will kill Ron and Iggy if you don't."

"Kill me, why me?" Iggy couldn't help but wonder aloud. Yet at the same time he was proud to be a person of interest to the Signore, so to speak. It was the first time he was considered a threat to anyone and a dangerous person. "Well just let them try and get this queer. There will be hell to pay."

"Really, who cares," Bob was bordering hysteria. "They're going to cut your…your things off too, and then…"

"Shut up Bob," Ron covered his friend's mouth. "It's true they think I turned the phone on and of course I did but they're not sure. Andrew just wanted revenge for being made a fool of by Iggy."

"I still don't get it, why me? I didn't go in the room?"

"But you did go into the stall with Andrew, remember..." Ron was interrupted.

"And the Signore saw you kissing Ron in the hallway, so he thinks you and Ron are in cahoots." Bob finished Ron's unexpressed thought with his best friend punching him in the arm. "Owe that hurt, asshole I'm just trying to let the Detective know all the facts."

Malone was now conspicuously leaning over the bar. Luckily only the backs of the guests could be seen as they were focused on the stage and the explanation of the Blessing of the Statues by Cardinal Spellman after they were transferred to the barge the following day. "What the hell, you risk your life for this artist and then go rogue with your feelings. I thought you guys were studying for the priesthood not a brothel for gays."

Susan stepped in before Ron's honor and pride in what they were attempting to do was totally shattered. "Detective, don't jump to conclusions. They were not having fun, shall I say. They had to distract that Signore guy who caught them near the meeting room."

Ron shot her a smile. Just maybe she did understand him.

"I see and you chose to kiss as the distraction. I think I'm getting behind the times. So what happened after that?" The middle age Detective stated rather somberly.

Inside the meeting room, the Signore had silenced his three henchmen and had them focused on the issue at hand. That was whether or not someone had deliberately set the phone on intercom and presuming so if they overheard what took place. In the end, he concluded that the kid as he called Ron had to be found. "He said he worked for the UN so there must be a record of employment and that should lead us to him."

"And what about the girl and the other punk?" asked Westridge.

The Signore smiled. "I think they may have hurt the pride of my men and nothing more but that we will learn when we find the kid. And one more thing, Gaglioni must also be found and dealt with. Westridge, I leave that to you. My men will help you as they know him. Now split up. I can still hear the speech making."

Andrew had opened the door.

"Not that way. We'll use the service corridor which connects to the kitchen and prep room to these meeting areas and the Reception Hall." He led them to a door partially concealed by the bookcase which lined the wall opposite the sofa. Stephano carried with him the leather folder which contained the map of the World's Fair and route of the Pieta to the grounds as well as a list of the times when the docking was to take place, the blessing ceremony and the transfer to the flatbed trailers. If their plan failed at the dock, the backup plan involved the flatbed trailer.

Malone had heard enough. He worried that confronting the Signore may be considered entrapment. He had no warrant and he was on International ground and thus had no jurisdiction. Nevertheless he had decided to risk it. He waved to Van Buren and O'Hara to follow him down the hallway. It was totally deserted except for the Latin School guys he had assigned at the bathrooms. They verified that no one had entered or left the rest rooms.

Arriving at the Meeting Room door, Malone told Van Buren and O'Hara to flank the door. He would knock and open it. "If this Battista guy really has mob ties God only knows what kind of fire power they may have."

He knocked. There was no answer. "This is the police open up…" Only silence so he gave the door a hard shove. Virtually falling into the empty room he walked to the phone. There was a crunching sound under his feet as he neared the side table. Pieces of broken glass lay on the carpeted area in front of the sofa. Van Buren and O'Hara had entered with guns drawn. "Put them away; they've fled the coop."

CHAPTER SEVEN

OUT OF LUCK

Malone was having the meeting room dusted for fingerprints. O'Hara was picking up the pieces of broken glass with the hopes of finding an identifiable finger print. In the meantime the Signore had unobtrusively entered the preparation area next to the reception hall. He struck up conversations with the actual catering staff of the gala. Wearing his credentials and dressed to kill, the staff was only too willing to discuss how they should bring out the next serving of hors-d'oeuvres. He even suggested that they do so when the speeches were concluded. The distraction enabled each of his co-conspirators and his body guards to slip past the workers one by one. The exit door of the prep room was near the stage area which was crowded with guests listening to the speeches. The four men who were at the table just mingled in with them as no one had any knowledge of who they were or what they looked like. The Signore though easily recognized was supposed to be at the gala as a supporter of the arts. His presence was taken for granted despite his reputation. There wasn't a sane person who dared to mention that gossip and expect to live to tell about it. Yet there was no evidence of his unsavory connections. He had been seen earlier by dozens of people speaking with everyone of note. Even the Cardinal, Ambassador and the Captain of the barge Challenger on which the Pieta and Good Shepherd would spend the next night, could provide him with a solid alibi of never leaving the reception area. His problem was to slip away and not be recognized as he did so.

Andrew, Stephano and Giuseppe had a more challenging time of it. The four behind the bar and Clarence not more than ten feet from the Prep Room door all could recognize them. They were forced to mingle with the crowd and make their way to the other side of the room and then follow along the window wall to the opposite side of the room. At all times they had to keep a look out for Ron, Bob, Iggy, Clarence and Susan who was known to them as Christine. Such large men in fine attire and of handsome qualities could not help but to attract attention which they did not desire or need at that moment. They of course had no idea that the one they sought to "rub out" was also present at the gala. And that's when their luck ran out, at least for one of them.

The four unknown men at the meeting managed to infiltrate the crowd virtually unnoticed. They even formed a barrier for the Signore Battista so that he could be seen and yet move along without hindrance. He was able to slip out of the reception hall with hardly a person seeing him actually leave. The speeches had ended and the band resumed playing. The crowd once again began to spread out as new trays were brought out and wine once again served. The milling about of two hundred people had made a perfect screen for the Signore to get out. A host of others were also taking the opportunity to leave. The main reason for the gathering had ended with the speeches outlining the movement of Pieta to the World's Fair grounds. His henchmen having a more difficult time knew that they were recognizable. They had to make every effort to blend in with the moving mass of people, each seeking to speak with this dignitary or that clergyman of note.

Detective Malone remained at the bar in the corner of the room for it gave him a good vantage point to view the entire room. To his left stood Brother Anthony and on his right the artist, Giovanni Gaglioni. He had to use the eyes of the artist as Ron, Iggy, Bob and Susan were huddled behind the bar until the detective felt it safe enough for them to come out of hiding. Now that he felt confident that the artist was not a participant in the plot to steal the Pieta, he was quite comfortable to use his eyes. Giovanni was more than willing to scour for the Signore and the henchmen among the guests.

"Mr. Gaglioni, do any of these people seem familiar to you?"

"No one, sir; and you may call me…how do you put it? ah… you may address me by my given name, Giovanni, if it pleases you."

Malone actually cracked a smile and his face lite up most pleasantly. "It pleases me, Giovanni; and stop calling me sir, if you must, just Detective or just plain Malone will do."

A bond of trust was being established between them. In the midst of this bonding moment, Giovanni suddenly did a double take toward the window wall. He was sure he spotted one of the henchmen but said nothing at first. He focused and then without warning began to run toward the window wall. Malone was taken by surprise as was Brother Anthony who tried to follow the artist into the milling throng of people and was swept sideways toward the stage area. Malone called to him but didn't want to frighten the guests.

He bent over the bar; "Giovanni bolted from us. Don't know what he's up to and us having reached such a nice friendly attitude too."

Ron couldn't wait, he jumped up and over the bar. Bob and Iggy walked around it. Susan jumped up to her feet and watched the testosterone leap as if he was some kind of medieval knight on a quest. She smiled as Ron leapt over the bar. *Perhaps it was Dudley Do Right of the Mounted Police coming to the rescue,* she mused. She would have been more accurate if she thought of him as the Lone Ranger jumping off a rock onto his horse, Silver. In either case she called to Ron and the others to be careful. Her gown gave her limited mobility so she took an empty bottle of wine. She wrapped her fingers around its thin neck. Then in a very lady like manner sat herself on the very barstool where she flirted with Stephano and waited. For what she couldn't tell you; but she knew someone nasty might be coming by her and she was prepared.

A continuous flow of people were leaving and Malone's men were hard pressed to keep watch for the red bow tie as that's all they knew about the Signore. They had no idea that he had ditched the red tie and sported one from a waiter who now wore his. Battista had been gone for a while when Giovanni tried to rush through about a hundred people remaining for more free food and drink. While Malone pushed through dozens of cocktail holding and designer clothes dressed people, Van Buren spotted the red bow tie. "O'Hara, I think I see the red bow tie. Follow me. I'm going to check it out." Pulling out his badge he ordered the people in his way to spread out. There was a growing reaction of fear as he made his way to the tall man who sported the tie. "You stop, I am a cop."

There was no response, only his back now faced Van Buren. "I said stop." Van Buren ran up to him and tackled him at the ankles. He and the tray he held went flying into the posh crowd. Screams began as the waiter fell into a portly man and an equally stout woman, bounced off them hit O'Hara on the rebound and landed at the feet of Van Buren. Scared half to death, the waiter lay on his back with his hands raised behind his head.

"I'm just a waiter, I didn't steal any wine, honest."

The frightened people around the scene now became the outraged citizens who were protesting the excessive violence at such a celebration of faith symbols coming to America.

"Just go about your business," Van Buren ordered executives, bank presidents, high society ladies and gents, Bishops and Abbots and one who just happened to be there with Father Gregory, a woman identifying herself as Mrs. Gertrude Liguri, the mother of Susan. She had stooped down with the priest to help the waiter to his feet.

"Look at him Father, the poor man. Let me help you." Mrs. Liguri and the priest took his hands with Van Buren's permission and got him to his feet.

"I am so sorry sir, but our description said the suspect was wearing a red bow tie and yours is the only one here that I've seen."

The waiter informed him that it wasn't even his tie, "a distinguished looking man in the prep room had asked me to exchange ties with him. He said that his rental came with this one which he said made him look like a clown. He paid me fifty bucks for my tie. It only cost two, so I did it. Is that a crime?"

"No sir, you are free to go. O'Hara I think the Signore is long gone." Van Buren thanked Father Gregory and Mrs. Liguri and apologized to the crowd around him and O'Hara.

During that surge to the scene of apprehension of the waiter, hardly anyone noted that two men left. They simply became one of a number of people trying to escape the pursuit of the criminal who wasn't a criminal at all. No one was really noticing Malone catching up with Giovanni.

They now blocked one side of Stephano's exit route. Ron rushing past the fleeing guests blocked the body guard's other flank. He was now trapped between Malone and Giovanni and Ron, who now had Bob and Iggy backing him up.

"It's him Detective, it's one of them." Ron threw his thin but well packed body into the large steel of a man. He bounced off and collided with his backups. The three ended up on the floor as Giovanni broke away from Malone and came to their aide. He walked right up to Stephano stepping over the three cassock wearing seminarians on the marble floor.

"You, you wrapped Sheila in a tarp like trash to be thrown out." Giovanni pounded on his chest and began to weep.

Stephano stood motionless and let him pound on him. The artist never saw Malone behind him with his gun pointing at the thug. "Giovanni, step aside, the law will take over from here."

The guys on the floor were now being ogled by several people who weren't caught up in the waiter chase. They helped each other up and gently took Giovanni away from Stephano. In doing so, they formed a blind spot between Malone and the thug. Stephano grabbed the gun out from under his tux jacket. He wildly shot so as to create panic rather than harm anyone in particular. One of the windows lining the wall behind him cracked resulting in a small spider web pattern but no shot out. The intent of the shot was successful. In the ensuing rushing of people and screams, he took hold of Ron, as he was the closest to him. It was no use to struggle, his immense arms held the lad tightly around his neck. The gathering crowd continued to run from the scene. Malone swung around with gun drawn. There wasn't a safe opening for him to shoot back without hitting the guests who were fleeing.

"Everyone stay back or this kid gets it right here." He had the barrel of the gun on Ron's temple. He began to back away from the window and toward the exit doors.

"No one is to approach this man," ordered Malone as the UN Security people were now on site as well. He allowed Stephano to move toward the doors in hopes that once in the main lobby they would be able to give chase if he didn't shoot Ron first that is.

The crowd became still and silent as their eyes followed Stephano now holding Ron under the arm and around his chest and keeping the gun at his head. Step by step Malone followed along behind the gapping people. Bob and Iggy began to follow them. "You two, stay put or else." The only hope of distraction and possible escape just vanished before Ron's eyes as his friends froze in place. Sweat poured off Stephano's brow as he moved slowly, his eyes looking for Malone. They had reached the bar where Susan sat with bottle in hand and no one the wiser. She looked at Malone who nodded "no" and then hit Stephano on the head with the bottle.

He screeched out "shit" rocked back and that was all that Ron needed. He kicked Stephano where the sun don't shine and pushed away from the dazed man's arm hold. Blood trickled down the side of the thug's head. He instinctively took hold of his groin and his head at the same time and staggered backwards. Malone appeared out of nowhere and brought him down as the crowd began to applaud. Ron still angry and fired up ran to them on the floor and kicked the gun out of Stephano's hand. Within seconds Malone had him in cuffs and Van Buren and O'Hara came running to take him away. Giovanni pushed his way through the gathering crowd and came once again face to face with Stephano now being held by Van Buren. Those sad eyes had a glimmer of satisfaction as he looked at Malone, Ron and then to Susan. "Grazie," he simply said and walked up to the thug and spit in his face. "May you burn in hell with the Signore."

The Detective took hold of the artist but too late. The spittle ran down the shocked thug's face. His hands were cuffed behind his back which prevented him from wiping away the insult. "Giovanni, that won't bring her back." He pulled him off Stephano and placed him in the arms of Susan. Speaking to O'Hara and Van Buren he told them to bring the suspect to the meeting room at the end of the hall. Being on International Territory, he had no jurisdiction and had to get permission to make the arrest. But that red tape wouldn't prevent him from interrogating him.

As he was taken away, Stephano spoke to Giovanni, "I liked Sheila. She was kind to me."

Lowering his head, the artist tried in vain to wipe away the look of hatred from his face. His thoughts were now of his own shame for his part in the plot to steal the Pieta. It didn't matter that he was unwittingly involved. The words from Stephano sank into his tortured grief stricken brain, he lifted his head. Susan was brushing his hair from his eyes more to comfort him and show support than because it was a bother. Gazing into her eyes, he noticed something. "Ron is fortunate to have someone like you to care for him."

"Ron…me? You don't understand…ah capisce, at all. Ron is studying for the priesthood."

"Ah si, I see him in the cassock of the priest to be sure. But I also see his eyes and your eyes at this moment. If I were to carve a statue right here it would be of two lovers in an embrace just before the kiss as they looked into each other's eyes."

Susan was turning a beet red as she glanced over to the oblivious Ron now talking with Malone, Bob and Iggy as to how to get Stephano to talk. The plot to steal the Pieta was known but how to prevent it and capture the accused murderer was quite another story.

"Don't be silly Giovanni. There's no chance; I mean God Himself has called Ron to serve His Church."

"Si, the Almighty is very persuasive." The artist took her hands into his own. "Such a pity, isn't it? You lost the one for whom you care to the Lord and the one I cared for is now with the Lord."

They walked toward the window with the bullet-hole in it and gazed out over First Avenue. A small church could be seen; from its steeple slim and white topped with a Cross the sounds of a chime could be heard but only faintly by them behind the thick glass. They chimed out the 11:00 p.m. hour.

The remaining crowd began to murmur and mill about as the prisoner was taken out of the Reception Hall. Most of the high profile dignitaries had already gone but the stalwart ones stretched out their brush with the famous just a bit longer. And so it was back to discussing who had been arrested, why that man spit in his face, how did the New York Police get involved, and what did that man called Giovanni mean by the theft of the Pieta which in their minds was utterly impossible. The band had stopped during the commotion and was now packing up. The party was over and everyone knew it. Within minutes, the hall was empty except for the staff, Ron and his buddies, the Detective and his men, Giovanni and Susan, and the prisoner in the meeting room with O'Hara and Van Buren. That is almost everyone; for Father Gregory, Abbot Lawrence and Mrs. Liguri were rushing to Susan now that they could get near them.

"Let me pass," demanded Mrs. Liguri to Officer Jones who stood between her and Susan and the artist at the window.

The Latin School guys were with Brother Anthony near the bar. Jones was being helped by a UN Security guard.

"Jones, let her pass," ordered Malone from across the room at the bar. He then waved to Father Gregory and the Abbot to come to their students.

The contrast between the tall, robust, balding, fifty-five year old Abbot with German heritage and the short slender forty something year old Asian priest was quite evident as they scurried to the bar area. Each with lines of worry across their brow, they made their way to their students and their fellow Monk, as members of the Benedictine Order were called.

Jones stepped aside. "I was just protecting them madam."

"Indeed, I understand." She ran up to her daughter. "Susan, sweetheart, are you hurt?" Mrs. Liguri wrapped her arms around her daughter.

Giovanni sighed at the sight of motherly love and thought of his own family back in Abruzzo Italy. His thoughts were like a vision of those innocent days of dreaming to become a great artist like his idol, The Divine One, Michelangelo. He saw his days at the Academy in Florence where he was discovered by the Signore. He was remembering how he plucked him out of oblivion and gave him a chance to create something out of the marble. Even if not from his own mind, it was still a chance to prove that he had what it takes to be a sculptor. A tear drop trickled down his cheek as all the joy of those memories was destroyed earlier that day.

Jones walked over to him and placed his hand on the artist's shoulder. "Missing your Mom, sir?"

At the bar, Malone was filling in Abbot Lawrence and Father Gregory on what had taken place. He talked about their suspicions as to what was being attempted. Finally he felt compelled to let them know that some of their students had become involved in what he called the situation. He had to include Brother Anthony in that discussion. The brother was involved in some of what happened when he was sticking like glue on

Giovanni all night. "You see the artist was a murder suspect until just a few minutes ago."

He could not give them all the details as he didn't know them all himself. In fact it was Ron, Bob and Iggy who had the most information of what was actually being planned in that meeting room. That knowledge led to the attempted capture of the wrong Signore and led to the capture of Stephano. The focus had been on the apprehension of the murder suspect. Now with his eluding them it was changing. "Your students have information on a plot which involved stealing the Pieta soon to arrive at the dock."

"I am stunned Detective Sargent Malone," the Abbot began. "I spoke with this man who you say is behind the plot to steal the precious Pieta and a murder as well. He seemed charming and most supportive of the Church's role in bringing the art work to the United States. Are you sure it was him behind the heinous crime and this plot of which you speak?"

"If that man, over there by the bullet riddled window is telling the truth and if your own students, Ron, Bob and Iggy are being truthful then, yes, I am confident that Carlo Battista known as the Signore is our primary suspect at this time."

"Then of course, Father Gregory and Brother Anthony will be at your disposal to assist with our students but Detective, only Clarence is over twenty-one, so be prudent in using them. I shall phone our Prior, Father Henry back at the Abbey and have him contact their parents."

Ron, Bob, Clarence and Iggy had moved closer to the clergy and the Detective to listen in.

"Father Abbot," began Clarence. "I can take responsibility for these three as I have been with them almost from the beginning when we escaped from the warehouse when that one just arrested with two others took the body of the poor woman and wrapped her in a tarp."

The Abbot crossed himself. "May God have mercy on her soul; but Clarence, I cannot allow you to be placed in such danger again. I mean escaping from a warehouse in the middle of New York, chasing down a potential murderer and thief. I would be remiss in my duties should any of you are hurt or worse."

Ron couldn't hold his tongue any longer. "Reverend Abbot, we're not little kids, we're nineteen and Iggy is twenty years old. Girls are considered adults at eighteen and guys have to register for the draft at eighteen but we cannot vote or sign legal papers until we're twenty-one. Now I ask you, is that fair?"

The Abbot was not about to be dragged into a societal issue, nor one of sexual discrimination nor one of legal principals within the law. He walked between Ron and Bob and pulled in Iggy with them and faced Clarence and the rest of the guys. "Now, you call me Father for that is my role with my flock of which you are part as you are students of the Abbey's Latin School. Thus I shall not debate the justice of that which is; rather I must act on what is best for all of you legal age or not. Clarence will answer to Brother Anthony regarding you three. The rest of you, my sons, will answer to Father Gregory and assist the Detective Sargent here as best you can. None of you however may place yourself in mortal danger again. You will be in constant communication with the Detective and should anything arise, you shall alert him before taking any action on your own. Am I clear on this?"

Ten voices replied in unison. "Yes, Father Abbot."

"I am most pleased to hear that. And now Father Gregory and I shall take you six back to the hotel if the Detective doesn't need you. Brother Anthony will stay with these four. I believe they should be present when the suspect is interrogated for they are eye witnesses to what he did with the others in that warehouse. But I do hope Brother; that you might bring them to the hotel soon."

Brother Anthony sought a sign of that possibility from the Detective. Malone took the hint. "Yes Abbot, we shall have a little talk with this Stephano person and then they will be returned to the hotel by squad car to insure their safety." Malone then called to Jones to bring the artist and Susan to him. "And what about Susan?"

"Yes, what about Susan." It was Mrs. Liguri speaking. "My daughter could have been killed by that Stephano person. She's told me quite a bit about what happened right here at this bar and in some kind of meeting room."

"Mom don't yell at the Detective, please. He's just doing his job. I told you that Ron…and the other guys needed my help to distract Stephano and that's all's to it."

"Indeed, distract a man so that a murderer might be found. So Detective again I ask what about Susan?"

Malone had dealt with many parents over his tenure as a Detective and now as Detective Sargent. He was not about to lock horns with a protective mother. "Ma'am, for now all I need from Susan is a statement as to what actually happened at this bar and in the meeting room with the murder suspect. Jones here can take it and then she's free to go unless I need to see her again."

Susan knew where this was headed and she had no intention of being babysat by her mother. Taking her by the arm she escorted her Mom away from the Detective. "Now the Detective may need not only my testimony but also my help in identifying anyone who was in that meeting room. So please don't baby me in front of those men. I am a woman and I can handle myself. Ron and the guys are there just in case anyway."

"I know sweetheart, but you're only going to be twenty. When you're a mother, you'll understand what it means to see your child in danger." She stroked her daughter's long hair behind her shoulders.

"I get it. But for now, I need to help Ron. He can't do this alone, though he thinks he can. But like most men, he's wrong. He's needs a woman's help to get it done right."

The trim mother with the elegance of a true southern lady who could be at the Queen's court smiled proudly. "There is no doubt in my mind that you can complement whatever those young men have in mind. But remember who you're dealing with sweetheart. They are future priests. Don't let your heart get in the way." She purposely used the plural and not just Ron's name.

Arm in arm mother and daughter returned to the Detective. "My Mom will be returning with the Abbot to the hotel. I'll hitch a ride with Brother Anthony and the guys after we give our statements."

The issue was resolved. The Abbot left with the six, Father Gregory and Mrs. Liguri. The Detective walked down the hallway with Giovanni and Officer Jones. Brother Anthony followed with Iggy, Clarence and Bob clustered about him. At the end of the entourage came Ron and Susan.

"So your Mom let you stay; that's cool."

"I told her, that you needed my help."

"What, I'm no kid. I don't need your help."

"That's exactly what I told my mom you'd say."

"Susan Liguri, you drive me crazy."

"Ron De Cenza, that's the second time you said that to me tonight." She took hold of his arm and he let her do so.

The first stop for the entourage was the room where the Signore held his meeting. Malone directed everyone to swing around the window side of the table and not to touch anything, especially the side table and the meeting table. Prints would go a long way to help identify who attended that meeting, he explained to them.

Bob slipped back to be with Ron. Susan dropped her hold on his arm. "Ron, I've got the notebook."

"Shush, keep it in your pocket until we see where this is heading."

"Isn't that withholding evidence or something? A concerned Bob asked.

"You two stop drawing attention. Bob, give me that notebook. I'll hold it in my purse."

"No way; I almost got killed for this." He put it back under his cassock and into his pants pocket.

"You two are such children. It would be safer with me. No one would think I would have it so they wouldn't even ask me. But if the Detective asks you Bob Wentz, are you going to lie to the police?"

Turning crimson in the face, he admitted that he could not. "Okay, okay, I'll give it to you to hold after we get out of here. Is that cool with you Ron?"

No sooner had the words left his lips than Malone began to go over what happened in the room as he knew it to that point. What he didn't know is what was said or who was at the meeting besides the three henchmen and the Signore. He began with Iggy.

"Just how did you get involved in this situation," Malone asked.

Poor Iggy was beside himself, what with Hollywood handsome Brother Anthony standing right next to him and he having had such a crush on him when he arrived at the Abbey for Latin School. He was mortified about having to talk about meeting Andrew in the bathroom and what transpired there, so he didn't. He also didn't say that he kissed Ron in the hallway to distract the Signore who was on his way to the meeting room. He gave the minimal facts that he saw Andrew in the men's room and that he was complaining about being treated like a camel and he needed to pee badly. He didn't realize who he was until a large man in a red bow tie entered and they talked about what was going to take place shortly.

"I had to become a non-entity at that point, so I left but he came out right after me so I took hold of Ron and shoved him against the wall like we were talking and the big man spoke to me as he passed."

"Well what did he say?" Malone asked.

Iggy tried to avoid the gutter talk part of him being a gay hustler type. "Oh, he just was surprised that I was…"

Susan began to laugh.

"Miss Liguri, is what Iggy is saying funny to you?"

"Well Detective Malone, in a way it is in that what I heard was that Iggy had to kiss Ron to make it look like they had a thing for each other which of course they don't being holy joes going to be priests. Anyway they were trying to throw the Signore off track about them trying to hear about the meeting and all. And it worked too."

"Well young lady, you seem to know a lot about something you weren't there to witness. Iggy, is Susan exaggerating or not?"

Ron had to save Iggy from himself so he jumped in. "Detective Sargent, it's true; we had to make a split second decision and that was the most outrageous thing we could do on the spare of the moment. Iggy was just trying to clean it up to save me from embarrassment because we are future priests."

"I see," Malone paused and then grinned. "Apparently it certainly wowed someone." He turned, the grin was gone and his focus was intense. "Now what about you Bob; I know that you and Iggy were in the room next door. We shall go there next to talk with the suspect."

Bob became weak in the knees and began to wobble. Ron took hold of his arm and pulled out the very chair on which the Signore had sat during the meeting. He placed Bob onto it. All the while Bob was trying to get the notebook out of his pocket. He just got it in his fingers when as he sat it slipped and fell down inside the cassock to the floor. Not having it in his possession was actually a blessing.

"Sorry all this talk of plots, murder, the shooting and all, has me all upset. You were asking me about what Iggy and I heard, right?"

"That's correct, so what did you hear?" Malone replied.

Bob swung around in the chair and kicked the notepad toward Susan. Why he did so was a mystery even to him. Perhaps a separation from it made would make it easier for him to lie about its contents so that he and Ron could figure out a plan. Or maybe it was just that he felt Susan would keep it safe. In either scenario, he didn't want to reveal its existence just yet. He was saved from his predicament when a knock on the door interrupted the questioning.

O'Hara popped his head in. "There you are; that guy won't talk. What should we do?"

The artist answered. "Detective Sargent let me go in there."

Malone turned away from Bob shaking in the signore's chair. He looked deeply into the somber face of Giovanni Gaglioni and sank into deep thought. He glanced at O'Hara with a questioning wrinkling brow as if he were about to ask him what he thought about the idea but that would be out of the question to ask a uniform cop what he should do next. While in his thoughts he studied the faces of his lineup of persons of interest in this situation. His eyes narrowed as if to suck into his mind whether these young people had valuable information and the artist the sincerity to help and not once again attack the suspect. They were all filled with apprehension and well he knew it as he made his decision.

"We'll all go in there… just maybe seeing all of you may show him that saying nothing isn't really going to help him or his comrades."

UN Lobby

CHAPTER EIGHT

CIVILITY AND PANIC

When Malone gently pushed open the door to the smaller meeting room where Bob and Iggy had listened in on the Signore's meeting, the first thing he saw was Stephano sitting behind a small table. His hands still cuffed behind him. It was obvious that no one bothered to clean him up as yet. Behind him his entourage had crammed so close as to be touching his back. He stepped aside and invited his entourage to enter. They filed in each with various degrees of anxiety about seeing this guy who could then identify each of them. Should he ever get hold of the Signore, their very lives could be in danger each were thinking yet remaining silent. Only Giovanni didn't care; he was convinced that he could get the so called body guard to help them in some fashion. Stephano's words about liking Sheila had stayed with him. A feeling of regret that he had spat upon him as they did to the Christ whom he carved in the marble began to eat at him.

"Uncuff him and get him a wet towel," Malone ordered.

Van Buren squeezed past the entourage of people entering and ran down the hall to the men's room. O'Hara was removing the cuffs. Stephano rubbed his wrists and placed his hands on the table as if he knew that would be the next order. It was not. Rather it was a question. "Do you need a glass of water?"

"Yeah," Stephano curtly replied. His eyes staring right into those large cocoa color eyes of the artist.

O'Hara went to the bar where a small refrigerator as many college students use in their dorm ruins was located. He took out a pitcher of water and poured it into a plastic cup. While this scene was unfolding, Susan and the guys remained silent and just watched for what would come next. They didn't have to wait long. Giovanni took the cup from O'Hara and brought it to Stephano. For the longest time, the artist just stood next to the suspect with the cup in his hand. Stephano didn't ask for it or even make a gesture to receive it. They just both looked at each other and waited for one of them to say something. Malone motioned to O'Hara to back off. He too wanted to see this scene play out.

Giovanni placed the cup between the palm-down hands resting on the oak wood table which had been highly polished so that the cup actually had a reflection.

"Did you really mean what you said about Sheila?" he asked quietly, his hands shaking as he placed the cup down.

Stephano looked up never touching the cup. "She was nice to me, even when the Signore got mad at me."

"She was nice to me also," Giovanni replied.

Then there was silence again as they just continued to stare at each other and wondering. Wondering how such a vivacious woman who usually could control the beast within the Signore could be murdered with such viciousness. Only the artist knew how violent the act was but the body guard saw the Signore become a Mr. Hyde on more than one occasion.

"The Signore, he is a very jealous man."

"Now I know but it's too late to take back what he saw between Sheila and me. He made sure of that, didn't he Stephano?"

"I was not there to see anything Giovanni, you know that. My job was to help crate the statue you made for the Signore."

"And what did you find?"

"Blood everywhere, all over the statue. There she lay in the arms of the Holy Mother and lying on Jesus, covered in a veil. Someone had to have done that, someone who cared for her. The Signore would not do such a thing."

"Is that how you three knew that someone had to have been in the warehouse besides you?"

Stephano finally took the water. He sipped from the cup and licked his lips. "We had a job to do but I wouldn't let them throw her into the river, I wouldn't let them do that. I'd kill them first."

Giovanni's composure was breaking down. Malone could see it, so could everyone else. Ron walked over to him and placed his hand on his shoulder. "Listen, this is too difficult for you. We've heard enough."

"Enough, is it enough to know that Sheila is lying somewhere cold and lifeless and unwanted?"

"My friend, she knows how you feel. She knows that she is wanted; that you want to find her and bring her to rest in peace."

"So the Church tells me, but now I don't know. I can't believe that such a man who brings art to the world, beauty to the world, can be so cruel. Why does God allow such things? I ask myself. I ask you who study to serve the Church," Giovanni turned to the others. "And you can any of you tell me why God allows such things to happen?"

Only Brother Anthony found some words but before he would speak them he asked the artist if he really wanted an answer, one which he may not like to hear. Only when the artist nodded "yes" did he speak.

He walked to the table and stood on the other side of Stephano so that he could look into the eyes of Giovanni and Ron. "God does not allow such things to happen. What he allows, if you call it that, is for people to make their own decisions on how to live their lives, how to treat each other, how to show love and yes even to choose hate."

A glaze seemed to cover Giovanni's eyes as he looked at Brother Anthony and then embraced Ron sobbing. "He chose hate, the Signore chose hate."

"That he did my friend and we shall catch him before he can hurt anyone else." Ron twisted his neck to seek out Malone. "Won't we Detective?"

Ron led the artist to the sofa while Malone was now to take his turn with Stephano. "A person you say you liked has been killed. And now millions of people may be spiritually hurt when your boss implements some kind of plan of which we know almost nothing…"

Bob plunked himself next to Susan, who was on the other side of Giovanni. "Give me the notepad Susan, this has gone too far." He had made his decision to bring light to the darkness of the Detective Sargent's case.

Susan leaned over so that she could make eye contact with Ron. "Give it to him," he firmly stated.

She opened her shoulder bag on the little gold chain and took out the notepad. Iggy smiled at Bob and Ron. "It's the right thing to do Ron. Go for it Bob."

It was so quiet when Van Buren when arrived at the doorway. He was holding wet and dry paper towels in his hand. Towels which Stephano could use despite a bar towel being given to him. He walked in as Malone watched Bob take the notepad and garner the courage to read from it. Not that he and Ron or Iggy didn't want to share what they learned. It's just that they had this ultraistic t idea that they could do what the police might not be able to do. That was to lure the Signore and the others into the open in a way which would give them the upper hand. If Battista and his buddies knew the police were on hand, they may simply leave the country and lie low. Van Buren handed the towels to Stephano and backed away to be with O'Hara behind the prisoner.

The notebook shook in Bob's hands as he flipped over the cover of the tiny pad. He took a deep breath as if to breathe in courage. It became increasingly clear that once it got out that Iggy, Ron, he and Susan were involved in getting this information that they would all be in danger. Each of them might as well be wearing targets on their backs. Not only would they be hunted down by the Signore and his goons, but also by those four men mentioned in the notebook and whoever they controlled. Nevertheless, he began with how Ron delivered booze to the meeting room next door and in the process turned on the intercom of the phone there. How he and Iggy listened to what took place. They heard it all; the nonsense of Ron getting fifty dollars for his service and the Signore bemoaning the fact that such a handsome boy should be taken from the women of the world. They heard about the snickering when someone touched Ron where they shouldn't but couldn't tell what that was all about. Ron quickly pointed out that had nothing to do with the meeting. They were just having fun at his expense. So Bob continued.

He finally got to the part which Malone and his officers needed. There were four men at that meeting he told Malone and all. He called them by name along with their responsibility based on what they said around that table next door.

"One was Francesco Mondera who I think said something about heavy equipment being needed. Then there was Jeffrey Rafferty. He was getting some kind of boat for the Signore. The next one was Antonio Penne who was in charge of trucks and cars should they be needed. Finally there was this guy named Ben Westridge. He sounded like a mean guy who would make sure any trouble would be handled. But the most important thing is that Stephano was at that meeting with those two guys Andrew, who made a pass at Iggy and Giuseppe who Bob had followed."

Malone didn't hesitate. "Van Buren get a read on those names; see if they have records. You boys did a fine job and so did you Susan. However it does mean that all of you are in danger and I promised the Abbot that I wouldn't allow you to be endangered."

"It's too late for that," observed Ron. "Stephano here will get this out as soon as he gets his phone call, right?"

The goon with the heart leaned back in his chair. "And what if I could help you? How would that go with my case and sentence?" He looked at the artist but was thinking of the kindness Sheila showed him. Somewhere in that heart there was tenderness. Somewhere in that muscular body there was a growing revulsion over what had been done to Sheila.

Malone didn't have a case as yet, not until the red tape of capturing Stephano on International Territory was resolved. But Stephano didn't know that. "Listen carefully. I can't do much here in the UN but back at a police station in Manhattan things would be different." He offered him special consideration and a plea for a lighter sentence if convicted. At the moment Malone knew that he was only guilty of aiding in the stealing of the Pieta and the hiding of a dead body. He was confident that he could help Stephano.

"Okay then," Stephano shared what he knew. "Each of those men are responsible for some part of the switch, you know to replace the real Pieta with Giovanni's copy."

He went on to say that in the beginning he thought they were to crate Giovanni's statue for the Cathedral as a memory of the Michelangelo's Pieta's visit.

"I thank you for that Stephano," Giovanni said as he placed his hand on Stephano's shoulder.

Such an act of kindness was not in his experience. "Like I said, Sheila was nice to me and you've been duped because you're an okay guy. So like the preacher there said, I choose to do a good deed. Am I saved preacher?"

Brother Anthony almost laughed out loud when he said that Stephano was at least on the way to repentance, he was already saved because of Jesus; he just had to accept it.

Malone's mind was spinning with what they could do to stop the switch, find Sheila's body and then capture Battista and his cohorts after they admitted or were caught in the act. "Listen up it's after one o'clock; my men will take Stephano to a holding area in the Secretariat Building for an overnight stay. Tomorrow we shall all meet at your Hotel at 9:00 in the morning. Hopefully by then the UN Security Force will give us Stephano as well. Bob, may I have the notepad?"

"Sure detective, but my handwriting is kind of messy what with the nerves and all." He handed Malone his notes.

"It will make for good night time reading, thanks."

When they entered the United Nations lobby it was totally deserted except for the presence of three uniformed UN Security people and another in a regular suit. The one in the suit presented Malone with the release granting him holding power over Stephano until the protocol was signed for transferring him formally to the New York Police Department the next day. Stephano would not be staying in the UN but in a Manhattan Police Station. He would be on Malone's turf and that meant interrogation and formation of a plan to capture the men listed in the notebook.

The next order of business as they entered the squad cars was what to do with Giovanni, who was now homeless and penniless. Brother Anthony took care of that issue and invited the artist to stay with him and the seminarians at the hotel. As they drove off for 48th Street and 5th Avenue that little chapel Giovanni and Susan looked at from the window began to chime out 2:00 a.m.

Malone was relieved as Stephano was taken to the holding cell in the 19th Precinct. Located between Central Park and the East River on 67th St. it was conveniently located to the United Nations complex.

"That's it men, he's safely away; go home and get some rest. Tomorrow it starts all over again."

That was welcomed news for Van Buren, O'Hara and Jones who had been with Malone since early in the day when all hell began to break loose. Malone had one more thing to do. He walked back to the holding cell to make sure Stephano would be alone through the night. No other prisoners were to be placed with him, he ordered. The Precinct Commander was most accommodating in making sure that would happen when he called her from the UN location.

Back at the hotel Brother Anthony was standing with Giovanni, the guys and Susan in the lobby. Since Father Gregory was the brother's roommate in the full hotel. It was determined that Giovanni would stay in Ron and Bob's room as it would be improper for the priest and brother to share a bed. It was already a stretch that they shared a room.

Susan pulled the chain of her purse over her neck. "I will be glad to get this off my neck."

Ron, his pals and the artist looked at her with a lack of understanding as to why that would be so important. "Yeah, I bet it's heavy." Ron didn't know what to say as it was just a little sequined thing which couldn't weigh more than a half pound if that he figured. "So have a good night; say hi to your mom for us. See you tomorrow?"

"Right, tomorrow…so you want me to help you then?"

Ron left the guys in the middle of the lobby and took Susan's arm, guiding her around the corner to the elevators and out of sight from the others. "Listen Susan, about what I said earlier. I was just being a jerk. If you hadn't done what you did with Stephano this night may have been a total bust. At least we got that Stephano guy."

The words of her mother of all things were ringing in her head. 'Do not let your heart get in the way, they are becoming priests,' she had told her. "It's all right, I was rather mean spirited. I wanted to show you that I could be of help and am not some helpless girl."

"And that bottle clunked on his head sure did that," Ron laughed.

"Thanks for that, but I didn't knock him out so…"

"So nothing, it was well placed and saved my ass."

She smiled thinking of his cute ass. "Thanks again; well good night, see you tomorrow."

"Yeah, tomorrow it is but which is today already."

The elevator door opened and she stepped into it and waved bending sideways to see him smiling at her as the door closed. As for Ron, he raised his eyes to heaven and began a little conversation. *"Lord, this isn't good, I feel that tingling again down there but there's going to be no repeat of what happened last time."* He pulled down on his pants to give his thing a little breathing room, a necessity which wouldn't have been acute were it not for the style of guy's pants being tightly fitted.

"Hey, Ron let's go up."

Ron about jumped out of his skin. "Crap Bob, you scared me half to death. After tonight, give a guy some warning that you're right behind him."

It wasn't only Bob but the others as well standing there and watching what had just taken place. Brother Anthony took the high road and said nothing other than they should get some rest. Bob on the other hand took off his jacket and handed it to Ron without a comment, which for him was the high road. They all entered the elevator with Ron holding the jacket in front of his groin area at belt level.

Giovanni as he entered wearing Ron's jacket asked if he should have given Ron his jacket back.

"Oh no, Giovanni," replied Iggy. "He wasn't cold, he just wanted to hold onto something for comfort, isn't that right Ron?"

"Very funny; come on Giovanni this is our floor."

Driving up Central Park West, Sacha was entrusted with getting to the Signore's apartment to see if the police had arrived there. Battista was sure that if whoever listened in on the meeting had heard everything that the cops would be searching his place. A bright moon hung low in the sky on a clear cool April night which was soon to give way to the dawn. The trees in Central Park were already budding and by the time the World's Fair opened its gates the unfolding of the leaves and greening of the grass areas would give the city its spring season. None of this mattered to the Limo driver and confidant of the Signore. He pulled up directly in front of the tall brick building with plaster decoration so common in buildings built in the 1920's when the rage was adding dignity to buildings not just functionality. He felt safe to approach the building. He only saw the doorman under the canopy leading to the entrance doors. No cop cars could be seen.

There was no mistaking the Caddy limo of the Signore. The doorman hustled right to the curb prepared to open the limo door for the big man with the cigar as he referred to Battista.

"No need Stan, he's not with me. So has it been this quiet all night?" Sacha sticking his head out the window looked up and down the sidewalk. Maybe there were plain clothes cops around or hiding across in the park he thought.

"Yes Sacha, it's been a quiet night. The news said that there was some excitement at the shin dig at the UN tonight; did you hear anything about it? Wasn't the Signore and Miss Sheila there?"

"Yeah some punk was arrested for shooting at the window the Signore and Miss Sheila weren't even there." He couldn't say anything about Sheila so he just left it as he said it. He left early, after the big wigs gave their speeches. So when did you come on duty?"

"It was about eight at night. You know, I work through the night until 6 in the morning."

"Right, I forgot. So what did Sidney have to say when you relieved him, anything interesting?"

"Not really, just that Sheila looked so pretty when they left this morning. And that they never came back to change for the party at the UN. She's such a sweetheart, always with a smile for me and a good tipper too. She gave Sidney twenty bucks just for opening the door for her the other day. What a lady."

Sacha instantly became silent and reflective; thinking of how many times he took her down 5th Avenue and up Park Avenue to shop and always she got him a treat or a little something for his place in Queens. Most of all his thoughts flooded with her insisting that he come to lunch around the Rockefeller plaza because she knew at Christmastime he enjoyed watching the skaters and in the nice months, he liked being outside to watch the fountain and have a coffee and roll. "Yes, she sure was Stan, quite a lady."

"Was? Sacha did something happen?"

"What, oh no not that I know of; just the wrong words that's all. So listen, I need to run up and get a few things for the Signore. You'll make sure the limo is okay here for a few minutes for me, right?"

"Oh sure," Stan replied but was thinking of the 'was' word and why he was only gathering things for the Signore.

Sacha slipped him a twenty more so as a memory of Sheila and ran into the lobby. The Signore certainly didn't need a lot of clothes; he had a whole closet full in his other home in Greenwich Village.

The Brownstone on the north side of Washington Square was what is called a safe house, for him that is. It was not in his name and could not be traced to his associates at that meeting either. Inside the historic row house one entered a world of another century. Works of art hung on its walls. Sculptures from antiquity stood on marble pillars. Flowers adorned every room in the three story house and they were changed every few days on a rotating basis to reflect the season and the Signore's mood that week. One would think they entered a museum, not the house of someone who came from Little Italy in Manhattan. Battista grew up on Mulberry Street as had the children of generations of immigrants for over a hundred years. Now when he walked down that street the vendors, the neighborhood people still there and the business owners of the restaurants lining the street would greet him and fall all over him. They hoped that he'd stop in their place to eat or buy a fashion for his lady friend. For well over two years, that Lady friend was Sheila who would be on his arm. Then he would check out his own businesses on Canal St. where in store front buildings mainly Asian guys would be pushing knock off purses with the big names that Sheila bought on 5th Ave. However, behind that tourist trap a more lucrative business for the Signore busied itself with a variety of clandestine operations not the least of which was what would take place when the Cristoforo Columbo docked at 44th Street pier.

Sacha hurried got out of the elevator at the 10th floor and hastily made his way down the floral print carpet in the long hallway. Candelabra light fixtures on the wall gave the appearance of royal luxury. He entered not just an apartment but a house called an apartment. It had two floors, a marble staircase leading upstairs and like the Brownstone many art pieces which would bring thousands at any auction. And yet all of this was not enough for the Signore, he thought as he entered his boss' bedroom and then the study adjoining it.

Pulling a small suitcase from the huge closet filled with suits by Armani to mention the Signore's favorite designer, he placed into it quite carefully a few of his personally preferred comfort wear, cologne and from the safe in the study, a leather portfolio. The contents of that folder would provide him with a tidy sum of money once he got out of town which was his plan all along. He had set his sights on the Island of Malta in the Mediterranean Sea not far from his ancestral Italy. No extradition and safe from most prying eyes was his primary concern. Now with the Sheila problem and the possible leaking of the plot to those who listened in on his meeting, that dream of retirement now became one of necessity.

Clicking the suitcase shut, Sacha took one last item. It was a photo of Sheila which was on the Signore's 18th Century Colonial style desk. It was for Stephano, if he ever showed up. "Oh shit," he exclaimed as he looked at the photo. He picked up the phone on the desk and nervously dialed; his fingers so shaky that he could hardly fit them into the dial. "Giuseppe is that you,"

"Of course it's me."

"The Signore gave no orders regarding the things which belong to Miss Sheila. What should I do?"

"Hold on; the Signore is taking a rest, let me ask Andrew." There was a clunk as he dropped the phone. Running upstairs to the body guard's room, he shook him from a sound sleep.

Andrew jumped out of the bed in his shorts and grabbed for his gun on the side table. "What's happened Giuseppe?"

"It's Sacha on the phone; what should he do with Sheila's stuff?"

"How the hell should I know, let me get my pants on. I need to think."

"Andrew, there's no time to think. We have to wake the Signore."

"Go ahead, you do it and end up like Sheila or at best that asshole artist who caused all this in the first place." Andrew picked up the extension phone. "Sacha, pack up her stuff, anything you can find and bring it here to the Brownstone."

Sacha began to yell that there would be a shit load of stuff. "Wouldn't that look suspicious?"

Andrew yelled into the phone. "Just do whatever you can. Once the police get a warrant they'll be there. Somehow they'll be able to connect the Signore with Sheila's death even if they already haven't done so."

"All right, calm down, I'll do my best."

"You do more than that asshole. Your life, my life, the Signore's life depends on keeping us away from a murder charge and then it's off to sunny whatever that island is called and basking in the sun."

Sacha hung up the phone and shouted, "Faggot" to it. He then pulled out three large suitcases and crammed in all he could into them. Every bottle of perfume, jewelry, loose photos, pieces of lingerie, dresses and shoes…so many shoes that it was impossible to get all of them in the suitcases. Those he shoved into garbage bags and threw them down the garbage shoot. Sheila's presence with the Signore was removed from sight. Or so he thought until he dragged the suitcases through the living room. Pausing in front of the fireplace he noticed a grouping of glittering trinkets. Taking a closer look, he realized that they were souvenirs from the Signore's trip with Sheila to Italy. Playing it safe he placed them in the duffle bag which had his boss's special things. He was sweating profusely and tired beyond belief. The necessity of saving his boss and his own ass took precedence over any thought of rest in his mind. That island was becoming all the more attractive to him as he thought of what might happen to him if he was connected to covering up the murder. He was beginning to understand that Sheila's death was no accident. Even more compelling to him was the reality that he helped those four men at the UN reception escape with plans to steal Michelangelo's Pieta. Finishing with the stuffing of the souvenirs into the bag he began to think of his parents.

Sacha was the son of immigrant parents who escaped the Ukraine after the Soviet Communists took control to pursue their dream of freedom. Dragging the bags to the foyer he began to see that the freedom they sought and which could have been achieved by their son was now gone. Only the thought of a prison cell ran through his mind. He carried the stuffed suitcases over the marble floor one by one. He worried that they would scratch the stone. His eyes reddened as he thought of his parents' dream for him and the kindness of Sheila.

Sheila herself was the daughter of immigrants; in fact she was actually one herself. She came with her parents from Ireland as a young girl. They came over in the early 1950's, over a hundred years after the big wave of Irish immigration due to the potato famine. When the Murphy's sought a better life it was because of hard economic times particularly in the far west counties like Mayo, which was her family's home.

Once he had lined up all the suitcases in the grand foyer with its Austrian crystal chandelier hanging overhead, he buzzed down to the doorman for help.

"So Sacha, is Signore Battista going on a trip?" Stan eyed the baggage but didn't let the driver know that he was aware that the suitcases belonged to Sheila. He had seen her with various pieces when they went off to the Poconos for weekend trips.

Thinking quickly, he replied that they were planning a trip to Europe and would be leaving right after the Opening of the World's Fair. "Until then, they are staying with friends closer to Flushing; you know where the Fair Grounds is located."

Exhaustion was setting in from the pace of what he had to do not to mention that his day had begun early in the morning of what was now the previous day. He cut through Central Park from Central Park West to get to the 5th Avenue side. Immediately found on the other side was the Metropolitan Museum of Art. He knew a guy who was a security guard there and was sure he could park in the curator's spot for a couple of hours of sleep. He'd be gone before anyone arrived to open the museum.

CHAPTER NINE

BIRDS, BEES AND COVER-UPS

Bright sunshine peaked through the little crack left when the guys closed the curtains in their room. It announced that it was to be a perfect April morning. White fluffy clouds were scattered across the city and the blue of the sky was not shut out by shadows of the skyscrapers or haze. Traffic was building and horns were blasting but none of that was heard by Ron and Bob in one bed and Giovanni Gaglioni in the other double bed. His bushy almost black hair sticking out from under the covers was all that could be seen. The restful breathing sounds were quite the contrast to the shot ringing out at the gala at the UN Reception Hall.

Ron was up against the wall and Bob's one leg was sticking out over the bed. It dangled in the space between the two beds; so close was he hanging on the edge of the bed. Even in sleep they seemed to be conscious of not creating an occasion of sin by possibly touching each other during the night. And so the leg covered with his blue PJ's bottoms which had little white lambs on them hung off the bed.

Only the constant ringing of the phone on the table between the beds began to stir them. Certainly the bells of the Churches of New York were not penetrating into their world of sleep. The twenty-eight year old artist opened his eyes and pulled down the covers. He pulled himself up to a sitting position. His bare chest carpeted with light brown hair shivered slightly as the air hit his skin. He looked at the ringing phone but did not attempt to answer it. Rather, he slid off the bed and shook Bob.

Bob opened his eyes and saw the hairy chest first. He couldn't move fast enough as he bolted away and began to shake Ron. "Oh my God, Oh my God, it's Brother Michael, he's after my body. Ron, Ron, wake up."

The frightened artist jumped back from their bed and threw himself over the edge of his.

Ron threw off the covers and grabbed hold of Bob. "Christ pal, wake up. Open those eyes." He shook him.

"You used the Lord's name in vain Ron. I think." His back was to Giovanni, who now had a full view of the blue flannel PJ's with the lambs, for Bob was kneeling on the bed and quivering in front of Ron.

"Really, you're quoting me the Second Commandment. Turn around, it's only Giovanni; and get your hands off me." He shoved Bob away.

Bob did not turn around rather he became upset about how Ron spoke to him. "Well you did break the 2nd Commandment, so there and another thing, any guy who stuck his thing against another guy shouldn't worry about that particular guy holding his shoulders."

Ron jumped up on the bed, pulled open his gray sleep shorts and looked down into them. "You're full of shit; everything is okay down there." He let the elastic band snap back on his belly, flinching from the sting it made. "You must have been dreaming."

"Well not of you, that's for sure. We're buddies and that's all and I'm not too sure if we're even that after how you talked to me." Bob slid backwards and fell off the edge of the bed at Giovanni's feet. "Oh it was only you, I thought…well that chest of yours reminded me of another person we know."

Giovanni looked down with pity at the sight of a young man in what he would term toddler's sleepwear. "I think you called me Brother Michael. Is he with your people going to the Fair?"

Bob looked up at Giovanni as Ron now lay across the bed and hung over the edge of it looking down at his best pal in the world whom he just insulted. "No, he's not with us, he's in jail."

Giovanni was perplexed as well as a bit shocked to hear that a Monk would be in jail. "Is there religious persecution in the United States, land of the free?"

"Let me explain Giovanni," Ron began. "This Monk was not really a Monk at all. He was in the Abbey under false pretenses."

"And they put him in jail for pretending to be a Brother; that is really strict."

Ron pulled himself up and sat on the edge of the bed. "Well it's more than that; you see he was also stealing from the Abbey and…"

Bob interrupted. "And don't forget that he also wanted you sexually."

"So then you like the men, Ron?"

"Does it look like I like the men; I just insulted my best friend for him thinking that I did something to him which I would never do. I'm sorry Bob."

"It's okay; I see that what happened to you could have you upset about the possibility…"

"There was no possibility. I'm okay down there now."

"Well you don't have to yell at me. I just thought after what happened last night that there might be a repeat of the last time you two were together." Bob looked up at Giovanni. "He had a little problem with his thing."

"I do not understand what this 'thing' is of which you speak. Do you Americans have something to aide you in your love making?"

"Oh no, I think we do it like you do in Italy," Bob answered quite cavalierly.

Ron couldn't take it any longer; he jumped off the bed and stood in his sleep shorts and undershirt in front of Bob and Giovanni. "My pal here is talking about me getting a hard-on last night when Susan smiled at me and said good-night." He looked down with a now reddened face at Bob. "So there are you satisfied now, a man whom we've known for less than a day knows what happened; which was nothing as you can see."

Giovanni smiled and stepped over the now emotionally crushed Bob. He swung his arm around Ron and pulled him close with a smile. "I do not understand this term 'hard-on' but I can guess from what you have said. And I wish to ask if your Papa has ever spoken to you about these things?"

"You are kidding, right? This is America; we learn sex from the street talking and some from more progressive schools. We don't talk about it with our parents; that's for sure."

"But your name, it's Italian, no?"

"That it is Giovanni and I'm proud of it. But we are American in our ways. I am not familiar with how they do it in Europe."

"I cannot speak for all of Europe, for certainly in Britain and probably Germany, I think it's more like what you describe. But I come from Italy the land of Romance and love. We take love making very seriously but we have fun too. We laugh at the boys who get the 'hard-on' just like you did. And then we fight to protect our honor, just like you did, but we use the fists too."

"Okay Ron," Bob stood up. "Hit me right here." He pointed to his chin.

"Don't be a jerk." Ron took hold of Bob and gave him a hug. "And get rid of those PJ's your Mom bought you. You're a man now."

The "Birds and the Bees" talk ended abruptly with the phone ringing again. "Probably a wakeup call reminder like last time," Ron walked to the bathroom. "I got dibs on the first shower."

"Of course your majesty and don't be insulting my Mom; oh and I'll answer the phone too." Bob had picked up the phone as he yelled over to Ron. "Room 601 is up; so don't call again."

"What? Hold on…is that you Bob?"

"Holy cow I am so sorry Brother, I thought…well I thought it was just the operator calling to wake us."

"In either case Bob, that would be rude. Now the reason for my call; the Detective Sargent has just called me. He's sending a car so that we might join him at the Police Station and once again talk with this Stephano person. Are the three of you presentable?"

"Ah, I don't think so, we've been…well we've been having a talk about customs in Europe as opposed to America."

"I see. Well shake a leg; the squad will be here in a half-hour."

Bob placed the phone down and called out to Ron in the shower. "Hey, that was Brother Anthony; the Detective is picking us up in thirty minutes."

There was no answer. Giovanni went to the door and tried it. It was unlocked. "I will hurry him." He walked into the bathroom as Ron was stepping out of the shower just as Bob was telling him that wasn't a good idea; that his pal was very private about his privates.

"Hell, what's this about?" He grabbed a towel and wrapped it around himself.

"I beg your pardon. Do not misinterpret."

"Well you are an artist who idolizes Michelangelo; one wonders."

"It is true that the Divine One thought the male body was beautiful and I do too; but I also love the female body as the splendid example of beauty."

"So you swing both ways then?"

"I swing, as you say only one way; with the women. So have no fear of me that way. Not all people in the arts are how you say…swinging with the same sex."

"Wow, don't get heated about it. I just thought…I mean I didn't think; that's a big problem for me sometimes. So why are you in here when you knew I was taking a shower?"

Giovanni explained that he took it upon himself to hurry Ron so that all of them could be ready when the Detective's car arrived for them. "So I have 'dibs' on the next shower time if you don't mind." He dropped his sleep shorts and entered the shower, pulling the curtain closed. "I do not want to offend you or make you jealous." Giovanni smiled at Ron as he stuck his head out of the curtain.

"Yeah, well I think I'll just finish drying off out there and give you privacy." Ron stepped back into the bedroom area. Bob was laying out his clothes for the day.

"We don't need our cassocks today right?"

"Wrong, we have the ceremony at the 44th Street Pier with the Cardinal when the Pieta arrives. Put it in that satchel bag you're always dragging around with you. Can I put mine in there too?"

"Gee, I don't know; maybe I don't want mine to get all wrinkled; my Mom would get upset if I don't look my best."

"Oh, you're still mad at me." Ron slipped on his jockey shorts and grabbed a pair of black pants. "It's okay; I'll get a shopping bag from the gift shop."

"You just do that; that won't attract any attention. You did notice that they are gold, right?"

"You're being an asshole; you do realize that don't you?"

"And you were a big prick to me and I don't mean that as a complement."

Ron smiled. "But I'm glad you noticed." The attempt at sexual humor didn't work. "Shit Bob, come on…I said that I was sorry what else do you want?"

Bob stopped folding his cassock. He looked up with a quite serious expression. "What I want is not to be treated like some kind of side-kick Tonto and you being the Lone Ranger. What I want is for you not to insult my Mom."

"Whoa now, I get the sidekick thing, but I love your mother almost as much as my own Mom. So don't go there. It was a PJ comment and that's all it was. After what happened at the Abbey I would think you'd never wear them again."

"She packed them after I was packed and I was chilled last night so I wore them. It's not like anyone would see me in them; but then you invited Giovanni to bunk with us."

"Shit, are you jealous of a man almost ten years older than us?" Ron sat on the bed next to Bob's satchel while buttoning his blue cotton button down collar shirt.

"I heard those Italians say a term I didn't understand but I got the gist of it; *va fungu*. I'll go to confession later for telling you to do so."

Ron lunged for Bob and pushed him. He fell onto the other bed. "Well…well fuck you too. And I won't confess it because you deserve it. You forget that I understand some Italian, mostly the bad words." He began to laugh as he sat back down on the now ransacked bed. "Our moms would wash out our mouths with soap even though we're nineteen because we said the most forbidden of all swear words."

Bob sat opposite him and began to unbutton his PJ top and laughing as he did so. "They are kind of hideous aren't they? You know I did protest when she bought them. I told her that I wasn't ten anymore."

"More like five…"

"Don't you start again; I'm trying to make up with you."

Suddenly everything got serious and silence filled the room just as Giovanni came out wrapped in a towel to see the two of them exchanging a hug.

"And you thought that I was attracted to the men?"

The two burst out laughing. "Don't even go there Giovanni. It's too early in the morning."

Bob hurried into the bathroom with his underwear and black pants. Ron took one look at Giovanni and realized that this guy had only what he was wearing last night and the borrowed cassock. He pulled out a package of Jockey shorts from his suitcase. "These are brand new, never been worn by me. We're the same size, so they should fit. I have another pair of pants here and a shirt like I'm wearing but in white, will that be okay with you?"

Twenty minutes later the three were at the elevator and heading down to the lobby with all three cassocks stuffed into Bob's satchel to which he attached the leather shoulder straps so that he could carry it without using his hands. He appeared more like a pack mule as a result, but Ron kept that opinion wisely to himself. Giovanni mentioned that he hadn't time to shave just as the elevator stopped at the third floor. The doors opened and Susan and Mrs. Liguri were standing there. Susan was dressed in a full skirt of navy blue, a ruffled white silk-like blouse and a jacket which matched the skirt. She was wearing her hair down over her shoulders, which is what Ron thought looked best on her rather than the beehive type hairdo she sometimes wore at the Abbey. Not that his opinion mattered since he was going to be a priest and was not to have a girlfriend. No one noticed what Mrs. Liguri wore. In Susan's hands she held an Abbey school jacket; that one in particular noticed. He also tuned into Susan being kissed by her mother right in front of everyone as she told her to have a fun day.

"I'll see you at the ceremony later."

"Okay Mom," Susan entered the elevator as Bob and Ron called out morning greetings to her Mom.

"See you later as well boys."

The elevator doors closed. Susan handed Ron the jacket. "Here, I knew Giovanni had your jacket so I got another one. You're both are the same size, so it should do. Why are you looking at me that way? My mom's here as part of the Souvenir shop which will be in the Vatican Pavilion. She's helping to set it up this morning. Naturally she brought samples from our store at the Abbey and that's how I got the jacket. So don't even think that I went out of my way."

Before Ron could even think about a witty response the doors opened and they walked into the lobby now filling with all kinds of seminarians and religious. They were to be part of the ceremony. Their job was to line up on the dock as a welcoming guard of sorts for the Pieta and The Good Shepherd statues. No one however was to be on the dock or barge during the transfer of the crates from the ship Cristoforo Columbo to the barge Challenger.

"Ah… thanks anyway," Ron, stumbling over his words, took the black leather jacket with gold lettering and put it on. "That was very thoughtful of you."

While they joined Brother Anthony and Father Gregory who were speaking with the other guys, Officer Jones entered the crowded hotel lobby.

In the Brownstone on the north side of Washington Square another discussion was being held over the breakfast table on which bowls of fruit and plates of sausages and scrambled eggs sat in front of the Signore, Giuseppe and Andrew. All of this was prepared by Giuseppe who fancied himself as a good cook. All were dressed as if it was to be an ordinary working day. For the Signore, that meant a three piece suit, which was gray silk accented with a royal blue tie and pocket handkerchief of the same color. For his body guards, it was a suit coat and pants of navy blue with white shirts. Giuseppe wore a red tie and Andrew a striped blue and white tie. The conversation however, made it abundantly clear that this day was not a usual one.

"Where is Stephano this morning?" asked the Signore as if he didn't have a clue to his whereabouts.

Andrew explained that a call was received last night from the Manhattan Police Station where he was being held. The Signore began to exhibit signs of frustration when he asked why his man wasn't released. Andrew stayed calm and proceeded to elaborate that he felt it advantageous not to keep him on the phone too long as it would mean a possible trace could be made. That decision was proclaimed to be a sound one by the Signore. He then went on to ask if his lawyer was called and sent to the precinct. That reply did not go over well when Andrew explained that the lawyer could not be reached in the wee hours of the morning and that the call had just been made prior to breakfast.

"He should be on his way to the 19th precinct as we speak, Signore."

The skewed up red face began to soften and the veins at the side of the Signore's head became less evident. "Then he should be released soon."

"I am no lawyer sir, but he was taken into custody on what is considered International Territory; that may pose another problem for us."

The Signore pushed his plates away glaring at Andrew. "I have lost my appetite. I need to speak with my colleagues. Get them here to the Brownstone."

"They have all been contacted but none will come for fear of being identified. They have suggested a place nearer to the 44th Street dock area where the switch is to take place anyway. Here is what I wrote down." Andrew handed the Signore a large sheet of paper folded in half.

The Signore read it and reread it before he spoke. "But this place, it's near the warehouse. Cops will be swarming all over the area."

"Exactly what I said to them; but their response was that who would look for you or us in a place near where the…" he paused so as to choose his words wisely. "Ah…accident took place."

Battista had his back to his body guards also now serving as administrative assistants as it were. He stood in front of a buffet cabinet on which was a Sterling Silver Coffee urn and china cups and saucers. He grasped the handle on the urn tightly but kept calm. Pouring some coffee and then adding sugar and half and half for he never used plain milk and no cream for that was bad for his arteries he would say. He expressed that perhaps they were correct. That too many people who could identify them coming and going from this place may put everyone in jeopardy. He walked with his coffee in hand to the front of the house where a large grouping of windows looked out over Washington Square. Hanging over them were gold and brown damask curtains with sheer lace panels between them. He stood there looking out onto the green area next to New York University. He paused in silence, which was most unusual. Andrew and Giuseppe didn't dare disturb this pondering mood he had entered.

"All this, I think I will miss," the Signore turned to see his two body guards under the arch between the dining room and the parlor. He walked to some of his art pieces and stroked the marble ones as if they were pet dogs. Then he set his coffee down on the coffee table in front of the Italian provincial sofa. The table was also of dark oak in that style. Panels of marble were inset in three sections of the wooden frame. The ivory marble, with brown highlights were complemented by the draperies. The entire room in fact blended together in a style of opulence and at the same time threads of beauty.

The clock on the marble mantle was from Switzerland and was a gift from Sheila of all people from their last trip abroad when they had seen the Alps and then gone into Milan to stock up on the latest fashions for her. It began to chime out the 9:00 a.m. hour. He gazed at it as if he didn't remember its origins until the last chime sounded. "What a shame; the accident that is, what an unfortunate thing."

Even his men found it difficult to accept what he was implying not after they were told to clean up the mess he had made.

"It was all a terrible accident brought about by that…that person who I brought from nothing to all of this. He wanted to be another Michelangelo and I gave him that chance. And what did he do; he killed my Sheila."

The silent men exploded with one word, "What?"

"Ah, yes you think that I did such a thing to that woman I held in my heart. I only tried to wash away my grief, that's all."

"Then Signore, let's go to the police and get this straightened out." Giuseppe said.

"We don't have to run away," added Andrew.

"It is too late, my friends, it is too late. The die is cast and we must follow through with our plan." Suddenly the Signore's entire demeanor changed. "There is only one person who dares to say that I killed our beloved Sheila, only one and he must be eliminated. Once that happens, this tale I have just stated shall be the only truth of what happened. There is no one who can refute it. Where's Sacha, we must go to our meeting and then find Giovanni."

"But sir…" Giuseppe began.

"But nothing, I already know that the police have the hammer which they are calling the murder weapon. I also know that Giovanni's prints are on it as they should be. I was wearing a pair of gloves of fine Florentine leather. They could not have been mine." He noticed the side glances of his two men and immediately added. "It was a chilly morning so I wore my Florentine dress gloves."

Whether his henchmen bought it or not was irrelevant; there was another more urgent matter.

"One thing more, Signore," began Giuseppe. "What about Stephano?"

"They will not break our Stephano, no matter how hard they try. The lawyer will be there soon to get him out in any case." He rose and returned to the window. "Ah, he's here; let Sacha in Giuseppe."

When Sacha entered the parlor the Signore took hold of him and embraced him, kissing him on each cheek and then the lips. "We must leave to implement the plan. Then we must find the artist. Capisce?"

"Yes Signore, but shouldn't I unload the things before we risk them being found?"

The room was suddenly filled with the unknown. A growing sense of regret for what would follow pervaded it. Once Sacha told him that the car was full of Sheila's things so that no proof of their relationship could be found, the Signore exploded. He demanded to know how a driver would presume to remove things from his apartment without his approval. He learned that his men did not want to disturb him from his rest so Andrew had given the order. In size the Signore and Andrew were not far different, so when he confronted the body guard, real threat could be felt. Blood rushed to his head as his fear grew. He knew that Giuseppe, if given the order, could and would end his life. The Signore was now in his face, screaming about respect and loyalty.

"You dare to speak for me. That is betrayal. You are no better than that artist."

Andrew was in no position to counter the barrage. His boss was on the edge and he knew it. So he simply presented his rationale for making the decision. "Signore, you needed to rest. Today, your entire future depends on your plan working."

Something clicked in Battista's angry head. He stopped yelling and went back to the window. Sacha and Giuseppe saw the signs. Their boss was thinking. He was becoming reflective. Watching him turn from Andrew was a good indication that he would not give the order of finality.

Battista didn't notice that they were still in the room. Rather, he peered out the window and then turned to the fireplace mantle. Placing his hands on the cool marble, he focused on a photo displayed in a shiny frame.

It was a gaudy fake gold one with tacky looking symbols of Rome molded on it. Yet it sat amongst artistic treasures and artifacts which collectors would crave to possess. The photo within it was why it sat there. It was an image of him and Sheila in St. Peter's in front of the shrine where the Pieta was displayed. That was the day he learned of the permission to allow it to be displayed at the planned World's Fair. He was now remembering his words to Sheila. He had leaned over and whispered just before the photo was taken. *'One could be the greatest thief in history as well as the richest.'* He then pointed behind them. Sheila's laugh was captured in the photo. *'Carlo, that would be impossible,'* she had replied after she realized he was dead serious. The next two years would see him consumed in planning to prove her wrong. That included discovering Giovanni Gaglioni and plucking him out of oblivion.

He slowly turned away from the mantle. Facing Andrew, whose eyes were still filled with fear, he smiled. "Andrew, my boy, you look upset." He walked up to him and patted his cheek. He then kissed him on each cheek and then on the lips. "I realize you did what you thought best for me. The decision was wrong but your heart was in the right place." The Signore twisted his head to glance at Sacha and Giuseppe standing as if they were one of the statues on the pillars. He placed his arm around the waist of Andrew and pulled him close to him. "Sometimes we all make mistakes, no? Like when our Andrew here was thinking with this thing between his legs." He grabbed Andrew's crotch and gently squeezed his genitals. "It was all about the boy in the toilet stall, wasn't it? You had forgotten all about my safety then, didn't you?"

The body guard forced out a smile, "Never again Signore, never again."

"Ah, that is good to hear. Don't you think so boys?"

The two statues nodded, "Yes."

Battista patted Andrew's groin area and walked across the parlor to the two statue-like men. They instinctively dropped their hands in front of their family jewels. "And now we have, because of this unfortunate decision, to make it go away. Sacha," he patted his cheek and playfully went for what was being shielded behind the hands. Sacha flinched and Battista laughed. "Do not worry; you are safe until Andrew desires you." He laughed again and then instantly became serious. "You will drive us to the meeting with my colleagues. Then you will go to the apartment and return all that you took from it. You must make sure it appears just as you found it, capisce?"

"Yes sir, I understand."

"That is good. So now *Andiamo*... let us go." The clock, it is clicking away our time." The Signore pointed to the gift from Sheila on the mantle.

Tip of Manhattan with Ship Docks

CHAPTER TEN

JOY AND SORROW

The 19th Precinct Police Station was buzzing with activity when Brother Anthony entered with the guys and Susan. The Detective Sargent Malone had arranged to create an interrogation environment out of the line-up room. Since that area had a double mirror on one wall, he planned to place Ron, Bob, Iggy and Susan behind it. They would, he thought, be able to verify whatever story Stephano spit out. Officers Van Buren and O'Hara were stationed at that room where Stephano had been transferred.

Malone having been called out of his preparations by the Precinct Commander reported to her. With the Commander were Security people from the UN. They presented him with the transfer papers. Stephano was now under his jurisdiction. Offering his gratitude profusely, they then departed with the Commander. Malone stood alone amongst the row of desks where officers busily completed their follow-up paper work. He was reviewing the document and complementing himself for having the foresight to have everything ready for the questioning as soon as he got the papers in his hands. Not only was he now able to begin formal interrogation but he could also call for a warrant to allow his people to search the apartment on Central Park West, though he already felt that he had probable cause to do so.

His self-congratulatory absorption was disturbed by the voice of Brother Anthony. "Detective Sargent, we're here to assist you."

Malone looked up from the papers. The Brother was standing directly in front of him on the opposite side of the desk which had seen its better days. He had his own line-up which began with Giovanni and curved around with Susan, Iggy, Bob and Ron. That placed Ron right next to Malone and away from Susan as he intended.

While Malone was welcoming them and expressing his delight with the transfer documents having come at that very moment, into the Precinct walked a dapperly dressed man. His bearing was formidable; that is he carried himself with a posture of arrogance. Some might call it dignity but Malone would not. He wore a navy blue pin striped suit and carried a brown leather brief case. Zeroing in on Malone and his gathering, he walked to the only unoccupied side of the desk and excused himself.

"Pardon me; I am looking for a Detective Sargent Malone."

"Well you have found him. What might I do for you?"

"You may direct me to my client, one Stephano Rondini." He withdrew a paper from his brief case and handed it to Malone. "He may no longer speak to you without my presence."

The Detective Sargent was not pleased. His wonderfully executed plans were being destroyed. "So you're Attorney Arnold Wicksham?" He held the notification letter loosely as if he could care less as to who stood before him.

"I am and I wish to see Stephano Rondini immediately. Where is he being held?"

"He hasn't been arraigned as yet. We have to set bail."

"Then it's fortunate that I have arrived. We shall post the bail whatever it is."

"I see. Well just hold on; I'll get someone to schedule the bail hearing."

While this cool exchange was taking place, Ron had slipped away. He was wandering down the stark looking hallway with fading gray paint. He spotted Van Buren and O'Hara. "Hi officers, I was just looking for Stephano."

"Where's Detective Malone?" asked O'Hara.

"Ah, he's held up but can't I just say hi to Stephano. He kind of trusts me."

"Let him go in O'Hara, he's technically not under our jurisdiction yet anyway."

Ron didn't mention the UN document. He just thanked them and went into the lineup room. Stephano was sitting at a small table to which he was handcuffed. He looked tired as he eyed the mirror across from him. His suit coat was gone as was his tie. A virtually sleepless night added to his disheveled appearance rather than the usual one which accentuated his tall, dark and handsome magazine cover image. At least that's how most women would refer to him until he opened his mouth. Then his lack of formal education and street language would do him in.

"Hi Stephano," Ron greeted him as he pulled up a chair not opposite him but next to him.

The thug wasn't feeling much like what he was hired to be. He looked Ron up and down. "You look different."

"Well, I'm not wearing my cassock. Just me in these with my school jacket; I'm not a priest yet." He stood and pretended to model. It brought on a smile across Stephano's face.

"A priest huh, so you really are a Holy Joe then. You weren't pretending."

"Well I wasn't as you say, being false with you. But I wouldn't call me a Holy Joe. Just this morning we were talking about peckers and swearing up a blue streak."

"Peckers, you should talk to Andrew. He likes peckers. The Signore caught him in the bathroom with your friend; was he hot about it."

Ron grinned. "Well Andrew is hot in another way. Where is he anyhow? I think my friend has a crush on him."

"Well fuck me, are you kidding me? Andrew and that kid; sparks will fly I tell you. Don't let the Signore find out."

"Oh heaven forbid; I would make sure that they meet discreetly."

"Huh?"

"You know in secret; like when he's off duty."

"Oh I get you now," Stephano said.

"Then you'll help me fix them up?"

"What the fuck, sure I will. Someone in all this mess should have a good time before it all goes to hell. But it can't be until after tomorrow."

"I don't get you; why not?" Ron feigned confusion. He had a pretty good idea of what that 'mess' as Stephano called the plot to steal the Pieta was.

The cuffs clinked as Stephano tried to lift his hands and express himself. "Listen kid, you may like peckers or tits or whatever but one day you'll be one of those Holy Joes, so I want to confess to you. Can you forgive me my sins?"

Ron was getting unnerved. He couldn't lead this guy on and offer him absolution. Not only would it be invalid but it would be beyond sinful. It would be disgraceful to his calling. "Listen Stephano, I will call a priest to hear your confession. I know one. He's with me and would keep your confidence, I promise."

"Shit man, I know you're just a kid with a dress…ah cassock or whatever. But I trust you. First time I ever trusted another person except my ma."

"I am honored to be in the company of your mother, Stephano. But Malone will be in here soon and then I won't be able to talk with you anymore."

"So then let's get to it. I fucked so many women that I've lost count. I beat up guys and left them for dead just because that's what I was hired to do. I stole from God only knows how many good people and some rotten ones too. And now I am covering up a murder and planning the biggest heist there ever was."

Ron didn't know how to react. He certainly had no clue on what to say which might sound forgiving as the list had appalled him. So he stuck with the present. "Stephano, that's a good start. True repentance however means to make up for what you've done and in your case what you are planning to do. At least one sin wouldn't be a sin at all."

"Well I can't un-fuck someone can I so what can I do?"

"You can stop a crime, you can be nice to women and respect them in the future, you cannot beat up guys because someone tells you to and you can stop stealing."

"I get you. I won't be ever getting out of the joint so I don't have to worry about the women or the guys. But just let me be straight with you. Those women, they liked me. They thought I was a cool dude with lots of muscle and lots of dick, if you get my meaning. I never hurt a one of them; but shit did we have a good time for a while. But then the job took me away."

Ron glanced at the Mickey Mouse watch on his wrist. He smiled thinking of how he made fun of Bob's PJ's while he had a cartoon character tell him the time. Snapping back to Stephano's confession he assured him that many people would agree that he had some fine qualities and that his physique was admirable. "I am sorry that your life turned out the way it did. But there is something you can still do about the murder and that heist you mentioned."

Stephano made it clear that he had nothing to do with murder. He explained that the Signore just told him and the others to clean up a mess from the accident. When they got there only Sheila was there he told Ron and she was lying on top of Jesus. He thought that only the artist Giovanni would be so thoughtful for he saw how kind she was to him. So he figured Giovanni either tried to rescue Sheila and he killed her by mistake or that the Signore caught them at something and he killed her. He was little help on that issue. Then he switched to talking about the heist as he called the plot to steal the Pieta.

"Today when the Pieta is placed on the barge, that's when it's going to happen."

Ron's heart began to pound faster and faster. His mind was spinning with ideas on how such a thing could happen and what anyone could do about it, let alone him and his pals. "But Stephano, there will be hundreds of people there. I will be on that barge with my friends as part of the welcoming ceremony. No one could possibly attempt to steal the Pieta."

"Sure but the Signore isn't stupid like you or me."

Ron wanted to take exception to that statement but kept his mouth shut.

"He's not the Signore for nothing kid. He's going to do it at night when the security is made up of his own men." Stephano stopped as the door to the room opened and Arnold Wicksham walked in.

"Stephano, I am your lawyer. Say not one more word to anyone." Wicksham turned to Malone who followed him in, behind the glass stood

Brother Anthony, Giovanni, Bob, Iggy and Susan. "Release this man. His bail is being paid. And who is this kid, what are you doing in this place?"

Ron spoke for himself. He told the lawyer that he was at the gala last night and that Stephano was a nice man who had saved him from a guy who tried to touch him where he shouldn't. He went on to say that he was at the police station to write a paper on police work, and that's when he found Stephano here and came to say Hi and thank him again.

Malone unlocked the cuffs as the lawyer ripped his department apart for their shabby security of their prisoners. He stated that the young man could have been an assassin hired by the real murderer named Giovanni Gaglioni.

"Kiss my ass Wicksham right in Times Square. This kid is nobody; he worked at the UN gala last night. We had him checked out." Malone turned crude to deflect attention from Ron to him.

Behind the glass, the artist began to weep. He kept stating over and over that he would not do such a thing. "Sheila was kind to me. She liked me and I gave my heart to her. The Signore, he is behind this accusation, this I know."

Back on the other side of the two way mirror, a frustrated Malone watched quietly until Wicksham walked out with Stephano. Then he turned to Ron lifted him out of his chair by his collar. "What the hell do you think you're doing? I could have you arrested."

Bob slipped behind Brother Anthony who was consoling the artist. He motioned to the others to stay put. Presenting himself at the door Van Buren and O'Hara blocked his entrance.

"Let me pass; or I'll call the Commander of this facility and sign a complaint of police violence against an innocent person." There was no giving in on their part. So Bob pleaded. "He's getting too rough with my friend guys. Come on, let me pass."

Bob entered the room as Malone was brushing down Ron's hair with his hand and straightening out his shirt collar. "Sorry Ron, but I think you screwed up the entire case by being in here. Nothing you were told is admissible in court. What the hell possessed you to talk to this guy? Thank God he was handcuffed."

Coming around the table from the other side, Bob stood next to his friend. "Shit Ron, you had us scared half to death."

"And you should watch your dirty mouth. Aren't you studying for the priesthood too?"

"I apologize. I was just worried that you'd hurt my best friend in the whole world, so I needed to come to his aide like any good sidekick would do."

The two began to laugh as they draped their arms around each other.

Malone didn't know whether he should be pissed or laugh with them. So he stayed on point. He wanted to know what Stephano, if anything, confided in Ron. He was disappointed to learn that it was mostly about his having his way with women, stealing like a Robin Hood and beating up men. And then Ron dropped the bombshell purposely leaving out the part about Giovanni as that wouldn't float well for the artist.

Malone was elated. He hugged Ron and slapped him on the back. "Kid, you may have done something the world should thank you for."

"But Detective, it won't be at the ceremony. It will be tonight when all the people are gone."

Bob interrupted. "Ceremony, Ron we need to move our ass."

Malone shot him one of those "that's a no-no" look of reprimand. He then directed Van Buren and O'Hara to arrange for their transportation to the 44th Street pier on the Hudson River.

By the time they arrived in a scant ten minutes thanks to sirens blaring and squad car escort, the crowds were already building. The tooting of the three red tugboats' horns was announcing the movement of the ship Cristoforo Columbo toward the dock. The festive platform holding the Cardinal and a host of dignitaries was filled with excitement. The ten seminarians from St. Benedict's Abbey now wearing their black Roman Cassocks were shown to their positions just past the stage area. Hosts of other seminarians and members of Religious Orders lined the dock itself. Ron poked Bob as they walked past the festooned platform. He pointed to the Cardinal resplendent in his red robes. A light breeze fluttered his long crimson cape. Then he saw him, two rows in back of the Cardinal and Church prelates. It was the Signore Battista. He was horrified. He and Bob were standing just below the stage nearest to the end of the dock.

"I can't believe it. Bob it's him."

"Holy sh…I mean cow. Does he have the balls…oh God, I mean the nerve to be here." His eyes were glued to the big man beaming a smile. "Ron, do you think they'll arrest him?"

"No way, and disrupt the ceremony; they'll probably wait until it's over…" his opinion was cut short when he saw Giuseppe and Andrew walking to the back of the stage. "Crap they're here too."

Swearing or not was no longer Bob's concern. He began to panic. He began poking Iggy next to him who then poked Clarence and so the alert went down to all ten guys. They were no longer watching the ship come closer to the dock. They were watching the Signore Battista on that stage for any kind of reaction or emotion which might alert them as to what was about to happen. There was not the slightest indication of joy, nervousness, even excitement on the face of Battista. Cheering was now rising to a deafening level as the crowds went wild. They waved American and Vatican flags and were yelling welcome Pieta, welcome Good Shepherd.

Just as they thought all was ready for the ship to dock a large hoisting crane on the pier opposite the one on which the welcoming students and religious stood began to swing over a large crate with an orange color painted top. It swung over a barge identical to the one on which the Pieta was to be lowered from the ship. It was not the Challenger onto which it was being lowered. The crane was straining to hold the crate steady. It began to creak and then the metal cable rope holding the crate slipped. Little by little it let the crate free fall then held it until it hit the deck of the barge. People began to scream thinking it was the actual crate from the ship holding the Pieta. The crate slammed onto the deck. Some of its wooden slats cracked. An announcement was being made that what was just seen was a test run for the transferring of the actual Pieta. Running along the pier with the crane were Detective Malone, Van Buren and O'Hara and a couple dozen other police officers. In a flash, Giovanni broke ranks from the guys and began to run to that pier as well. Ron and Bob made a dash to catch up with him. Brother Anthony and Father Gregory managed to keep the other guys in place. Susan watching with her Mom from the visitor's section had no recourse but to watch the scene unfold. Though their view of what was going on was obscured by the platform lifting up the stage well above the gathering crowd.

Several crew members were on the barge assisting the police with climbing down a ladder. Ron didn't wait; he spotted a loose mooring rope and swung down to the deck on his own. Then holding the rope for Bob who descended like it was the high school climbing rope. Giovanni spotting them shouted that he was coming down. Holding the rope taut, the artist made his way down quickly. Those powerful sculpting arms had no issue with holding his weight as he came down. Before Malone and his team reached the cracked crate, the artist and the boys were standing in front of the container. As soon as the announcement was made that the box was the test crate, the artist felt sure that it was his Pieta being lowered.

The three stood in front of the cracked slats. Giovanni moved forward. A yell from Malone to halt did not stop him. He grabbed hold of the broken piece of wood and began to tug on it. Ron and Bob ran up to help. They managed to pull down two broken pieces before Malone arrived with a large crowbar and tools to pry the wooden slats open. Giovanni dropped to his knees. He had seen the white tarp embedded within.

"This is not Michelangelo's work my friends. This is my Pieta."

Ron and Bob knelt beside him; placing an arm around him. Giovanni did not know what Andrew, Stephano and Giuseppe did with Sheila's body but Bob, Iggy, Clarence and Ron did. The two who were there held the artist tightly. Malone and his team took over. They removed the outer section and then an inner section. There situated within the three walls remaining was a large white tarp covering something big and heavy.

Malone took a step back and turned to face the kneeling threesome. "Giovanni, you in particular may not want to stay as we uncover whatever is under that tarp."

"Detective Sargent, I know what's under it. You will find the statue which I carved for the Cathedral. Why it's here I do not know. What I do know is that Signore Battista is behind this and yet he is here right on that stage. If he planned this why would he be here in broad daylight?"

"That's not the point sir. There's obviously dried blood pooled at the edge of the tarp."

"Yes, this I expected you to find some as it's my blood. I hit my head on the statue during the fight with the Signore. There may even be some from Sheila for I placed her on the statue to be held by the Christ and his Holy Mother. But then we had to run away before I could say my farewell."

"Then we shall proceed. Officers, gently pull the tarp up and push it over toward the back of the container."

The officers wearing their dress white gloves so as not to disturb any evidence with their fingerprints began to roll it up. The white marble of the sculpture was visible to them. Blood was splattered on the marble itself. They rolled up the tarp a bit more, an arm fell down. They stopped. Van Buren called out to Malone. "Detective, come here." He said no more and had the officers close ranks so as to block the view of the statue. Malone knelt down and lifted the tarp. He shook his head from side to side.

"Van Buren, bring the boys and artist forward."

Holding onto Giovanni they approached the few steps. Grief began to flow into their hearts. Ron and Bob knew what they were about to see. Giovanni not as yet seeing what was behind the wall of officers still felt what they were to about to see was his worse fear. As they knelt before the statue, Malone and O'Hara lifted the tarp to reveal the entire statue. The blood soaked lace shawl covered the body but Giovanni knew that they had found his secret love.

"Sheila, we have found my Sheila," cried out Giovanni but so softly as to hardly be heard except for those standing near the statue.

Van Buren was on his walkie-talkie communicating what Malone dictated. No one is to know what we have found here he told his officers. "Van Buren, tell central that the casing broke but the statue is fine."

Central replied that the crane was faulty as reported by Signore Battista. The ship's crane and the actual barge were now being brought in."

"Battista, how did he know? Why would he allow such a thing to happen?" Malone was in shock. The guys were beside themselves. Malone took hold of himself and told Van Buren to inform Central that they would secure the damaged crate and move the barge away.

Word was delivered to the stage that all was well. The so-called test proved the Signore Battista's concern about improper equipment. Everyone began to shake the hand of the Signore. Only he knew that in his meeting with his co-conspirators they had changed the plan. The switch would take place on Land near Flushing Bay's dock area.

Back on the barge, Giovanni was beside himself. "Battista, it could not be. Why would he betray what you heard from that meeting?" He was speaking through his tears.

Ron replied that something was fishy about all of what just happened but responded to Giovanni's grief first. "Right now, let us pray for Sheila and have her taken to a place of peace."

As they did so the mooring ropes were being released and the flat barge began to move. It would be guided to the other side of the pier so that the ship may get near to actual barge to be used, The Challenger. An ambulance was waiting on the other side and a stretcher was lowered to carry the body of Sheila off the barge. Giovanni insisted to carry her body and place it on the stretcher. Ron and Bob assisted him as best they could. Malone was most cooperative and let them pray over the body. Afterwards, the stretcher with her body was to be lifted up to the pier by ropes. He told them that they would be allowed to carry her to the ambulance. Giovanni asked if he could accompany the body to wherever it was to be taken. The answer would crush the artist and shock Ron and Bob.

"I'm afraid that I cannot allow that at this time Giovanni. You must stay with me."

"I don't understand." His sad blood shot eyes revealed his broken heart.

"Detective, what's going on here? Why can't he go? He needs to be with her." Ron stood next to Giovanni, who couldn't comprehend the directive.

Malone pulled Ron away from Giovanni and motioned to Bob to follow him. He walked to the front of the ambulance. "Listen to me and listen carefully. Unless we find evidence to the contrary, the hammer will be proven to be the murder weapon. Right now only Giovanni's prints are on that weapon."

"Oh my God, he's being framed for murder." Ron exploded, "No way that we'll allow this to fly Detective."

"So then get me evidence to prove otherwise. Ron, you and your pal here are to stay away from Battista. You're in danger whether or not what you reported from that meeting was just a show for your benefit or the actual plans gone wrong."

"No way in hell Detective." It was Bob who shouted the defiance. "We're sticking with Giovanni."

"Good, do that. I shall place him in Brother Anthony's care and he will be confined at the hotel until the real statue is in place at the Vatican Pavilion. Then we shall see where we go from there. You may break the news to him. It may be accepted better from you."

The Cristoforo Columbo was now in view. The spray from the water cannons of the Fireboats were shooting arches of water along its route. Cheers from the crowd and jubilation on the stage platform were echoing across the dock area. Not a soul on the stage or in the viewing area had a clue as to what was found. In fact it was doubtful that many of them realized that a copy of the Pieta was in the crate which fell. Even the dignitaries thought the entire demonstration was a test to prove that the original crane would not sustain the weight of Michelangelo's Masterpiece. The Captain of the ship was now communicating with the Captain of the barge Challenger as the test one was gone from the berth. As a backup to just such a problem, the ship was provisioned with its own hoisting equipment. It would sustain weight well beyond that of the marble of the Pieta. All was set for the transfer to the barge, the Captain communicated with a sigh of relief that the treasure would soon be off his hands.

Almost totally unnoticed against this backdrop of water spraying across the river, tooting tugboats and waving flags was the artist. On the opposite pier, he was standing alone at the back of the ambulance. His head bowed down and hands folded in prayer as the now bagged body of Sheila was lifted into it. Also part of that scene behind him was his statue. It was now slowly being carried away on what was being called the "Test Barge." The resealing of the crate had begun so that it could be moved.

Into that solemn moment walked Ron and Bob. They said nothing at first; just stood next to Giovanni and watched as the doors of the ambulance were closed.

Malone was in conversation with the driver. He was told that no sirens were to be used when they departed. The pretense was that it would upset the people gathered for a time of joy. However, the Detective Sargent had another plan stirring in his head. Van Buren and O'Hara had already been assigned to perform the task after the ambulance left.

Ron placed his hand on Giovanni's shoulder. "Don't worry, she'll be guarded now."

"Grazie…thank you, but to make sure, I want go with her."

Ron brought his other hand up and pulled Giovanni away from the ambulance. "Listen to us Giovanni. It's the hardest thing you'll hear today. Bob and I have to tell you something which may upset you. And it's not just that you can't go with Sheila."

"But please don't get mad at us. If it was up to us, you'd be in the ambulance right now." Bob had inadvertently set off an explosion of sorts.

"What are you saying?" the artist pushed away from Ron. Bob stepped up to him, his heftier size blocking his path. "I must be with her. She's all alone."

Bob brought him into a bear hug. "She's with God, Giovanni. You above all people should know that."

Giovanni could see the ambulance slowly pulling away. He struggled with Bob. Ron had to get involved. He took the artist by the arm and swung him around to face him. Tears were streaming down his cheeks. "Why do you act this way?"

"We're only trying to help."

"Help? Help to break my heart more than it is; that is all you do."

The ambulance was on the road leading out of the dock area. Ron dropped his hold. "We are so sorry, but the Detective thought we should tell you. It's not just that you can't go with Sheila. You must stay at the hotel until all this is cleared up."

Malone stood with Brother Anthony who had just arrived. They were at the junction of the pier and the strip of land adjoining the road along the river. Giovanni glared at him and pushing past Ron and Bob ran not to the Detective but to the end of the pier. A back-flash of something quite similar simultaneously flooded the mind's eye of both of them. They began to shout at the artist to stop. He picked up speed and the boys sprinted to catch him. Brother Anthony's eyes bulged from his head as he saw the unfolding drama. More than any on that pier he understood what disappointment and depression could do to a person. The Brother was quite a strong man with a physique to match though concealed under the robes of the habit. He shoved Malone away and ran toward his students and the artist who was headed for the end of the pier on the Hudson River. Giovanni had abruptly stopped at the edge of the pier. He stood motionless gazing down into the dirty water with oil slicks shimmering in the sunlight. Ron and Bob came to a screeching halt about an arm's length away from him. Right behind them, Brother Anthony arrived.

"This is not the way to honor Sheila," Ron began. "It will not bring her back."

The artist spoke softly replying that it was not an act of honor but an act of union. He would join her in death he told them. "I was a walking dead person when she lived on this earth. I knew that she and I could never be together. And now, I might as well truly be among the dead. No one would care. The Signore would be delighted."

Ron was too naïve about the depth of love to counter. However, one thing Giovanni said gave him an idea to pursue. "Exactly, you are playing right into the hands of that bastard Battista. If you jump, he will win. There will be only the hammer with your prints on it. You would be considered just another murderer who ended it all when he was caught."

The Blessing of the crates on the Barge Challenger by Cardinal Spellman had ended. The throngs were departing the dock area. A cordon of guards was taking up positions near the barge. The two statues would remain on the vessel overnight. In the morning it would make its way around the Battery and up the East River to Flushing Bay. Moving toward the corner of the stage area away from the 44th Street Pier was Battista. Just below him on the ground were Andrew and Giuseppe.

Stephano had arrived too late to get into the secured area since they had his credentials. He had to wait until the ceremony was over to get past the crowds leaving. He made his way toward the stage. As he did so he came to the barricade separating the secured area from the observation area for other guests. Leaning against the sawhorse were Susan and her mother. He stood next to them about to jump over.

"I know you," Stephano commented.

Susan turned and gasped. She dared not say anything and yet she had to say something. Her mother would have a fit, if she knew who this person actually was and what he did for a living. She responded with the truth just not all of what she knew. She responded that they had met briefly at the gala the previous night at the United Nations. Stephano hadn't been in his line of work and not realize that she did not wish the older woman to know the circumstances of their meeting. When she introduced that woman as her mother, he knew to play along. He kissed the hand of Mrs. Liguri when introduced. Then he went on to explain that he was in security work at the UN gala which is why he was there.

After a brief chit chat about the pomp and glitter of the previous night and what just took place, he did jump over the barricade. Susan called out to him. "Oh Stephano, one moment," she turned to her mom. "I'll be right back." Ducking under the sawhorse, she not too quickly walked to him. "Thank you for not letting on that we met in that Meeting Room. So I see that they did release you."

Stephano explained that his boss had made bail for him. "Now I must go to him. Tell your friend, the skinny one, that I will meet him right here tonight. I was to be one who guards the crate with the Pieta; that is if no one knows that I was in the jail."

"Okay, how's 8:00 p.m.?"

"Fine, that's a good time." Stephano ran off toward the stage area.

Susan sashayed back to her mother. She was in no uncertain terms told to stay away from that Stephano person. She insisted that he was too old for her. 'In any case any man who kisses a woman's hand these days is up to no good,' she went on to say.

"Why Mom, are you saying that he was trying to pick you up?" Susan grinned.

"Don't be ridiculous. He's much too young for me. In any case your father wouldn't approve."

"Papa is in heaven Mom. He may want you to find love again." After embracing her mother, they walked off sharing memories of Mr. Liguri.

The tension at the end of the pier was easing up. Giovanni was talking to Ron and Bob. He no longer was facing the water. He was facing them. What his new friends had said began to fill his thoughts. Whatever he was to do to avenge the death of Sheila, the least that would accomplish anything would be his removal from what was to happen. His death would truly play into the Signore's hands. His head began to swirl with the thoughts of Sheila, his death, the Signore's pleasure, the failure of the plot to switch Pietas, the new bonds with the young men of the Abbey and the cute young woman who reminded him of Sheila. He became unsteady. His feet moved on the boards extending to the beam which ended the pier. He swayed from dizziness, grief, confusion and thoughts of death.

Ron took a chance and lunged for him. Grabbing hold of the artist around the waist and pulling him down to the boards of the pier. He lay on top of the artist who suddenly smiled.

"Ron, I told you that I do not swing with the boys."

Brother Anthony and Bob with hands folded in prayer burst out laughing. Ron rolled off Giovanni, sweat pouring off every part of his body but seen mainly on his brow and matted down hair from fear and relief and yet laughing. The Detective ran to the two on the boards. He knelt down beside them relieved that what he was about to do would still be possible because Giovanni was to be the key to his plan.

"You gave us a scare Mr. Gaglioni."

Lying flat on the boards, his one hand holding onto that of Ron, he replied that he regretted his actions and would cooperate with the law of the land. The air about them seemed to be lighter and warmer as they all once again felt the breeze off the river, and the warmth of the sun. The gloom at the edge of the pier was being replaced by the bright sunshine on their faces. Yet the temperature was only hovering around 60 degrees. Since all of them at that point were still in their cassocks or Habit that sensation of warmth was becoming even more exaggerated. Malone seeing their discomfort rose and pulled up Giovanni who pulled up Ron. With joy and relief Brother Anthony embraced them as did Bob. Even Malone got into the act. When the Detective got to the brother, Ron snickered a bit. *I wonder what this macho policeman would think if he knew that he was embracing someone who did go for the guys.*

Once Malone saw that all was stable, he called to his officers. It was time to implement the next part of his plan. As Van Buren, Jones and O'Hara approached, he reiterated what the artist had to do. Brother Anthony accepted the responsibility to insure that he would be with him at the hotel. As for Ron and Bob and their friends, they would once again be told to keep away from Battista and his goons. Satisfied that everyone would be safe for the time being, he walked off the pier with his officers.

Malone shouted back, "A Squad will take you back to the hotel."

"Thanks," Brother Anthony replied.

The Brother, the artist and the two seminarians were left standing alone. To the left of them high on the stage platform was a large man wearing a silk suit, black fedora and smoking a cigar. Ron noticed him as they began to walk off the pier. Whether or not the man noticed them, Ron wouldn't hazard a guess. But as for him, he knew that the order to stay away from that man could not be obeyed. But he'd take the ride back to the hotel first.

Within minutes Malone was out of sight. The man with the cigar walked down the metal stairs of the platform to meet his men, his heavy steps creating a clanging sound like a cracked bell. At the same time the one who was saved, the one who pledged to watch over him and the two who would disobey a certain Detective were entering the squad car.

All that remained to be seen were uniform police stationed at all access points and plain clothes security people along the pier overlooking the barge with its precious cargo symbolizing the salvation of humanity. A stillness as one in prayer had fallen over the scene where joy and sorrow had taken center stage.

CHAPTER ELEVEN

CRACKING THE CASE

Three events were beginning to unfold simultaneously. Each event would further bring their participants on a collision course. More importantly, would be the permission given to the Cardinal Archbishop of New York City. Pope Paul VI, confirming the agreement for New York to host the most revered religious sculpture in Christendom, had set off in the mind of Battista a plan which would take from civilization a precious gift of the faith.

Pacing the white marble floor of the hotel lobby were Iggy and Clarence. When Susan returned with her mother, she found the guys waiting impatiently. They managed to create a chit chat about the ceremony with them. All the while they were seeking a way to find out what had taken place at the police station. If they would have heard one more story of the thrilling ceremony, they would have screamed. Luckily for them, she came to a part of her retelling of the welcoming experience which did interest them. Since all the guys from the Abbey were at the ceremony, Iggy and Clarence were quite aware of the flags and horns and shouts of welcome. It was clear that none of them knew about the finding of anything in the damaged crate. All of them thought that a test had been made.

"And then this impertinent young man kissed my hand." Mrs. Liguri paused. She glanced at her daughter. "Okay, he wasn't pushy; he was trying to be polite."

The boys made no comment but their expression of "what goes on here" to Susan spoke louder than any words could.

She continued after Susan reminded her of his good looks and politeness. "You're quite right, I suppose honey; but there was something about this Stephano person which didn't sit right with me. I suppose his flirty ways bothered me."

Iggy was having a time of trying to control his melt down after Stephano's name was mentioned. He wanted to tell that he was a henchman of the Signore long thought to have mob ties. Instead he just kept the lid on until she finally excused herself. Susan told her mom that she would have a Coke with the guys before going up to their room.

As soon as she was out of sight, Iggy pounced on Susan. "My God girl, you saw that thug? Did he recognize you?"

"And what's he doing out of jail in the first place?" Clarence ever acting as the more mature big brother felt that he had the most important question.

Susan explained about the bail being paid. Then she went on to address those of Iggy. She told them that he did recognize her. That brought up concerns for her safety. She calmed them when explaining that he played along with her story of just meeting at the gala.

"In fact," Susan went on to say. "He gave me a message for Ron."

No sooner than those words left her lips then who should walk in but Ron with the others. Iggy didn't hesitate to jump from the conversation circle set up in the corner of the lobby. Leaping from the gold, black and ivory brocade sofa and circumventing the circular wrought iron coffee table with a glass top, he ran to Ron.

"Whoa, Iggy, you're talking too fast. What happened to Susan?" Now Ron was getting concerned. He pulled Iggy away from the revolving doors lest he be trampled by incoming seminarians like them just returning from the welcoming event. Looking beyond Iggy he saw Clarence and Susan on the sofa. "Get rid of Brother Anthony and Giovanni and come with Bob. I'll be with Susan and Clare."

Ron pushed through the swarms of incoming people and ran over to her. Ignoring Clarence completely, he plopped himself between she and him. "Are you all right? Iggy said something about trouble, Stephano and you. He babbled so that I didn't get it."

Clarence, a bit perturbed at the snub, had moved his butt over to let the incoming Ron hit the cushion and not him.

"Good grief, that boy needs to take a pill. All that my Mom said was that we saw and spoke with a man named Stephano at the welcoming ceremony." She looked up at Iggy having just gotten to the sofa. Ron leaned back into the accent pillows relieved. She looked like at him, his cassock soiled from climbing ropes and running on the pier, his usually well-groomed hair a fright and new sweat forming on his brow from worrying about her. None of that she knew about. To her he appeared as a poor Monk depriving himself of amenities and a bath and she told him so.

"Really, you think I stink. You met Stephano and all you have to say is that I'm a mess. I have you know that I had to tackle Giovanni so that I could save him from committing suicide." He tried to get up but Clarence pulled him down.

"Dear God, Ron it's like what you did for Brother Anthony."

"Clare, zip it up. I never told Susan about that night." He turned his back to her to face him.

She pulled on his shoulder. "Ron De Cenza, look at me, right now." The voice was stern, but filled with concern.

A voice came from behind the sofa. "What about 'that night'?"

"Oh shit, nothing Brother Anthony…nothing at all." Ron tried to redirect. "So I thought you'd take Giovanni to your room to get cleaned up after our long day. Susan says I stink."

"Brother, I said no such thing. I said he looked like a deprived Monk…"

"Susan, you do realize that I am a Monk." He was having a bit of fun with her. The last thing anyone would think about Brother Anthony was that he was deprived, emaciated, or carrying about a sack of ashes to make him look impoverished or melancholy. More likely they would see his appearance to be meticulously well ordered. Most would think of Adonis when he appeared. He was so well put together and so good looking that people would say it's a waste that he should be celibate.

Ron was feeling more and more uncomfortable being seated as he was virtually on top of Susan and Clarence. The fact that their little conversation circle was filling up also made for more eyes to be cast their way. He suggested that they move to another location which wasn't so visible. That's when he noticed Bob's appearance. He looked down at his cassock. He thought of what Susan had just observed and about what his mother would say. 'It looks like an elephant chewed on it.' He cast a side glance at Susan. So he amended his suggestion to going to their rooms, freshening up and changing. They would meet for dinner in an hour and discuss what happened at the ceremony.

Susan felt vindicated in her opinion of Ron's appearance. She told him, that he had come to his senses. But that was only done to make the others laugh. That was her redirection effort. She pulled Ron back just as the others entered the elevator and the doors closed.

"Ron, I didn't want to say this in front of everyone. Stephano wants to meet with us at 8:00 p.m." Of course she knew quite well that he said it was Ron with whom he wished to meet. There was no way that she was going to be left out of solving what she called the mystery of finding Sheila. She had yet to learn that the body of Sheila was found. The mystery for Ron and his best pal Bob had become one of what happened to the plan to switch Giovanni's Pieta with Michelangelo's masterpiece.

While the message was being delivered in the hotel on Lexington Avenue, Stephano approached 8th Avenue from west 44th street on foot. He was not alone. The Signore Battista and his colleagues were with him. They stood on the busy corner waiting for Sacha to arrive.

The Signore was feeling like a new man. He was at the side of Stephano patting his cheek. It was not the one on the body guard's face. He expressed his pleasure that all went well at the police station. He desired to hear what happened there after they got to a more private location. The black limo pulled up to the curb. Sacha jumped from the car and opened the door. The Signore entered followed by his men. In seconds the limo was just part of the traffic flow. Battista knocked on the partition window dividing the front from the rear of the limo. Instantly it was lowered. Sitting next to the Signore was Stephano while Giuseppe and Andrew were told to take the pull down seats.

"Before we begin, let's have a little something to drink. We celebrate Stephano coming back to us." He patted his cheek. This time it was the one on his face. He nodded to Andrew who immediately picked up the crystal bottle and poured out the scotch into matching glasses. "Salute," cried out the Signore. He gulped down the drink without taking a breath. "And now, Sacha I must ask. Is the apartment in proper order?"

Sacha was pleased to report that everything was back exactly as he had found it. Battista verified what he was told by probing questions about things which he knew reflected Sheila's presence in the apartment. "Even the gold frame from the Vatican?"

"Yes, sir, it's back on your desk in the study. Oh, and the souvenirs from Italy are on the mantle where Sheila had arranged them."

"Va bene, and there was no trouble?"

"All went well. No police were at the apartment even as I left."

"Excellent Sacha; now to the New York State Historical Society, our friends await us there. We have some history of our own to create."

Sacha knew better but he couldn't hold his tongue, "Signore that's only a couple of blocks from your apartment."

"Precisely my dear boy; we shall be able to keep an eye on our Detective friend, eh Stephano?"

A sudden chill ran up the spine of Stephano. *Could his boss know that what he intended to do? Did he know what happened at that police station?* Impossible he thought as he replied, "Signore, you are so clever, as to be in plain sight though you are the hero today and should not be worried."

"Listen carefully, all of you; even heroes fall. Even such as Julius Caesar who ruled the world as he knew it, was brought down by his closest friends. You must always be on guard my friends." The Signore placed great emphasis on the word 'friends.'

The limo arrived at Columbus Circle where Central Park began on the south end. It continued on Central Park West, the road parallel to the park. Sacha drove into a gated area of the Historical Society Building at 76th Street. Just a few blocks up from there, an unmarked black police vehicle arrived. It stopped in front of the canopied entrance area to the fashionable residence. Through the tinted windows Malone could see two Doormen. It appeared that one was taking over for the other. He quickly exited the sedan just as Van Buren and O'Hara came out of the glass and brass entrance doors. The officers stayed in place at the doorway when Malone ordered the two men to stay where they were.

They appeared like Nutcracker characters from the Ballet in their spiffy Uniforms of Navy Blue with gold trim around the collar and cuffs. Their hats of matching material with a black leather brim above which was more gold braid finished the look. It was however their frozen stance that turned Stan and Sidney into wooden figurines. They were frozen in fear, not of the police in particular but from the thought of how the Signore would react should he find out that they were speaking to them. They had no choice but to cooperate in any case.

Malone began with simple questions. They gave their names, the time of their shifts and length of time on the job. Then he moved onto more pointed ones. He presented them with photos of the Signore Battista and Stephano because that's all he had available to him. Battista was well known and had many public images and Stephano had the mug shot taken at the 19th Precinct Station. They identified Battista as the Signore who lived in the building. They recognized Stephano as one of his security people but didn't know his last name.

"There are two other security people," added Stan. "One is called Giuseppe…"

"And the other Andrew," continued Sidney so as not to appear uncooperative. "I'm afraid that we know them only by their given names."

Malone asked them to give his men descriptions of the two who had no photo. "But first, were any of these men in this apartment since yesterday?" He was disappointed to learn that none had been in the apartment for almost two days. Then he caught a break.

Stan recalled that Sacha had been by. Malone sent Sidney to his officers to give the descriptions. He took Stan by the arm and strolled over to the street light just out of ear shot. "Who is this Sacha and why didn't you mention this earlier?"

The woodenness of his appearance was softening to butter. "We were talking about the guards and the Signore. Sacha is only his driver. He never goes up into the apartment. That is until yesterday."

"So what happened yesterday that was so unusual?" asked Malone, softening his tone.

Stan explained that Sacha arrived and asked him to watch the limo while he ran up to the apartment. He had no idea why he had to go there since no one was at home. The Signore and Miss Sheila went out early and hadn't returned he told Malone. "And then something struck me. I was buzzed on the intercom to come to the apartment and help him to bring down several large suitcases. Well naturally, I did. When I entered the foyer as I had done on other occasions to bring a package to Miss Sheila or deliver the Signore's cigars, I noticed something was missing."

Malone's ears perked up. Stan went on to say that directly in front of the foyer was the entrance into the parlor. A huge marble fireplace faced the entrance hall. He said that he always admired the beautiful way the marble was carved.

"Are you actually saying that the fireplace or the marble was missing?"

"Oh no Detective, not the marble of the mantle but what was usually on it. Miss Sheila had mementos of their trip to Italy last year. They were all gone. But who was I to say something? I helped with the bags and that was that until this afternoon."

The questioning ended abruptly. When Malone asked what happened earlier, Stan didn't know. But he did say that Sidney had told him he saw Sacha and that maybe he could shed light on the subject.

"Thank you for telling me how to do my job, Stan. I'll get right on it. Now if you'd be so kind as to go to the officers and give your statement and send Sidney to me."

The two Nutcrackers switched places. Malone got right to the point. He asked about Sacha the driver. Sidney said he saw him earlier, not long before the Detective's men arrived. "I had to help him carry the suitcases into the apartment."

Malone then asked Sidney two questions which were of special interest to him. Had he ever been in the apartment before and did Sacha mention anything about the couple taking a trip. He learned that Sidney often was in the apartment as his shift was during delivery hours and postal hours. As for the trip, he said that Sacha mentioned a trip to Europe or some place. That brought on yet another question. Were the suitcases he carried heavy? Sidney replied that they were quite hefty. Another question came to mind. "Sidney, you've been most helpful. Do you like this Miss Sheila like Stan says he does?"

"Oh yes Detective; everyone likes her. She never treats you like a servant or inferior. Why do you ask?"

Malone became quite somber as he told him that they had found the body of Miss Sheila near the Hudson River. He made no mention as to how it was found.

Sidney cried out to Stan. "Our Miss Sheila is dead Stan, she's dead."

Running to Sidney with the officers on his heels, the two held each other. Each exclaiming that such a good woman who had no enemies should be found at the river like trash was too horrible to imagine.

Malone took advantage of their sorrow. "Then gentlemen you would want justice for such a good person wouldn't you?"

Both echoed a strong "of course."

The Detective asked just one more question. "Sidney, your colleague told me that he saw mementos on the mantle of the fireplace…"

"Yes, I've seen them often," Sidney replied. "Miss Sheila even told me of all the places where she got them on the trip last year."

"Good, thanks and now here's the question. Today you helped this Sacha person bring up the luggage. Were those items on the mantle?"

Sidney was confident that he saw nothing on the mantle as they dropped off the bags. He also noted that Sacha stayed in the apartment for some time after he left. He had presumed he was getting it ready for the Signore's return.

Malone thanked the doormen and told them he'd be in touch. They asked if he would inform them when the funeral for Miss Sheila would be. They would like to pay their respects. They left arm in arm. Sidney said he'd have a cup of coffee with Stan before he went home.

As they left Malone overheard them. "Poor Giovanni, his heart must be broken."

"Ah yes poor boy, he loved her in silence since he came to this country and met her." Stan squeezed the arm of Sidney to comfort him.

The Detective Sargent wanted to call them back but decided against it. He mulled over their words. *"Why poor Giovanni and not poor Signore Battista?"* he thought.

Once the doormen went into the lobby for their coffee, Malone turned to his officers. He had a question for them as well. "Van Buren, O'Hara when you entered the apartment to search it did you find anything unusual, say nothing on the mantle over the fireplace?"

"No sir, everything seemed in order. The closet had women's clothes, the one dresser lady things and the bathroom had even more lady stuff," replied O'Hara.

"And that mantle in the living room, it had a bunch of trinket type souvenirs on it. Kind of out of place with all the fancy posh artsy stuff around that room, we thought," concluded Van Buren.

"Indeed, quite…but then they were probably bought by this Sheila Murphy while the artsy things were acquired by Battista given his art world connections. Let's go up. I want to have a look."

The hotel elevator doors opened at the 6th floor. "This is my floor. I'll see you at dinner and then to the meeting with Stephano. Where did you say that was?"

Susan grinned like a Cheshire Cat. "I didn't, so don't get cute with me. I'm coming with you."

Ron pushed the emergency stop button on the floor selection panel. The doors stayed open and a clunking sound was heard. "You're driving me crazy. How can I protect you with those kinds of people?"

"Protect me? What am I some helpless wench in the middle ages? This is 1964 Ron De Cenza and I can do what I want."

"Who said that you couldn't, certainly not me; I know better. But be reasonable; these are vicious people and I don't want your head bashed in like he did to Sheila. It doesn't mean that you're incapable of handling a situation. But this is out of our league, Susan."

She patted him on the cheek lightly. "You're cute. But no it won't work. I come or I don't tell you where Stephano will be."

The alarm sounded just as Ron punched the emergency button to put the elevator in operation again. "Shit, now look at what you've made me do."

"Watch your mouth Father Ron. See you at dinner." She pushed him out the closing doors."

Like a five year old, having a temper tantrum, he stamped his feet on the plush carpet. "Susan Liguri, you'll be the death of me yet." He clumped down to Room 601 while unbuttoning the over fifty buttons which closed his cassock. "And this is a shitty way for this to… ah fuck…come on and unbutton."

The door of room 601 opened. Bob stood there with his cassock and the one loaned to Giovanni in his hand. He was somewhat surprised to see his pal. "I thought I heard someone say the 'F' word so I came to see what was going on." He looked at Ron pulling on the cassock buttons.

"This damn thing won't unbutton. Ah shit," Standing in the hallway he wiggled out of the partially open robe and stepped out of it. "I don't know how women do this every day." He kicked the cassock right into Bob.

"You must have been with Susan." Bob caught the garb of seminarians and priests and added it to those hanging over his other arm.

"She's driving me crazy. Now she wants to come with us to meet Stephano."

"What?" Bob grabbed hold of Ron's arm pulled him into the room. Then he looked both ways down the hall and slammed the door shut. "That is crazy. It's too dangerous…wait a second, what meeting with Stephano?"

Ron pranced into the room. Giovanni was sitting on the edge of the bed quietly watching the tantrum taking place. The sight of such passion actually brought a smile on his dower face. Now unzipping his pants and letting them fall to his ankles. Then he kicked them off right into Giovanni. Even that didn't calm him. Standing in his underwear and unbuttoning his shirt which he then tossed on his bed, he proclaimed that is was just easier to unzip than to unbutton. "I'm going to take a shower. Susan said that I stink."

Giovanni stood, folded the kicked pants and placed it on Ron and Bob's bed. Bob was hanging the cassocks in the closet ignoring the tantrum all together.

"May I suggest; that it be a cold one Ron. That always did the trick for me after I had seen Sheila."

Standing at the bathroom door in his Jockeys and socks Ron turned around. The tantrum was over and the reality of where he stood and how he appeared sunk in. "Oh Shit, I'd hug you Giovanni but you know not like this." He pointed down to the obvious. "I am so sorry. Acting like a child isn't proper when you've lost the two most important things in the world to you."

"Two?" Bob asked as he closed the closet door.

"Sure, the woman he loves and the Pieta he created."

The pall of sorrow began to descend on the room. Ron fought it off. "Listen, stand by the bathroom door. I have a lot to tell you… but with your backs to the doorway."

"Oh for God's sake Ron, Iggy's not here. No one wants to see your ass."

It worked. He knew Bob would just have to make a comment.

"But it's so cute," he dropped his shorts and jumped into the shower. Another loudly yelled "shit" followed and out the socks came as they were tossed over the shower curtain.

Bob and Giovanni stood dutifully as directed with their backs to the door. Bob asked Ron if everything was all right or if he should wash his back for him. That brought on several more expletives and then a loud laugh. A head stuck out from behind the shower curtain. "Bob you're an asshole."

"I know and it makes me so cute that I can't stand myself."

Giovanni had a flashback to his teen years. Even then he did not see himself in this kind of banter when something important was at stake. At the same time he knew that he never had a chance at such friendship either like Bob and Ron or Sheila and him. He was a bit envious. He being almost ten years older than the two made him feel that he had to take on the role Clarence usually played. He leaned into Bob and whispered. "Should we not be talking about what we are to do next to avenge my Sheila?"

Bob turned pale. "Oh man, we do this all the time. Sometimes the rest of the world is just not present to us. You're right; we need to get back on task." He turned to look into the bathroom. "So are you done washing your pits so that you don't stink for Susan?"

The head popped out again. "Asshole, I don't smell and yes I'm coming out. So turn around or…"

"Or what; let us marvel at that little thing of yours."

"It's not little and shut up; I have important things to tell you."

Bob smiled at Giovanni. "We're back on task." He turned away from Ron. "Ok, let's hear it."

"I forgot my underwear. Would you get me a pair?"

"So now I'm not only your sidekick but I'm your servant too."

Giovanni walked to the now open package of new shorts which Ron had given him. He pulled out a pair and threw it over his shoulder. All was well. Pushing his way between them he told them what Susan had said. "So guys, Susan said that Stephano wants to meet with us. I know it's at 8:00 p.m. but I don't know where. That means she has to come with us."

"Do not be afraid; I shall go too," began Giovanni. "Stephano knows me and liked Sheila. He will not harm you."

Ron was pulling up a clean pair of black pants he had just taken off the hanger in the closet. His back was toward them. Zipping and turning around his eyes caught those of Giovanni. They were burning with desire to avenge his Sheila. The look had changed from nonsensical comedy back to a deep sorrow that overshadowed him. It tugged at Ron's heart. At the same time he knew what he had to do. He decided to scrub that thought but first he'd try something.

"Giovanni, the Detective said that you had to stay with Brother Anthony."

Without hesitation the usually soft spoken artist responded. "Screw the Detective Sargent. I'm about to be indicted on a murder charge. You'll need my help."

Ron and Bob were hanging onto each other arm over shoulder over arm. They stood with feign surprise in their expression but with genuine pleasure in their hearts. "Screw, the Detective Sargent," they shouted. "But not too badly; we do need him eventually," Bob whispered.

"Okay, then that's settled." Ron went to the door. "I'll go get Susan. And you guys had better get presentable. Your clothes look like an elephant chewed on them." He quickly exited as Bob threw a shoe at him.

"You jerk; you probably used all the hot water up." Bob opened the door off which his shoe bounced. Looking down the hall, he yelled at Ron. "The least you can do is to have someone pick up our cassocks to clean and press for tomorrow's practice run at the Pavilion."

Running backwards, Ron told him that would be no problem. "I love you pal just remember that before you come to dinner."

The pledge of love brought the heads of his classmates out their doors, so loudly had he shouted it. But it was one in particular which took interest in exactly what he said. Brother Anthony popped out of his room and got to the elevator at the same time Ron pressed the up button.

"Ron, you pressed the up button and why would that be? Dinner is on the main floor."

"Oh hi Brother; I'm just going to pick up Susan for dinner that's all," his face reddened like that of a ripe tomato. It was only a lie of omission but still it bothered him to do so with the very man he saved from death back at the Abbey. A man who became more than a Monk to him; he was an older friend like Clarence, the older Brother he never had.

"Is that so, well I'll just hop on and go with you. That is, if that doesn't upset your plans."

"Why of course not Brother, not at all," he lied. This time it was not one of omission; it fit the guidelines for breaking the commandment not to bear false witness. Together they rode the elevator up to the 9th floor. "Susan's room number is 911; odds are this way." They had only taken two steps when Ron broke down his resolve. "I can't do it Brother. I can't lie to you; not after all we've been through."

"You mean when you saved me from death and damnation."

"Not only that; you tried to save me as well and got shot in the process."

"Ron, that's all behind us now. But thank you for your honesty. Tell me are you having problems with celibacy or is something else going on?"

"Oh Brother Anthony you don't know half the problem. There's hope though, I'll be twenty in July. It will get better right."

"Let me just say that I am twenty-eight and it's still a struggle. But for me it's a bit more complicated."

"I know about the gay thing, but that's not why I said what I said to Bob. It's not that kind of love. He's my best pal and he'd cut off his right arm for me and I for him."

"Rather like the Lone Ranger and Tonto such a noble and enduring friendship. No it's more than that. Weren't they also blood brothers?"

"So you watch the TV reruns too; are Monks supposed to watch shoot 'em up shows?"

Brother Anthony laughed. "Well so far no one has said that it breaks the Monk rules. Ah, here is Room 911."

Ron knocked on the door. Susan opened it. She was dressed not for dinner but for something else. Wearing pink Capri pants, matching pink socks, white tennis shoes, and a hot pink blouse what could be seen of it under the Abbey school jacket. "Oh hi, Brother Anthony; you brought Ron, how nice." She grabbed a tiny black leather shoulder bag off the hook next to the door and closed it behind her telling them that her mother had already gone down for dinner with some lady friends from the Vatican Pavilion's gift shop.

Standing at the bank of elevators in silence they waited for what seemed to be hours and yet was only a couple of minutes. Susan couldn't take it any longer. "Okay, Brother, let's be honest here. Ron and I are going for a walk after dinner."

"Is that so, and will you two be alone on this walk?"

"Ah, come on Brother; you know that I can't lie to you." Ron almost came clean. "We won't be alone. Bob and Giovanni are coming with us."

"I see. You do realize that Giovanni cannot go anywhere without me. I promised the Detective Sargent."

The elevator doors opened. They let it go without them.

Like school children caught for misbehaving, Ron and Susan stood before the Monk with bowed heads. "We were going to ask Iggy and Clarence to distract you by taking you for a walk to Times Square to see it at night with all the lights and people going to the theater."

"I don't understand Ron. Why would you want to deceive me? Where are you four going that it's such a secret?

There was a small bay window area just in front of the elevators. It contained a couch, an arm chair, table and lamp. Taking a seat there, Ron felt obligated to share their plan. By the time they finally arrived at dinner, Brother Anthony had been filled in on what was really going on.

Central Park

CHAPTER TWELVE

THE SHOES

The last orange and crimson explosion of sunset streaked across the Manhattan sky. The final breath of day cast its brush strokes across Central Park and into the gray granite building known as the Historical Society. The Signore's limo was parked behind the building concealed from view. Inside the three story structure the Signore and his men took stairs to the second floor. Waiting for them in the reading room of the Library were his friends. He walked into the vast space appearing like the inside of a Roman Temple with its white columns surrounding the room. His triumph at the dock ceremony and the genius of the last minute change for the switch brought him some joy. Then he looked about the library. It wouldn't work; he announced that the meeting was to be moved. Such a vast space which needed much light would attract attention. Since the museum was closed that kind of attention was not wanted. He suggested that they meet in the Coffee Bar on the first floor. Though intimate, it afforded refreshments and privacy which had no windows to emit light onto Central Park West. The four men seated around the light oak table were disgruntled with having to move but they did so anyway.

As they walked down the staircase with only security lighting on, Francesco Mondera decided to question the Signore. "Carlo, why is it that our men are waiting with the cars while your men are here with you?"

Battista in his usual style patted his cheek. "My dear Francesco, have you never heard of the story of Julius Caesar. I wish to follow an example which he did not. It's just that simple."

The blank look on Mondera's face said it all. He hadn't a clue as to what the Signore meant. He turned to look at his colleagues, Ben Westridge, Jeffrey Rafferty and Antonio Penne. He found equally empty expressions of ignorance as to what the Signore referred. On the other hand Giuseppe, Andrew and especially Stephano were totally aware of what he was saying. The Signore told them only that day to be on guard at all times. As they walked past the galleries and exhibits Battista tried to strike a happier note. He began to complement Francesco for having substituted a crane that could not possibly hold the weight of the Pieta replica. The move was successful.

Everyone was patting him on the back and offering him their special blend of cigar. Battista forbade the smoking of anything pointing out that it would leave a telltale sign that someone was in the museum after closing hours. They settled instead for Andrew preparing espresso and Giuseppe taking some biscotti from the display case. The remains of whatever they used would be taken away with them.

The five men settled around the round wrought iron tables in the tiny café. It reminded the Signore of sitting in a piazza in Rome or Florence. But that thought also brought an image of Sheila as she was with him on that trip. He had to get down to business to remove that memory. The next step which was to be taken was to be discussed. But not before the Signore continued to accept accolades for his genius idea to sabotage his own switch plan for the Pietas and replace it with the fiasco of dropping the copy in a fake test scenario.

"I tell you Carlo, that you are a genius among men." Ben Westridge, who was in charge of muscle and security, was earnest in his praise. "Now it will be so easy to implement the next phase of the plan. Everyone thinks the highest degree of security has been put in place after that…that test."

"You are too kind Ben. But now we begin to change history."

"We have already begun Carlo," stated Rafferty. "The test barge has begun to move the Pieta copy to Flushing Bay while all the excitement was taking place at the 44th Street Pier.

"And by now it is being lifted onto an exact replica of the flatbed truck which is to receive the real Pieta." Antonio Penne was pleased with his announcement. But felt obligated to present a cautionary point as well. "Tomorrow will present the challenge. We must switch trucks. There may be confrontation by those not under our control."

"That would be unfortunate," began Battista. "However, in the possible confusion shall I say, we shall present the duplicate truck as the real one by how we protect its cargo. While those not loyal to us take it to safety, we shall drive away with the Michelangelo Pieta. We have only one problem remaining and I think that I saw him on the pier receiving the fake statue. The one who betrayed me and murdered my Sheila was on that pier with the police and some religious people."

Westridge, the one in charge of security, rose from the padded chair. "You saw the artist, this Giovanni Gaglioni person? Carlo, why didn't you send in your men and get to me? He's a loose-cannon out there, one who knows too much."

The nostrils flared and the thick eyebrows seemed to spike upwards as the Signore glared at his men. He was remembering that the artist escaped while they were supposed to get rid of him. "Do you not think that I don't know that? But he was with the police and I was up on that stage." He suddenly became silent. His countenance relaxed. "The police, that's it. Stephano you know who is in charge don't you? Of course you do," he rose and slowly walked up to him. The nervous body guard stood face to face with him waiting to be chewed out at best. Instead Battista patted his face softly. "You, you shall go to the policeman with a story of how you admired dear Sheila. You shall tell them that you knew of the artist's love for her. You must tell them that you wish to speak with Giovanni. Say that you wish to console the artist as you both are filled with grief especially since her body has not been found. You will tell them that I have gone away to mourn. Tell him that you have something to give him which Sheila would have wanted him to have, but that he would have to come to the Central Park West apartment..."

Battista stopped his direction. He asked why Stephano, in fact all three seemed to be so agitated. He studied them as they stood with their backs to the coffee bar, the hot steam coming from the just made coffee warming their backs. Did they dare to tell him the truth that Sheila's body was in the crate which fell on the test barge? Their eyes gave them away no matter how hard they tried to keep a stern posture and expression. He walked up to each of them and looked into those wide eyes darting about as they tried to see each other's reaction. Westridge had enough.

"Carlo, stop the drama. Is there something wrong with your men?"

"My men are loyal to me. They are not like Brutus who pretended to be a friend and then thrust a knife into Caesar. Go Stephano and do as I told you. And stop at the apartment to see if Sacha was right in saying that it is as it should be."

Stephano still fuzzy about the reference to Brutus bolted like lightening. He ran to the parking area and found Sacha with the other drivers and protectors. "The Signore has ordered me to seek out that Detective who arrested me and check out the apartment. Are you sure you returned everything exactly as it was?"

Sacha replied that he was definitely positively sure that all was as Sheila had it when they left the apartment on what would be her last day. He looked saddened as he said the last words. Stephano patted him on the back. "I am sad too; she was a kind woman to us. After tomorrow this nightmare will be over. We will be free."

"Free, my parents came to America so that I may know freedom. And here I stand a slave to a sometimes mad man who plans to rob the Church itself of a great treasure so that he could live like a king. None of us will ever be truly free Stephano, my friend. Sheila understood that. She is the only one truly free now."

Stephano began to run out of the parking garage onto 77th Street. Sacha remembered something. He called him back.

"The shoes Stephano, the shoes; I forgot about the shoes. We can be free."

"What the hell are you talking about? What shoes, how can they make us free?" He looked at his watch. It was past the hour he was to meet Ron. "Listen, I need to get going."

Sacha took hold of his arm. Something he would never do to Andrew or even Giuseppe and live to tell the tale. "This is worth waiting for; Sheila's shoes are in the closet as I said. Some however I never took to the

Brownstone. I threw them in the trash, you know down the shoot to the basement." A sense of relief, no more than that came over Sacha. It was the feeling of being a free man, though perhaps a dead one still walking around. "Get in the limo. I shall take you to the apartment and show you."

"Sacha, I cannot. I am meeting someone and I'm late already."

"A woman, when all this is happening, when we are about to become free you are worried about a woman."

He was getting antsy. "Sacha, it's not a woman, capisce. It's that kid from the party who served the Signore at the meeting. Now I've got to go; the Signore ordered me to see the police."

"The kid, I thought Andrew liked young peckers, you too?"

"I'm no queer; he is going to help me save the Pieta and say good-bye to Sheila. No one knows that Andrew, Giuseppe and me…" he took a deep breath. "We put Sheila in the crate with Giovanni's statue. When the crate fell, the police had to have found her body."

Sacha cut him off. "Get in the car. I'll take you to see this kid."

Sitting silently next to Sacha in the front, Stephano began thinking. More than that of the possible consequences of what he was about to do. He wondered who that Brutus, the Signore mentioned, was and whether or not Sacha was also a Brutus.

Small crowds were still milling about the barricades in front of the entrance to the 44th Street Pier. Moored there was the barge Challenger on which sat two crates. The larger one had a spotlight shining on it. The bright orange painted top glowed. People stopped to point at it. They wanted to be a part of history. In the morning the barge would set out down the Hudson River go around the tip of Manhattan called the Battery and up the East River to Flushing Bay. There a flatbed truck was parked. All was ready to take its precious cargo to the Vatican Pavilion on the Fair grounds. In the driver's seat taking a nap was its driver who just happened to be in the employ of Antonio Penne, a colleague to Signore Battista. He had no idea as to what was about to take place in the morning.

Leaning on the sawhorse where she first met Stephano was Susan. Directly behind her were Ron, Bob and Giovanni. Absent was Brother Anthony, who having most of the truth shared decided the best thing he could do to help was for him to appear to be with Giovanni at the hotel. There he would wait being contacted.

Anxiously the four stood waiting for Stephano's arrival. They openly questioned his honesty and commitment to whatever he had intended to tell them if anything.

A deep voice behind them asked who they were calling dishonest. The four turned around to find Stephano standing there still dressed in his suit, though his tie was loosened. He grabbed hold of Ron by his jacket collar and pulled him close. "I told that girl that I wanted to meet with you. And you've brought him." He pointed to Giovanni.

The artist pulled Ron from his grasp. "Knock it off Stephano, I insisted on coming."

"But why, you who killed Sheila why would you come?"

"Don't be a jerk man." Ron pulled Giovanni next to him. "Look at his head. Your boss tried to kill him and he's the one who killed Sheila."

"Then all his talk of an accident is a lie?" Stephano was filled with a growing queasiness in the pit of his stomach as the truth sunk in.

"No shit Sherlock, of course he lied so that his buddies would help him steal that crate down there." Bob showed no pity for the confused would-be Brutus.

The truth was overwhelming for Stephano, who was trying to be noble in his betrayal of his boss. But a light illuminated within him at that moment. He understood the analogy the Signore was making though he still didn't understand the context. "This Brutus must have been a friend of this Julius Caesar guy, and betrayed him just as I am about to do," he said aloud. "So who knows about this guy Julius Caesar?"

All four offered a history lesson.

"Well tell me on the way. And you artist, tell me about Michelangelo and why it's so important that we save his statue." Giovanni sprinted up to be next to him, anxious to begin his illumination. In his thoughts he planned to tell him how Michelangelo created the Pieta, the David, the Ceiling of the Sistine Chapel, The wall of the Last Judgment, the Battle of the Centaurs, the Madonna and Child. He stopped himself as the works of his five hundred year old idol danced in his head. *"No,"* he thought. *"I shall focus on the Pieta alone for that is enough for Stephano."* He began to enlighten the dull if not dark mind of the man who hid the body of his secret love as a way to honor her.

Left slightly behind were Bob and Susan. An evening breeze with a chill in it began to come off the river behind them. Susan pulled her jacket more tightly around her.

"You shouldn't have worn shorts in April."

"Really, and what makes you the fashion expert? And besides, these are capris not shorts."

"Whatever they are, they have exposed your legs. All I'm saying is that in April it can get cool." Bob decided it was best to shut his mouth at that point.

Susan looked at him for a brief moment as they now walked in silence. "So you really like him don't you?"

Looking at her with full understanding he chose to play ignorant as he had no intention of discussing friendship with her as he was still ticked. But he couldn't fully commit. "Who's him?"

She began to laugh. "Are you for real? Like you have no idea as to who I'm talking about; well you're a liar Bob Wentz, so there."

He was frustrated now that she caught him in some kind of cover-up. At the same time he was furious that he felt forced to admit the obvious. All of that began to tear at him because he didn't want her to think the worse about them.

She felt his struggle and could guess as to why. "You know that sometimes a friendship goes deeper than love. It's like a love but different. There's a chemistry, sure; like when you two banter about being the Lone Ranger and Tonto. Dumb boys stuff…"

"It's not dumb; it's something we can relate to."

"So you admit that we're talking about Ron," she offered softly so as not to upset him further.

She failed. "Yes, okay, you're right, Ron and I are close friends; but don't you be thinking it's something else…"

"Perish the thought; Ron in any kind of physical connection let alone with a guy is almost unthinkable."

"If you weren't a girl, I'd say something that wasn't very nice right now."

"So you're going to tell me to go to hell? It wouldn't be the first time I was told that."

"I can see why. You can be overbearing…no frustrating…no a pain in the ass, yes that's it. You're a pain…"

"I get it; you don't have to go on. So tell me Tonto, how's your friendship going?"

Now Bob was really getting to the boiling point. "Don't even go there Susan; we don't play roles. We just talk about their ease at working out things together."

"And now who's the liar, Bob Wentz? But one thing is true in what you've said. You two do work well off each other or we wouldn't be walking with a mob boss's thug and a guy accused of murder."

"Thank you for that, but we're just friends and nothing more."

"I really do understand Bob; I'm sorry if I implied anything else."

His heart was touched and began to melt. "You're forgiven. So what now do we hug?"

She didn't answer; she just threw her arms around him. "I always thought Tonto had the best ideas."

"Yeah, me too, but don't tell Ron. He thinks I'm jealous because if people really were put on the spot, they'd say he was the Lone Ranger to my Tonto. And you know that's okay with me. After all it was Tonto who saved the Lone Ranger's life just like I have done and may have to do before this is all over tonight."

Susan placed her arm under his and they sprinted up to the others.

Stephano was already on overload as Giovanni went on and on about the symbol of Salvation, how the Holy Mother with her look of acceptance held the Lord so the world could behold his sacrifice, how the Christ was serene and at peace no longer suffering. The view of the limo at the corner of 44th and 8th gave him the chance to stop the lesson. "There's the limo. Sacha will take us to the apartment to find the shoes. We'll talk about these things on the way." Stephano ran up to the limo and opened the door.

Susan releasing Bob and taking the arm of the artist so that Bob could go to Ron's side, expressed concern about getting into a car which belonged to the very person who they were attempting to prove guilty of murder and theft. Ron reassured her that Iggy and Clarence knew of the meeting with

Stephano and were expecting a call within the hour as to how it went. They entered the car with trepidation, blind courage and an unspoken question. *"How will these shoes prove anything?"*

When the limo pulled up to the canopy covered walkway of the apartment building on Central Park West, the two doormen could be seen talking together. It was unusual Giovanni thought as Stan should have replaced Sidney by now.

"Oh God, that's the Signore's limo." Sidney was frozen in fear.

"Just play it cool. He's probably come home to…well to make the arrangements for the funeral. Don't say a word about the police having been here." Stan walked to the limo's passenger door and opened it. When Stephano came out, his composure stiffened. But then Giovanni appeared and he felt the grief within him. "Mr. Gaglioni, my dear man, we just heard." He took the artist's hand apologizing for being so demonstrative.

Giovanni embraced Stan, who motioned to Sidney to come to them. "Our Sheila is gone Stan." He turned to Sidney weeping for him. "You loved her too, didn't you Sidney?"

"She was kind to everyone but your love for her, Mr. Gaglioni… that brought sunshine out on a dull day. We shall miss that smile she gave you whenever you came into her presence."

"Well I liked her too, you know." Stephano was feeling left out.

The doormen swung around. "Of course Stephano, she always had a way to make you feel important didn't she?" They took his hand and shook it.

"Well, yea, that she did. That's why I'm here, to be Brutus."

"Brutus sir, I don't understand."

"You don't have to, he just had a history lesson that's all," Giovanni explained as the others got out of the car. "Stan and Sidney, this is Ron De Cenza, Bob Wentz and Susan Liguri from Wisconsin." Bob and Ron held their tongues as they were about to explain that one was from Chicago and the other from Oak Park which was right across the street from the Windy City border. They saw the look on Susan's face which was telling them to skip the explanation. "They are here to help us prove that I am not a murderer and at the same time save the Pieta."

Sacha had rolled down the window so that he could call to them. "I've got to get back to the Signore and those…those assholes, pardon my words Miss."

"I am not offended. I believe that term is warranted."

Sacha smiled. "So let me quickly show you where the shoes are. I have to get back and take the Signore, Giuseppe and Andrew back to the Brownstone. Tomorrow everything will take place. Then if I can, I will come back to get you after dropping them off."

"You know Sacha, I didn't ever think too much of you. You just drove us around and yes sir to this and that is all I heard." Stephano placed his arm over the shoulder of the driver. "I see now that you cared for Miss Sheila too."

"So it appears that many did; but now we must catch the real murderer and save the Pieta." Giovanni noted.

What amounted to a small entourage now blocked the sidewalk entirely. They hastily walked to the brass and glass doors. Stan told them that the police had already searched the apartment. Sacha informed them that they wouldn't be going there but to the basement where the trash shoot dumps the garbage. The issue of how shoes could help catch a murderer was about to be resolved or so they who had placed their trust in the limo driver hoped.

Stan was to remain on duty as normal or suspicion might arise as residents came and went from their dinner engagements. Sidney said that he would take them to the trash bins and then stand guard at the service entrance where it would be safer to exit from after whatever was being done was completed. Sacha had one concern and that was when the trash pickup would take place. He was relieved to learn that it wouldn't be until the next day.

Going toward the elevators, Ron noticed a phone on the Doorman's desk. "Sidney, would it be okay to make a call?"

"Yes, of course Mr. De Cenza but now when so much is at stake?"

Ron returned a look of pride. Someone actually thought he was a full grown man like his father. He shook it off. "It's really important. But first, Sacha you spoke about a Brownstone. I need to know what that meant and where it's located."

The driver quickly told them about it being a safe house which only the Signore, he and the body guards and also Sheila knew about. No one else was allowed at that house just in case something happened, which now it had. From there they would be able to skip town he told them and that's what had to be prevented. "So once we find the shoes, I'll have to leave pronto. Then I'll come to pick you up. I'll take you through Greenwich Village and to Washington Square, where the house is located."

"Right," Ron turned to Sidney. "Please take everyone down to the basement. I'll be right there." Ron went to pick up the receiver on the phone. Bob already had it and handed it to him.

"I already dialed the hotel."

"Hi yo Silver, you're the best pal."

"Tonto rode Scout." Bob lightly punched him on the shoulder. "It's ringing."

"Hi, Room 624 please. Clarence, listen…yes it's me Ron and you must do as I say. I don't have time to explain. You and Iggy must get to Central Park right now. Bring a couple of the other guys if you can. If what I saw is what I think it is then there may be a little trouble. What you cannot do is tell Detective Malone anything about this. Do tell him to go to a Brownstone on the north side of Washington Square in an hour or two. There he'll find Battista…"

"Ron De Cenza, have you gone nuts. He's the one who killed Sheila you said…"

"I also said to just listen. Across from Central Park West apartments at 76th Street I think I just saw a couple of guys in suits hiding behind a lilac bush in the park. If they are who I think they are, our asses are going to be kicked."

"Guys in suits in the park, right. And exactly who do you think they are?"

"Giuseppe and Andrew; so Iggy comes into play here. He'll know what I mean. Tell him to do his thing, the one he started in the men's room. Tell him he's brave and that I'm sorry to ask him to sin again."

"Sin, what the hell…okay, okay. I'm on it. Call Malone; send to Brownstone in Washington Square, Iggy and me to Central Park. Got it; but then what?"

Ron needed to think but didn't have time to do so. He turned to his pal.

A shrug of the shoulders was returned and then. "Tell them to go to the Brownstone after Iggy does his thing to distract them. We'll meet them there with the shoes if we find any. Make sure the guys are at Central Park…"

"So that they can take care of the situation; good idea Bob," Ron explained the plan to Clarence. "Okay then, see you at the Brownstone in a couple of hours. Remember north side of Washington Square, the one with the fancy drapes, no blinds and pots of flowers on the staircase. Oh, and tell Malone to stay back until we get there with the shoes."

"Shoes, what the hell…"

"Just do it Clare, literally the life of Giovanni depends on it."

"Right, Holy Mother of God, what have you done now?" Clarence hung up confused but resolved to follow through. The late vocation as he was called due to his age was a big guy. What he needed to subdue the thugs in the bushes if it came to that were others capable of doing just that. He placed his hand on his roommate's shoulder. "Iggy, you need to sin again."

Sitting at the desk in their room, Iggy was trying to figure out the conversation from a one sided viewpoint which is all he heard. He didn't even ask what the sin was. Iggy just gulped and ran to the bathroom. Clarence followed and stood at the door. What he saw was the twenty year old dousing himself with Old Spice Men's cologne. "So Clare, what's up? Sounds like we have to sneak out of the hotel; is Ron in trouble?"

"Not exactly, at least not yet but that I think depends on how successful we are in distracting a couple of guys hiding in bushes in Central Park."

"So he must think Andrew is one of those guys, right?"

"So it would seem," an even more confused Clarence said. "I think we'll need Jim Beck and Matthew Sullivan to come with us to the park. If it's not Andrew and he's not open to your," he paused for just the right words. "Well your allure then we'll have to take them down so that Ron, Bob and Susan can get away with the evidence."

"Susan, is he crazy to let her go with them?"

"I don't think he had a choice, if I know Susan at all." Clarence went to the phone to call Jim and Matthew's room.

Bob and Ron ran from the elevator along storage sheds holding residents' stuff, as Ron would call his special trinkets or Christmas decorations. They found Giovanni and Stephano in the trash bin sifting through bags and loose garbage. Sacha was watching and saying yes or no to whatever they picked up. The driver himself couldn't risk returning to the Signore with the stink of garbage or a mess on his uniform, so he could not join them in the search. He and Susan stood at the edge; she was holding the pants, shirt and jacket of Stephano. It might have seemed that stripping had become second nature to him after his ultimate strip down for the Signore. The reality was that he too couldn't risk stains or smell on his clothes when he had to report back to the Brownstone. So there they stood just outside of the trash heap hoping something was found. Luckily for them the Signore had distinctive garbage bags which were plastic and not paper. He was even secretive with his trash and a plastic bag didn't break as easily.

When Ron and Bob came running up to them, their eyes focused on what Susan was holding and not on what the two men in the trash heap were holding up. "Susan, you could at least turn your back."

"Are you for real Ron? You're afraid that seeing a guy in his underwear will what excite me?"

"For shit's sake that's not what I meant. Give the guy some privacy. He had to get naked the other day for the Signore…forget it, you wouldn't understand."

"Ron De Cenza there you go again thinking that you could tell what I'm thinking. If you look at the guys in there you would see they can only be seen waist up, so grow up."

Bob was already catching a bag of what felt like shoes while this blow-up took place. "Will you two cut it for now? I think they may have found something." He handed the bag over to Sacha.

He carefully opened it. It was indeed full of all kinds of shoes ranging from tennis shoes to elegant pumps with high heels. Giovanni and Stephano watched him as he pulled out two shoes. One was a tennis shoe and the other a black leather high heel with a gold trim. Giovanni was identifying the pump. He remembered her in them on a special evening that she and the Signore had going to the opera. On that night he was allowed to take a break from the statue and go with them at her insistence. He smiled at the thought for she said she couldn't understand a word of the Italian opera and that Giovanni could help with the translation as most of what the Signore knew was in dialect Italian mostly bad words. She kidded him with a tickle under his chin. He huffed and puffed but knew it to be true, so he let the artist accompany them to Carnegie Hall.

"As it turned out," Giovanni began, "it was Verdi's La Traviata. You know that it's a story of love being revealed as death draws near. Who would have thought that it would be a prediction of things to come?" He began to weep. Stephano, the only one near him, chose to console him. The artist pulled himself together. "Grazie Stephano, and now the other bag; we must find the other bag of shoes."

Susan stepped between Ron and Bob. She took hold of their arms. "I guess he's a thug with a heart."

Sacha tied the bag up and turned to her. "Make no mistake Miss, even when he was completely naked in the limo the other day had one person dared to make a remark, that person would not be around today. But yes, you are right; he does have a heart and Sheila has touched it or he would not be standing in garbage tonight."

While the search continued, across the street in the lilac bushes Andrew and Giuseppe waited in Central Park. Andrew was holding himself, "I got to pee bad."

"So go already, nothing's happening."

"What here like a dog?"

"No not here, go over by those trees. I don't want to have to stand in it."

"Christ it must be ten o'clock; I might get mugged." Andrew was reacting to the sounds of the Church bells.

"Then pee your pants. I don't care. But just maybe one of your kind will be around and give you a quickie."

Andrew grabbed Giuseppe by his suit coat lapels with one hand and a strangle hold on his tie with the other hand. "Just what the hell are you implying asshole?"

"Cool it. We have a job to do. Everyone's heard the story of you and that kid in the men's room stall and the Signore catching you at it. It's cool man; I don't think getting a blow job is a big deal no matter who gives it to you. So go pee and get lucky."

CHAPTER THIRTEEN

FAILURE

That chilly breeze which started at the river was building up a little steam. The young leaves of the lilac bush began to rustle as the wind made its way through the branches. Andrew dropped his grip on his partner and laughed. "You're right. Who the hell cares these days how you get off as long as you can get off? I'll be right back. Watch to make sure no one mugs me."

"Right, I'll just do that little thing and not watch the Signore's apartment building."

Andrew pushed through the branches of the bushes and stomped off to a clump of trees next to some large boulders which stuck out of the ground all around the park area. Their massive size in some parts gave one a sense of awe to know that this bedrock is what was holding up the foundations of the giant skyscrapers throughout the city. He climbed up on the rocks and perused the area for potential muggers. Seeing none he slid down one and took a leak, watering the large clump of trees behind the rocks. Zipping back up, he heard a crunching sound. Someone or something was approaching him.

The night sky did not afford him a lot of light. The surrounding lights of the city pretty much obliterated the stars in the sky and the moon was shielded by a light covering of clouds. The Park's lamppost near which the lilac bush grew didn't shed its light to the rock formation. Giuseppe now stood under it as he occasionally looked at where Andrew had gone.

He figured that it was safer under the lamppost while alone just in case a mugger tried anything. Why one would even consider such a move against these two stalwart men of massive shoulders and strength of a Hercules one could only guess. But they were well dressed and that made them a prime target for those seeking money, drug deals or forbidden sex at that time of night in the park.

He could see the top of Andrew's head behind one of the rocks. His attention went back to Stan the doorman.

Andrew was looking over the rocks as he saw a shadowy figure coming his way. "Hey, you, I wouldn't even think about it."

The figure came a little closer and stopped. "Are you Andrew standing back there in the rocks?"

"What the hell…who wants to know?" He reached for the gun under his suit coat.

"Well if you are Andrew then you should know me. I'm the guy you almost had fun with in the men's room at the UN Gala yesterday"

"No shit, well come on little closer but not too close so as I could see you." He tucked his gun away. "That's far enough. I can see you plainly… shit little man, haven't you had enough. I heard that you had a fling right in the hallway with some dude who paid you."

The aroma of the Old Spice was filling Iggy's nostrils. Did he smell too tempting or too much like bait to catch a thief?" It was too late to think. He had to act and distract this giant of a man in more ways than one. Their eyes were locked now. Iggy dropped his hands to his side. He started to flick his right hand giving a signal to his classmate Jim to move out of sight. At that very moment Matthew and Clarence appeared on the walkway where the lamppost stood with Giuseppe leaning against it. They walked directly up to the thug.

"Hi there," began Matthew. His Midwestern twang had not yet been refined with college vocabulary. He could pull off the tourist thing better than the more mature Clarence who'd rather be at the symphony than in a park under any circumstances. Matthew began to spew tourist information questions and bullshit which would make his farmer buddies proud. Giuseppe was trying to get them to move along but they just kept on talking. So he got to the point before the big guy got too perturbed.

"So I heard that in Central Park a guy can find anything he wanted is that really true?"

"I ain't no faggot; so move along."

Mimicking the Herculean, Matthew responded. "Well we ain't no queers looking for a good time but we are looking for a good time. I just thought with you looking like you do you might have connections with ladies who want to have a good time with young guys, well at least one young guy." He poked Clarence in the ribs.

Giuseppe didn't know whether he should be pissed off or just laugh. Luckily he chose the latter. "I ain't no pimp either. But at the lagoon, up ahead, you'll find ladies walking."

Matthew got all excited, an Academy Award performance level of excitement. "No kidding, wow, and you think they'd take a kindly look at me and like have their way with me."

"A good looking kid like you instead of the old men usually around that pond, tonight's your night kid. Go for it."

Matthew started to jump all over Clarence. "Hear that, oh shit, I think I'm getting hard already."

At the rocks Iggy had now moved to be right in front of Andrew. The big dude had his hands all over him. But he kept on getting him excited. "Oh man kid, you make me so hard. Come on go down on me before I burst."

Iggy just stood there smiling ear to ear. "Is this to be free big man?"

"What do you mean? I thought you liked me."

"I do big guy, I do. I was just wondering if you wanted me to pay you for the privilege."

He had gotten to Andrew. He bent down to pull up his pants and get money from his pockets. Just as he did so, Jim pounced on him at the ankles. He fell into the rocks and hit his head and went down for the count. Pulling out drapery cords stolen from their hotel room, he tied Andrew's hands behind his back and then pulled up his pants as it was the descent thing to do in his mind. Iggy squeamishly slipped his hand under his coat and pulled out the gun, holding it in his hanky.

"Oh God Jim, is he…"

"No, he's just knocked out. Come on." Jim jumped onto the rocks and climbed to the other side. He could clearly see Clarence and Matthew with the guy under the street lamp. No one else was visible. "Now be quiet, we'll come from that guy's backside and surprise them. What gives with Matthew? He's like going crazy jumping around and pouncing on Clarence. Whatever he's doing it's a good distraction. Let's get going."

"What do I do with this?" Iggy held up the gun.

"Well first off, give it to me before you drop it. I was in ROTC, I can handle guns."

The hand off was made. Jim kept it wrapped in the hanky and shoved it in his belt under his school jacket. Then they stealthily made their way to Giuseppe. The guys didn't even see them approaching as they crept along the bush line.

In the basement of the apartment building the second bag was finally found. Sacha had gone as it was getting too late. The Signore expected to be picked up at 10:00 p.m. and go to the Brownstone. His cohorts were to split up and go to their assigned areas to insure that the switch was made without incident in the morning.

They were confident that they had the right bag in that it only contained shoes. Both Giovanni and Stephano could remember some of them. Susan turned her back to the guys as they walked out of the trash bin. Stephano grabbed hold of a pair of pants held in her hands. One look and he realized that they could not possibly be his and handed them to Giovanni. Taking the other now slipping out of her hands, he quickly dressed. The five of them now stood around the two bags and waited for Sacha's return. Sidney was at the service door as their lookout.

Out on Central Park West, Stan had seen something going on in the park across the street. Clarence came running to him heavily breathing. "Excuse me, you don't know me, but I think that you've met Ron de Cenza and Bob Wentz."

Stan was unsure as to how to react so he didn't.

"Listen to me, Ron and Bob sent me to capture two rather boorish men known as Giuseppe and Andrew. Now it's imperative that they know that these men are indeed… shall I say all tied up." Clarence pointed to Central Park and the lilac bushes across from them.

The doorman's eyes lighted. "I am so sorry. I do know the boys of whom you speak and if you were able to get the better of those two you mentioned then all I can say is that you are a far better man than I."

"I am most gratified. However, I need them quickly…you see one of them is not quite all put together as far as being fully dressed is concerned."

"I see. You must be talking about Andrew," Stan grinned as he led Clarence to the lobby of the building. "They are in the basement collecting evidence to prove the innocence of poor Giovanni. So sad that he lost Sheila; she was so good to him and all of us."

"So I've been told. This Giovanni, is he the artist?"

"Yes, quite a handsome young man, talented too from all I've heard; and so in love but never did he let on to any of us. We just saw it in his eyes whenever she was around." He picked up the lobby phone to call the police. "You do want me to call the police I take it?"

"Of course, you do that and I'll go tell the guys and Susan. How do I get down to the basement?"

Clarence was guided to the elevators and told to press LL for lower level. "You'll find them by the service entrance door with my colleague Sidney or in the trash bin."

The late vocation wanted so badly to ask why they would be in the trash bin, but time was of the essence. "Tell the police that Andrew is behind some rocks beyond the walkway and Giuseppe is tied to the lamppost by the Lilac bushes." Clarence pressed the LL button. The brass doors closed with a light thud and he was gone.

By the time Stan had finished calling the police Iggy, Jim and Matthew were crossing Central Park West and headed his way. In the distance sirens could already be heard. Moments later Clarence returned with Sidney. He had been told that his friends were off to Washington Square. Jim Beck was presenting the thugs' guns to Stan when they walked out of the lobby.

Seeing Clarence only with the other doorman Iggy told them that they would have to get going before the police arrived. "I'm afraid that we must get going. They may need our help with the next capture…"

"Oh my God, you are talking about the Signore' no doubt." Stan looked at the guns which he held by the nozzle with his fingers. Sidney took them from him before someone got hurt he noted while shoving them under his uniform coat and into his belt.

"Exactly," Clarence confirmed. "I believe his name is Battista. In any case we do apologize and ask for just one more favor. Would you whistle for a cab, it would expedite our departure."

Stan did so and a cab pulled right up to them along the curb by the canopy's end. As the guys entered the cab he asked what he should tell the police.

Iggy answered. "Tell them that those guns can be found to be used in other crimes by the men we tied up. That should do it."

As the cab sped off, a squad car with flashing lights pulled up along the very same curb line. Bells of the city's church steeples could be heard ringing out the 10:00 p.m. hour.

The Signore was not too pleased when he entered the limo while listening to those very same chimes. The displeasure was not directed at Sacha. In fact his presence made him a non-suspect in the betrayal. He was certain that Stephano was his betrayer after his Police Station visit. Wicksham's report that Stephano was seen talking with some young kid there seemed to confirm his feeling. At that same time the people of his four cohorts were driving them away. He was alone in the car, something which almost never happened. All his body guards were gone. One of them left to be his Brutus; this he believed with every fiber of his being. The other two were directed by Battista to stop him before he could betray him or worse.

In this melancholy state they arrived at the Brownstone. "Sacha, I don't want to be alone tonight of all nights. Come in, have a drink with me."

"Signore honors me; may I fill the car with gas first so that all is ready for tomorrow?"

"Ah, tomorrow…of course get the gas and then return for the drink. You should not drink and drive in any case," he laughed at his attempt to be amusing.

Sacha did accompany him to his front door to insure that he entered safely. A butler appeared at the door. It was a shock to the driver. He remained silent but Battista saw the surprise look on his face. "This is…" the Signore paused, I forget your name."

"It's Anthony, sir."

"Yes, I remember now." He looked at Sacha. "He was just hired. This is his first day though I did not expect him to be here at this hour. My connections in my business have placed him here so that I may be comfortable if my people aren't around. Lucky for me, isn't it as they aren't with me tonight." Then he turned his attention to Anthony. "You look more like one of my body guards than a servant young man. The women, they must fall all over you. You do like the women with the big breasts and long legs?"

"You make me blush Signore, may I help you with your hat and coat?" Anthony removed the items and placed them in a nearby closet. "It's late, are you retiring or will you prefer a drink?"

"A drink, this night I think I need several. Now Sacha, go do what you have to do." It didn't even dawn on Battista that he had paraphrased the Scriptures when Jesus told Judas to go from the table of the Last Supper and do what he had to do.

"Yes Signore, I will be back as quickly as possible." He left slowly.

Once in the limo, he drove around the Square and back up to Columbus Circle, then onto Central Park West. It was half past ten when he arrived at the service entrance of the New York Historical Society where the heist of the Pieta had just been planned. It was only a block away from the apartment building but afforded a concealed area away from the police search soon to begin across in Central Park or so they thought. Standing there were the Seminarians, Susan, Giovanni and Stephano, the Brutus whom Giuseppe and Andrew were to stop permanently. Stephano had not been stopped but was boasting about the finding of the shoes. He held up the two bags to Sacha's delight. As he relished in their success, Giovanni explained that the shoes demonstrated that someone was in that apartment. It would prove that Sacha, who moved items, returned them and threw some of them in the trash. So when the police searched earlier that day, they thought all was as it should be. This will prove otherwise. He became gloomy however as they went down Broadway. Its lights and fading glory beckoned them to enjoy the night. Ron saw the gloom like a pall come over the artist.

"Giovanni is everything all right. We found the shoes, isn't that great?"

He looked out the window at the passing flashing neon lights. The throngs of people still milling about the streets, the theater billboards inviting them to come and see Hello Dolly and Fiddler on the Roof. One a story of grand old New York and the triumph of love and the other a tale of hatred and yet hope, tradition and family. How he wanted to experience family once again. How he desired to bring the tradition and glory of the Renaissance to New York. He looked across to the pull down seat. "Ron, all of you, we have accomplished the impossible. We have the shoes. They will prove Sacha's story when he tells it, but they do not prove that I am innocent."

"But it does conjure up reasonable doubt to the crime. In any case we shall have to catch the Signore in the act of theft tomorrow or confront him in a way to show his guilt as the murderer of Sheila."

"Ron is right Giovanni, don't lose hope now. We shall trap him like the police can't." Bob placed his arm around the shoulder of the artist. "Buck up, it's not over 'til it's over. So Ron what's next?"

"Simple, Stephano here will go to the Brownstone as planned. We will meet the Detective Sargent by the Arch of George Washington and hand over the evidence to him. Hopefully that will be enough to confront the Signore in his own house and at least take him into custody for questioning."

A soft spoken voice added something which brought all of them into shock and rejection of the proposal. "And I shall go with Stephano as his captive, along with Sacha. They will say Stephano caught me at the apartment trying to find money to escape from the city. And Sacha got involved when he came to the apartment to fetch Stephano, who was sent there to watch who came and went into it in the first place by the Signore, so it's believable. It will also remove any thought that either of them was involved in a plot to betray him."

Bob saw a positive side to the proposal. "We'd only have to worry about Giuseppe and Andrew messing up the plan."

"But that will not be a problem if Clare and Iggy got to them first…"

"And were successful, let's not forget that part Ron." Bob squeezed the artist's shoulder. "Have faith Giovanni, you don't know the guys of the Abbey like we do. They're formidable."

"Truly they are," Susan confirmed.

The limo was now at Washington Square dominated by the huge granite arch dedicated to the First President called the Father of the Country. It shone brightly in the darkness surrounding it from the spotlights hitting it at all angles.

Susan, Bob and Ron jumped out of the limo right in front of the Arch. Under it stood Detective Sargent Malone. Sacha drove off with Stephano and Giovanni to a reception which could turn violent or worse and here they were on the other side of the park. It would take them a few minutes to circle the square lined with historic homes of another century to the north side. That, they thought, would be just enough time for the three to inform Malone of what they found. They stood on the pavement holding the two bags of shoes. Malone, Van Buren and O'Hara ran to them. Before they could even be reprimanded for disregarding the Detective's order, they held up the bags of shoes.

"These shoes belong to Sheila Murphy, the murder victim. We found them in the trash which proves Sacha's story that he was in the apartment and tried to remove Sheila's presence from it."

Van Buren and O'Hara took the bags. Malone before chewing them out revealed his own little plot. They walked up to a squad car and in the rear seat was a young man. Malone informed him that this was the butler hired for Battista who didn't know anything about the plot or the murder. He was just to keep the Signore comfortable because Battista's friends in the art business were under the impression that he was grieving and needed to be watched over.

"Well if this is the butler why is he in the squad car?" Susan asked. "Shouldn't he be with the Signore?"

"But he is with the Signore, Miss Liguri." Malone was quite proud of himself in his statement.

"I don't get it."

"Simple Bob, a replacement butler was sent instead. In size, appearance and demeanor he was similar to that man. You might know him as Brother Anthony."

"No shit, Brother Anthony is with the Signore." The shocked Bob became the concerned Bob in an instant. "We just sent in Giovanni as a prisoner of Stephano and Sacha."

Malone went ballistic. "Van Buren, have that house surrounded. O'Hara put the bags in the squad. Then this man must be brought to safety. You three are in grave danger of arrest amongst other things so don't try me any further. For now just follow me."

While Van Buren called squads in on the radio and O'Hara had the real butler driven away, Malone and company made their way with haste across the square to its north side. That in itself was no easy task as the Square was still filled with tourists arriving in droves to the city for the opening of the World's Fair.

Inside the Brownstone the Signore was being served a glass of wine by his imitation butler. Sitting in a plush arm chair next to the fireplace he could not help but to see the Swiss Clock and the St. Peter's photo of him and Sheila. Brother Anthony took advantage of the melancholy state.

"Sir, that's a lovely photo. St. Peter's interior isn't it, the one in Rome?"

"Huh, oh yes, that was almost two years ago now, before she betrayed me."

"I am so sorry sir, so she is gone from your life now, it that it?"

"Gone forever but there is one more Anthony who is not and he is the true betrayer." The Signore Battista held his tongue and thought before he spoke. "He murdered my Sheila who is in that photo. Lovely wasn't she. Now she is gone."

"Murder, I shudder at the thought. When, how...I mean how awful for you." Brother Anthony was trying too hard to ingratiate himself with Battista.

"For a butler, you ask a lot of questions Anthony; but this night I do not mind. I feel alone..."

A pounding on the door ended their exchange as Anthony hastened to the door. "Sir, are you expecting someone?"

"No one knows that I am here but my men. It must be them."

When Brother Anthony opened the door, there stood Giovanni between two men. The artist and he exchanged eye contact but said nothing. Anthony clutched the brass door knob of the heavy oak door. The hall light gave color to the stained glass window inlay. His knuckles were white from grasping so hard. If Giovanni made any sign of knowing him Malone's plan would bite the dust. He decided to play the butler role to the hilt.

"Good evening gentleman, it's rather late to be calling. May I help you?"

"Who the hell are you…where's the Signore?" Stephano, playing his role tried to intimidate the butler.

"I am unimportant but unless you tell me who you are, this rather imposing door shall be closed to you. So who are you and what do you want of this Signore person?"

Sacha cut in with a more civil tone to the stranger. "Tell the Signore that Sacha and Stephano have brought him a gift. He'll know who we are."

Standing at the side window of the parlor, the shadowy figure of the Signore was watching. The voices were loud enough for some words to be understood. When he saw that one of the men was Stephano whom he suspected of betrayal he began to second guess himself. For with him as he turned under the porch light was his driver who was holding onto his personal Judas, the artist. He pulled back the sheer curtain just slightly to make sure that what he was seeing was true. "So I am wrong about Stephano, he comes with the one who betrayed me," he muttered to himself. He was now delusional in convincing himself as well as everyone else that the artist actually killed Sheila. He dropped the drape and continued to watch the scene unfold.

"Indeed, do hold on a moment," Brother Anthony slowly closed the door.

Giovanni stood nervously between the two men as he thought someone would who had been taken by thugs. He looked around and saw only tourists roaming the square. "That guy, the butler, I know him, so play along if we're going to pull this off."

Back at the Central Park West apartment, Stan was speaking with two police officers under the canopy. He was telling them that he saw a mugging or something taking place right across from where they were standing. He pointed to the Lilac bushes and lamppost." I heard shouts." He lied with a straight face to protect Clarence and Iggy as well as those who had just left the basement. Sidney standing at his side nodded agreement. The officers told the doormen to stay put and that they would go check out the area in Central Park.

"Good they're gone Sidney, so where did the others go?"

"I only know that Sacha was to pick them up a block away at the Historical Society Building. They found two bags of shoes and went off with them."

"Shoes, why would that be so important, I wonder?" Just as Stan asked the question which neither could answer the officers returned holding drapery cords.

"Okay, something or someone was tied with this at that lamppost all right."

"But there should be two..."

"How do you know that there were two people involved? I think we need your names and ID gentlemen. Then you will come with us to the park and tell us what you really saw."

While Stan and Sidney tried to cooperate, at least give the appearance of it, down the street at the Historical Society parking area two men appeared. The Signore's limo was gone as Sacha had made his pick-up. But Ben Westridge had not left as yet. He was just entering the concealed lot from inside where the heist plan had been discussed. He never knew that Sacha had been there. His two men ran ahead of him to start the car. They saw movement next to the black Ford LTD. Taking no chances they drew their guns. "Show yourself or we'll let you have it right here," they yelled as Westridge froze in place. Two rather beaten up and disheveled men jumped out from behind the car. Giuseppe and Andrew came forward with their hands raised.

"Don't shoot; we're the Signore's body guards. I'm Giuseppe Mortelli and this is Andrew Jackson."

"Okay men, lower your weapons. I know these men." Westridge holstered his gun and walked between his men. "What the hell happened to you? His remarks were aimed at Andrew in particular because his dirty appearance and bloody head stood out.

Andrew explained that the Signore had sent them to watch their partner Stephano. Their boss had a funny feeling about his body guard since he was arrested and questioned by the police. Then he had to explain why they appeared with no weapons on them and so rough in appearance. They had to admit that they were mugged but separately because Andrew had gone to take a leak. He never addressed the intimate details of the encounter.

"The Signore is in danger Mr. Westridge. Your men may be needed." Andrew then asked if he would take them to the Brownstone. The very mention of the safe house brought on more questions.

Unlike the art dealer Battista, Westridge kept a low profile and that meant an ordinary Ford LTD black in color and not a limo. Andrew and Giuseppe squeezed in with Westridge in the back seat. By the time they arrived at the Brownstone they had explained why the house on Washington Square was known to very few people, none of whom would be in their circle of friends. Westridge was not offended. He always felt that Battista's artsy friends were a bunch of snobs anyway. The Ford slowly made its way to the north end of the Square. Squad cars could be seen parked by the George Washington Arch so they avoided going past that area.

"That's the house," Andrew pointed to the one with the flower pots on the stairs. "Stop, there's someone at the door. I think its Stephano. You can't mistake that physique even in the dark."

Westridge poked Giuseppe, "is this guy for real...physique, who the hell notices a guy that way?"

Giuseppe chose to shrug his shoulders and play ignorant. This gave Andrew a chance to jump out of the car and run toward the stairs. He stopped as he heard their voices. There was no doubt, it was Stephano and Sacha was with him with the artist. He grouched behind the stone staircase. Giuseppe moved up on him and knelt beside him. "Are you nuts, running away like that from Westridge. His men were ready to help us. What gives?"

The artist is with them, something's fishy; they seem too chummy." Andrew sent Giuseppe away to tell Westridge's men to go across the street and move up on the house from the other side.

"As I said, that's Brother Anthony, guys. I know him. Why he's the butler for the Signore I have no idea." Giovanni was no longer being held by his arms and his revelation to Battista's men was being overheard.

"Signore Battista," began Brother Anthony as he scanned the area by the fireplace. "Oh there you are, sir." He walked toward the windows. "Three men are asking to see you. Well actually only two of them spoke."

Battista was only half listening to what he thought was his new butler. He had just caught a few words of the men on the porch. It was beginning to dawn on him that something was not as it appeared. His doubts about Stephano flooded his mind once again. Disappointment with Sacha followed. But what mattered the most, were those words from Giovanni that he knew the butler. When Brother Anthony repeated his statement, he had already decided to play along.

At the sidewalk level behind the century old stone stairway, the crouched Andrew also heard those words. "Christ, they're working with the artist."

Andrew looked about and waved to the men across the street to move in. Giuseppe was now with them. He had to make a move quickly; for he could see coming up behind Giuseppe and the Westridge guys some policemen. What he hadn't been able to see were Ron, Bob and Susan behind the cops with Malone.

"Well look who's coming home." Andrew stepped onto the first stair.

The three men turned. Instinctively they took hold of Giovanni's arms. "Why shouldn't we be, we have a present for the Signore." Stephano jerked the artist's arm so that he'd appear to be captive.

"Then why was he talking about the butler being a Brother Anthony, who's that? The Signore doesn't have a butler."

"Listen faggot maybe if you'd zip your fly and not worry about every pecker that comes your way you'd know he hired him because we were not here to be with him."

Andrew looked down at his fly and in that moment Stephano flung himself at him. They tumbled onto the street. The cops coming up behind Giuseppe and the others shouted for them to halt. Giuseppe split as did the other two and the cops now followed by Malone and company were on their heels.

Just as Stephano attacked Andrew, the Signore had given orders to his butler to admit the men at the door. Brother Anthony went to the door. The shouts and screams beyond the door could be heard by the Signore for they were certainly heard by him. He paused behind the door and then swung it open and closed it behind him. The farce was over and he knew it. He stood on the stoop over Sacha and Giovanni watching the two rolling in the gutter of the street pounding on each other. Tourists began to gather at the edge of the park as the thugs ran through them.

"I told you to keep back." Malone realizing he had company shouted to Ron, Bob and Susan.

"Too late, we're here now." Ron just kept running. Susan spotted Giuseppe heading for the side of the house.

"Ron, look there, it's Giuseppe." He ran off to the side of the cops and went for the thug.

Sacha and Giovanni ran down the stairs and headed for the Square right into the cops. "Stop police," Van Buren shouted. The two froze in place. O'Hara and Jones continued to the street where they were almost run over by a black Ford headed for the alley. The roaring of the car's engine and rumbling of its tires on the brick road scared the wits out of Andrew and Stephano. They rolled to the curb, pushed each other away and ran off. Stephano was tackled by O'Hara. Andrew got to the alley.

Brother Anthony now stood in front of that impressive door. The plan had failed. The Signore was now watching the entire scene from the parlor window. He now saw Anthony run down the stairs behind his driver and the artist. "Am I really to be murdered like Caesar and have betrayers all about me?" he yelled while running to the back of the house. He paused briefly to grab a gun from the bureau drawer in the dining room. Turning he blew a kiss as if to say good-bye to his not so safe house. Running down into a small courtyard he opened the iron-gate and stepped into the alley just as a black Ford screeched to a halt and a panting Giuseppe came up the alley calling to him. Westridge opened the door. Battista and Giuseppe jumped in and off it went almost crashing into a cab which had stopped at the alley opening on the other end. It stopped to let out passengers. Clarence, Iggy, Matthew and Jim got out of the car. Iggy recognized a face in the Ford which almost hit them.

"I'd know that guy anywhere. Andrew was in that car."

Ron came running out of the alley. "Shit, they got away." He bent over trying to catch his breath. The guys from the cab rumbled off as they ran up to him as he sat down on the pavement of bricks. "It didn't work, the plan didn't work guys. God's just not on our side in this."

A hand came to rest on his shoulder. Its owner had just placed his finger to his lips and motioned to the guys to silently step away. "God doesn't take sides Ron; I think that you understand that as a future priest. Humans have free will and make their own decisions right or wrong."

Ron looked up and saw the smiling face of Brother Anthony in his butler tux. "It looks good on you. Don't let Susan see you in that, she'll lure you away from the Monks."

Brother Anthony laughed. He knelt next to Ron and whispered. "She'd have a difficult time of it, wouldn't she Ron? Now if you sent in Iggy like you did to lure Andrew tonight then maybe there would be a chance but I doubt it. I made my choice to serve the Lord and I'm committed to it. But you're right about one thing. Our plan failed and so apparently did yours."

Riding with Westridge, another was realizing that a plan had failed. It dawned on Battista that after what just took place a connection would be made to the murder of Sheila. The whole city would be looking for him. The entire plan to steal the Pieta was now in jeopardy. He remained silent with his thoughts as Andrew and Giuseppe spewed oaths to get their revenge.

Ron having caught his breath took hold of the hand of Brother Anthony. He hoisted him up. "Well guys, let's talk about Plan B."

Iggy turned to Clarence. "I didn't know that we had a plan B."

"I don't think that we do, but something tells me that our friend does or at least it is in the works in that brain of his right now."

A silence fell over them as they gathered about to learn what brilliant plan was being cooked up now.

Washington Square

SOLIDARITY AND DEFIANCE

Clarence locked arms with Iggy who locked arms with Jim who did the same with Matthew. They caught up with Brother Anthony and Ron and locked arms with them. Running across the street from the Square were Bob and Susan. Seeing this sign of solidarity massing at the end of the block they were drawn to it like a magnet attracting metal.

The solidarity brothers stopped as they saw them coming. The two stood in front of them. They also locked arms with each other.

"So is this little wall of unity open to girls?"

"And Tonto…don't forget the sidekick."

When the laughter stopped Bob and Susan were arm in arm with them. They walked right in the middle of the street pretty much filling the road. It had been blocked off by the police so their monopolizing it wasn't a problem except for Malone. He was flaming mad as he stomped toward them with fire in his eyes. But when he saw them laughing and in the arm lock his demeanor changed. It softened and became appreciative of what stood in the middle of that street. He placed his hands on his hips and tried to carry off an authority stance.

If anyone could appreciate authority figures it certainly were the guys in the group. Their whole experience at the Latin School of the Abbey in Wisconsin was that of following the rules laid down by the Abbot, the Prior, their Lain professor and the whole Church. Authority was something they respected even when they rebelled and took matters into their own hands as they just had. Susan on the other hand attended Loyola University in Chicago where questioning rules and who made them was common practice. Nevertheless she and the guys stopped as the Detective Sargent approached.

Behind him at the stairs of Battista's safe house were Van Buren and O'Hara. They were tending to the cuts and scrapes on Stephano the aftermath of his fight with Andrew and almost getting run over by Westridge's car. Sacha and Giovanni flanked the injured former body guard sitting on the cold stone steps.

The lights on the squad cars spun out bright color giving an eerie feeling. It was as if they had just walked into a war zone. Tourists and neighbors in the other fine homes along the north end of Washington Square stood about gawking at the line of young people now being confronted by the Detective Sargent. The solidarity brothers and sister tightened their grip on each other's arms. It seemed to be an effort to stand firmly as one against the barrage that they were sure was to come. They were wrong. Malone rather than shouting and berating them was almost caring like a father to his children with whom he was disappointed. He did so as he paced back and forth looking into each of their faces as he spoke. He kept his hands clasped behind his back to avoid wagging a finger at them.

"What you did tonight was very foolhardy. Giovanni has shared Ron's plan. Clarence, you of all those in this line of culprits, for that's what you all are, should have known better. And you Brother Anthony, a Monk has joined them in their…well I don't know what to call it. Maybe it's a call to bring justice were none existed. Maybe it's just defiance and impatience with the way things are done. Or maybe it's because of a bond you feel exists between you. Whatever it is, it destroyed my efforts to get to the truth about Sheila Murphy's murder and the plot you insist is in the works to steal the Pieta. And now Battista is out there, God only knows where." Malone stopped. He saw in Ron's eyes a spark. Something was buzzing around inside that head of his. An idea was being born. "It appears Ron De Cenza that you may have something to say."

The bright cocoa brown eyes which his gym teacher once told him to keep shining always seemed to sparkle in the flashing lights surrounding them. First he apologized for keeping the Detective in the dark as they sought the shoes. Then he told Malone that he could offer a defense for what he and his friends did. He amended that thought as it would be a waste of time which was so important. For as the Detective pointed out the Signore Battista was out there in the city or fled from it. He had been rescued by person or persons unknown to anyone.

"So Detective Malone, I was thinking…"

"Yes, everyone here can see that; your eyes give you away."

"Oh, okay then," Ron got a little flustered and embarrassed. "Well then, like I was saying; tonight was a bust both for us lined up here and for you. But now that I think of it, not entirely a failure. The Signore has seen that Giovanni is alive. He will want to get to him. So I don't think he fled the city. You and your men by seeing his reaction and flight now know that there must be some guilt in him. We found the shoes which proves that Sheila's things were as Sacha says returned after initially taken away to remove her presence in Battista's life. And we still know that there is a plot to steal the Pieta before it gets to the Vatican Pavilion. And since that takes place tomorrow, in all likelihood between the 44th Street Pier and the World Fair grounds something has been planned to steal the statue."

"And you no doubt have a theory about how this will take place."

"Yes sir, I believe that we do."

"We?"

"You look surprised Detective. Did you think my ideas just pop into my head? I am not that egotistical." Ron smiled. He glanced along the line of his mates and then into the eyes of Susan. "Something that Bob and Iggy put in their notes when they were listening in on that meeting between the Signore and those four mysterious men no one knows struck me."

"Well are you planning to share this brilliant thought with us or not?" Malone's hand were no longer behind his back but on Ron's shoulders, but gently placed.

The bells in the steeple of the Churches of the City were chiming out the Midnight hour as Ron squirmed with a bit of discomfort with Malone being in his face. He managed to suggest that they finish the thought back at the hotel. "It's getting a bit chilly and I think Giovanni and Stephano should be in on this."

Malone dropped his hands and agreed. He called his men to get the squads lined up. "You'll be under our protection, all of you. Just get into the police cars and we'll meet later to finish this conversation." He then ordered that no sirens or flashing lights were to be used. In fact each car should travel to the hotel by different routes. If anyone in that crowd watching them were people put there by Battista, they would find it difficult to ambush all the cars. Ultimately they all would have to get to Park Avenue and follow that up to Lexington Avenue where the hotel was located.

Riding in O'Hara's squad was Clarence, Brother Anthony and the artist Giovanni Gaglioni. Clarence had purposely slid over to the opposite door which then forced the artist to seat next to Brother Anthony no matter how they entered. Acting as the big brother even to the actual religious Brother and the artist as he was a good eight years older than either of them, he knew that they had to talk. As the car crossed Manhattan mid-town and turned onto Park Avenue, Giovanni was the one to break the ice.

"Are you angry with me, Brother Anthony?"

It was an uncomfortable question for in it was truth. He was upset that he wasn't able to keep his pledge to Malone to be with Giovanni always. He pledged that to keep the artist out of the holding cell until the whole matter of murder was cleared up. Now here they were literally squished against each other and acting like ten year olds who got in a fight on the school playground. Finally, he said something. "I wasn't able to keep my pledge to the Detective Sargent."

"Brother, before you answered this calling to serve God, did you ever know love?"

"I presume you are speaking of human love even the expression of it in a physical way."

"You are partially correct. However only on the human love part; you see I loved Sheila with all my heart, but never expressed it in a way other than a touch of hands or an exchanged smile. We tried to honor the Signore by keeping apart as much as possible. But this love burned in us. We had to talk, we had to see each other if nothing else. The Signore, he called it betrayal. He was cruel to Sheila and I could take no more. I tried to protect her and got this to show for it," Giovanni held his head where the bandage was on his brow to the side of his head over the ear. "She gave her life for unexpressed love. I had to do something to avenge her. Can you understand that? I had to do something even if it meant deceiving you. Yet even that failed. I was punished for what I did beyond anything you can imagine."

The heart of Brother Anthony wept over the pain Giovanni was experiencing. He had only known abusive sex acts from one blackmailing him because of his being a homosexual. He never knew but he did dream of a love expressed by a smile or touch of the hand. How lucky Giovanni was he thought, to have such a love which elevates one above just the chemistry of attraction to a spiritual union. He managed to get his arm up and over Giovanni's shoulder and gave it a squeeze. "You are one lucky man. For you have experienced what I or even Clarence so quietly sitting so as not to disrupt our bond may never experience. I am not angry. True I wish that I could have been with you to help you avenge that love. Yet I understand the fire burning within you which ignited that desire to first find where they had hidden Sheila's body and then to avenge her death. Next time let me join you. I would be honored to help you."

"You have already done so, Brother. And it would appear that you may get that desire fulfilled as well for are we not to plan yet another attempt to capture that beast who killed Sheila?" He brought his arms up, placing one over Brother Anthony and one on the shoulder of Clarence. "Clarence, thank you for arranging us this way," he whispered. The three then rode in a quietness brought on by exhaustion and a sense of baring one's soul, lifting from it a burden.

Inside the hotel lobby, the guys of the Abbey Latin School were pacing the black and white marble floor. With them was their Latin professor Father Gregory. He was praying the Rosary. It was after midnight. Only a skeletal staff was on duty at the reception desk. The seminarians, religious and tourists had returned from their various outings to see the crate on the barge, have dinner and enjoy the city lights. They had gone to their rooms long ago. But not Frankie, Andy, Quinlan and Jerry all of whom had stayed back, not by choice, in order to receive word from the others so that they could communicate real danger to the police. They never got a call and thus the pacing.

When the guys started to come up those stairs into the lobby, it was like welcoming home long lost family. Father Gregory allowed the rejoicing as he took Brother Anthony aside for a quiet conversation. He had kept the events of the night from the Abbot. Once assured that all the students and Susan were safe and unharmed he stopped wrestling with his decision. It was short lived. Once he learned that Ron had another plan to prove Giovanni was innocent, the struggle was renewed within him. When he learned of the plot to steal the Pieta, he began to pray the beads again.

Ron and Bob slipped away from the welcoming chaos. They were asking the clerk at the reception desk if there might be an easel with markers and a pad of paper which they could use along with an open meeting room. Standing right behind them was Malone. He had no intention of being left out of any future plans and was resigned to the fact that these lads and lass would not give up. Receiving their supplies and a room assignment they rushed off to Meeting Room 101 just off the lobby area. On the way they called to Susan. Her immediate job was to inform Father Gregory and Brother Anthony to get the guys ready to come to the meeting in ten minutes and then to join them.

The ten minutes flew by and the guys rushed into the room to find a souvenir map of New York City taped onto the wall and a drawing of Manhattan, the East River and the Flushing area across the river from it. Flushing was a former garbage dump and was the location of the World's Fair. Ron was attaching the World's Fair layout map to the easel. Sitting right in front of where Ron, Bob and Susan stood were Giovanni, Stephano, Sacha, and the Detective. His officers were posted at the doorway and in the lobby.

"Okay, I think we're all here, so settle down and let's get started." Ron shot a look at Susan who then moved to the map on the wall. "That is what New York City looks like. On the Hudson River side at 44th Street the barge Challenger sits with two crates on it. One holds the Good Shepherd Statue and the other Michelangelo's Pieta." Susan pointed to the area being described. She drew a red circle around the area on the map. "Tomorrow that barge will move from the pier and around the tip of Manhattan called the Battery. It's supposed to go to Flushing Bay. Once there a truck will transport it to the Vatican Pavilion." Susan drew a line outlining the route as he spoke. "Tonight we failed to trap the Signore Battista who we believe is the real murderer of Sheila Murphy. He's a big shot in this city with many high society connections but also the Detective believes, with the mob. Those of us from Chicago understand what that means.

Bob bent over to Iggy. "So now he's from Chicago because he understands the mob reference."

Ron wrinkled up his nose at his sidekick best pal and continued. "That's all water under the Brooklyn Bridge let us say. We need to focus on tomorrow and here's why. Bob and Iggy took notes on a secret meeting Battista had with four guys none of whom we can identify. Until that is, we learned their names and what their job was in the plot they were forming. Susan and I know what they look like as does Stephano here who was Battista's body guard, Sacha who was his driver and Giovanni our artist friend who has carved a replica of the Pieta. Battista had planned to switch Giovanni's statue with Michelangelo's and make millions by holding the real one for ransom. But the Detective Sargent here has pretty much put an end to that part of the plan. The replica statue at this moment is being confiscated and taken to a safe place off the river. That means the Signore Battista will have to go to a plan B as well. And I think we can all agree that it would have to be an aggressive one. With certainty I can say that it may bring harm to those protecting the Masterpiece."

Stephano rose. "And let me tell you that these men are not nice people." He sat back down.

"Thank you," Ron continued. "So why are we here? It's because of something Bob said about one of those men. His name is Antonio Penne. In the plan to steal the Pieta he is in charge of ground transportation. Bob heard him say over the intercom of the phone that he would be there with a backup truck just in case."

Frankie from Quebec rose. "So what's that mean?"

Stephano turned and glared at him. "Shut your face and let the kid finish." Sacha patted his shoulder telling him it was just a question and not to get upset. He meant no disrespect to Ron.

"Well Frankie, it means that if their Plan A failed that a Plan B would kick in and this Antonio guy would make sure it was successful. Well their Plan A did fail. The crate with Giovanni's statue fell onto a barge. It was well planned to do so. Battista got all the credit in this test as he called it. He wanted it to fail because it covered up what the others wanted which was to switch the crates at the pier. Battista knew too many people would be there and it was too risky. However, when the crate with the Pieta in it was brought onto land and placed on the flatbed truck, that switch would be less obvious. The fake truck would be one of many bringing exhibits to the Fair grounds. Our job is to identify that fake truck and steal back the real Pieta."

To say that all hell broke out would be understating what took place when Ron dropped the Pieta bombshell. For another hour the details of how that could be accomplished was debated and evaluated. One thing was for certain, Malone would send undercover men to Flushing Bay immediately. It would be their job to be disguised as dock workers and members of Religious Orders arriving to serve as part of the welcoming event. By the time Ron and his classmates arrived in the morning, the truck should have been marked. Stephano, Sacha and Giovanni would be indispensable as they could ID most of the main characters in the theft of the century, should it be successful. Father Gregory was to get them cassocks so that they could blend in with the others. It was done.

Malone insisted that they all get some rest. "Tomorrow…later this morning really, will see our Plan B defeating Battista's Plan B. But only if we can all stay on task, be rested and know exactly what our part is in the stealing back of the real Pieta. All you Abbey school students will be placed near the Vatican Pavilion and along the route to it. Each of you will have a walkie-talkie so that you may communicate what you see when the truck bearing the Pieta makes its way onto the grounds. Now go get some rest this all starts up at 8:00 a.m. this morning. Stephano and Sacha, I have arranged a room for you here at the hotel. It will be easier to keep you safe."

The guys left with Father Gregory and Brother Anthony. Van Buren went with Stephano and Sacha to insure that they had everything they needed. Malone assigned a few of his officers to guard the hotel. He left with Susan to escort her safely to her room. Ron and Bob remained with Giovanni. Since they were roommates they would go together back to their room after the maps and drawings were taken down. No one wanted to risk having the wrong eyes seeing them.

When they entered their room on the 6th floor, Giovanni threw himself onto his bed. He just lay there looking up at the ceiling. Bob and Ron taking turns in the bathroom got ready to get some sleep. They sat on the edge of the bed and tried to talk to the silent artist.

"Giovanni, are you okay?"

Bob received so answer. So Ron tried.

"You know we have to be up and ready to pull off our own switch in six hours. You are an important part of the plan."

The single window over a table with a phone and small lamp let in slivers of city light. In that shadowy environ Giovanni turned his head sunken into a pillow. One of those slivers of light shone on his face. It was streaked with tears.

Bob took hold of Ron's arm. "Crap, what did we do?"

The reply came from the artist. "Not you my friends, the Signore. What did he do? He tried to kill me. He did murder the love of my life. Now he plans to steal the treasure of the Church…no of all civilization to become richer than he already is. And yet no mention of him was even made at the meeting. The only important thing was to get the real Pieta to the Vatican Pavilion." He boosted himself up on his arms and swung his legs over the edge of the bed. "Do not worry. I shall help you in any way that I can." He walked to the bathroom.

"He's right Ron; we ignored the whole murder thing."

"Not quite, you, Susan and I will not let Battista off until we prove he is guilty of murder. And this is how we're going to do it. I only hope that we can pull it off."

By the time Giovanni came out in his sleep shorts and returned to his bed, the guys were under their covers. Slipping into bed he tried not to disturb them. As he lay down and pulled up the sheet and blanket he heard Ron's voice.

"Giovanni, you are our friend. We shall get Battista, this I pledge to you. So rest up, all hell will break loose when sunrise comes."

Sunrise did arrive and it was heavenly. The crisp 50 degrees was to increase as the day progressed. The sky was crystal blue with just a patch or two of cumulus clouds dancing across it. At the 44th Street Pier the barge Challenger was already under way down the Hudson River. Tourists came to wave good-bye to the crates holding the Pieta and Good Shepherd statues. As it made its way on the crowded waterway, once again the tug boats tooted and sprays of celebratory water arches followed it. At the tip of the Battery, throngs gathered to watch it pass by.

Up the East River in Flushing Bay near the dock area a flatbed truck waited with Penne's driver. Other flatbeds were there to receive the Good Shepherd statue crate and the official truck which was to receive the crate with the Pieta was closest to the dock. It would take most of the day for the barge to make its way around the Battery and up to the bay.

Sitting in the back seat of a black Ford LTD were Ben Westridge and the Signore Battista. The men of the other co-conspirators were scattered between the Vatican Pavilion and the dock. Outside next to it stood Andrew and Giuseppe, cleaned up and fighting mad. Andrew still ached from the tackle on the stairs and his face was bruised around the right eye and onto the cheek. He kept fondling the new gun under his jacket. No longer in a suit but in dock worker's clothes he felt demeaned. Giuseppe however thought the opposite. He felt that it made it easier for them to mill about with the workers. Those dock workers would transfer the Pieta to the truck; he had told the complaining colleague. In the driver's seat sat Westridge's man enjoying their bantering.

Behind the Ford was a dark blue Buick sedan. Sitting in that back seat were Francesco Mondera and Jeffrey Rafferty. Some of the men on the docks were also their people. It was their job to distract with many trucks crowding in the area and mooring of the barge at the dock. All was ready for the heist that would make history.

Arriving on the actual grounds of the World's Fair main gate were the Abbey Latin School guys and their mentors. Already in the Vatican Pavilion were Susan and her mother who were helping to set up the gift shop. The Vatican Pavilion sparkled with its gold dome like crown which at night shot out beams of light. Its delivery doors at the rear were wide open to receive the statues. The staging area for the Pieta designed reverently and beautifully by Broadway set designers was ready. Bathed in blue light with the huge plain cross in the background, a pedestal to hold the Pieta waited for the masterpiece. Flanking the sides of the display were votive lights cascading down wired ropes.

The Fair's Carillion rang out the 9:00 a.m. hour. Flags of the nations fluttered from the gentle April breezes. They provided a global ceremonial welcome all along the path leading from the symbol of the Fair, a gigantic silver metal globe called the Unisphere. It rested in the Fountain of the Continents which had a ring of water spouts circling it; their streams arching toward the Unisphere creating crystal-like droplets cascading off the sculpture. The fountain, the flags as well as the sculpture of the world would give visitors the sensation of being at an International event. The sculpture was to symbolize unity of all people. That lofty goal couldn't be further from the truth in 1964. But it served as a constant reminder of what might be accomplished with people of all nations gathering to share their culture, art, music, food and customs.

Malone's officers were handing out walkie-talkies to the guys of the Abbey School. They were to use them when reporting anything which seemed improper during the escorting of the truck with the statue. Inside the Vatican Pavilion a rather excited Susan was receiving hers. She was thrilled to be a part of the effort to save the Pieta. It was short lived as a buzzing sound was heard coming from the walkie-talkie. Malone was being contacted. The somewhat garbled words were clear enough for Malone. A flatbed truck had been identified as being at the dock area before it was supposed to be there.

"Susan, don't move from this Pavilion. Ron and Bob are at the dock and so is the fake truck." He ran off with Giovanni, Stephano and Sacha.

Each of the Abbey guys as well as Giovanni, Stephano and Sacha were attired in the black Roman cassocks to be part of the welcoming guard of honor. This meant that the artist, body guard and driver of the Signore were to line up with them from the dock up onto the road especially created for the Fair. They were to blend in and spot anyone in the Signore's employ.

Inside the Ford the Signore was checking his watch as the bells rang out a song. "Good all is well. The barge should be here soon. By then Antonio should have all his trucks at the dock area."

Ben Westridge was not so confident. "That's all well and good but the fake Pieta couldn't be brought here. Thanks to your men placing the dead girl on it, it's now part of a crime scene. So when we tried to move it from the Hudson River we were denied a route. Our only recourse now is to hijack the actual truck with the statue." He had no idea that the replica statue was actually off the river and in police hands.

By this time Battista was a possessed man with only one thing in mind; that was to kill the artist Giovanni Gaglioni. He had seen his world begin to collapse through the curtains of his so called safe house. Seeing Sacha and Stephano on his stairway with the artist convinced him that the Ides of April could very well be his end of days. If he didn't get rid of Giovanni, he would end up like Caesar. Statue or no statue the artist must be eliminated. "You worry too much Westridge. In the chaos of traffic and exhibit deliveries we shall simply take the truck out as we came in. By the time that they realize the Pieta's truck was not in the traffic jam, we shall be on our way." He got out of the car and placed his credentials over his neck. He had one more chore to get done. "Let's take a look around the dock and road to the Pavilion." He was speaking to Giuseppe and Andrew. "Part of the chaos to make this job successful will now have to be the elimination of the artist."

"Signore, is this wise to just walk amongst these people," asked Giuseppe.

"What if someone recognizes us," Andrew still hurting was not looking for another fight or a situation which had him running any kind of distance.

"You also worry too much. Westridge' people are watching us like the angels. We need to end Giovanni Gaglioni in a manner which creates panic and confusion. This will conceal our getaway with the statue. And to do that, we need to find him."

"Exactly, and what better place than right here; there is no way he'd miss seeing the Pieta." Andrew shoved his fist into his hand. "Giuseppe you take the pier, I'll take the Fountain area…"

"And I'll stay by our truck." The Signore walked toward the flatbed which would soon be called to pick up the crate. As he approached the truck some commotion was taking place. He kept his distance. Andrew was already on his way to the Unisphere fountain. Giuseppe he could see moving toward the dock. He dared not call out to him. He squeezed between some of the religious lining the road commenting on the growing excitement of the historic day. All the while he watched the exploding events at the flatbed truck.

It was as if lightning had struck. The Detective Sargent having reached the dock area pressed the call button on his walkie-talkie. It was a series of beeps rather than words. Only his people would know that it was a signal to attack the driver of that truck now being eyed by the Signore. Van Buren and O'Hara climbed onto the passenger and driver side of the cab. Van Buren shoved his gun through the open window and ordered the driver to get out. In a matter of a couple of minutes it was all over. The driver was taken away. Malone ordered one of his people to back the truck off the dock road and block all other traffic from entering until the Pieta was on its way to the Pavilion.

The Signore watched his Plan B bite the dust. His dream of making a fortune by holding the Pieta for ransom had become a nightmare of murder, intrigue and betrayal. Yet there was one light of hope which remained. The artist would be found and eliminated. He backtracked to the Ford, but decided to avoid both cars as they were now in a forbidden area. Police were gathering to order them and all other vehicles away from the dock area. It would only be a matter of time before his co-conspirators were found to be among the cars and trucks. He decided to find Andrew at the Fountain of the Continents and then search for Giovanni. It was too late to get to Giuseppe.

On the other side of the roadway Giuseppe was watching the police activity with other dock workers most of whom were not the men of Antonio Penne or Jeffrey Rafferty. He was dressed to appear as one of them but couldn't ask each one if they knew the Signore, so he felt and was alone. Feeling helpless he too decided to make his way to Andrew.

The blaring of horns and tooting of boat whistles announced that the Pieta had come around the bend of the East River by LaGuardia airport. It was nearing Flushing Bay. The excitement began to build again as the police action with its brief disruption had subsided. No one knew, except for Malone and his men what had taken place. It was made to appear that a traffic issue was being addressed. All eyes were on the dock. The barge had been sighted. There could be no doubt as to what the crate sitting in the center of that barge was. The bright orange color painted on its top end served notice to all. It held the priceless masterpiece.

Vatican Pavilion

CHAPTER FIFTEEN

REVENGE IN THE HEART

The excitement of the approaching barge was reaching a crescendo level. The cheering and thrill of the moment was infecting everyone including Ron and Bob. Everyone was feeling relief when their walkie-talkies were communicating the apprehension of the truck and its driver. A comfort level began to set in that perhaps all would be well. After all, now with the Signore's truck having been identified as not being the actual one to transport the Pieta it became clear that his Plan B had failed

Victory was thought to have been achieved. Giovanni however, was distracted by someone else. Sacha and Stephano were watching the docking of the barge but not Giovanni. He had caught a glimpse of Giuseppe in the crowd now swarming to be near the pier. Despite his dock worker appearance, hat and beard growth, there was no doubt about who he had seen. He was also the only one frantically shoving his way through the throng and away from the dock.

"It's him, there's Giuseppe," he called out. He broke away from the others and ran towards the man going against the traffic flow of people. Even the guys of the Abbey were now caught up in the push of the crowd.

"Wait up Giovanni." It wasn't easy to go against the flow but Ron finally caught up to him. He grabbed hold of the artist's arm. "Are you sure it was Giuseppe?"

"Let go of me. Yes I'm sure and he will go to protect the Signore, so I must follow him."

Ron released the sleeve of the cassock he was wearing. "Okay, I understand. Bob and I will help." Holding his walkie-talkie he got hold of Bob. All he said was that he should come to him. He did not want to create a panic not with the Pieta so close. Once Bob caught up to them which was no easy undertaking as the wave of people wanting to be by the water to see the arrival of the barge was now overwhelming. Giovanni and they were hard pressed to see Giuseppe. They began jumping up and down trying to look over the heads of the growing crowd. Finding the man who was going against the flow had become increasingly more difficult. That didn't stop the artist.

"There, see…there he is," Giovanni pointed to the right side of the moving mass of people.

They now focused on the man who they thought to be Giuseppe. For the moment their attention was drawn away from seeking out the Signore or Andrew. They would not have seen them in any case. The disruption and the flow of the crowd toward the dock allowed Battista to reach the symbol of the World's Fair. There he found Andrew looking for Stephano.

Battista was taking off his overcoat. The struggle against the crowd and nerves of the defeat of his dream raised in him the fire of hatred and revenge. "It's over. The cops have the truck." He threw his coat as if it were a piece of trash to the side. It landed on the popcorn vending cart. A slight clanging sound could be heard when it hit the metal of the cart. Both men ignored the sound. Battista had removed his Beretta from his coat as well as a small box of bullets for it.

"Then we have to get out of here, fast."

"True Andrew, but first we have a visit to make."

Andrew walked toward the cart to retrieve the overcoat.

"Leave it. It will throw them off and keep them searching around this fountain area. We shall, however be in the International pavilion area." The Signore had already developed a Plan C as the crashing sound of the water fell into the basin surrounding the Unisphere. The goal of that plan was the elimination of the artist. "One of the pavilions is not being used, follow me." They walked off toward the Indonesian Pavilion which was closed due to a conflict with the government of the United States and

President Lyndon B. Johnson. "We'll bide our time. My credentials will keep us safe for now."

The sun shone upon the bay as the moored barge's crane went into action to deafening cheers. The crate was without incident lifted onto the flatbed truck, the authorized one. A roar of the throng followed. Once it was on, the Good Shepherd statue crate was placed on the truck as well. The procession of the truck was about to begin. The guards of honor realized that they had a job to do. Order was returning to the scene. The Abbey guys lined up with the other seminarians and religious nuns, brothers, and priests to form the line of welcome up to the Pavilion of the Vatican. It seemed that victory had been achieved. The statues were safe. Stephano and Sacha made their way to the pavilion. They had thought they'd find Giovanni, Ron and Bob there after they had disappeared in the crowd. Having heard of the truck incident, they too realized that it was over for the Signore. The fear of reprisal was now their concern. They understood the personality of the Signore Battista. He would never give up.

Giuseppe had made it to the fountain centerpiece as the crates and the procession of the statues began. Virtually no one paid the slightest attention to him. The Signore and Andrew were nowhere to be seen. He now had no idea what he was to do. His reflection didn't last long. Running at breakneck speed toward him despite the long cassock were Giovanni, Ron and Bob. Their eyes locked on him. First he made a move toward the road from which they had just run. Then he made a move toward the International pavilion area. Each time he was thwarted when Bob moved to block his way and Giovanni ran to block his alternative choice. Now those two simply followed the circular basin of the fountain and closed in on him, while Ron backed up Bob. His only choice would be to run through the fountain itself.

"It's over Giuseppe, just give yourself up," Ron shouted to him.

"Tell us, where the Signore has gone," yelled Giovanni.

"Va fungu, assholes, you'll learn nothing from me because I know nothing." His dialect of telling them to fuck themselves in Italian was rather crude. He made a dash through the spraying waters of the fountain. Ron ran back to intercept him as did the others. Just as he jumped from the basin soaking wet and hardly able to move so drenched was he, Malone appeared with some of his men. The truck and the people escorting it were behind the truck forming a procession as they sang hymns. Malone was in front of the truck. Jones and O'Hara hearing the shouts, saw Giuseppe emerging from the fountain and ran toward the saturated man. Ron got to him first and flung himself in his path. The impact was as if he was hitting a brick wall. Ron bounced off and fell to the ground. Giuseppe stood over Ron with his gun drawn. Bob and Giovanni froze in place, one behind and Bob in front. The delay however gave enough time for the officers to reach them. The procession didn't even see what was happening for they were on the other side of the fountain going to the right of it. From the Coca-Cola Pavilion where the Schulmerich Carrilion was housed, the escorts of the Masterpieces clearly heard the song its bells now rang out. In honor of their arrival, the bells were playing the Ancient Hymn "Pange Lingua." More than any other hymns used at Mass this one by St. Thomas Aquinas was familiar to all those in the procession. And so they took up singing its verses in Gregorian Chant style while the screaming vulgarities of Giuseppe were absorbed by the cascading waters of the fountain.

"Given for us, descending, of a Virgin to proceed, Man with man in converse blending. Scattered be the Gospel seed, Til his sojourn drew to ending, which he closed in wondrous deed…" their voices blended to bring the choirs of angels to earth.

"Get the hell away or I shoot this kid right here." Giuseppe grabbed hold of the collar of Ron's cassock and tried to pull him to his feet. "Get up asshole," he pointed the gun at his head, "Now."

"Let him go jerk, the cops are here." Bob shouted at him. Giuseppe tightly holding the cassock pulled Ron in front of him and faced Bob. While this confrontation took place, behind him Giovanni inched closer. O'Hara was right with him. Continuing to plead for Ron, the sidekick drew all of Giuseppe's attention to him and not what was stealthily happening behind him.

"Kill him and you're dead too. So what's the point?" Bob shouted as the splashing water drowned out his words to anyone not near the scene.

"Shut your face. Let me pass." He shoved Ron forward as he took a step. The words had hardly left his mouth when Bob nodded to Ron. Instantly he feigned collapsing. Giuseppe had to hoist him up to his feet.

Giovanni body checked him as he did so. The gun went flying into the fountain basin and he followed it. In seconds O'Hara and Jones stood at the water's edge with guns drawn. In the background the sounds of singing faded while the crashing waters of the fountain doused Giuseppe as he crawled back onto the pavement. O'hara pulled him up. Jones took hold of his arms and brought them to his backside. He then placed on the cuffs.

The artist, Lone Ranger and Tonto were embracing one another. "That was brilliant Bob, all that shouting at him to distract him."

"I almost peed myself though. What if he just shot you?"

"That pal, he wouldn't have done. It would remove his only leverage." Ron threw his arm around his pal. "Holy…cow, the procession there it goes. Come on we need to get a move on. And please don't tell Susan or the guys what just happened."

"Of course not, Tonto might get too much praise for saving your ass."

"Asshole, I love you but it would scare her and God only knows what Brother Anthony and Father Gregory would do." He gave his pal one of those humble looks with cast down eyes and a tilt of the head. Then he squeezed his arm and gave it a light punch.

The three ran off leaving the police with Giuseppe and joined the end of the procession. Giovanni noted as they got into step with the procession that one was down and that only two remained. It was a reminder which was more of a prophecy.

Once inside the Vatican Pavilion all those who were guards of honor to the Pieta wanted to watch the placing of the Pieta. All were crowded on what would be the double tiered moving walkway. Totally unaware of what just took place they peered through the gigantic plastic glass panel. The Pieta was just being set on the pedestal. The lights were being tested one last time to insure all went well. An announcement was made that the two moving sidewalks, one elevated a little higher were going to have a trial run. With a light jolt they began to move. The Abbey guys and all the others found themselves slowly moving. The bells of the Carillion still filled the air around them. Everything seemed to be running perfectly. The thought of Giuseppe being hauled off was becoming a memory not to be shared at that time.

When they got to the other end of the display shrine they were escorted off and told to take a look at the rest of the Pavilion. Part of their duties at the Pavilion as Seminarians was to act as tour guides. It would be their responsibility to guide the visitors to the moving walkways and insure that they safely got on and off. So naturally they were told to familiarize themselves with everything in the pavilion. That included running around back to the beginning of the moving belts and trying it again.

Iggy and Clarence were at the walkway when Ron, Bob and Giovanni ran up to them. Each one was eager to experience the masterpiece which had gotten so close to being stolen once again. To behold and give thanks that in some small way they had helped to save the priceless treasure made them swell with pride as they once again embraced, then pounded on each other's arms with light punches. The five of them took positions on the lower belt. Their eyes began to water and their heartbeat pounded in their chest with excitement but also with a foreboding of what still had to be done. They had helped save the masterpiece but the mastermind behind the attempted theft and the murder was still at large. But now a brief moment their eyes were affixed on the Pieta. There it was shining in the white lights surrounded by blue lighting as if it was suspended in space in heaven.

"This is so cool, right Giovanni."

"It is as you say quite cool Bob."

"After this how about going to the gift shop and check out stuff?" Ron asked with the thought of the Signore and Andrew still free slightly fading from his thoughts.

"Right, isn't Susan working there?" Bob snickered.

"Don't start with me Bob. I only want to see if she can get us a discount on a small statue of the Pieta. I think my Mom would like it."

"Oh, really, well my Mom would want one too. Okay let's go."

And so, for a brief time, the pursuit of the Signore took a back seat. They entered the gift shop on the other side of the Pavilion past the Chapel area where the Good Statue was to be on display. Susan was radiant in a turquoise blue plaid print skirt which fell below the knee. It was a requirement to work at the Pavilion. She wore a long sleeve white cotton blouse and a jacket which matched the skirt in color. A ribbon of that same color was tied at the top and kept her crimson locks behind her shoulders. She was a pin up girl for a Catholic School no doubt about it.

Bending over the counter the three watched her loading the shelves. "So can we get some help here?"

Recognizing Ron's voice, she didn't bother to turn her head. "We're not open yet, come back tomorrow."

"Tomorrow, that's a long way off. Can't you make an exception?"

She still played around with the shelf arrangement. A smile was on her face. "So who do you think you are the Pope? Come back tomorrow."

Giovanni didn't see the fun in the exchange. He was taking it quite seriously. "Susan, it's us. We wish to buy a Pieta statue for their Mamas and you are being rude."

She jumped up feigning a look of surprise. "Giovanni, I didn't know you were here." She flowed right into her Southern Belle personality. "Well bless my heart if you don't look good in that cassock, just like a priest." She kissed him on the cheek. "So what would your mother like? Oh, hi boys, I'll be right with you." She shot a grin at them.

"It's not for my Mama. It's for the Mamas of Ron and Bob. You have the discount for them, no?"

She couldn't keep up the act. She began to laugh. "Okay guys, so what's on your mind? I thought you'd be patrolling to look for Battista and his goons."

"We needed some comic relief so we came here," Ron shot a grin back to her.

"Will you two stop?" Bob was flustered. "We just cornered Giuseppe and he's in police custody. But we still have to catch a murderer. I think we don't need to squabble like we're twelve."

Ron and Susan instantly became serious. "Sorry guys," they said in unison.

The Carillion was ringing out the 11:00 a.m. hour and playing a tune. They stood silently and were counting the chimes when it dawned on Susan what had been said.

"Giuseppe, you caught him?" she threw her arms around Ron.

He pulled at the collar of his cassock. His faced was a nice shade of pink but getting darker by the second. He squeaked out some words. "Ah, it was really Bob who made it possible."

"Yes Signorina, he was most helpful."

Not letting go of Ron, she turned to look for Bob. "Why you sweet thing there you are all quiet and shy." Letting go of the sweating Ron, she ran around the counter to the other end and kissed him on the cheek.

"Aw shucks, Dorothy, it weren't nothing at all." He giggled and rubbed his cheek.

She knew what he meant. He had done that once before back at the Abbey. "Is that so, well come on boys, let's go down the yellow brick road." Dragging Bob with her and locking arms with Giovanni, who hadn't a clue as to what was happening they took hold of Ron and skipped out of the gift shop singing that famous song from the movie about a girl, and her three pals. The only problem was that they left by the door which led into the chapel and found themselves in front of the statue of the Good Shepherd. Arms dropped and singing stopped.

"This sure ain't Kansas Dorothy," Bob's voice shook while at the same time trying to not be in awe. He made the Sign of the Cross as did everyone. "Do you think Jesus is offended Ron?"

Ron looked around the Chapel. He saw some of his friends kneeling in prayer. "What I think is that Our Lord appreciates that we just had quite the experience catching that thug. That we were being silly but for a good reason; but it would be nice maybe if we pray a Hail Mary, Our Father and Glory Be just to make sure we're okay with Him." They found an open kneeler and had a conversation with the Lord.

Trying to be as reverent as possible they were leaving the chapel when Sacha and Stephano ran up to them.

"Where's the Detective Sargent?" Stephano was excited.

"We haven't seen him since we got into the pavilion. Maybe he's questioning Giuseppe someplace."

"Well there's no time to lose Ron. I swear that we just saw Andrew near the Globe fountain."

"No way, that's where Giuseppe was just caught."

"I tell you we saw him and that means the Signore is around, he has to be."

Now it was Giovanni who became agitated. He wanted to know exactly where Andrew was spotted and in what direction he was going. "This is the answer to my prayer. I will avenge Sheila." He took hold of Stephano by the shoulders. "You will take me to where you saw him, yes?"

"Okay, get your hands off me or I'll slug you. Sacha, go find the Detective Malone and tell him where to find us."

"Ron, what does he mean by 'avenge Sheila'?"

"I don't want to even think about it Susan," he began to frantically unbutton his cassock. "He can't go alone with Stephano. Damn these buttons." He tugged at them to the breaking point.

"Calm down Ron, here let me help." Susan slowly unbuttoned each one without difficulty. "You're just too upset, that's all."

"We've saved that man all week from certain death and now he wants to walk right into the lion's den. I don't understand it."

"There all finished," she pulled off the cassock and folded it on the counter. "I'll come with you. Everything is closing up now anyway. My Mom is going back to the hotel with everyone else."

Susan was quite observant. The Pavilion was emptying out. Iggy and Clarence wandered in the gift shop looking for Ron and Bob. When they saw Susan unbuttoning Ron's cassock they tried to not react or make a comment. They did however go up to Bob who was taking his cassock off without any help.

"We're going back to the hotel, are you guys coming with us?" asked Clarence still with an eye on Susan now stooping down so as to reach the lower buttons on Ron's cassock.

"I don't think so. Giovanni is hell bent on finding the Signore. He just heard that Andrew has been spotted on the fair grounds."

"Andrew, he's no match for him. I should know." Iggy looked around at all the religious artifacts surrounding him. He felt embarrassed even to hint at how he knew how strong Andrew was. "We got them once, so we'll do it again. I'm coming with you."

"Don't leave me out. Someone with a bit of sense has to watch over you." Clarence was assuming the role of big brother once again.

There was almost a feeling of separation as four more cassocks were folded and placed on the glass top counter displaying a variety of Rosaries. One by one the guys and finally the artist placed their cassock next to Ron's. Except for Giovanni, who had used his as a disguise, the cassock was a symbol of their vocation. It reminded them that they were to serve the People of God through the Church. It reminded them of their responsibility to bring peace and comfort to others. And now as they stood facing that symbol neatly laid upon the counter top, they were feeling something quite different. Giovanni burned with revenge in his heart. The four guys wanted to protect Giovanni from doing something rash, something he might regret. At the same time they wanted justice for their friend. The challenge would be how to bring justice to the heinous crime and not more bloodshed. As Susan watched and helped with this ritual like disrobing, she saw that difference between their calling and their need to seek justice.

"Well there you have it. All lined up quite nicely." She looked into their eyes and knew what was in their hearts. She saw the fury, the struggle to be men of peace yet also of justice, and the bond of friendship so strong as to risk themselves on behalf of their friends." So what do we do now?" she asked with a slight smile.

"What we do first is to say good-bye to you," Ron insisted.

"No way; that's going to happen. I said I'm coming with you and that I am."

The torrent of protests about her safety didn't chip at her resolve at all. Finally, the obvious had to be stated. Stephano was the one to point out that Andrew and the Signore were dangerous men. "They would not hesitate to shoot you any less than they would kill the guys."

She didn't flinch. "Listen Stephano, you don't know me. But these guys do, well not Giovanni of course. They know what we've been through back in Wisconsin at the Abbey. I know what you are planning to do is quite heroic in your minds but ridiculously dangerous should you actually find them somewhere on the grounds of the Fair. The odds are that they are long gone so don't get yours shorts in an uproar. I'm coming along." She slipped the chain of her purse about her neck and walked to the door. "Well are we going on this wild goose chase or not?"

Stephano looked at her with wide eyes and respect. The guys followed her lead and walked to the door. They entered an empty Pavilion and passed the Pieta exhibit. Standing in a line in front of the darkened display except for a security spotlight on the statue, they paused. Ron felt compelled to say something. He reflected on the symbolism. "Jesus gave his all for his friends, actually for all people and Mary was there with him until the very end. See how she now holds him so tenderly. At the same time she is also presenting his sacrifice to the world. Whether or not we are being noble and seeking justice or just looking to get even, to be avenged, we only know in our hearts. But we are all together on this venture, 'all for one and one for all' as the Musketeers would say. We can only pray for God's blessing and guidance to do the right thing."

Susan looked at this young man who suddenly spoke like a philosopher and theologian. Her heart sunk a little in that thought. For now he had distanced himself from the pursuit of the ordinary things of life. He seemed to be at the brink of a celestial understanding of love.

They walked out into the bright sunshine, surrounded by the message of the World coming together. They sought to find two people who would destroy such common purpose. Once at the fountain where Giuseppe was captured, they decided to divide up into smaller groups. They would cover more territory and not be so obvious, as they searched. Stephano took Iggy and Clarence and Giovanni went with the Three Musketeers.

Except for security people and some police presence all was quiet. The workers, Pieta guards of honor and official guests had left to rest and get prepared for the grand opening rehearsal. Stephano chose to retrace their steps back to the dock. He thought the Signore might have a boat ready to use for his escape. On the way they came upon Sacha who was with the Detective Sargent and Officers Van Buren and O'Hara who just returned from sending Giuseppe off to a holding cell. Malone was not thrilled that once again the Abbey guys were taking matters into their own hands.

"I have one murder yet to prove and a heist attempt which must be kept a secret and now this. "O'Hara, you come with me. Van Buren you help Stephano. Maybe you'll be lucky and find those other men who were at that meeting. As for Battista, if he's smart, he's long gone." Malone and O'Hara headed for the fountain. "Keep in contact with the walkie-talkie."

He called out as he held up his, "Now if only that De Cenza kid kept his we'll be able to find them." He then hung the device on his belt.

Inside the closed Indonesian Pavilion Andrew had returned and reported that Battista's plan to bait the artist worked. He was sure that Sacha had seen him.

"Those traitors; we will deal with them in due time. But first, the artist for once he's out of the picture they cannot prove that I murdered Sheila."

"You, Signore, I thought you said it was Giovanni."

"Yes, yes it was all an accident which he started. Now tell me again, where did they spot you?"

Running aimlessly from street to street connecting the Pavilions, the huffing and puffing seminarians and Susan finally yelled to the artist.

"Giovanni stop; this isn't getting us anywhere." She bent over to catch her breath. "We have no idea where Andrew could have gone. But if there is one thing I do know, it's that he wanted one of us to see him; why else would he be alone and right where Giuseppe was captured?"

Battista is baiting us; so let's nibble at that bait." Those cow-like eyes sparkled.

"I know that look Ron, what's going on in there," Bob poked Ron's head.

He was hesitant to put forth his idea because it did have an element of placing someone other than himself in danger. On top of that the person in that position is the very one who Battista accused of betrayal. And so they sat alongside the Indonesian Pavilion, totally unaware that inside was the very man who sought to get rid of Giovanni. And if he was successful it would be virtually impossible to prove that Battista actually killed Sheila Murphy.

Susan began to walk up and down past the boarded up doors of the pavilion. "I wonder why this place is still boarded up. The Fair is due to open with a big ceremony."

Bob tried to peek through the slats covering the glass area of the doors. "It looks like nothing is in there from what I can see."

"That's because the United States and Indonesia had a falling out. They're not coming to the Fair. I think the President disinvited them. It was in the news just before we came to New York."

"Shit Ron, that's it; what better place to hide than in plain sight and in a building no one would expect to have people." Bob was excited, so was Giovanni. They both began to pull on the wooden slats across the doors. One of the doors opened. "Holy crap, it's open."

Ron and Susan ran over to them. "Don't make any noise. If they are hiding in here we don't have to advertise that we're here. Remember we're just baiting them not confronting them. Okay Bob, open the door a little bit." Ron poked his head in. It was dark save for the sunlight coming in through windows high up on the façade of the building. Displays or at least places for exhibits were set up but were empty, at least those which he could see. He popped back out and closed the door gently. "So I guess we go with my idea since we're all here. Giovanni what we don't need is to be cornered in this place by Andrew and the Signore both of whom surely have guns. I'll go in and act like well like a lost tourist or something. Surely if they're in here they will hear me. When I think they can see me and I them, I'll make a run for it. Andrew surely will chase me down. That's where you come in Giovanni. You need to be at the fountain. Bob and Susan will go with you. Bob will stay out of sight with Susan. You will be alone."

"I understand. But why would I be just standing there at the fountain?"

Susan opened her purse and pulled out a map. "You'll be studying this. It's a map of the fair grounds. And I will be with you to make it look believable." She turned to Ron who was about to object and she knew it. "Ron De Cenza, he can't be there alone. It will be like an alarm saying that it's a trap."

He caved as did everyone. Ron was insisting that Bob also be with them. The suggestion didn't fly.

"Are you crazy? There are two of them with guns in there, if they are inside and only one of you…" he shuddered. "Two of us can split them up because we could run away in different directions."

Susan insisted that Bob was right and Giovanni agreed. Bob and Ron opened the door which despite the boards across it and not being used made no audible sound. They disappeared in the shadows of the welcoming room. At that moment his walkie-talkie began to buzz. He shut it off. He wasn't able to hear the message.

"Ron De Cenza, if you can hear this, my men are with your friends. They are searching the dock area. I am on the way to the fair grounds. Repeat on way to fair grounds. Meet me at the fountain." It was the Detective Sargent Malone's voice which went unheard.

The Carillion was ringing out the 3:00 p.m. hour. Susan and Giovanni slowed down their sprint and stopped at edge of the fountain's basin which faced the street leading to the closed Indonesian Pavilion. They held the map between them and began to search their surroundings by glancing over the map. The sparkling water shooting up into the gleaming hollow Unisphere sculpture came splashing down causing a spray to hit them. Being on edge the water hitting them was startling. Jumping away from the fountain, they shook the water off the map, totally unaware of the Signore's overcoat lying across the popcorn cart directly behind them.

In what would have served as perhaps the gift shop or office area of the pavilion a hushed silence pervaded. Andrew and Battista heard something. In the stillness Battista was sure he had heard something.

"Andrew that was a buzzing sound like a radio was being tuned in."

"I heard it too." He nodded to his boss and smiled. "I think I should get myself seen again. I'll go to the fountain again, it's the most visible spot and in an open area."

"Good thinking," The Signore patted his cheek, the one on his face. He leaned into Andrew and whispered. "You will live in luxury when this is over because you have stayed loyal to me in my darkest hour."

"You are too kind Signore," Andrew took the liberty of kissing Battista on each cheek as was customary. He then slipped out of the room with the hope of luring out whoever was around.

Coming into the welcoming atrium he headed for the doors. Ron and Bob prepared to be seen as soon as they could see Andrew. As much as the goon wanted to catch whoever was in that pavilion so too did they want to be seen. A little dispute arose as to who would run first. Ron worried that Bob had never completed the mile run back in college before they entered the seminary. Therefore he could be easily caught in Ron's mind. They agreed to both be seen simultaneously. Andrew hopefully would pause to choose which one to chase. That would give them time to get out of the pavilion and into daylight. Neither one would consider what would happen if Andrew decided to shoot at them. They were crouched opposite of each other behind small display cases designed in a style to accentuate the products of Indonesia. One of them had empty shelves but the one where Bob was had jewelry pieces in hand carved wooden boxes. Bob slipped his hand up and found the glass door unlocked. He peeked around the base and saw no one so he grabbed hold of one of the wooden boxes. What good that would do against a bullet was anyone's guess but it gave him something to throw. And that's what he did. Andrew jumped around and fired toward the sound of the crashing box. The bullet smashed through another glass display. The sound of shattering glass brought out Battista just as Ron and Bob made a dash for the door. The light from the open door attracted Andrew who gave chase. Battista was still at the office door and did not see them.

As if on the wings of Mercury, they ran toward the Unisphere Fountain of the Continents. Andrew was a tough man but was not a runner. The guys managed to outdistance him. Yelling for Giovanni and Susan to get away, they came into their sight. The map went flying as the artist took hold of Susan and pulled her to a popcorn vendor cart behind which they hid. Giovanni recognized the black overcoat immediately. He grabbed the coat. "This is his, the Signore." He began to search the pockets, for what he didn't know. "Look here, these are the gloves." He grew sullen. The dried blood of Sheila had been seen.

Susan had to get him back to the moment. "The gloves, that's great. It will prove that he was there in the warehouse. And if that is Sheila's blood or even yours when he hit you, you're on your way to being proved innocent. Maybe your Signore guy isn't that smart after all."

He placed the gloves into Ron's jacket which he was wearing. His heart beat thumped faster now just thinking that Battista may be coming into sight. Just as he was about to toss the overcoat aside, he felt something else, something hard which hit his leg. He removed it and slipped it into his pants pocket.

Coming into the Fountain plaza was Andrew. He was clearly visible now. Giovanni patted his pocket and dropped the coat. As he made his move to attack Andrew out in the open, Susan held him back. She saw a gun in Andrew's hand. The dark eyes scanned the basin of the fountain.

The figures of Ron and Bob running around the basin of the fountain were easily identified through the spray of water. They were sprinting toward the cart when Ron saw the artist holding the overcoat and taking something out of it. He had no time to process what he saw. The thug fired a shot, through the spouts of water it went for its mark but grazed the stainless steel structure of the sculpture instead. Ron pulled back Bob and yelled for Susan to stay down. Giovanni took hold of her and shielded her. She struggled out of his hold and ran toward Ron.

Andrew took aim following her, knowing he might be able to hit two with one bullet. His finger pressed against the trigger, the hammer of the gun pulled back ready to release its deadly cargo. It was as if all was taking place in slow motion but it was but a fraction of seconds. The echo of the shot pierced the ears of security people and Malone who was just coming onto the plaza of the fountain. The shot had gone wild for at that moment Giovanni had tackled Andrew at the ankles. Artist and thug tumbled across the plaza, the one trying to get the gun and the other trying to shoot the artist before he could do that. A knee rammed into the groin of the thug. Another shot was fired as Andrew screamed more in shock than in pain. Giovanni froze in fear which enabled Andrew to throw him off.

"Now asshole, it's your turn." Andrew swung around and aimed for Giovanni.

Malone on the other side of the fountain drew his weapon. He knelt and waited for the boys and Susan to get out of range, but could not do the same for Giovanni. He was too close to Andrew, he had to take the shot or the artist would be dead. Through the arches of water spouts he gazed and fired.

Andrew was hit. His body twisted with the shot digging through his left shoulder. He fell onto the rim of the basin. He was trying to push himself up when Bob jumped on him from the rear as Ron grabbed his hand holding the gun. It flew out of his hand. Ron jumped for the airborne gun, caught it in mid-air and threw it into the crystal blue water of the fountain. In seconds Malone and O'Hara were on him and pulling a rather soaked Bob off his back. Ron was cursing himself that he just got rid of what he might need to get Battista as he ran toward Susan. She was kneeling next to the rather dazed Giovanni, who was assuring her that he wasn't hit.

"What the hell were you boys thinking? I tried calling you but I had no response." Malone was holding onto Bob and called for Ron to come to him. Andrew was leaning on the rim of the basin breathing with difficulty, blood oozing out of his shoulder now spread across his shirt. "Bob, see that coat over there by that cart. Get it and hold the sleeve against the wound to stop the bleeding." He looked down on Andrew. "And you jerk don't move or you'll bleed to death."

Frozen in place alone in what seemed a vast emptiness about him, Ron glanced at Susan now helping Giovanni to his feet and they turned to face the Detective Sargent. "There's no time to explain," began Ron. "Battista is in the Indonesian Pavilion."

As soon as those words were absorbed in the ears of Giovanni, he bolted from Susan's hold and began to run.

Susan shouted, "Stop Giovanni stop, you'll get killed."

Ron swung around to catch a glimpse of Giovanni running off. Susan gave chase. He tried to cut her off. "Susan, stay back, he's after Battista." She refused and ran with him. They were outdistanced already. Not until Giovanni was at the doors, trying each one did they finally catch up. "Giovanni let the police take him. It's over. He has no way out."

The plea fell on deaf ears. Pulling Susan away from the door which wasn't locked, Giovanni paused to look into her pleading eyes. "Mi dispiacere, I am so sorry Signorina." He pulled it open. Ron made a move to block him. "Get back Ron, this I must do."

Looking over Susan's shoulder he saw Malone running hard with Bob, Clarence and Iggy who had caught up with him. "Stay back Susan, I mean it. We don't need three people dead." She stepped aside, the thought of what he said causing her eyes to fill with tears. Ron followed Giovanni into the Pavilion.

As he entered he heard Giovanni shouting. "I am here Signore, show yourself or be the coward who can only kill innocent women."

When Ron reached Giovanni, he was a perfect target standing in a ray of sunshine toward the middle of the atrium. He pulled the artist back into the shadows.

"Leave me be Ron. I want him to see me." He tried to break the hold on his arm. In doing so he dragged both of them into a shaft of sunlight. A shot rang out. The glass of the display case next to them shattered. Ron pulled the artist to the ground.

Again Giovanni shouted. "Show yourself coward."

From the shadows on the other end of the atrium another shot was fired. It rang through the building splintering a bamboo lined wall of the atrium. Battista kept moving in a circular pattern keeping the atrium wall on one side of him. Giovanni and Ron back in the shadows after dropping to the floor crawled toward where the shot was fired.

At the doors Malone was now with Susan who was telling him what Giovanni did and how Ron followed him in. Stephano, Sacha, Bob, Clarence and Iggy were with him. His men were stationed around the building at any entrance or exit area. Stephano, hearing that the Signore was in there slipped behind Malone and ran into the building. "Stay back, all of you," Malone ordered. "Jones, make sure Susan and those lads are out of danger." He then followed Stephano in. Both had their guns drawn. It would now be a gun fight more in their favor. Malone accepted the fact that Stephano was there and armed so he used him. Telling him to go to the right, he then went to the left in a circular movement along the walls of the atrium. In the center were Ron and Giovanni. And somewhere in between was the Signore Battista. It was only a matter of time before someone spotted him.

Giovanni was shouting again. "You killed Sheila. She was only kind to you and you smashed her head."

A voice full of fury and hate rang out in reply. "You, I gave you everything. I plucked you out of nothing and made you into something. Yet you betrayed me. I spit on you." And spit he did though on the floor.

"And I spit on you, a liar and murderer."

Battista spun around and there stepping out of the shadows was Stephano his once body guard and confidant. "Et tu Brute, you too betray me who loved you."

"You are no Caesar, you are scum who lies and cheats and kills. You said the artist killed Sheila but first that it was an accident and here I stand to learn the truth from one whom I served loyally."

Battista held his gun steady aiming it at Stephano. "You are right; I am no Caesar for I shall kill those who have betrayed me. Show yourself artist."

Giovanni pushed Ron away and stood in the center of the atrium just twenty feet away from Battista and Stephano. "Here I stand Signore. You are the betrayer not me, not Stephano not Sacha. You betrayed our trust in you by what you have done. You lied about the Pieta I created for you. You killed the only person who brought kindness to us. And now you stand ready to kill me. Well here I am. I look forward to joining my love, yes Signore my love. With all my heart I look forward to joining her, so your gun holds no fear for me." His steps were slow and almost indiscernible. Malone was now at Ron's side on the floor.

"Detective, please don't confront. Giovanni doesn't care if he dies and surely he will if you attack Battista."

Twenty feet had now become ten feet of separation of the Signore from the artist. "That's it come closer so that I can't miss." Battista swung his gun first to face Stephano and then pointing it at Giovanni.

"Shoot me Signore, get it over with."

"No never, you shall not kill him," Stephano yelled at Battista as he ran toward him.

The Signore swung his gun and shot. Stephano reared backwards as the bullet pierced his chest. He collided with the display case of jewelry and plummeted to the floor. It was just enough time. Giovanni lunged for Battista and brought him down. Giovanni was no match for the larger man but he was holding his own. Stephano lay just a few feet away from Malone and Ron.

Before Malone could get up, Ron had crawled to the side of Stephano. He was dying in his arms. "You are a good boy, you will make a fine priest," he said with his last breath.

Ron traced the Sign of the Cross on his brow and set him down gently. Perhaps it was the only kindness since his youth that he had experienced. Ron crawled toward the wrestling Giovanni and Battista. Malone was now standing with his gun drawn but didn't have a clear shot. Ron filled with righteous indignation and blind courage pounced on the two rolling on the stone floor. He landed on Battista's arm and kicked the gun out of his hand. As he leapt to retrieve the weapon, Battista managed to keep Giovanni in his grasp.

"It's over Battista," shouted Malone. "Let Giovanni go."

The much larger man placed a strangle hold around the neck of the artist. He pulled him toward the wall of doors. "Stay away, I will snap his neck." Ron backed off not having found the gun. Malone firmly held his gun waiting for a clear shot to Battista's head.

Inch by inch Battista moved toward the doors. Malone, knowing that on the other side of them waited his men. Whatever he was trying to do was doomed to failure. So Malone stayed in place. He waved his arm to Ron to do the same. "Stay put."

Giovanni had become silent. Ron could see that his hand was moving, his fingers grasping down into his pocket. A silvery object was pulled out. In the shouting match going on, Battista didn't see the finger press the knife and a blade appearing. The artist suddenly came to life and resisted. The surprise loosened Battista's grip just enough for him to turn and plunge the knife into Battista's lower chest.

A screech of pain boomed out as he fell against the door. "So now you know what it's like to kill." The weight of his body banged against the door which was then pulled open. Falling backwards his arm let go of Giovanni who was pulled back by Ron. The Signore fell sprawled at the feet of Bob and Susan. They had pulled open the door when they heard the shouting just beyond it. Bathed in sunlight standing in the doorway were Ron and Giovanni. The words of the Signore rang through the artist. He was still holding the knife with the blood of Battista dripping from it. They didn't move. Like the statue he had carved from the marble, they stood looking at the man who did pluck the artist from obscurity but who also lied to him about how the statue would be used and killed the love of his life. Ron reached for the knife loosely held in Giovanni's hand.

"You can let go of it now, my friend."

"He told the truth. I have killed. I am no better than he was."

Life came back into their stone-like bodies. Ron turned him and embraced him. He whispered into his ear. "Evil is defeated, you only defended yourself, my friend."

"No, it was more than that. I didn't care if I died but I knew that he wanted to live. I took that desire away from him."

"We are only human. He was about to take your life. He did murder again, his own man who had served him with blind loyalty."

Behind them Malone appeared in the doorway. Sacha made his way toward that door and had slipped by unnoticed. He found Stephano's body, knelt down and cradled it in his arms. "You are free now my friend."

The Carillion was ringing out another tune honoring the arrival of Michelangelo's Pieta. It was a familiar hymn known by everyone around that doorway. "Holy God we praise thy name, Lord above we bow down before thee…" The sky above them was turning pink as the sun began its descent. The waters of the Unisphere Fountain of the Continents splashed as if nothing had happened. The sirens began to pierce the silence. That stillness had pervaded across the fair grounds and inside the Vatican Pavilion where a lone light shone upon Michelangelo's Pieta. No one would ever know just how close it came to being stolen. Malone let the door behind him close and quietly moved closer to Ron who held onto Giovanni. The Signore lay still on the pavement. O'Hara kneeling next to the body placed his fingers on Battista's neck. He nodded to Malone that it was over. Bob glanced at the overcoat he was absentmindedly holding. The same one he used to help Andrew until the medics arrived. Now realizing that it belonged to Battista he began to lay it over the body. Susan helped him adjust it so that the face of the Signore was completely covered.

Ron watched his best pal and the one who made him crazy with pained eyes as they reverently placed the coat over the body of Battista. He glanced at Giovanni who despite all that had happened made the Sign of the Cross over himself and was praying. The final words of that prayer entered Ron's heart. "…pray for us sinners, now and at the hour of our death. Amen"

He turned and looked into the eyes of the Detective Sargent. "Stephano told me that I was a good boy and would make a fine priest. I just don't know if I'm good or will ever become a priest."

The Detective Sargent looked into those distraught brown eyes of the questioning young man. His mind reached back to his own Catechism days and from them he chose the words. "Ron, aren't we taught that we were created to know, love and serve the Lord? We travel on this path of life never quite knowing where we are going but yet have a focus. On that path we may fall in love…the kind which Susan has for you or the bond between Bob and you…different kinds of love. The greatest of these is remembering that God is love and connects us to each other."

Malone was rather proud that such words were coming from his often irreverent mouth. He knew he had struck a nerve when he mentioned Susan and that it had created only more doubt in Ron. But he went on. "Ron, you and those you love all served your Church and our community well this day. It was not the kind of service which you would expect in terms of what you are thinking. Yet, it was placing your life on the line to save others. Didn't Jesus say that there is no greater service than to give one's life for a friend? I don't know what your future holds but I do know that what you did during all of this was good." The Detective was now quite pleased with his words of guidance. He smiled, one of those fatherly expressions offered to show encouragement. His hand rested on Ron's shoulder while he was slipping the knife out of the lad's hand.

Ron looked at the blood on his hand. He lifted his eyes slightly to avoid the glare of the setting sun but more so the eyes of the Detective. Those words of the Detective Sargent were heard by more than just him. He saw tears streaking down the cheeks of Giovanni, Susan and Bob. In his own eyes water gathered as once again the words of Stephano rang out in his thoughts of the future.

'You are a good boy and will make a fine priest.'

Unisphere

The Pieta Exhibit
New York World's Fair

EPILOGUE

The blood had been washed away and the tears had dried but the words of Stephano to Ron still could be heard even days later. Perhaps it was the funeral for the one time body guard of the Signore Battista and that of Sheila Murphy which kept them ringing in his thoughts. It was a most unusual one in that Sheila or Stephano had no family. It fell to the artist Giovanni Gaglioni who loved Sheila in secret and to the driver of the Signore, one Sacha Dumbroski, to arrange for the service. The two had the support of the seminarians of the Abbey who would serve as the pall bearers as well. Susan and her mother took on the responsibility of seeing to the flowers and one thing of importance to Giovanni. That was to insure that the Irish lace shawl which Giovanni had placed over her was cleaned and placed around her shoulders once again. Thanks to Abbot Lawrence and Father Gregory permission had been granted to conduct a double funeral at the historic old Cathedral of St. Patrick's on Mott Street at the entrance of Little Italy.

It was a very small funeral. The mass was celebrated by the Abbot with Father Gregory assisting. In terms of attendance it was quite intimate, just the Abbey guys, Brother Anthony who read from the Scriptures at the funeral mass and the Detective Sargent Malone, Officers O'Hara, Van Buren and Jones. They had grown quite close to Ron and Bob, taking on almost fatherly roles which were a mixture of pride in their persistence in getting to the truth and frustration when they placed themselves in danger. Their relationship with them as well as Iggy was not soon to end. The three would be testifying at the trials. While the avenger artist and his pal Ron confronted Battista, his co-conspirators were captured before they even left the grounds of the World Fair. Their testimony would be needed at their trials as well as those of Andrew and Giuseppe, the two body guards captured at the Unisphere Fountain of the Continents.

Sacha because of his cooperation in the apprehension of Battista was already granted a sentence of probation based on his helping to cover-up Sheila's death.

As for Giovanni, there was nothing to prosecute as he was not involved with the plot to steal the Pieta and certainly the murder of the woman he loved. As for the stabbing of Battista, the D.A. had ruled it to be self-defense as part of the struggle. Thanks to the Archdiocese of New York there was a tiny light of hope shed on him. It was decided that the Pieta he created belonged to him and thus its sale would be left to him. A Basilica Church in Chicago had already heard of the statue and offered a bid to purchase it.

The cars were now returning from the small Catholic Cemetery in Queens where Sheila and Stephano would rest in peace, a peace they rarely experienced in life. Giovanni yearned to have been the one to be next to her for eternity. But it was not to be. He would have to go on with life, how he would do so would be the question. The answer he was still forming in his grief stricken mind.

The caravan of police cars and unmarked cars were making their way to the grounds of the World's Fair. It was a mild spring April afternoon, with the sun shining brightly on the day before Opening Day. Hundreds of people were in their Pavilions and Exhibit Buildings making those last minute adjustments to their displays. The excitement was building as each hour passed bringing the opening ceremony closer. But for those silently looking out the windows of those cars as they approached the Meadow Lake Gate at the end of the Flushing River, those fluttering flags of the nations, revolving towers of the New York Pavilion, the heavenly chimes of the Carillion announcing the 1:00 P.M. hour and the Unisphere sculpture of the globe gleaming in the sunlight raised little joy.

At the same time they understood how important their roles were to the success of the Vatican Pavilion. Susan and her mother would be part of the staff operating the gift shop. The guys of the Abbey were to be the guides at the Pieta Exhibit. After all that had happened since that day when they found a bloodied Giovanni at that warehouse doorway, everyone sought to find purpose and hope in what was to be the highlight of their lives. Brother Anthony had arranged with the Pavilion of Spain to provide a luncheon at their café outside along the flowing waters known as the Fountains of the Fair. Afterwards there would be a final run through of their duties on opening day at the nearby Vatican Pavilion.

By the time the Carillion was chiming out the 2:00 p.m. hour the luncheon was ending. The Detective Sargent and his officers had greeted everyone and were offering their final good wishes to Father Gregory and Brother Anthony. He had wished to do so with Ron and Bob as well but they were not to be found.

"I do apologize for the boys' absence Detective Malone; it seems that those two are missing again."

The Detective Sargent shot a glance of "oh no, now what" to his officers. He forced out a smile in an effort to hide his fear that those two were up to something which might drag he and his team back to the Fair grounds. His bushy reddish eyebrows lifted high onto his brow. It gave away his true feelings despite his words. "Well I suppose all of this has been too much for them, Brother Anthony. I think I'll walk with you to the pavilion if you don't mind."

"That would be most pleasant. Perhaps they ran off to see the Pieta before the crowds come."

"Perhaps Brother, but…" he held his thought for a moment, wondering if by some remote chance they would actually already be in the Vatican Pavilion. Cracking a slight smile he soon dismissed the thought. "We are talking about those two aren't we?"

Brother Anthony laughed as they walked onto the path. The sun glistened off the cascading fountains rushing alongside them in a series of mini water falls created by a slightly descending slope of the manmade waterway. "I think I see what you mean Detective. We are talking about Ron and Bob. But they'll show up; of that I am quite sure."

What neither of them knew was that Ron was not with Bob at all. He sat quite alone at the basin of the Unisphere fountain. He had rolled up one of the long sleeves of the white shirt and loosened the black tie. His cassock which was worn at the funeral service was nowhere to be seen. He was dipping his hand into the crystal clear water lifting it out and then watching the water drip from it. This he was repeating over and over. It was rather morose in a way for it was reminding him of the blood from the knife he had taken from Giovanni after the fight with the Signore Battista. He kept repeating what Stephano had told him about being good and making a fine priest. He gazed transfixed on each drop splashing down and creating small moon craters in the azure blue water of the basin.

Suddenly he punched the water. The result of the impact was an explosion of chlorine treated water splashing in his face. "Shit," with his other hand he took hold of a handkerchief in his black pants pocket and pulled it out. "What a dumb ass you are Ron De Cenza," he wiped his face.

"Well now, that's the first time I heard you admit that…" Bob was walking toward him from behind having come out of the Court of the 1939 World's Fair which was also held in Flushing Meadows.

Ron swung around at first not realizing who was speaking. "Who the hell…oh, it's just you. Well don't get all excited. I just got wet that's all and was aggravated with myself."

Bob stopped in his tracks about twelve feet from his best pal. He held up a cassock. "What do you mean by 'it's just you,' like I'm a nobody to you? Well go to hell pal…"

Ron interrupted him. "Who said that you were a nobody? I never said such a thing. I was just surprised that's all. Don't get all hot and bothered over it."

"Well it just seems like you take me for granted. You know I left the luncheon worried about you," Bob was calming down and took a few steps forward. "I guess we're all upset after everything and sensitive." He lifted up the cassock hanging over his arm.

"You're of German stock; you're not supposed to be sensitive…"

"What? There you go assigning things to me. Well I'm my own person and if I say I'm sensitive then I am. And you're an asshole if you think certain people can just be clumped into one pot just because they come from a certain background.

Coming to his feet while rolling down the sleeve of his shirt, Ron became emotional and found that he couldn't control it. So he tried to change the subject. "Is that my cassock?"

Bob looked at the cassock. "Well who else could it belong to? Certainly none of the other guys could fit their ass into this." He swung it up as if he was about to throw it but thought better of it. "I found it in the bathroom and knew it was yours right away. So I've been looking all over for you. Given who you are, I went back to the Indonesia pavilion..."

"Knowing who I am; you just did the same thing that you accused me of doing. Just because I am of Italian heritage therefore I must have that Latin blood boiling in me. I'm not that gruesome as to want to see the spot where Stephano and Battista were killed." Ron was now about six feet away from his friend, the brother he never had. Tears were flowing, like those drops of water did from his hand, down over his reddening cheeks. "Go away, look at me...no don't look at me. Go away."

Seeing his pal in this state melted away the anger. Instead of walking away, he approached Ron. Bob took one step then paused, another step and another pause until he was face to face with his distraught friend. "Tonto would never dessert the Lone Ranger." He placed his arm around his pal.

Ron let him. A quivering tremor could be felt flowing through his body. The silence between them just standing there was only broken by the geyser-like eruptions of the spouts of water of the fountain. Each of them was trying to find words to express themselves. And each of them found that to be most challenging in that just the right ones had to be found so as not to make the other upset. Being men of nineteen as they both would point out obliged them to try to find the courage to face the future and stand up for what is good. But that idea of manhood was what was being questioned in Ron's mind as he reflected on those words of Stephano and also of what the Detective Sargent told him. Was he really a good person? It was he after all who supported Giovanni in his quest to avenge the death of Sheila. It was he who knew of the knife's existence in the overcoat on the vendor's cart. It was he who knew that Giovanni had found it and kept it. It was he who kept silent about this knowledge of the knife. And it was because of that silence that Battista was dead by Giovanni's hand. But it might as well have been his hand which thrust it into the Signore as far as he was concerned. Finally, his voice was found. It cracked a bit but it was found.

"The Lone Ranger would never have left Tonto to go on a wild goose chase to find him."

A squeeze of fingers on his shoulder was felt, "But I found you and am here to help if I can. But first let's get you cleaned up and into your cassock. We have to rehearse our parts for tomorrow's ceremony."

Ron's big cow-like cocoa brown eyes now red with emotion looked into his friends blue eyes, as blue as the waters of the fountain next to which they stood. It was probably the first time he even noticed how blue his pal's eyes so filled with concern were. "Christ, don't look at me that way. I think I'm turning into an Iggy. Your eyes, I see they're like blue but not only that they are full of light…"

"Stop right there," Bob shook Ron hard. "Wake up and listen to what you just said. You of all people know that you can't just turn into an Iggy…I mean a gay guy. Do you want to have sex with me? Now that's a choice. Do you want to have sex with Susan? Now that's another choice. But should I be gay today and then tomorrow maybe not; that's not a choice. You are what you are. You just come to understand it better over time and choose how to live that life of the person who you are."

"My God, Bob, you've become a philosopher."

"Well that's Tonto's role, to bring what shall I call it…clarity to a situation. So here's your cassock. Put it on and we'll talk about this tonight."

"I can't Bob." Ron pushed the cassock holding arm away from him. "Stephano said that I'd be a fine priest but I'm not sure of that. I get a boner any time Susan touches me. I helped Giovanni kill Battista. I swear a lot. I see how blue your eyes are. I constantly break rules and give a hard time to people like the Detective Sargent. I hardly ever pray kneeling down in a quiet fashion; you know just God and me in a conversation. It seems like unholy things are attracted to me like the Signore's sidekick was to my ass in that meeting room." He couldn't go on with his litany. He turned away and began to walk around the fountain basin.

Bob chased after him. Pulling on the collar of his shirt he brought him to a halt. In no uncertain terms he impressed upon him that they were only nineteen. Clarity and understanding doesn't happen overnight. But more than the cliché answer he began to speak to each of Ron's protestations about his vocation. He pointed out that he and all the guys were young and feeling their oats, as his father would tell him. Getting a hard-on when a pretty girl is around is a natural thing not often sought after. He went on to point out that if swearing was to be grounds for not being a priest then almost none in the seminary would qualify. Cleaning up one's language was part of maturing into the vocation. As for Giovanni, he pointed out that both he and Ron were about to be killed by the Signore Battista. What choices were there than to stop him in any way possible. And as for unholy things being attracted to him; whose fault was it that they had the good taste to admire a good looking guy. Or just maybe part of his calling was to see things that are wrong and try to fix them and that may result in more than just uncomfortable situations arising. As for praying, Brother Anthony made it quite clear that a conversation with God didn't have to be on one's knees or on the beads of the Rosary. There are all types of prayer. Personally Bob thought that God liked just plain talking. When he got to the 'blue eyes' part, Tonto didn't quite know how to respond. He chalked it up to being a sensitive guy and shouldn't priests be honed into the feelings and needs of his flock.

"So there you have it pal, put on this cassock. We are being called to service and that's all it is right now for us."

Ron embraced his pal. "And don't you ever tell a soul about what I said about your eyes or so help me I'll punch those lights in them out." They both laughed as he put on the cassock and began to button it up, "So what now my friend?"

"Hey I'm only the sidekick in this duo; you're the one with the ideas."

"Well then I say we should look for the good in what we have done here at the World's Fair and ride off in the sunset shouting," Ron paused as he took hold of the last button near the hem of the black cloth of the cassock. He smiled broadly as having accomplished the buttoning without cursing and returned to his thought. "Hi Oh Silver up and away. Tomorrow is another day."

Lifting up their cassocks they began to run down the Court of Nations Road toward the Vatican Pavilion.

"Hey, Tonto you forgot one thing in your pretty speech."

"Huh, what's that?"

"You didn't argue my point of breaking rules and challenging authority."

"That's because that's what you do all the time, so I couldn't lie."

Ron came to a grinding halt, taking hold of Bob's arm as he did so. The force of stopping while at full sprint caused them to trip over their cassocks and crash onto the stone walkway. Lying there laughing their asses off, they never noticed the shadow coming over them. That is until the sun was blocked from their eyes.

Bending over them were Susan and the Detective Sargent. Susan immediately saw Ron's reddened eyes and knelt beside him. She stroked the cheek of his face. "So what's so funny, boys?"

Ron couldn't answer; he just flipped onto his belly with a slight groan. Detective Malone grabbed hold of Bob's hand and hoisted him to his feet.

"Is Ron feeling sick Bob?" Malone asked tongue in cheek as he watched the blush spread across Ron's face when Susan touched him.

"Oh no Detective Sargent it's just that the Lone Ranger fell off his horse. He'll be up and at full speed ahead in no time at all."

Ron turned his flushed face to the side so that he could see Bob. "Thanks pal."

Bob went down on a knee and looked at Susan opposite him. He had to say something but what? "So *kemosabe* is every little thing okay down there?"

Ron looked up at his pal. "I think all's fine. I just need a little help getting up."

Bob smiled at Ron and then looked at Susan. "I think in that regard, Susan should help you."

They both began to laugh hysterically. Susan simply let them be and stood at the side of Malone. "Boys, I don't think I'll ever understand them what with all that Tonto and Lone Ranger stuff."

"Ah, now there Miss Liguri, I can help. You see the Lone Ranger and Tonto were best buddies and they went around righting wrongs and solving problems and giving hope. Not too different from those two rolling on the ground like little boys, which of course they will always be in one way or another."

Susan flipped her crimson locks behind her shoulder. "I guess that's what future priests should do."

"Oh no Miss Liguri, that's what all of us are called to do but maybe without the rolling on the ground part."

"I think I get your point. Okay, boys, let's stop the nonsense. I get it, so let's get to work."

The two on the ground lay on their backs and looked up to her bending over them. Ron flipped back on his belly just in case. "You do?" they responded in unison.

Bob jumped to his feet and pulled up Ron. Susan squeezed between them. "Yes, I do boys. So bless my heart if we won't make a great team."

Ron was confused. "So what are you saying; are you becoming a nun?"

"No sweetie, I am not becoming a nun. But I am beginning to understand who you are and that's enough for me for now." She turned to look for Malone. "Isn't that right Detective Sargent?"

The tall man dressed in black looked more like a minister than a cop but he agreed with her.

Susan slipped her hands under the arms of Tonto and the Lone Ranger. "Let's just say that this duo needs to become a trio. Now what would be a good name for me? Let's see…there's Dale Evans but she's already with Roy Rogers. And there's Wonder Woman, but that's too Sci-Fi for us for now. Well then there's Scarlet and I am from Georgia originally but that's been done as well. Then of course there's our favorite, the girl from Kansas but we've already done that too. Oh dear I think this will take a bit of time, right boys?"

The guys leaned back and looked at each other, their eyes communicating that they were confused but accepting of it nonetheless.

They began to walk and realized that they had left Malone. Susan brought them to a quick halt. "Detective Sargent, come along, you never know when we might need you again."

He locked arms with Bob and off the four walked down the Court of Nations Road as the Bells of the Carillion rang out their song of the hour.

Ron couldn't stand it any longer; he just had to say it. "Susan, I don't know what's going on here, but you drive me crazy."

"Well bless my soul, dear boy, that's exactly what I am supposed to do; so Hi Yo Silver and all that jazz y'all."